Dancing with Bear

Karen Lorene

Lorene Publications 1420 Fifth Avenue, Suite 108, Seattle, WA 98101
www.LorenePublications.com

ISBN:0961830263
ISBN-13: 978-0-9618302-6-7

TO DON

For all the times he suspended disbelief

and

believed

CONTENTS

ACKNOWLEDGMENTS

Do all novels take fifteen years? *Dancing with Bear* did. The story came about due to a fascination with sub-cultures—sub-cultures that generally are, if not despised, ignored. Hence this romp is full of ministers and trailer courts and chainsaw artists and widows and accordion players and bartenders and precocious children. During the years of putting these people into a novel, I have many to thank.

Thank you to:

Sue Jostrom, editor

The amorphous Super Group who has read and critiqued much of this story, and presently consists of: Harriett Connor, Kristina Danilchik, Sharon Goldberg, Netter Hansen, Sue Jostrom, Susan Landgraf, James Stark and Vladimir Vulovic

All those writing teachers over the years, especially Priscilla Long

Facèré staff who, because of their competence, give me time to write: Mēgan Corwin, Madeline Courtney, Trudee Hill, Dana Shaw, Lorraine Vagner and Susan Welch

Madeline Courtney, for her time formatting the book

Trudee Hill, Dana Shaw, and Madeline Courtney for final proof readings

Cappy Thompson, for her cover art

Susan Welch, for the cover's typography

Kait Rhodes, for her glassblowing expertise

Dear readers, who I hope will follow these assorted imaginary friends to the very last page

And lastly, to sundry and assorted people whose names I will remember the minute *Dancing with Bear* comes back from the printer.

Thank you all!

Karen Lorene
Facèré Jewelry Art Gallery Owner
Writer

1

COMES A CALL

A six-legged bear. Four-inch claws. A gurgling growl.

Paul's legs churn through molasses. A tree ahead. His hands reach. His fingers grasp. Tree bark peels like scabs.

Below him bear paws slam the tree. Whup! Whup! Whup!

A branch overhead! Almost safe! His arms are like sludge, like cooked noodles, like Jell-O. His heart pounds.

Claws scrape his heel, engulf his foot. The tree shakes and the bear yells in a hollow voice that echoes up into the mountains and over the valleys—echoes and echoes, "SHALL WE DANCE? SHALL WE DANCE? SHALL WE DANCE?"

Paul laughs at the joke until he looks down. He has no legs. He can't dance. He can't climb. He can't move or wiggle or breathe. He can't... even when his mom's voice calls, "You can do it! You can do it!" He can't.

Paul gasps for air. Through a glaze of July heat he pushes away the twisted sweat-filled sheet. His flannel shirt clings like a second skin. A buzzing drills his head. A blue bottle fly pounds against the window. The whining makes his ears ache. The whining ricochets around the room. The whining is chainsaw loud. Paul grabs yesterday's want ads and slams the fly. The fly curls around itself, pumps its legs, and dies.

Paul covers his eyes with his arm, he moans and groans and vows he will never drink again. He yearns for sleep and he would have dropped back into his nightmare dream except at this moment, incessant thuds bounce through the floorboards. From below he hears Brummer call with a huge laugh, "Get your lazy ass down here!"

1

"All right, already," Paul mumbles, slides out of bed and stomps the floor in reply. "I'm coming! I'm coming!"

He stumbles two steps across the room and pushes open the window. He drinks in the breeze off Mt. Grizzly—like iced whiskey. He shields his eyes from the sun and then sees from under his cupped hand an amazing sight. A limousine inches its way down Main Street. A Mercedes. White. The car oozes closer and parks directly below his window between a gun-racked Ford 350 and Paul's Jeep.

When the limo door opens, Paul can see loopy gold letters: THE REVEREND RANDI MACARTHUR CRUISEWELL.

More thuds reverberate through the floor boards. Paul yells, "Brummer, cool it!"

Paul leans out the window and watches a small, round jellyroll of a man emerge from the limousine. The man glows: white suit, white vest, white shirt. Across his belly drapes a gold chain. Gold winks at his cuffs and gold flashes from his little finger. His hair is a glorious, whipped meringue of white.

The man glides under the porch overhang and disappears. Paul closes the window and heads to the sink. He splashes his face with water. Above him the mirror is not kind. Red eyes. Another day's growth. Thirty-four? He looks old. Older. He looks like Bear. Damn it. To erase the image, he finger-combs his hair and pats down the stray whiskers of his beard.

From a chair Paul grabs a fresh, un-ironed shirt and yesterday's jeans. He reaches under the bed for his boots. It hits him that finding his boots is no longer difficult. They're there. His saws are gone. Sold. Another month and even the money he got for them will have been spent.

Outside, he stands on the landing above the back parking lot. The air smells of pine and cedar. Around the base of the trees, raccoons have had a party. Garbage everywhere.

Paul descends the stairs to the back door of The Big Drinkers' Bar. Before entering, he tucks in his shirt, pulls at his collar. Presentable? Maybe Elsie won't notice his hangover. But, no question, Elsie and Travesty John have made it clear. They're cutting off his tab. A force, those two, and last night's parting words were, "That's it Paul. No more drinks." Never? Probably never. Hard to imagine.

Paul pushes the back door open and bumps Burps. He nudges the dog. "Git. Git, big boy." The baggy St. Bernard unravels himself and heads for the belly of the pool table. The click of the dog's toenails on the broad-planked floor makes Paul aware of an unnatural silence: no pool balls slam, no espresso machine hisses, Roger Miller doesn't sing. Brummer and the rest of the crew aren't razzing each other. Everyone's attention is glued on the gnome-like man in the doorway. In the slant of sun the man's hair glows. His short body casts a long shadow.

In the length of that shadow stands Elmer Spitzky, a lanky logger in loose jeans and fluorescent orange suspenders. Elmer rolls his pool stick between his hands, back and forth, back and forth. Next to him, Ace Johnson rests his rounded belly against the pool table and tilts his head as if to catch words the visitor is about to speak. Brummer, gray-haired, gray-mustached, John L. Lewis eyebrowed, stands waiting in bib overalls and a waffled, long-john shirt. Brummer places both hands on the rim of the red mahogany pool table.

At the bar, Elsie folds foam on the top of a latte and hands the cup to a hiker. Her polka dot Bakelite bracelets make hollow clapping sounds as they slide down her arm.

By her side, Travesty John keeps his hand on the porcelain beer pull. He waits.

Even Burps waits. He sniffs the silence.

Paul catches a slight movement as Ace Johnson elbows Elmer Spitzky. Elmer raises his eyebrow and winks at Brummer. Except for this exchange, no one has moved.

The stranger at the door steps forward. He holds a manila envelope. He extends the envelope to focusing distance. In a voluminous voice he calls, "GENTLEMEN!" A moment passes. He lowers his voice and repeats, "Gentlemen." He turns a half-circle on the back of his heel as his eyes make contact with each frozen figure.

"My name's Cruisewell. The Reverend Randi MacArthur Cruisewell. I'm on a mission." It was as if he put a beat between words. One-thousand-and-one, one-thousand-and-two. "I'm looking for…" One-thousand-and-three. "Mister…" One-thousand-and-four. "Paul Whitinowsky."

All eyes turn toward Paul.

Startled by the announcement, embarrassed by the attention, Paul stands stalk still. Deer in the headlights. Raccoon in the garbage can. Cruisewell walks toward Paul. He holds the envelope just out of reach and smooth as a do-si-do, he tucks his hand under Paul's elbow. He partners Paul to the bar.

Reverend Cruisewell hops onto a barstool. He drops the envelope in front of Paul and with two stubby fingers, signals Travesty John to pull beers. Travesty's eyebrows furrow and he turns to Elsie with an unspoken question and not missing a beat, she pulls a single beer for the out-of-towner. She places a Coke in front of Paul. Defeated, Paul studies the envelope.

The large type on the front reads: PAUL WHITINOWSKY, MINISTER CANDIDATE. He squints at his name as if the large black letters aren't in focus, don't spell his name, aren't attached to the paper, couldn't possibly mean him. Paul swivels on the barstool to watch Spitzky and Ace and Brummer concentrate on a number seven ball. Totally entranced. All of them. They act like Cruisewell doesn't exist. They act like they haven't suckered Paul.

Reverend Cruisewell clears his throat and when Paul turns to look at the diminutive man, he becomes aware of the minister's small, corn-on-the-cob teeth and his manicured hand at the knot of the perfect white tie under the starched white collar of his perfect white shirt. The pinky ring sports a fat diamond and a prism of light splashes around the room. And the fingernails? If he hadn't seen Jackie Gleason play Minnesota Fats in *The Hustler*, Paul wouldn't have believed those fingernails. The immaculate hands make him want to sit on his own hands—logger's hands. Scarred. Once tough. Hands going soft.

"Paul? You with me?" Cruisewell demands. "You and I need to talk." His voice grabs Paul. It beckons. It pleads. It implores. And immediately a series of words skip through Paul's brain: *goofy, silly, foolish, idiotic.* Then the word *serious* joins the list when Cruisewell demands, "Pay attention."

Paul scoots back on his barstool trying to think of some way, any way, to escape.

Cruisewell continues, "Yes, Paul. You." He runs his finger across Paul's name on the envelope. He pushes the envelope an inch closer to Paul. He points with his diamond-dressed pinky at the bold black letters. "Paul Whitinowsky! That *is* your name, isn't it?"

"Right," Paul affirms. "I can read ... my name ... but..."

Cruisewell's voice drips with assurance. "Of course you can read your name."

Paul's headache roars back, an ice pick in his right eye.

The Reverend pulls back his shoulders like a banty rooster about to crow. He proclaims, "You are exactly, exactly who I am looking for!"

"Yeah? Your mistake." Paul concentrates on making his voice firm. His eyes narrow. He speaks low and clear, loud enough to stop his pool-playing friends, "A BIG UGLY-BUTT MISTAKE!"

Ace laughs and yells back, "Couldn't have chosen a better guy!"

Spitzky leans to make a perfect shot. "Ab-so-lute-ly!"

Before Paul can move, Cruisewell pulls a single sheet from the envelope. "This. Your application?"

Just as Paul is ready to stop the whole stupid nonsense, Cruisewell continues, one beat away from begging. "Look. Look here. You are my man. Just give me a minute. I'm going to make it worth your while."

Paul hears "money" in that last sentence. He accepts the piece of paper. Studies it, front and back. It states his name, his address, his schooling (to which someone has added college graduate and a couple years of graduate work in forestry), and a long rambling paragraph about seeking truth and direction. It's too much.

"I'm sorry Reverend. Really sorry, but my so-called friends have played a joke." And, with that, Paul pushes himself off the barstool. "I'll be right back."

He strides across the room. With each step he slams his heel into the pine wood floor. Paul has the attention of Ace, Spitzky and Brummer. They watch. Paul leans over the pool table and grabs the cue ball. He lofts the ball from his left hand to his right hand and his friends watch as the ball arcs back and forth. On the last loft, Paul jabs the ball in the air, as if at any minute he might bean one of them.

"Enough, already. This is not funny!"

Ace and Spitzky step back. Brummer grins, takes a deep breath and says, "Now, now, Little Bear."

"Don't! Don't say a word and don't use that stupid name."

"Now, Paul . . ."

"And don't you 'now Paul' me." Paul's voice drops to a whisper. "I'll get rid of this idiot and after I get rid of this idiot, I'll. . ." Paul has no clue what he'll do. These are his best friends and he can feel a laugh bubbling up inside his belly. If he was on the other side of this joke he'd have howled. So, before he gives himself away, he makes like Clint Eastwood, and stares his meanest, maddest stare and, without speaking, heads back to the bar. For effect, Paul slams the cue ball so hard on the bar, Cruisewell's beer jumps. The ball rolls down to Travesty John's waiting hand.

Everyone is silent.

Elsie grabs the manila envelope from the river of spilled beer and hands it to Reverend Cruisewell. Like a mother demanding her children settle down, she calls to the room, "I want no more squabbling. All of you … mind your manners!" With that Elsie guides Paul and Reverend Cruisewell to the back booth. She wipes the table clean and with authority says, "You two sit here. Paul, it appears your guest has come a good long way. The least you can do is listen. I'll put on music." Elsie turns and flips her bar towel at the other men and calls, "And you idiots, get back to your game."

Everyone does as they are told.

Burps pulls his bulk from under the pool table, lumbers the length of the hall toward the back booth and flops his rounded body on the floor. His chin rests on Paul's boot. A comfort.

The clatter of pool balls resumes. *"Chances are..."* smoothly slides off the tongue of Johnny Mathis.

Cruisewell stares at Paul. Clears his throat. "Thank you. We need just the littlest amount of time to explore the possibilities. Don't you think?" His eyebrows ratchet up asking Paul to say 'yes.'

Paul can't even remember the question. He covers his eye to hold his headache in place. Is the guy institutional? An ax short of a blade? Is he a sham or just stupid? His come-on a trick or temptation? Is he bogus or beneficent? Words tango in Paul's brain. How is it possible this strange man doesn't get the joke?

With all the energy Paul can muster he addresses Cruisewell, "I've got this really bad headache. I don't want to hurt your feelings, but I need to leave. You have been misled. There's nothing more to talk about."

Smooth as a pull on a crosscut saw, Cruisewell answers, "Wrong, my friend. We've only just begun."

2

STRIKING A DEAL

Had Paul been sitting in the front of The Big Drinkers' Bar instead of the back, had he been shooting pool with his buddies, had he been experiencing his normal out-of-work, do-nothing morning, had he not been cornered by an idiot-stranger, he might have noticed the single eagle silhouetted by the glacier on Mt. Grizzly, soaring and diving, and it might have crossed his mind that the magnificent bird was stalking prey.

Paul speaks in a firm, subdued voice, "I apologize for my friends." He slides the envelope back towards Cruisewell. "You've been had. I'm not your guy."

"This isn't your application?" Cruisewell asks with equal parts disbelief, dismay, and confusion.

"Not in a million years."

"But it's your name?" Cruisewell's voice begs Paul to say yes, to succumb.

"No way would I have applied to be a minister, anywhere, anytime."

"But it's a *perfect* application." Reverend Cruisewell waves the paper in front of Paul. "Why are you so sure you're not interested?"

Paul squeezes his eyes shut, places both hands palm down on the tabletop as if to brace himself and declares, "No, no, and no. Never."

Cruisewell's shoulders slump, his eyebrows sag, his mouth quivers. "One more chance?" His voice, full of defeat, pleads, "One more minute?" He shakes his head and his hair loses a bit of its loft.

Paul fears Cruisewell might cry. Frantically, he looks for Elsie. He signals her. Maybe she'll understand how needy he is.

Cruisewell's head rests in the palms of his hands. His muffled voice begs, "I care. I care about you." He looks up and catches Paul's fixed gaze. "Guys like you I can help!"

Elsie places glasses of water in front of the two men. "Anything else?" she asks. Paul can see the concern in her eyes, but not enough. "I'll bring you a menu," she says and scoots away.

Paul eyes the back door. Four steps away. Freedom. This is like one of his worst nightmares. Maybe, just maybe, he'll wake up.

Cruisewell hiccups.

What if the hiccups turn to sobs? Desperate, Paul asks, "Is there anything else that would help? Maybe there's someone else."

No answer.

"You can't believe this is for real!" Paul tries to keep the irritation out of his voice. "What could you have been thinking?"

Cruisewell looks up. His eyes grow large. His eyebrows jig and across his face slides a hint of a smile. "I go where people need me!"

"Need you?"

"I believe you have been called. And, indeed you need me."

"Called? I don't know what that means, but whatever it is, I don't want to know." Paul can barely contain his frustration. "Believe me, I don't."

"You need to know about both."

"Both what?

"About not being a minister. About not being called."

"Double negatives make me crazy!" Paul is near losing it; his voice is loud, ends in a nervous laugh.

"There! Just that. A logger who knows double negatives. It's time for you to move. On! Upward!" Cruisewell reaches out, his palms open. It reminds Paul of a come-to-Jesus pamphlet from some long ago Sunday school class. Cruisewell's voice brightens with hope. "Why not?"

"Because," Paul's voice cracks, "It's crazy!" He stops himself from saying, "You're crazy."

Cruisewell picks up the application. In a calm, steady voice he reads: "My name is Paul Whitinowsky. I am a thirty-four-year-old ex-logger in the dying town of Twist. I have spent my whole life logging. I love the forest. I love the guys I work with." Cruisewell stops reading. "I'd guess you mean those guys over there." He nods toward the pool table.

"Who else?" Paul shakes his head in disbelief. "Enough..."

"No! Listen." Cruisewell continues reading: "My logging days are over, but I am young and I need a job. I'm good with people. I can tell a good joke. I can take a good joke. I am interested in peoples' lives. I care when they hurt. I love seeing people get together and solve problems, or just celebrate." Cruisewell looks up. "Great word! Celebrate."

"I wouldn't have thought those clowns knew the word."

8

Cruisewell snaps the paper and reads as if Paul has not spoken: "I have just spent the last six months taking care of my father, Bear Whitinowsky." Cruisewell looks at Paul over the application. Cruisewell's eyes fill. "This is the part that got me. You wrote, 'He's a son-of-a-b_____,' and you left out the word 'bitch!' I like that! So damn sensitive!" Cruisewell reads on: "My dad needed me and I was there." Cruisewell looks up. "Now here's where it gets interesting." With his little finger he finds where he had stopped reading: "You asked for the downside of my character. I guess you should know that if I don't get out of Twist, I'll end up a drunk. The other downside is that I have money problems. I need a job!"

"Oh, brother," Paul groans. "Stop!"

Cruisewell is undaunted. "Don't you want to know the part that clinched the deal? Made me drive all this way?"

"No." Paul sits forward, rubs the bridge of his nose, squeezes his eyes shut. He opens one eye. Cruisewell's waiting. "How in the hell did my so-called friends find you?"

Cruisewell's voice brightens, "I put an ad in a Seattle newspaper, *The Stranger.*"

"An ad? For a minister?" He shakes his head in disbelief. "*The Stranger?*" Paul can't resist saying, "That's appropriate."

"In Seattle. Lots of people place ads to meet people. I thought it was a great idea." Cruisewell's eyes narrow as if he is wrestling with a hard problem. Then he lifts his voice as if directed by a baton. "You know, I can hear it in your voice. You *are* interested."

"No!" Paul spits.

Cruisewell's shoulders slump a notch, his hands drop into his lap, his head dips and the top twirl of his hair slides across his forehead.

Paul hurries to add, "Cruisewell, I'm sorry. I suppose you're an interesting guy. You're probably a *great* guy and it's nice you came all this way, but you've got to understand, I'm a logger. My dad was a logger. We go way back."

"So?"

"If there is something I am supposed to do, it's logging. Besides, I'm not what you'd call religious."

"Oh, no problem. Me neither. I'm not what you'd call real religious."

"You're a minister for God's sake!"

"Indeed!" Cruisewell answers, all smiles.

"But, my 'not religious' and your 'not religious' are nowhere near the same."

Cruisewell sweeps his hand through the air as if to sweep away the 'religious' question. "I help people! Like you! Create families! Bring purpose! Bring joy!"

Paul laughs and pulls at his beard. This conversation reminds him of the time Elsie tried to teach him the Texas swing. They both agreed he had inherited Minnesota feet. But at least she gave up.

"This is a great, great offer," Cruisewell insists.

Paul yearns for bed. For silence. For cold beer. For revenge.

"Great terms," Cruisewell adds.

"Terms? I don't need terms. I need a job. A logging job."

"Not going to happen, Paul."

"Says who?"

From a sleek white leather folder Paul has not noticed until this moment, Cruisewell extracts a chart. Lines cross in red and green over a grid.

"See this line. It crosses this line. Trees and loggers. Kaput."

Paul studies the chart. No question 'kaput' is the right word. He sighs, "You don't even know me."

"Your application."

"I told you. I didn't write the damn thing."

"But it captures you. And I checked the references."

"What references?"

"Ace Johnson and Elmer Spitzky."

"Oh, great." Paul points to the pool table. "That's them playing pool."

Cruisewell ignores Paul. "They said you were well liked." Cruisewell's hand slips inside his vest. He unfolds a document, turns it toward Paul, and points to a figure: *Thirty thousand dollars.*

Paul stares at the number. "Now, you are really messing with me."

"Not enough? There's also up-front money."

"You're crazy. Thirty thousand's twice what I made last year."

"Well, you have to guarantee me six months."

"Six months?"

"Well, the first six weeks you use to prepare. Correspondence lessons. Live here in Twist. Get used to the idea. Say your goodbyes."

"Then what?" Paul shifts his body. Pushes his spine against the bench back. He can feel it coming. He's getting sucked in. He desperately tries to get Travesty John's attention. He *really* needs a drink.

"Then you move to Seattle for your ministry."

"Yeah, right. *My* ministry."

"I've a few things to finalize, but yes, a ministry in a trailer court."

Paul bursts with laughter and before he can say another word, Cruisewell gives him a stern look and with eyes narrowed proclaims, "Don't make fun. It could be the other way around. There are those who make fun of Twist loggers. Makin' fun doesn't become you."

"Sorry, it just hits me as so … I don't know, impossible. Not something I can get my head around."

"You were condescending."

Paul goes silent. He *was* condescending. His image of a minister to a bunch of folks in a trailer court is ludicrous. Cruisewell is ludicrous.

Cruisewell continues, "Well, at least we've got past that. Six months, and I'm sure you will see the rightness of my offer and the rightness of this opportunity."

Paul meets Cruisewell's stare and can barely believe the words coming out of his mouth. "Okay. For just a minute, let's pretend there is such a situation. I accept the deal. But what if it doesn't work. You've paid me and I'm a complete failure. Then what?"

"Either you stay, or if you decide you can't, you make a good faith effort to find a replacement. Other than that," Cruisewell beams, "Nothing!"

"Let me get this straight. I work six months. If I don't like it, I find somebody else. That's it? The next ... what do you call it? Candidate?" Paul wants to say 'fool.' "Does the next candidate get thirty thousand dollars?"

"Well, everyone needs an incentive."

Paul shakes his head. "This is a scam, right?"

Cruisewell lets out a deep sigh, his intensity and earnestness slide away. He looks up, sad and disbelieving. "Trust me. This is straight. Straight as it gets." Cruisewell slowly shakes his head. "It never dawned on me someone would think this idea was a scam. Incomprehensible."

"Incomprehensible? The whole thing, and please, please don't be insulted, but the whole thing is nuts." Cruisewell doesn't interrupt. Doesn't look as if he'll disagree. Paul is on a roll, "And on top of it, there's your ring. That car. Limo, whatever you call it. All this stuff!"

"I'm a minister!" he says with a bright smile.

"That's what I mean, for God's sake! Ministers are supposed to be poor!"

"Ministers are not poor! They're blessed! I'm blessed! I could make you blessed! Believe me! Don't you want to be blessed? Have a job? Some income? Something? Anything?" Cruisewell's staccato questions hit Paul head on.

Paul reaches for the glass of water. He takes a huge swallow hoping somehow the water will wash away the words, the temptation, everything.

"You know how to hurt a guy," Cruisewell says. "But never mind, we won't even think about that, in time it will be clear, in time you'll understand, for now I have a concern."

"*You* have a concern?"

"Well, two concerns." Cruisewell flips through the application, his lips moving, his voice mumbling. He finds a page. LEGAL ACTIONS AGAINST YOU. He points to the word: DISMISSED.

Paul, inexplicably, is suffused with relief. For a moment he knows the answer to a real question. "Oh, that. It's nothing!"

"Want to talk about it?"

"No! I don't want to talk about it! Especially if you use . . . if you use that damn syrupy minister's voice." Paul feels mean. Paul feels like yanking out Cruisewell's larynx. He is aware that Cruisewell is using a stupid, irritating voice like he thinks Paul is some kind of yokel or a kid or just plain stupid. "You talk like you've got a mouth full of sugar! Powdered sugar!"

Cruisewell's eyes water.

"Don't! Don't get weepy on me!" Paul begs.

"How's this?" Cruisewell lowers his voice. He sounds normal. He asks, "Would you like to discuss item number one later? What about we go on to item number two?"

Paul moans, "What in hell is item number two?"

"Your beard. Your beard will have to go."

Paul burst out laughing. "My beard? What about your hair?"

Cruisewell lifts his hand inches above his head. "What's wrong with my hair?"

Before he can answer, Elsie appears carrying two plates. "I bypassed the menu. Here's a peace offering. Compliments of the boys." She tilts her head in the direction of the pool table and places in front of Paul and Cruisewell hamburgers and curly fries.

"Elsie, much appreciated. But I've a question: What do you think of my beard?"

"It could use a trim."

"Oh? Well, then what do you think of the Reverend's hair?"

"It could use a trim."

"Thank you. And be sure to thank my '*friends.*'"

Elsie gives Paul's head a scrub with her knuckles and a see-what-you're-missing smile to Reverend Cruisewell.

Cruisewell carefully bites into the hamburger, then dabs at the corners of his mouth with a napkin. There is something about the dainty precision of his action that makes Paul anticipate Cruisewell's next question. Paul slips lower on the bench as if to avoid the words.

"Seems we have a deal, then. Your beard. My hair."

"We do *not* have a deal."

"Well, then, tell me about my first concern." Cruisewell takes another bite, chews, all the time his eyes drilling Paul. After he swallows and neatly wipes his mouth again, he encourages Paul, "Go ahead. Get it off your chest."

Paul is tired and defeated. Unbidden, the words he's never spoken to anyone but the judge came to him and he tells Cruisewell, "I burned down my dad's cabin."

"Oh? Just burned down your dad's cabin?"

"That's the short version of a long story. I'll give you the short version of the short story. Then I'm going to eat this hamburger and then I'm going upstairs to sleep off my headache."

Paul stalls, hunting for words, trying to ignore the remembrance of Bear stretched out on the recliner. A recliner that became a bed that became his dad's final resting place. He sees the split-log cabin. He remembers the silence of the final days.

"Continue," Cruisewell says with soft encouragement.

"My dad had an accident. Hit by a widow-maker. Slow dying. Not to ruin your lunch, but there was an overwhelming smell to that cabin. Ever been around gangrene?"

Paul doesn't wait for Cruisewell's answer. "After dad was gone, I burned down the cabin. Killed the smell. The judge understood. It wasn't arson. As he put it, it was a logical act. He told me to never do it again. I assured him I wouldn't. He dismissed the case."

Silence holds them like dance partners in a slow waltz.

Paul takes advantage of the moment. "Okay? I've answered your question, you answer mine."

"Shoot."

"What is it with this ministry thing? All the white? All the pomp and circumstance? Recruiting me?"

"You'll just have to trust me on this. I'll give you a short answer. Time will certainly reveal a long answer. But for now? I had a tough childhood. I yearned for friends. I looked around and the most consistent example was the church. Truth? I loved the dress-up. I loved the singing and the meetings every day. Every evening. I just decided I'd start my own. So, here I am. It's not my only interest, but it's one of my most current. And, I must say, to date, the most fun."

Paul doesn't answer. It isn't the words. It's the sincerity. Cruisewell is one less notch crazy.

Cruisewell neatly folds the paper napkin and smoothes its edges. "Then we have a deal?"

Paul groans and wipes away the sweat that has gathered on his forehead.

"You're broke," Cruisewell says with a smile.

From across the room, the roar of Brummer's voice interrupts their conversation. "Paul!" Brummer beckons. "Get over here! Some guy's messin' with your Jeep!"

3

THE REPO-MAN

Paul hurries out the door. He can't imagine that someone in Twist, someone in broad daylight, would be messing with his Jeep. He bounds down the steps. Ace, Spitzky, and Brummer follow, carrying their cue sticks in a just-in-case-we-need-to-whop-someone-up-side-the-head attitude. Cruisewell, Elsie, and Travesty John join them on the front porch. Paul skirts the protruding end of the limousine and arrives at his Jeep just as a man with a flat-bar is sliding it down the Jeep's window.

"What?" Paul demands. "What in hell are you doing?"

The man jiggles the bar slowly and deliberately. It's all Paul can do to not reach out, grab the bar, and smash the guy's face. With clear blue eyes, the man stares at Paul. He doesn't smile. He tilts his freckled face. The sun shines through the coral-colored bristles of his crew cut and reflects off his clean, shiny scalp. He holds the bar higher. Tips it toward the tow-truck where his partner waits. Paul has no doubts. These two mean business.

With a clear, innocent, and unthreatening voice, the man says, "And you must be Mr. Whitinowsky."

Behind Paul, Spitzky demands, "And who the fuck are you?"

"It's all right Spitz. I can handle this." Paul waves Spitzky away and turns to the intruder.

"About the payment, huh?" Paul's voice is low, a throaty whisper, enough to keep his crew from hearing.

"You guessed it. I'm from Auto Reclaimers." His words are precise. Distinct. "Name's Gaylon Fowles." With a certain theatrical ease he transfers the bar to his left hand. He extends his right hand to Paul, and Paul, unable to avoid the contact, returns the grip, their clasp a hair short of an arm wrestle. Fowles smiles a smile of assurance and contempt.

Spitzky comes close, leans over Paul's shoulder, and barks at Gaylon Fowles, "We don't much like people messin' with our stuff."

14

"Wait, Spitz. Give me a second," Paul drapes his arm over Spitzky's shoulder and turns him around. "Go on back inside. This'll take a minute."

His team hesitates, then each gives Fowles a mean look and turns to go back to the bar. Spitzky, the last to leave, makes one last try and asks Paul, "He going to take your wheels?"

"Not if I can help it."

Spitzky's expression changes. He smiles a huge smile as if he's just had a brilliant idea. He reaches for his wallet. "How much do you need?"

"More than you got, Spitz. But, thanks. I'll work it out."

Spitzky shrugs. "Your call." He raises the cue stick as if to give Fowles the finger, and stops at the top of the steps. "If you need us we're here." With a last jab of the cue stick he goes inside.

Gaylon Fowles leans against the Jeep, his arms folded, his legs crossed at the ankle. He has an air about him: two parts boredom, two parts disdain. Fowles speaks with precision, "We aren't messing, as your friend so deftly put it, with anything we haven't a right to mess with. I'm here for the finance company. I'm here to get what's theirs."

"Mr. Fowles. Gaylon. Believe me. It's not a problem. I've been a little short. I'm sure you don't want to do anything that isn't right."

"Didn't cross my mind to do something wasn't right."

"I'm sure you wouldn't want to do anything this mean. Taking a man's wheels." Paul hates the whine in his voice. He clears his throat, wants to belt the guy. Instead he kicks a mess of dried dog shit under his Jeep and then studies the scuffed toe of his boot and studies the shine of Gaylon Fowles' black military boots and tries to think of an out. Something. Anything.

Gaylon Fowles isn't waiting. "Life's mean. Nothin' personal. Let's get this done. No money? We've got work to do."

"Give me a break." Paul realizes his hands are at his sides, palms up, pleading.

"I can't be worried about how someone does, or does not, make payments. If you want your Jeep, pay this." Fowles takes a bill from his pocket and snaps it open. "This month's payment and last month's payment. And a hundred bucks for my time. Cash." Sweat drips down Paul's back. Fowles continues, "I'm not here to argue. I'm not here to discuss philosophy, payments, your financial state. Got it? It's cash. Now."

Paul doesn't believe in prayer. He doesn't believe in miracles. He doesn't believe in divine intervention. But then! A strange thought slips through his brain. "I've got an idea! A great idea! It'll solve our problem."

"It's not *our* problem. It's *your* problem. And you've a solution? Just like that?" Sarcasm drips off the words.

"Right! You got it. Just like that." With a snap of his fingers, Paul turns and heads up the stairs. "You comin' or aren't you?"

Fowles looks over his shoulder, signals his partner and calls, "Watch this Jeep. Don't let nobody touch it!"

Paul waits at the top of the stairs and then pushes the door open for Fowles, all the time talking: "Stupid of me not to have thought of this. I've got a new job. Right now. A job with money. Up-front." Fowles follows Paul past the stares of his buddies to the back booth. Reverend Cruisewell, a curly fry suspended in front of his mouth, looks up.

"Reverend Cruisewell, meet Gaylon Fowles. Gaylon, meet The Reverend Randi MacArthur Cruisewell. You may have seen his limo outside." Paul gestures for Fowles to sit and says to Cruisewell, "Mr. Fowles is here on some important business." Paul stares at Cruisewell. Catches his eye. Holds it. Never once looks away. When they are seated, Paul waits until Elsie is busy with two new customers, then signals Travesty to bring a round of beer. Another miracle. Travesty brings three beers. Paul takes a huge swallow of the cool amber liquid. The beer eases his nerves, quenches his thirst, gives him courage. Anything is possible. He raises his glass to Reverend Cruisewell. "I was just telling Mr. Fowles that you have offered me a position…with an advance."

"Yes. Sure. Ah … the advance …" Cruisewell says with a hesitant slipperiness.

"I need to pay a small bill with Mr. Fowles and he will be on his way and we can conclude our negotiations."

Cruisewell smiles with pleasure. "Is that the small advance or the large advance?"

Paul pushes his back against the hardwood bench, straightens his shoulders, drains his mug. He makes a huge leap of faith—asks the prettiest girl to the prom, bets on the long shot, believes in the power of charm, and says, "The thousand-dollar advance."

"Of course." Cruisewell reaches into his pocket. Retrieves a silver dollar money clip. He lays a fan of ten one hundred dollar bills on the table. As if this was the most everyday of everyday occurrences, Paul reaches for five of the hundred dollar bills, tucks them into his shirt pocket, scoops up the remaining bills, and presents them to Fowles.

"My change is fifty," Paul smiles a winner's smile.

Fowles stands. He reaches for his wallet and throws five tens on the table. "A pleasure, Whitinowsky. I hope not to do business again." He drains his beer. "Cheers." He raises the empty mug to the room, and with a snappy, military stride, he heads to the door.

"And the receipt?" Cruisewell calls to Fowles' back.

Fowles turns. He crosses in front of the transfixed crowd, scribbles PAID on the bill, and throws the paper on the table. He turns to leave, applause follows, in time with each step.

"Mr. Fowles!" Cruisewell calls. "Your tool." He raises the flat-bar. Gaylon Fowles returns and grabs the bar. The entire room explodes with vigorous clapping in time to his leaving. Hoots and hollers follow.

Paul waves a thankful wave to his friends and slumps down into the booth. "Thanks, Reverend Cruisewell. You saved my hide."

"You can call me Cruise."

Elsie interrupts, "What more can I get you, gentlemen?" She leans over the booth to sweep up the three empty beer mugs. No question, Travesty John is due for an earful. Paul smiles at Elsie and pats her hand. He doesn't say it, but he can't imagine she didn't see how much he needed that beer: to cement the deal, to eliminate the repo-man, to soothe his exhausted body. He hands her a ten-dollar bill and says, "Thank you. Forgive me later."

Elsie turns, and as she turns he sees not the slightest smile on her face. That proverbial trip to the woodshed is waiting for Travesty.

At his side, Cruisewell takes out a pen and hands the contract to Paul. "I believe you have something to sign."

Paul stares at the paper. "We need to talk."

"We've talked."

"These were extenuating circumstances." Paul laughs an uneasy laugh.

Cruisewell pushes the contract an inch closer to Paul.

"You're going to make me sign?" Paul asks.

"I'd like to think you want to sign."

"Reverend Cruisewell, would you mind not using that syrupy voice? It grates. You use that preacher's voice and I feel like I'm falling into a pit, like I've just sold my soul to the devil, not to insult you, but that's how I feel."

"Interesting choice of words. You see, I can talk normal as the next guy. Hell, I can talk however you like, but I think what's important is that you recognize help when it's offered: recognize it, appreciate it, treasure it, value it, relish it, prize it." Cruisewell waits to be sure Paul has heard every word, then he continues, "Think of it this way. You're salvaging your soul. Here." Cruisewell pops off the end of the silver fountain pen and places the pen in Paul's hand. The slick, expensive pen feels like a silver bullet. Paul writes his name on the dotted line at the bottom of the contract.

"With that, I think it's appropriate we call you Pastor Paul."

"Another joke."

"No, I move things right along."

"So, change-o, presto, I'm a minister?"

"No, Paul, it's not a magic trick. You'll receive a correspondence course each week for six weeks beginning immediately. You get less than an 'A,' I send you a make-up lesson. First of September you report here." Cruisewell slaps a white business card on the table. **NEW DAWN IS BREAKING ADULTS-ONLY TRAILER PARK, SEATTLE, WA.**

"What in the name of Jesus-H-Christ is this?"

Cruisewell's head jerks back. "Not a great choice of words, Pastor Paul." He taps the edge of the card on the table and like a beat of a military march he says, "Your parish. Your assignment. Your call. Your job."

Paul winces, "But, it's in a trailer park?"

"Widows in trailer parks need ministers."

"Widows?"

"'Widows' doesn't necessarily mean old."

"What does that mean?"

"Well, agreed, most of them are old, but..."

"But, what?"

"One of them has this lovely daughter, lovely...."

Paul notes Cruisewell's voice has gone soft. "You sound more than a bit interested."

"No!" Cruisewell shoots back.

"Now *you* sound defensive!"

"No! Not at all! Let's discuss the particulars of our contract."

Paul eases his head back against the hardwood booth, sighs in defeat. "Okay, Reverend Randi McArthur Cruisewell, tell me the particulars."

"First, return my pen."

4

THE PARTICULARS

Paul signals Travesty John.

As if Travesty knows what Paul is going to ask, he looks to be sure Elsie is occupied at the front table then heads toward Paul's booth.

"Old friend," Paul keeps his voice low, "extraordinary times require extraordinary measures. Another beer for Reverend Cruisewell, and please," he looks directly at Travesty John, "please, one good shot."

"Better make it cash. Don't want this showing on a new tab."

"Yes. If I'm going to make you an accomplice the least I can do is spread the wealth!" Paul hands Travesty a ten.

Paul drinks the shot with one swallow, hands the glass back to Travesty. Travesty tucks the shot glass into his apron and whistles his way back to the bar.

A flush of warmth dances through Paul's body. He sinks further into the booth, hums along with *Lonesome Traveler*. The jukebox is so sympathetic. For a brief fuzzy moment, everything is possible. Even this joke.

He opens his eyes to Cruisewell's curious stare and punchy words. "Okey-dokey. All is well! Nothing like being op-toe-mistic! We're going to be a team. You and me."

Paul barely nods his head.

"Good. The first thing I'm going to do is pay Travesty John to cut you off." He raises a hundred dollar bill until Travesty looks up and walks over to their booth. "Want you to know. Paul and I are partners. This is for the past tab and the lost business I'm causing. You can feed him. That's it. That's all."

Travesty looks bewildered and pleased. He walks back to a waiting Elsie. She pulls Travesty into the kitchen and Paul knows beyond a doubt his drinking days are over.

"Now, for the particulars."

Defeated, Paul slides down, his legs sticking out in the aisle. Beaten.

"Sit up! Sit up and pay attention." He doesn't wait for Paul to right himself. He keeps talking. All business. "The trailer court is off Borealis Avenue in Seattle."

"Court? Thought it was a park."

"Park. Court. Whatever makes you feel good."

"I don't feel good."

"You will. It's a great place. You'll love everything about it. Might take you a few days. A week. These women are no fools. You'll come prepared."

The liquor's smooth warmth evaporates.

"Has a kind-of chapel. Has a parsonage. Needs a little work. Your job? Get everybody together. Advise when it's needed. Sometimes the women can use a handyman. Nothing difficult. Screen doors. Gutters. That kind of thing. But best of all? You'll get the habit of being a friend. Isn't anyone doesn't need a friend."

Paul doesn't interrupt. Cruisewell is uninterruptible.

"That'll have to go." Cruisewell points at Paul's face. "I mentioned it earlier, but I think without a doubt, the beard's gotta go. That a problem?"

Paul runs his hand along his face. "No, not a problem." Would it have mattered? Isn't this one big hind-leg of a trap? Isn't this a dance with too many steps? How can it matter?

Cruisewell picks up his pitch. "This ain't navel lint." His hand, like steel, reaches out and holds Paul's arm.

Whatever Cruisewell just said is undecipherable. Words swirl. Ideas skip a beat. Thoughts jitterbug.

"Trust me."

"Sure, can't think why I wouldn't trust you."

"Sarcasm does not become you, Paul."

Something about the intensity of the minister's voice, the grip of his hand, the fading buzz of the whiskey, the diffusion of the beer, all of it fills Paul with fear. He's agreed to an offer from the imaginary wanderings of a deluded mind. But the agreement has solidified. The agreement is solid. Solid but stupid. Stupid but sure. Sure like the biggest tree in the forest falling. Powerful. Final. Over.

Cruisewell claps his hands and rubs them together, gleefully. "This is exciting. I have grand ideas. I have money. Vision. Enthusiasm. I create new opportunities. I spread wealth, good cheer, friendship. I find partners!"

Travesty John slams an empty glass and a huge pitcher of water in front of Paul. "We're in the doghouse," he says and he turns and walks back to the kitchen as if he's not allowed to play anymore with the bad neighbor kid.

Paul looks at the water. No bubbles, no color. He's sinking, descending, drowning.

"You okay?"

Paul takes a deep breath. "Any more particulars?"

"Tomorrow, over-night delivery will bring you your first correspondence lesson. The lessons give all the information you'll need: sermons, ideas for the chapel, counseling suggestions, a diploma. Everything! You'll have to study, of course, but it's a kind of Johnny Appleseed ministry."

Paul sits stone still.

"September 1, you'll begin with eight parishioners. Good rent payers. Good tenants. You'll like them."

"Tenants? Rent payers?" Paul asks in wonder.

"Well, they rent from me, but that isn't important. What's important is that you're a great match. To them. To me."

Paul imagined reaching over, removing the top of Cruisewell's skull and seeing what was swimming inside. Sharks with huge gnashing teeth. Or, absolutely nothing.

"Reverend Cruisewell. I'm sure this might be a great idea. But..." Paul shakes his head, tries to find the right words. "Money can't buy this kind of craziness."

"Well, indeed it just did. The Lord works in mysterious ways. A new beginning! Salvation!" Cruisewell raises his empty glass to Paul. "You've signed! Any problems? We'll solve problems together. Solve problems in groups!" Cruisewell's hand pats Paul's arm. "You know what I mean."

Paul's eyes grow heavy, his mind grows numb. He doesn't know what Cruisewell means. He doesn't trust the way Cruisewell continuously pats his arm. He thinks his enthusiasm daft. Maybe since they hadn't shaken hands, maybe the agreement doesn't count. Maybe his friends will stop this movie by yelling, "Joke! Joke!" Maybe he'll wake up and that big black fly will still be trying to escape his hot, stuffy room.

Paul's thoughts are interrupted. "The pen. It's yours." Cruisewell pushes the silver-bullet pen across the table. "Seals the deal. Partners." Cruisewell raises his glass, holds it in the air.

Paul lifts his water glass. Their glasses collide. Water slops over the rim, streams down his unsteady hand.

Cruisewell gives a huge laugh. "Baptized!"

The pen rests inches from Paul's hand. And then it is in his hand. And it feels right. Perfectly balanced. As if destiny resided in a cold, clean pen.

5

LESSONS

The breeze lifts the curtains in Paul's room. Outside he can hear crows barking opinions. Pages of his correspondence lessons are spread over the bed. Pages slip lazily to the floor. Paul studies the next question:

If you have to create a Missions Committee, should you, as a minister:

A.   *Pray first*
B.   *Handpick committee members*
C.   *Outline the duties of the committee*
D.   *All of the above*

He circles D (so obvious it makes him ache) and reaches for his very last lesson: *Outreach.*

Eight widows need *Outreach? Outreach,* like a hook from behind a curtain plucking some poor soul into a congregation cooked from the mad ideas of a man with too much money and no sense?

Paul pushes the papers off the bed. He curls so the sun toasts his back. He tries to remember Reverend Cruisewell. He can't quite recall his face. He can remember the loft of his hair. He remembers the voice. How could he not? They speak by phone daily. The daily check-up. Lessons arrive and Paul hurries to finish before the phone rings again. After Cruisewell expounds on each and every question, Paul heads downstairs to the pool table. His reward. Today, he just can't study anymore. He closes his eyes and escapes into sleep.

Gulping air, Paul wakes from the dream of the branch breaking, twirling, slicing, crashing over his dad's head. In the silence that follows, Paul can see Bear's broken legs as if God were playing a vicious game of pick-up-sticks. And Paul blames himself. If he'd only been watching. If he'd only been closer. If.

A widow-maker. Strange word: widow-maker. By the time the tree slapped his dad to the ground, Paul's mom had been gone for ten years. Took the Greyhound in front of The Big Drinkers' Bar, right in front of his dad's crew. Better had he been a widower.

And, after the accident, with mangled legs, better had he been dead.

Paul reaches for a warm beer from under his bed and his hand pushes aside the crumpled papers on the floor. A front page of a lesson sports a *B*. Sometimes he gets a *C*. Once he got an *F*. Got an *F* for answering "give up" to the anecdotal question about what a couple should do about their God-awful marriage. As far as Paul could determine the couple shared a love of Chinese noodles and not much else. His lesson came back with big loopy letters over the answer sheet, "No, no, no! Never give up!" His next assignment was to write an essay describing an ideal marriage and by the time Paul finished he was lonelier than he'd ever been, felt totally hopeless, and wondered for the hundredth time what he was doing and how soon could he find someone to take his place. And if he tried to escape, he knew he would have to repay the money. Have to, or he couldn't live with himself. No matter that Cruisewell didn't seem to care much about money. Not the way he kept sending more. Unbidden. Unexpected. Crisp new bills.

Paul groans and picks up this past week's lesson: *Memorization*. He still has work to do. He read the entire Bible, well almost. He did skip some 'begats." Next? He had to memorize the names of all the books in the Bible. Paul closes his eyes and recites, "Zephaniah, Haggai, Zechariah, Malachi." He's getting there. But, he always screws up on Ezra, Nehemiah, Esther, and Job.

Why? Because it's so damn hard, that's why. And why would anyone *need* to know the names of the books of the Bible? But he's close. He asks Cruisewell, "Why do I have to memorize this s____?" he gets chastised for using the word 'shit.' And the answer to the question is: "Because." The real challenge came with a guarantee of another five hundred dollars. All Paul has to do is get his recitation of all thirty-nine names of the Old Testament books under twenty seconds. On the fourth day he's ready. Twenty seconds. Cruisewell calls. Times him. And another piece of Paul's soul flutters out the window, up over Mt. Grizzly, and disappears. Paul sleeps to the rhythm of, "Genesis, Exodus, Leviticus, Numbers, Deuteronomy, Joshua, Judges, Ruth, First and Second Samuel, First and Second Kings . . ." names that dig into his dreams.

6

AUGUST LOGGING DAYS

Out of absolutely nowhere, Elsie asks, "Want to work the bar?"

"Work the bar? Elsie, sweetheart, you're talking to Paul Whitinowsky!"

"Yes. No liquor."

"Well, sure, no liquor."

"Time off to carve."

"Time off to carve?"

"Paul, stop echoing me. We need you during Logging Days."

"God, I'd love that."

"You still need to work on your language. And how's your drinking?"

"You know. I've drunk so much water I…"

"I found a bottle."

"It was a warm beer. Horrible. Last one. Honest."

Elsie hands Paul an apron. "I'm going to miss you and your sweet lying ways. But I need an extra pair of hands for Logging Days and what with your lessons done, you need to keep busy. Working the bar will give you a chance to say goodbye to the whole town. And, here, my dear." Elsie flaps a registration form in front of Paul. "Fill this out. You can have time off to carve come Friday."

"Carve? Who says I'm going to carve? Besides, I've gone soft. A whole day of carving will kill me."

"No excuses. Like riding a bicycle. It'll come back. So, fill out the form."

Paul laughs and teases, "You're not my boss."

"For these last ten days I *am* your boss. Besides, I've already made a bet that you'll win."

"Who's betting against me?"

"Travesty." She nods towards the kitchen. "Now, don't look rejected. He'll bet me anything, knowing I never pay. So it doesn't matter that you'll win."

"Elsie, the idea of carving makes me hurt all over." Paul rubs his hands together then shakes them as if to relieve doubt and fear.

Elsie reaches to hold his hands. "Dear boy, I understand. But it's time you gave up comparing yourself to Bear. Time to move on. You're next. Time for a Whitinowsky to get back on top! Besides, I know your secret." From her pocket Elsie pulls a three-inch bumble bee in high heels. She hands it to Paul.

He thinks for a minute he will pretend it isn't his, but looks up to see a huge smile on Elsie's face as if there is no denying the carving's maker. "Aw, come on, woman. Those are secret."

"Those? There's more?"

"Where'd you get it? I threw it in the garbage."

"Well, you'll just have to thank the raccoons. They dumped last night's garbage and when I went to clean up the mess, I found it tucked under a half-eaten cinnamon roll. An appropriate hiding place, I'd say. So why are you hiding it? Hiding them?"

At just that moment the front doors burst open with a group with maps and compasses in their hands.

"Ooops, here come the orienteers!"

One yells, "Hamburgers and beers all around!"

"Man your station, Mr. Whitinowsky. Just don't forget you owe me a good story, and finders, keepers." Elsie takes back the bumble bee, tucks it in her apron pocket, and gives it a gentle pat. "And don't forget to register! To carve. A week from Friday."

The days fly by. Tending bar is heaven. No more lessons. Guy talk. The clank and clatter of the glasses and mugs. Out-of-towners begin to arrive.

By Monday Paul's thinking, maybe, just maybe it isn't insane to carve. Why not? He has the registration fee, thanks to Cruisewell. Why hesitate?

He's scared, that's why. Even while he has a dozen carving ideas bubbling.

By Wednesday business escalates. Main Street has jitterbug intensity to it. Concessionaires set up tents and displays: pots and bowls, tole ware, velvet paintings, macramé, popsicle-stick baskets, birdcages, tooled leather, beaded jewelry, fluorescent painted wine bags. More people arrive. Eventually everyone needs a beer.

Thursday. Logging Days opens. At the Twist High School baseball field crowds fill the bleachers to watch the truck parade and the tractor pull, the log toss, the barnyard scramble, and the sheep-shearing contest.

At the community center customers jury the canned peaches, beans, and applesauce. The townsfolk and all their relatives line up to purchase roasted corn, Republican snow cones, and Democrats' chocolate-dipped ice cream bars. The Daughters of the American Revolution chili pot bubbles along side a stack of cornbread.

Near the north end turn-around next to The Big Drinkers' Bar, a small traveling carnival opens with a twirling rig, a carousel, a dart throw, and a clown twisting balloons into swords and saws.

Thursday noon, carvers arrive from all over the Methow Mountains and each greets the other with high-fives and bear hugs.

Every so often Paul sneaks a look at the registration form.

"Time to do it!" Elsie says as she slides past Paul to deliver fries and onion rings to RV campers.

Paul looks at the registration form. Not much to it. Sign his name. No liabilities. Five hours of carving. No rules other than to respect the other carvers. The sentence makes Paul laugh knowing everyone's fair game and constant ragging is expected and returned. Jeering and cheering. He picks up a pencil. He will carve something crazy, something no one has ever seen. Huge and wild. He'll do anything he damn well wants. He signs the form. Then he studies his hands. Back to front. Not a callus. Bear would have sneered. City hands.

At five minutes to five, moments before the cut-off time, Paul waves a hand at Elsie and calls, "Be right back!" He walks to the front door of the community center where Brummer stacks forms and counts checks and cash.

Paul slaps the form down with two twenties and asks, "Lend me a saw or two?"

"Hot damn! I knew you'd give in. I've got my saws clean, sharpened, ready. For you. Can hardly wait to see you clean up!"

Paul takes his time walking back to the clamor and chaos of the bar. He thinks about tomorrow. He knows he's different. He knows he doesn't carve like other carvers with models and sketches. He dreams carvings. And except for Elsie, no one knows he carves palm-sized imaginings. Has carved them for years. Carved and destroyed dozens. Ever since his mom left. Something to do. Something to keep him from asking over and over, why did she leave? What had he done wrong?

To stop the questions, Paul started carving three-legged gnats and two-headed turtles and single-footed caterpillars. He never shows anyone. He has come to believe the wood tells him what to carve. Each time, for a single second, doubt bores like a wood mite in his brain, and then an image comes. And he carves.

There was a time he carved logs. He has never forgotten the last log. It was after his mom left. The memory is clear and unforgettable. He was fifteen. He carved in the junior division. Carved an owl with huge reading glasses, a pile of books at its feet. Came in third. That was also the year Bear's carving won in the adult division: a single carving of six bears, each standing on the shoulders of the other. Bear's carving sold immediately. Without help from his dad, Paul lifted his owl onto the truck bed. At home he lifted it out of the back of the truck. By himself.

"Dad, wait, wait…"

Bear didn't wait. He threw gasoline on Paul's owl. Lit it.

All the time it burned, Bear snarled at him, "No makin' fun! What do you think? You didn't think! Carving is serious. Your cartoon crap ain't hardly worth burning!" And Bear doused the carving with more gasoline.

Paul didn't cry. Despised his dad. Vowed he'd never carve again—not till his dad was dead and burning in hell.

Secretly he continued to think carvings and then one day with a knife he kept secret from Bear, he carved an alligator with a miniature umbrella. Fit in his palm. He continued to carve and then destroy each one. Bear never saw the carvings. Never. Paul burned them all. Once he threw a carving in the Monarch stove right in front of Bear. Wondered if his father noticed. Neither said a word. And now? He conjures a four-foot crazy, wild carving. It already holds an umbrella.

That night, on the stage directly to the right of Travesty John's Big Drinkers' Bar, three women in red cowboy boots and fringed outfits pluck their guitars, catch a sour harmony, and break into a calliope of twang. The crowd claps and stomps until the air vibrates. The trio is followed by a zydeco band, the Ha-va-na-gila Monsters.

Around midnight, slippery, sweaty dancers drain their beers and Travesty pulls the extension cord on the ornamental paper lights strung across the stage. Families and couples drift off toward pickups and campers and home.

Inside the bar, Elsie pushes Paul away from the dishwasher. "To bed with you. You need shut-eye. I'll finish up."

Paul continues to stack dishes. He wipes the bar for the second time.

Elsie watches. "Don't worry, Paul. Don't think of Bear. You'll do just fine." At the back door, Paul gives Elsie a hug. "Thanks Elsie. How is it you read my mind?"

"No, sweets, I read the sighs and the slump of your shoulders. No one is going to compare you to your dad. Sure, he always won. But this is now and you are you. Bear was Bear. You'll win! Go get some sleep."

When Paul wakes he can hear morning calls, setting-up noises. Generators chug. His clock reads seven-thirty. He leans out the window. At the end of Main Street a semi stuffed with four-foot logs maneuvers into place. The mobile crane from the mill reaches its long arm to place the first log. Upright. Ready for its carver.

By the time Paul dresses and stands on the front steps of The Big Drinkers' Bar everything is in motion: Lutherans have lined their tables with red, green, and yellow Jell-O salads. The Baptists display fresh baked marionberry, blackberry, apple, and hazelnut pies. The Unitarians put out crockery pots of mild beans and spicy beans—your choice. The Young Democrats maneuver freezers for the ice cream bars and across the street, the Sweet Adelines heat oil for corn-dogs. The Republicans wait. They've been ready for an hour with a self-serve buffet.

Paul walks down to watch the crane place logs. Once in place, high-school girls yellow-tape the areas for each carver.

Brummer joins Paul with two duffel bags as long as skis. "Here are your saws. Gas tanks full and look what I've got for you! Earphones." Brummer unboxes the earmuffs and Paul fits them over his head. Brummer exclaims, "Astounding! Never thought I'd see this day. Old-timers gonna think we're a bunch of sissies. But I guess it's better than being deaf like me and your old man."

Paul waves his hand as if to let Brummer think he didn't hear. He doesn't want to think about Bear. How was it his dad had any friends at all? How was it no one noticed his meanness? Sure he was a great carver, but … Paul lets the thought of his dad disappear. He can't imagine the answer.

After a three-corndog breakfast, Paul gets in line for his bib number and then heads for his assigned log. Around him the other cutters adjust their chaps, check their saws, complain that their neighbor's log is knot-free and their log isn't. Paul makes his rounds, greeting old friends. Five new contestants shake his hand. Two are women. Imagine that! Women competing.

Paul is half way down Main Street before he realizes he's doing what Bear did. The Greeter. No one asked him to. No one competed for the position. Because Bear was the champ? The West Coast winner? Brummer catches up with him and together they finish the rounds. It's better having Brummer by his side. Maybe Brummer will win. Paul chuckles to himself. Brummer won't win. He carves "Welcome Bears" and "Welcome Bears" never win. They sell. Not so bad. Given the times, everyone will want to sell.

Back at his log, Brummer lays out the saws between them. Paul pulls on his gloves. Adjusts his earmuffs. At ten o'clock, they wait the long last minute for the bell's clang. Time to start. And when it does, there is an immediate roar of chainsaws. The carvers appear to hug the saw's vibration. Paul grips the four-foot Sthil, grips the toggle, and pulls. The whine of the motor is as good as it gets. He loves the thrum and the weight of the saw.

He can almost taste the oil and breathes in the fumes of gas. The saw fills him with awe and pleasure, an extension of his arms, of his mind, of his heart. He bends to the chatter of the blade on wood. Wood chips shoot over his leather gloves and up his arms. The sour-green bite of newly cut wood catches at the back of his throat. Paul swallows the smell as if it were the best malt liquor.

At the first break, Ace, Spitzky, and Brummer gather around Paul. Brummer offers Paul a bite of marionberry pie. Together they all stare at the large, about to take shape carving, each wondering at the arc of the umbrella. An umbrella?

Ace nudges Paul's carving with the steel toe of his boot. "What's it?"

"You know it's bad luck to talk about a cut."

"Looks like he might be copying me," Spitzky says as he catches the chocolate covering of the ice cream bar in his hand. "Not a good sign when even your ice cream bar falls apart."

Paul answers, "Spitz, it's a sign. Carve big fat round bears and guaranteed…it won't ever fall apart."

"Don't mock old Spitz," Brummer cautions.

"Somebody's got to sell. Somebody's got to win. Right?" Ace asks to no one in particular.

Brummer joins the banter. "I may not win, but at least I don't have to cut mine up for fire wood. Bears I carve. Bears I sell. Your dad was no dummy, Paul. He knew." Brummer takes a last bite of pie and with his arm he wipes the juice from his chin.

Paul pulls on his leather gloves. He's glad the break is short. He doesn't want to hear about selling. He doesn't want to hear about who's going to win. And he sure as hell doesn't want to explain to anybody anything about what he's carving.

The warning bell clangs. "And…," Paul turns to Brummer, Ace, and Spitzky, and says, "…you better get back to your saws before I whup your asses."

Paul adjusts his earphones, pulls his saw into action, and forgets everything but what's in front of him.

At the lunch break, carvers stand with full paper plates, talking little, sizing up the carvings. Competitors are friendly, but tense. Paul walks the perimeter of the carving area as he eats. He checks out the competition: two eagles, two bears, a seaweed thing, an angel, two fishermen, a jumping salmon, a few indistinguishable carvings, and his carving. The umbrella covers the beginning of a bent leg, a leg about to kick air.

Paul is ready for the long, last cut.

Carving is sure and sweet. Paul uses a sixteen-inch saw to carve the underside of the umbrella. He carves away the space around the animal's head and steps back to judge what he has done: the rooster's head is back, beak open, there is pride in the stance, the rooster's comb slops over one eye. Each feather is distinct and cleanly cut, each feather groups to define wings, one wing holds the umbrella. The skinny, scaled legs end in curled talons. The bell-shaped skirt is a chancy addition. The high-kicking leg points a toe toward heaven and in the final hour Paul details a garter belt with a clump of four roses.

Paul reaches in his pocket. He knows extraneous material is pushing the limits, but the round red reflectors will make perfect eyes.

His competitors aren't doing all that bad. But, if the judges, just this once, give consideration to originality, Paul thinks he just might, could possibly, win. The only real competition turns out to be one of the women, Jesse Ann Henderson. Across from him an angel folds its wings. He watches as Jesse's torch dusts the feathers with charcoal edges. It's a great angel; but it's no worry. Paul can't remember the last time a woman competed. And she didn't win. Anything.

"Nice job," George Tipton calls to Paul as he marks his judge's chart and walks on to the next carver. Paul doesn't read anything into the comment. George has been a judge for all the years Paul can remember. George was an old friend of his dad. Who knows? He might hold it against Paul not to have maintained the family tradition of carving—carving every year—carving bears. On the other hand, George is a great friend of Elsie's, so maybe she's talked to him about originality. Maybe. Just maybe.

"Looks like a rooster," Brummer offers as he helps Paul wrap each saw in its oily picnic blanket. "A real rooster . . . except for the tutu and that sexy garter belt."

"You didn't finish it," Spitzky calls as he joins them. "You didn't burn the finish."

Paul is too tired to be angry at Spitzky and too tired to even verify Brummer's obvious analysis. He restrains himself from telling Spitzky that his carving looks like every bear Spitzky has ever carved.

"Thirty minutes 'till they announce winners, let's hit the bar," Brummer says, his arms extended, rounding up everyone.

"Meet you at the judges' stand," Paul calls as his friends head up Main Street. Paul finds a shady spot under a large leaf maple in front of the Post Office. George Tipton walks back by, finished with judging. He gives Paul a thumb's up. "As good as Bear's," he calls pointing to Paul's rooster.

Paul waves and nods and says, "Thanks." Avoiding the comparison was impossible. But it irritated and astounded him that Tipton couldn't see the difference. Sure, Bear's carvings were great. But damn, it was time everyone took a good look: in case they haven't noticed, Paul didn't carve a bear. He's carved one hell of a rooster!

Behind Paul, on the post office porch, one of Bear's earliest carvings stands guard. Without looking, Paul knows it by heart: worn white from weather, a crack from snout to foot, powerful, towering, eyes glowing black with marbles, an enormous tooth-filled mouth conveying Bear's signature grin. It was one of a dozen bears that dotted porches and yards and parks in Twist. His dad had been the best.

Paul wonders why no one has ever mentioned the 'extraneous' marbles.

7

A LESSON REMEMBERED

On the grass, Paul stretches out to watch the spectators pass. His arms ache. His eyebrows are heavy with sawdust. In the sweaty creases of his neck, he itches. Perhaps it is the sting of sweat in his eyes, or the persistent burn in his tired hands, but he suddenly remembers Bear backhanding him. He flinches involuntarily, as if the blow fell on his face, now, not twenty years ago.

"Pay attention, for crap's sake! You cut. You think *bear*. Get that *bear* in your head and he'll come out your fingers. You got that?"

Paul can't make sense of Bear's anger. Anger comes from nowhere. Not just at him. Sometimes at his mom. This time the anger erupts in the middle of their first chainsaw-carving lesson. Bear points and Paul cuts. The three-foot log grows arms and legs and a snout. The bear emerges. One paw up.

"Well, at least you got that right. Never forget. The paw's always up. You cut twenty bears, perfect bears, and then maybe, just maybe, you can take some chances. You'll have plenty of time to follow my example: bears walking high wires, bears rolling balls, bears hugging barbershop poles. For a long time you carve bears like every bear you ever seen at every gas station from here to Sunday. One paw up. And don't forget the eyes. You got the marbles?"

Deep in his pocket Paul has the marbles. Aggies. A line of smoke slicing each black world. His best shooters. In front of him the finished carving glows like butterscotch. His dad stuffs the marbles in the eye sockets.

Then, like the bear could actually see, Paul drifts into a dreamy state where he and the bear are friends. The bear knows who created him. The bear knows he has been given a gift of his best marbles. The bear thanks Paul for his existence.

As if his father has read his thoughts, Bear says, "Looks like he might start talkin' any minute."

"He's perfect. What if we leave him just like he is?"

Incredulous, Bear demands, "How's that?"

"Natural. Don't burn him."

"Leave it? Boy, you aren't paying attention!" Bear's voice has an edge. Bear's voice is so loud it attracts Paul's mom shelling peas on the porch. Paul hears the metallic ping as she places the colander beside her chair and then he hears her feet crunch the gravel as she walks toward them.

"Now, Honey." Her voice has the edge of pleading.

Bear's lips tighten and he demands, "You leave us be."

Paul winces at the sharp squeeze of Bear's fingers on his shoulder, into his bones.

His mom extends hands, pleading. Bear ignores her. He continues the lecture, "Down at the Arco station, what the hell do you see? Bears! Yeah, and what kind of bears?" His words grow colder. "Tell your mom. What kind of bears?"

Paul keeps his eyes down. Doesn't want to answer. Paul loves the pure buttery color of the freshly carved wood.

"Down at the Friendly Diner, you ever seen a bear natural?" Paul stands frozen. His mom steps back as if the distance between them will loosen Bear's hand on Paul's shoulder. "Be like putting a naked lady out there. Right, Maria?" Bear lets go of Paul's aching shoulder and reaches for his wife. She stands stock-still. Bear laughs. "That'd stop em. A carvin' of a naked lady. A 'Welcome Lady!' Hah!"

"Bear, let's have lunch," her words beg. It's the voice she uses to soothe Bear's outbursts. Bear pushes Paul toward the house.

Over lunch the harangue continues.

"We'll burn the hell out of that bear," his dad says and tears a dinner roll in half, runs it through the gravy drippings. "Natural? It'd be a sissy bear, wouldn't you say, Maria?" She remains at the stove, her back to them. Doesn't answer.

Paul sits at the table next to Bear. Paul can't stop his arm from moving straight out from his mouth and dropping in a vertical line to his soup bowl. Bear yells, "Stop that stupid robot stuff!"

That's when Bear's hand goes back and the next thing soup splatters over his mother's back, over the Monarch, over the kindling box. Immediately his mother is by Paul's side, her hand steadying. Reassuring. Healing. She says low and sure, "Stop, Bear. I mean it. Stop."

Bear glares. "Watch your tongue, woman."

His mother turns away from his words and Paul watches her at the stove, her shoulders rounded as she stirs and stirs an iron kettle of applesauce. It is as if the air has changed the kitchen smell from sweet to sour. The smell marks the moment.

Paul sits. Head bowed. His stomach aches. He never figures how one good minute turns into a bad minute. How one good day turns into a bad day. Everything going okay, then kapowie! Everything changes.

The remaining minutes at dinner are coated in silence until Maria lines the empty canning jars on the dough table. Jar clanks against jar and when the jars are perfectly arranged and rearranged, all the time Bear cleaning every morsel of food from his plate, Maria throws down her apron, walks past Paul, past Bear, lets the screen door slam, and strides to the garden. From where he sits, Paul watches his mom jerk weeds from between the tomato plants. Paul dares not move. He's a prisoner at the table. He despises the sound of Bear's chewing.

His mom comes back in the house only when Bear stomps out of the kitchen and heads toward the car shed. His dad disappears under the hulk of his Chevy truck—a project never finished. Clanking metal on metal is the only sound.

Paul stays inside doing homework. Maria silently fills one canning jar after another. Paul studies a Weekly Reader. In the right-hand corner of the front page is a picture of Machu Picchu. Paul dreams of living on that high, secret mountain. He holds back tears when his mom leans to give him a hug. Her touch is not enough. He yearns to be anywhere but here. Would the silence never end? Would anyone ever speak again? Would this be one of those horrible long, long silences? Days? Weeks?

Hours later, Bear comes in the house, his overalls stained as dark as his mood. He scrubs his hands and wipes them on a clean checkered towel. Maria ignores the black streaks. Bear doesn't speak. He doesn't touch Maria. The kerosene lamps flicker. Their light barely cuts the darkness that fills the house.

Later that evening Paul sits close to the stove to get warm. He feels drugged with the weight of sadness. He tries to remember the state capitol of Illinois and asks his mom.

Bear yells, "You don't know? Where were you, boy? Asleep? I drive you across the whole damned United States, drive through every state, and tell you capitols, and you don't know?"

Paul can't remember who answered or if anyone answered, but he remembers that day was the day the *BIG* silence began. Before the silence ended, his mom was gone. She packed the cardboard suitcase. She pinned a note on Bear's recliner.

Paul found the message when he got home from school: *Don't forget Paul's parent- teacher conference on Friday.* In perfect Palmer script she'd written: *I need sunshine. You'll find the Dodge on Main Street.* Paul never understood how she could have left. Without him.

When Paul is eighteen, he and Brummer shoot pool. None of the crew has arrived for the evening game. Paul has had enough to drink to ask Brummer, "Tell me about Mom's leaving."

Brummer leans over the table. Sights a shot. Doesn't look up. He talks, as if he were telling a story that has been told a thousand times, telling a story like it was a bad fairy tale, telling a story as if his best friend wasn't the one who had been left.

The story: on a Sunday, Maria parks the Dodge in front of The Big Drinkers' Bar. The guys quit shooting pool and they watch her pull the suitcase out of the trunk. She sits on the bus bench with hands folded. She wears a red hat with a red feather. She looks like something out of a movie. When the Greyhound drives into town and stops, it blocks the view of the three guys standing at the front window of the bar. When the Greyhound drives away, the bench is empty.

That car sits, unclaimed for a week. Testifying. On Friday night, Bear walks into town. Drunk. He fumbles getting the keys in the door. The bar crowd pretends not to watch. The crew never, ever speaks of it.

Paul aches for having not been there on that bench with her. Not having left with her. And he wonders out loud, "Was he ever nice to anyone? Ever?"

"Paul, believe me, he had his moments. Good and bad. Things turned as he aged."

"Right. He got meaner. He hates me most of all."

"No, believe me," Brummer shoots a clean perfect shot that ends the game. "He loves you Paul. He's so proud you're a logger. But he's competitive. And he's a black and white kind of guy. Let me buy you a drink. I'll tell you another story." They leave the crew at the pool table and at the bar, with no one else around, Brummer clears his throat, takes another swallow of beer. "We were kids…" and at that very moment, Bear bounds into The Big Drinkers' Bar to calls and yelps and high fives. Paul watches, always amazed that the guys are glad to see Bear. Everyone so glad to see his dad. A dad he's quit talking to except for the most mundane of every day talk.

Paul drains his beer and heads out the backdoor.

A week later, Bear is felled by a six-foot tree limb. He lives for three months. Paul stays at the cabin while gangrene eats away at Bear's leg. All the time Paul ignores Bear's steady mantra, "It'll get better by itself." Doc Able is finally there by the side of the bed. Bear is delusional and uses all of his energy to be angry. He's angry at the world, angry at his son's disobedience, angry at Doc for meddling. Then he dies. Angry.

It isn't until after Bear is dead, buried, praised (but not by Paul), that Paul with a vengeance decides to burn the cabin to the ground. With that decision, comes an answer.

Paul sloshes gasoline over the walls, over the floor, over the rocker, over the bed. The smell fills him with fear and a yearning to be done with everything about this cabin: his dad, his youth, his memories. He reaches for the wooden match in the tin holder by the Monarch and as he does, he brushes the box of Red Light Matches and from behind the tin, falls a white, folded paper. He strikes the match, runs outside, the paper crumpled in his hand. He watches the cabin as the flames eat everything he wishes to forget.

In the warmth of the fire he feels cleansed and satisfied. He sits down on the chopping log and opens the paper. There in the slanty, sharp slashes of his father's writing he reads:

Damn. Damn her to hell. She's gone. In front of the whole damn town. How could she? We had good days. Not every day, but lots of good days. She forgot. Forgot the day we waltzed. Forgot the day we said our vows. Forgot when we christened Paul. I can name a hundred good days.

I've written. I've called. No Answer. No second chance. Damn. How is it that what we had disappeared? Disappeared like Pa. One day he was gone. Gone and Ma was always on me. Grow up! You're the man now. Grow up! Act like a man.

The only good days I remember are logging days. Cutting days. And now with my legs a mess, there won't be anymore days with the crew. With anybody. I tell Paul I'm getting better. I'm not. I'm going. Now I'm the one that will be going away.

Maria left and Paul's as good as gone. He's around, but we're strangers. And I thought we'd carve together. Be a team. But he carves crazy stuff. Like he's making fun of me. Like my whole life I've been nothing. If only once my Ma had held me. Said I was a good boy. I never was the boy she wanted me to be. Now I'm dying and I can't say to Paul, You're my boy. You're good. I love you. The words aren't there. This letter – this letter, Paul, is for you. With the words I could never come to say. I love you. And should you ever see your mom again, tell her I loved her. Tell her I'm sorry. I never said it enough times: I love you.

Your stupid, stupid Dad,
Bear

The bell rings and snaps Paul from his revere. He stands and shakes his aching arms. His eyes wince at the continuous clang of the bell calling everyone to the judge's stand for the announcement of the winners.

8

JESSE AND HATTIE

Jesse's angel wins third place. Spitzky's bear wins second. When the first place winner is announced, all the competitors raise their saws to salute Paul. The rooster sports a ruffled blue first-place ribbon. Paul blushes and nods and accepts the high-fives and the back pounding and tries not to be as pleased as he is.

Across the cutting yard Jesse applies another coat of oil to her angel. She waves and gives Paul a thumbs-up. Even in her rumpled overalls she looks good.

"Nice work!" Paul calls.

Jesse reaches into her bib-overall pocket. She holds a folded check in the air and snaps her fingernail against it.

"All right!" Paul acknowledges her sale and feels a slight tug of defeat. He has won, but no one appears to want a rooster in their front yard, especially a high stepping rooster in a skirt. He watches as Jesse neatly packs her three Stihls in their cases, as neat as chefs' knives. She places the saws on a pallet along with her tool chest, compressor, and gas can and pulls the load to her camper. Paul watches, admiring her strength, her long stride, her sureness. He knows enough not to offer help to an independent woman like Jesse. Maybe she'd be around later and maybe he'd get up enough nerve to ask her to dinner.

Judge Murphy walks across Main Street and as he hands Paul his hundred-dollar check, he grumbles, "Women'll get a blue ribbon over my dead body." He steps away and then turns back as if he's forgotten something. "Keep that extraneous shit off your carvings if you enter the Nationals."

"No chance. I'm . . ."

"Just thought I'd warn you. If it weren't for Bear . . ."

Judge Murphy walks away and Paul's pleasure at winning vanishes.

Over a microphone at the stage next to The Big Drinkers' Bar, Travesty John announces, "SOUP'S ON!" Families, crews, dogs, and kids gather. Everyone moves into an amorphous line along tables of plywood covered with white butcher paper. Today's main meal is Elsie's famous "Growing Stew." The hearty, sweet-sour smell of Methow Mountains Cabernet bubbles around an assortment of Walla Walla sweets, Idaho potatoes, Yakima sweet corn, home-grown carrots, and Elsie's particular touch— Wenatchee Granny Smith apples.

Paul pulls his sore body up the back stairs to his room. He washes and changes into suntans and a crisp, white shirt. Standing on the front steps of the bar, he looks to see if he can find Jesse.

A resounding whack on his back turns Paul to Brummer. "Some carving, buddy. A chip off . . ." Paul's face tightens a fraction and Brummer changes course, "I knew you'd do it!"

"Thanks. Seen Jesse?"

"Not since the carving. She gave you a run for your money!"

"No question. She's good."

"Did you see the feathers on those wings? Brilliant."

"If Judge Murphy would just fall down dead, women might have a chance."

"Paul, trust me. You won because your rooster is the best. Besides, angels? Won't happen. Even without Judge Murphy, everyone wants bears and eagles and..." he chuckles with pleasure and just an edge of disbelief, "...roosters, of course!"

Paul turns and catches a glimpse of Jesse. She's deep in conversation with a woman Paul has never seen before. Paul waves and the two women move toward him through the crowd.

Paul nudges Brummer. "Well, here she comes. You can tell her she'll never win."

Brummer pulls on his suspenders. Smoothes his hair. Calls, "Hi, Jesse! We were just talking about you!"

"And we were just talking about *you*. Well, about Paul, anyway. Brummer, Paul, meet Hattie McFee. From *The Seattle Times*."

"Gentlemen," and Hattie reaches with a firm grip to shake each man's hand. "It's a pleasure. I'd love to get a couple of statements from you. Whitinowsky, isn't it?"

"How about over a beer?" Brummer suggests.

Paul slips behind the bar and pulls two beers. He notes them on his tab. His eye skips down the tally. With his abstinence, he is forty bucks away from a zero balance. What with rent paid, Cruisewell's generosity, and the hundred dollar bill in his wallet—Paul, these last few days, has become generous. And what with all the lay-offs, he is rarely turned down.

"Now, back to business. Tell me, how did you get into carving?" Hattie asks, pen at the ready.

Before Paul can answer, Brummer speaks, "It's his dad, Bear Whitinowsky. Bear was the best carver this place has ever seen, before Paul, of course. My best friend, Bear. And Paul? Well, Paul just seems to have gotten it by, what's that word? Osmosis? Right, Paul?"

"I guess."

"There's at least five of his dad's winning carvings right here on Main Street. I'll be glad to show them to you. Front of the post office? Bear's very first win. Nineteen-seventy nine. Then there's one in the park. A giant bear with a honey pot. There's a third at the Arco station. And more."

"Paul, you learned from your dad, then? And he's no longer carving?" Hattie asks.

"Well, he's no longer…"

Brummer interrupts, "Bear recently passed on. A great loss. A really great loss." He leans towards Hattie. "I've got an idea. Let me show you those carvings. Give Paul a breather here and when we get back, I'll bet you'll get yourself a good story." Brummer picks up his beer and reaches for Hattie's. Hattie looks from Paul to Jesse to Brummer and then follows Brummer out the door.

"What was that all about?" Jesse asks.

"Just Brummer being Brummer." Paul feels his face flush, fearful Jesse will see the obvious ploy of Brummer leaving him alone with her. "So, you sold your angel?" he asks.

"Brummer sure was bossy."

"Nerves, I would guess. I've never seen him be anything but nervous around women. I think he's takin' a shine to Hattie."

"Too bad. She won't be interested. In case you didn't notice, we're a bit more than friends." With certain sadness, it dawns on Paul what Jesse has just said. "And the great news is that Hattie's going to write a major story about the competition."

"I'll believe that when I see it."

"If you're worried she'll make fun or hold us up as yokels, you're wrong. She's Seattle's best art critic. She thinks our work is good, good as any city sculpture. Well, she might add 'edgy' but she still thinks it's exceptional. She's a fan, and a very nice person. And I don't say that only because she bought my angel."

"Oh! She's your buyer! Nice. How'd she learn about Twist?"

"We met through *The Stranger.*"

"Astounding. The whole world appears to meet through *The Stanger.*"

"Yes, thank goodness for the personal ads."

"Right, ah, right." Paul wipes down the bar, clears the empty beer mugs, avoiding the discussion of Jesse's friendship and avoiding an explanation of how he even knows about *The Stranger.* " 'Scuse me a minute. I might be a carver, but I'm also a bartender!"

A few more customers fill the bar. As he moves from table to table, Paul is slapped up the head by a huge sadness. He isn't going to just miss Twist, his buddies, the mountains. He's going to miss carving. He's going to miss Travesty John and Elsie. He forces himself to think about the fact that he won't miss being broke.

Minutes later, Hattie and Brummer push through the front door. Hattie's arm is draped over Brummer's wide shoulder. They straddle the barstools on either side of Jesse. Paul sets out another round of beer.

"Wait 'till you hear the story Hattie just told! Wait 'till you hear!" Brummer hiccups and laughs and wipes tears from his eyes.

Jesse guesses, "The Russian story?"

"Yes. Can you stand to hear it again?"

With an encouraging smile from Jesse, Hattie begins, "Before I was the art critic, I was the travel writer. I did a series of stories on women-owned businesses in Russia. I was in Georgia for a month. Got to know a number of women. One, Slovana Ostnick, was so pleased with my article about her; she expanded her business and sent me a photo. She named the new business *Hatties*. After me, of course. So there she is in front of her sign, beaming and proud." Hattie looks at Paul to be sure he's ready for the punch line. "She sells manure!"

Brummer laughs and his hiccups return. Jesse shows him how to drink out of a glass backwards. Brummer spills beer down his overalls and drowns the hiccups. Admiration written all over his face. That Hattie. Some woman!

9

A LECTURE

As if knowing Hattie needs Paul's full attention, Elsie gives Paul a pat on the shoulder. "I won't need you for awhile. Take advantage of the lull. Sit yourselves on the front porch. And, Paul, tell Hattie nothing but how wonderful we all are!"

Hattie raises her pencil, and in a "follow me" motion leads Paul out the door. They sit facing Mt. Grizzly and Hattie shows Paul her list of questions.

The list is complete. Paul is slightly intimidated about what Hattie already knows: the names and styles of saws, a list of past and future competitions, names of his crew, and a map with black dots: the location of all of his dad's carvings in Twist.

"So begin," she says with an encouraging smile.

"Let's stick to your list. Feels better than just yammering on about nothing."

"Your choice. But yammering is never about nothing."

Paul points to the first word on the list: *Saws*. "My favorite's the sixteen-inch Stihl. Like the extension of my arm. It cuts details. Maneuvers easily. Even smells good. But the forty-two-inch saw makes wonderful sweeping cuts. Creates the base." He looks at the list, "Next question."

"I'm ready. Tell me about the competitions. How they work. Who qualifies. Who judges. Criteria."

"Well, Twist has a competition every year. I've attended since I can remember."

"And competed?"

"I used to. Missed a few."

"How's that?"

"Well, when I was ten, I won the junior division. But it was a stupid carving."

"Can't have been too stupid."

"The judge probably didn't know what he was doing."

"Given how you carve now, you're probably not the best judge of that." Hattie waits for Paul to continue. Paul shakes his head as if to wipe away the whole idea. Hattie stays silent.

"I haven't competed since. My dad won every year. It seemed a bit futile to compete. After he passed, my crew pushed me to compete. I decided to give it a try. I signed up."

"Did you make drawings? How did you plan?"

"Ideas come to me in dreams. Night dreams. Day dreams. They appear. Like ear-worms. I have dozens of ideas I need to find in the logs. My next competition? Who knows. Presently, I've got some other distractions."

"Like?"

"Nothing much. What do you say we get something to eat? Travesty probably needs help."

"But, before that, come with me." She tucks her hand in the crook of Paul's arm and walks him to his rooster. Ten photographs later they finish.

"Well, dear friend, that's a start. I'll be interviewing others, but don't be surprised if I call again," Hattie beams with pleasure and waits for Paul to speak. Hesitancy is written all over his face.

"Hattie. How about you use the photo of the rooster? Just the rooster."

"Bad idea. This is not the time to be shy, retiring, or whatever you're thinking. This is a chance to let people see you. This will get your name out there. If you're uncertain about your future, this can make your future!"

"I'd prefer if you didn't."

Hattie taps her pencil on her pad. Paul can see she's not ready to give ground.

"Do the story. Picture the rooster. Feature Twist. But, I've got this new job. My employer might not like this kind of publicity. About chainsaw carving."

Hattie sighs and steps back, shaking her head in confusion. "Believe me. In all my years as a reporter, no one has asked that I write less."

"Let's do this. Write the article. Make it about the competition. When the Nationals are here, should I come back to compete, should I win, you can write whatever you like. The competition will be stiff. I'll be in or out of this job. I'll be able to handle it."

The determination in Paul's voice can not be ignored. Hattie closes her notepad. "Your call, Paul."

"I'd appreciate it."

"That's a deal. I won't use your name. An anonymous quote or two. But no pictures with your smiling face." Hattie shakes Paul's hand. "But, fair warning, I'll be following you, and one of these days…"

They return to the front porch of the bar and before they push through the doors, Hattie stops. "You've an exceptional talent, Paul. Your medium's unusual, but your talent? I'm amazed."

Paul is surprised at his irritation. He's turned her down. He's not explained a thing about why. He surprises himself when out of his mouth pop the words: "You mean, you can't quite believe real art talent exists with a chainsaw? Logs aren't quite legit?" Paul's words are clogging hard.

Hattie answers, "Keep on talking and I'm going to get a front page article out of you yet! Tell me, what's all the energy about?"

"Forget it. Not sure where that came from. Let's go inside."

Paul pushes through the doors to The Big Drinkers' Bar. He tries to ignore Hattie but she doesn't leave his side and keeps right on talking. "I meant what I said. I spent the whole day studying every contestant. I saw carvers who haven't a clue. They cut until the log's gone. And I saw carvers who made kitsch. And I saw some craftsmen. And then there's you, Paul. That rooster? You went right up to the edge and then you flew! It's not just interesting and well done, it's startling. A rooster with the freshness of Chagall."

Paul straddles a stool, accepts the Coke delivered by Elsie.

"Elsie, have a few words for Hattie?"

"She's already interviewed me! I raved about you. No question, it's going to be a great article."

Paul turns to confront Hattie, and then holds his tongue when she gently touches his arm.

"It's a great story. Everyone thinks so highly of you. I've already considered suggesting the headline for the article: *A Michelangelo with a Chainsaw*."

Elsie exclaims, "What a sparkling idea! You two keep talking! Travesty needs me at the grill." She heads to the kitchen and Paul says loud enough for her to hear, "That's nuts! The two of you are nuts!"

"No, my dear," Hattie says beaming. "This is opportunity. Opportunity has come knocking. For instance, do you know the name Jim Dine?"

Paul shakes his head. "Never heard of him. He a carver?"

"You might say that. But he's also a painter and a printmaker. Famous. World renowned. And guess what. He has a carved angel. It's in Bilbao. In Italy. Beautiful. But let me tell you, even with his talent, he doesn't have your edge. He hasn't your history. It might please you to know his carvings presently bring over a hundred thousand. Each, that is."

"Dollars? A hundred thousand dollars? That's beyond crazy." He hesitates and then in awe asks, "You're not joking?"

Hattie meets his stare. Her enunciation becomes very precise as if her words need to drill through Paul's skull. "I could have been in and out of Twist in a minute. I stayed. I talked to Elsie. It broke her heart when you quit carving as a young boy. She never doubted you were as good as Bear. Possibly better." Hattie reaches out to grasp Paul's arm. "So, give me space. Art's not an easy road. No quick millionaires. But I can tell you, there's an audience for your work. It would take some time, but if I were you…"

Paul interrupts, "I haven't got time."

"Artists make time."

"Not this one. I'm leaving Twist. I'll not be carving."

Silence hovers over Hattie and Paul.

"Well, sorry for the lecture. I just thought you needed to hear what I had to say."

She slips off the bar stool, takes two steps as if she might leave, then stops, turns around and offers Paul her hand, "Let's play some music. I hear you're a great dancer."

With the last beat of Hank Williams *Hey Goodlookin'*, Paul twirls Hattie under his arm and bows deeply. She roars with laughter and gives him a big hug. They collapse in the back booth and Elsie brings them a menu. "Keep on interviewing that knucklehead until he gets the message!" Elsie says. "Order whatever you want. I'm paying off that rooster!"

"Well, isn't that nice!" Hattie says with a laugh.

Paul smiles his pleasure and stifles an urge to tell Hattie he'll soon be in Seattle. He'd love to meet up with her there. He'd love to have someone to talk to about Twist, about cutting, about chainsaw art. But what would a tough-talking reporter think of someone headed to a trailer court to be a minister to widows? Not much.

"Paul!" Travesty calls before Hattie and Paul have a chance to order, "I could use your help." With relief, Paul excuses himself and for the next two hours pulls beers, takes orders, serves platters and baskets of food.

By the time Paul has a break Elsie hands him a note: "*We're back to Seattle. Stay in touch! I'll send you a copy of the story once it's printed. See you in the future! Hattie.*"

Paul tucks the note into his shirt pocket and Brummer steps up to greet Paul with a hearty slap on the back. "Ouch, easy on the shoulder, man. I'm totally out of shape. Not used to cutting! I'm feeling old and beat. Another half hour and I'm going to sneak upstairs and collapse."

"Not staying for the party? You, the polka freak? I'll have to dance twice as hard, for the both of us!"

"You do that. Besides, nothing worse than not enough women to partner. Polkas weren't meant to be danced alone."

10

LONESOME BED

Paul's last days fly by. As word spread like an ever enlarging circle dance, the bar fills with locals come to say goodbye. With more customers, Elsie needs Paul and Paul tending the bar gives him a chance to say goodbye to everyone.

The rooster is a major topic of conversation. All the congratulations sit well.

At ten o'clock the next to last night Travesty pulls the plug on the Wurlitzer, the loggers rack their cue sticks, late-staying customers turn chairs upside down on the tables—legs up like a dozen dead dogs—and The Big Drinkers' Bar folds for the night.

Paul grabs a mop to justify luxuriating in the easy companionship of Elsie and Travesty as they button down the bar. He thinks he would never tire of being in the presence of their gentle ease together. Elsie sets the dishwasher to washing. Travesty wipes down the bar. Burps waits at the back door. A cold breeze slips off Mt. Grizzly and circles a partner-less dance through Twist. Soon Paul will leave and the rooster will stand guard at The Big Drinkers' Bar.

Locking the back door, Travesty and Elsie follow Burps as he gallumps to their truck. Travesty, ever the gentleman, ever the lover, opens the truck door for Elsie. From the back porch Paul waves and calls, "g'night!" A double honk of the horn beeps 'goodnight.'

Paul lingers until the late night cold works its way into his bones and he knows it's time to face his empty room with his empty bed and the midnight news on his twelve-inch screen. Part of him wants to be gone. Part of him wants to never leave. It seems these last days with everyone aware he's leaving; he's been more lonesome than ever.

In his room the television is full of the anniversary of Laika, the space dog. Paul stands at the window, staring into the black space above Main

Street. He studies the dark and the far stars and he chokes-up thinking about the puppy eternally circling earth.

In time, Paul turns back the bedspread. The bed is too big, too empty, too cold. He crawls under the covers and he waits for sleep. He waits for the tiredness of the week to sink him into a night of dreams. Instead of dreaming, he aches. His shoulders ache. The blisters on his hands burn. He hates his aches and he loves his aches. The soreness eases over him like the hug of an old friend. He closes his eyes and he replays the cutting of the rooster. He conjures the vibration of the saw, can still see the wood giving way to the rooster. He loves that rooster. He re-visits every word Hattie said. He can't keep from thinking maybe she's right, maybe he's good. Then immediately he thinks she's both crazy and wrong. And maybe leaving Twist isn't the worst thing that could happen.

Paul falls into a restless dream-soaked sleep. Granddad, Sederius Whitinowsky, holds a dragsaw at his side, like a weapon. Around him trees fall and horses skitter and skids fly. Bear's father appears and Sed hands over the saw which immediately grows a motor and throbs as it cuts into a tree as wide as their cabin. Paul is about to offer help, to take over, when his mother calls from the front porch and Bear leaves the thrumming saw which cuts by itself and Bear runs to the front porch, arms open, and he and Maria dance.

When a bright morning sun hits his face, Paul wakes smiling, pleased that for once he's had a sweet dream. He slips his hands behind his head and takes in the new morning. He wonders about leaving Twist. Twist, his only home. Logging center of the Northwest. Real trees gone. Not that there weren't trees left to cut. Second growth. Third growth. But the big mamas? Old-growth? All hidden and forbidden. Hands-off. But along the roads and the highways, where forests once stood, acres and acres of cottonwood grow in four-year cycles. Pulp. How Paul feels about himself. Pulp. Sadness replaces sleepiness.

11

THE LAST DAY

Paul folds his suit, a suit not worn since his dad's funeral. He places it in the bottom of his suitcase. He lays his white shirt and his good suntans on top of the suit, tomorrow's traveling clothes. He curls his tie and tucks it in the corner. Five of everything: shirts, socks, T-shirts, shorts. He throws his worn work clothes in the waste basket. He works quickly ignoring the sadness that surrounds him. He snaps the suitcase closed. Damn. He forgot the stupid lessons. He un-snaps the suitcase. Slams the pile of papers inside. Cruisewell hasn't said so, but Paul fears he'll want to review the lessons. Question Paul. See if he has an understanding of what it is to "minister." Cruisewell's ever growing, ever evasive definition. Paul thinks the lessons are useless. Who cares about boxes of Kleenex, tithing, animal care, voice modulation, confessions. The word *confessions* makes Paul's stomach cramp. The lessons are nuts. Paul feels shame at how easily he has learned to correctly answer multiple choice questions. If Cruisewell only knew. And his stomach cramps again at the thought that he probably does know. And once again Paul side-steps the question, "Why am I doing this?"

Paul checks the room. His closets. All the drawers. He's ready. That's a joke. He'll never be ready.

Downstairs, Elsie hums as she slathers white-sugar frosting on a pan of cinnamon rolls. She looks up when Paul enters.

"It's good you've only today left, sweetie"

"How's that?"

"Take a look," she nods toward Brummer in the far corner hidden behind the *Methow Mountains Post.* "Went to work this morning and got a pink slip. Look and you'll see it's sopping up the coffee he spilled. He's down."

Before Paul has a chance to join Brummer to say how sorry he is, Spitzky and Ace enter the bar, stomping and shouting. "We need coffee!" They flag their pink slips to let Brummer know he's not alone. Ace yells, "The usual!" and Elsie starts whipping up eggs.

"Four down, wonder how many more to go. Hard to watch," Elsie says. "Well, I guess it's only three down, what with you actually being employed."

"Don't remind me."

"Think of it this way, maybe some haven't gotten pink slips."

"Yet."

"Travesty," Elsie calls. "Four breakfast specials!" And she gives Paul a nudge. "Git. Join your friends. Make it a good day."

Paul moves around the bar wiping tables, enjoying the smooth feel of wood under his hand. He makes his way toward the corner table. The initial exuberance of his crew has given over to a sad silence.

Travesty calls from the back of the kitchen, "Hey! It's much too quiet! Paul! Put a quarter in that machine."

Paul walks to the jukebox. Without looking he hits number thirty-two. The blended harmony of "Waltzing with Bears" glides through the bar. When the chorus begins, Brummer booms across the room. He pushes aside his chair, and flings his arms wide. With his pool stick in hand he lopes around the room, as if he were clutching a microphone. He jumps and turns, and gives waltzing a try. At the chorus, Ace grabs Spitzky and they waltz, stomping and swaying around the tables. Singing, off-key and loud. Paul can't resist. He grabs Elsie and joins in the dance. His voice the loudest.

At the end of the singing and the end of the dancing, Brummer calls, "Bring on the beer! Bring on the cinnamon rolls!" Paul heads for the kitchen, and Brummer calls, "Paul, get your ass back over here. Last day? Hell, you're fired!"

Travesty John brings a tray of beers and a single Pepsi. He slaps Paul on the back and says to the guys, "Let's party all day. No holding back. Paul, buck up. There isn't one of your crew wouldn't trade places with you. Pure envy. And so what if you aren't the best minister in the whole world. Who in hell cares. If it doesn't work out, and we sure hope it doesn't, you'll come back. Right? Six months isn't that long."

"Easy for you to say."

Travesty gives Paul a gentle push and announces, "First round on the house—in honor of the recently ordained— itinerant, illiterate minister!" The men cheer and Paul raises his glass. He likes the noise and the cheers, but he knows they are not envious. And if there was an emotion to describe how Paul feels, it would be more like: bewildered, bemused, baffled, confounded, confused, and just a bit concerned. What if Cruisewell is a crook? A scam artist? A total phony?

Paul joins his crew and he thinks, I wish I had a pink slip from Cruisewell. I wish I was one of them.

By the end of the day, the goodbyes are over. Elsie, Travesty, and Paul lock the doors.

"Come sit for a minute," Elsie sits on the back steps. She scoots over for Paul and Travesty to join her. "What a hole there's going to be with you gone," she says.

"I'll be back to visit. I'm sure I will."

"Not the same. Travesty's taking bets on when you'll be back, I mean, for sure be back. Want to join the pool? Place a bet?"

"No thanks. I'm squirreling money away. Escape money. Which brings me to the question, are you positive you want that rooster for the last of my bill? You sure you're not going to regret it? A sympathy purchase?"

"Paul, I've told you, we love that rooster." Elsie gives Travesty a gentle push. "Don't we, sweetie?"

"Without a doubt!" Travesty says. "And listen to this! I'm going to make a recording. Of a rooster. The door opens? The rooster crows."

Paul moans, "Oh, God. Then everyone will really hate me."

"No one hates you. They might think you're crazy, though."

"Or sold out," Travesty adds.

"But no one hates you," Elsie says and gives Paul a hug.

"Which do you think?" Paul asks.

Travesty answers, "Sold out or crazy? Guess I think what's important is what you think."

"I don't think. I can't."

"That bad?"

"Bad. Out of the blue, for no reason, Cruisewell sent me a note that said he'd be out of touch for a few days. He's recruiting."

"There's more than one of you?" Elsie's question is full of disbelief.

"There may be dozens of me. One of these days, someone's going to figure out what the hell's going on. It's scary. Like Cruisewell's dopey correspondence school. One whole lesson was on breathing. Breathing, for God's sake. I think that was the name of the chapter: *Breathing, for God's Sake*," Paul groans.

"Paul, it's never too late." Travesty leans so that Paul can't look away. "I can't believe you won't get back here. Back home. Back to cutting. The Nationals need you. Need your talent."

"The Nationals? I couldn't even qualify."

Travesty goes silent and then after a thoughtful moment says, "Listen up. I'll get you qualified. You have one win. You need two. There are a couple of small competitions north of Seattle. I'll come kidnap you, get you there, you'll win, and we'll have you back here in time!" Travesty extends his hand, "A deal?"

Paul swats Travesty's hand away. "No deals. I've got too much ahead of me."

"Like what? What's more important than competing? And, as I recall, your words, 'I think I'll vomit…no it was worse, you said puke…if I have to preach.' And, as you have clearly pointed out; there is no possibility of not preaching given that this trailer court is expecting a full-fledged minister."

"Maybe I'll just drive off the road tomorrow."

Elsie pats Paul's hand, "You'll be okay. Much as I would be pleased to have you stay, you'll do just fine. And someday you'll be back."

"But for now. Time to go." Elsie stands and pulls Travesty to his feet. Travesty kisses the top of her head. "Lover," he says to her, "*You* should be a minister."

"I *would* be a great minister, come to think of it. Don't you agree Paul? You and me."

Travesty pulls back in mock horror. "You'd run off with this slick-talking, woman-seducing preacher man?"

Elsie leans against Travesty, reassuringly pats her husband's protruding belly as she talks to Paul. "You want my advice Paul? Whenever things get difficult, pretend you're a bartender. Listen to those widow ladies. Someone asks a question? Answer by asking them what they think. It's simple. They do the talking. Guaranteed. Bartending is the best ministering I know."

"Wise, wise words," Travesty says and gives Elsie a big squeeze.

Paul wants Elsie and Travesty to stay right where they are, with him, hugging and assuring him that all will be well—forever.

"You ready?" Elsie asks.

"Ready as I'll ever get," Paul says and brushes off the seat of his pants.

On the back porch, they stand together. They look up to a sky bursting with stars. Silence surrounds them and then Travesty shouts, "Wait! Wait! I can't believe I forgot!" He unlocks the door and disappears inside the bar. Seconds later the porch light comes on and Travesty returns with his hand outstretched. He unfolds a copy of *The Seattle Times*. He hands the newspaper to Paul, "I feel like a fool. I can't believe I forgot this! A going-away present!"

Paul pages through the paper. Bewildered, he looks at Travesty John.

"Check the *Arts* section."

Paul flips pages. His heart skips a beat as his eyes land on a photograph of a rooster. His rooster! The fingers of his hand are just visible on the head of the bird.

"I can't believe it!"

"Read! Read it out loud. It's the best thing that's ever happened to Twist!"

Paul reads the title: *"New Art in the Northwest."* He continues, *"A new art form has hit the Northwest with the power of a chainsaw cut. Chainsaw carving, a relatively new form of folk art, better known on the East Coast and the South as Outsider Art, will soon be seen in major art collections around the world. Mac MacCaffrey, a prominent New York art collector, has put together a private collection on his game preserve in Maine. The collection is valued at one hundred thousand dollars. Pieces like this whimsical, but deconstructed rooster, are examples from the Logging Days Celebration in Twist, Washington. Unlike other Outsider Art pieces bringing in ten thousand to twenty thousand dollars, this Northwest rooster sold for under one thousand dollars.*

This art form deserves watching. You can quote me: chainsaw art is ART!"

Paul looks up in amazement. Elsie beams. Travesty grabs the paper and reads the caption under the photograph: *"Chainsaw art will follow the spiraling path that glass art has taken in the last fifteen years. Now is the time to invest!*

"Holy shit," Paul shakes his head in disbelief.

"Paul, you've got about twelve hours to quit talking like that."

"But, can you believe this?" he asks. He brings the picture of his rooster up close to his face as if closeness would make the picture and the article more believable.

"The newspaper came overnight. I was going to show it off to everybody, but then with all the sadness and then all the singing and dancing, I plum forgot." Travesty John points. "Look at the headline!"

Paul holds the paper at arms length and reads outloud: *ONE THOUSAND TODAY! TEN THOUSAND TOMORROW?*

"So, you don't really have to be a minister anymore if you don't want to," Elsie says.

Paul studies the picture. He re-reads the article. After a long silence, he looks up. "One thing you've missed, Elsie. The headline is a question, not a statement." Paul hands Elsie the paper. "Besides, I've no saws. I'm packed. I've got eight widows waiting for me. I'm committed. Maybe I *should* be committed!"

"Besides, it's my rooster," Travesty John says with a guffaw. "Touch it and you're dead meat! And, soon, that rooster's going to crow!"

Sunrise the next morning Elsie and Travesty stand next to Paul in the parking space in front of The Big Drinkers' Bar. Elsie plants a kiss on Paul's newly shaved face. She pats his clean chin. "You should have done that earlier," she says. "I just might have run away with you."

"The only catch is that we'd have had to take Travesty with us."

"Well, you're right about that," she says, giving her husband a hug.

Burps emerges from the bar and stumbles down the stairs to where they stand. The dog works his nose into the back of Paul's knees. Paul kneels to give Burps a hug, pulls back as drool escapes the dog's rubbery mouth. Even with the drool, Paul realizes how reluctant he is to push away the canine mass. Burps separates himself from the three of them, settles on the top step of the porch where he tucks the curve of his back into the feet of the rooster.

"Now. About the Nationals," Travesty speaks as if their previous conversation had been interrupted by seconds rather than hours. "There's got to be a way to get two more wins. If I can't get you to those wins, I'll just say you did. I'll lie. No one checks those applications."

"Great way to begin a career as a minister."

"Ah hah! You haven't even left and already it's a career."

"You never know. What if by some miracle I'm a natural? Maybe I'll love sermonizing, taking care of sick old people, advising newlyweds."

Elsie interrupts, "I'd suggest if someone's sick, you call a doctor. You know diddly-squat about marriage. And sermons? Thank God you're going into the miracle business."

"Just be sure your butt's back here," Travesty says as he throws Paul's bag into the back seat of the Jeep. "You get back. You win the Nationals. Sell a few carvings for ten thousand dollars. Pay back Cruisewell. Come home for good."

"Great idea!" Paul eases into the driver's seat. He leans out the window. "Guess we can't prolong this goodbye much longer." He reaches out his hand to their hands. "Thanks. Thanks for everything."

"If I believed in prayer, I'd pray for you, sweetie," Elsie says as Paul pushes the key into the ignition.

Paul pulls the Jeep on to Main Street. He turns one last time to wave. "Yeah, me too," he says to exactly no one.

12

ON TO SEATTLE

Beside him in the Jeep sits Elsie's parting gift: a Sears boot-box packed with a lunch of wax-paper wrapped fried chicken, still-warm soda bread and two Granny Smiths. The lunch nestles between an assortment of canning jars filled with her homemade treats. Paul knows he will have the taste of Twist for days to come: pickles, jams, peaches, apple sauce. With his free hand, he reaches for an apple and as he does, a note falls free: YOU PICKED A FINE TIME TO LEAVE US, LUCILLE. He smiles and savors the tart taste and with Kenny Rogers floating through his brain the WELCOME TO TWIST sign fades in his rearview mirror and he wonders how long it will take for the hurtin' to heal. Leaving is tough.

Paul hums the song as he takes the twists and turns through the mountains along the Winthrop Valley Highway. The demand of driving takes away some of the spider-like anxiety that creeps up his spine. He rolls down the window. The rush of cool air off the snowy peaks blows over his cleanly shaved face. Paul catches his reflection in the rearview mirror. Surprise. He's smiling. Maybe this whole adventure will be just that. An adventure. He reaches for a chicken leg.

The Jeep accelerates around the snaking curves between High Mountain Glacier and The Four Sisters. Above him the first fallen snow has dusted the broken patches of summer snow. Everything is fresh and new.

Three hours later, Paul drives through a stream of honking, swerving, speeding, bumper-to-bumper traffic. At the Eighty-fifth street exit off I-5 he turns. At the first light, he spreads his fingers, loosening his grip on the wheel. As the light changes to green, he dodges a minivan of sixteen-year-olds bouncing to the blare of rap. He inches around a woman in a station wagon with three children wailing in car seats. He allows a Harley biker with his girl friend attached to his leather bulk to pass. At a red light he stops and half way down the block he sees a railroad-car diner with a neon sign blinking, REX, EAT. Paul checks his map and re-reads Cruisewell's note: TWO BLOCKS PAST REX'S DINER, TURN LEFT.

The Jeep bumps over a set of railroad tracks. Paul stops to stare at the trailer court entrance. He thought he knew what to expect. He'd dreamt the trailer court. He imagined the trailer court. The trailer court in front of him? Nothing fit.

The fresh stark whiteness stops him. White pillars. A white arch. White gravel. At the base of each pillar are bursting red geraniums. The silhouetted words, TRAILER COURT, fill the space inside the arch. Everything about the entrance shouts 1930s. Embedded in one column, above the flowers, is a sign: NEW DAWN IS BREAKING TRAILER COURT. Directly across, on the other column are the words: ADULTS ONLY – NO PETS ALLOWED. Under the sign sit two children.

In unison the children wave to Paul. He wiggles his fingers in a return wave. The children wave more vigorously. They stand. They follow his Jeep as he maneuvers the white gravel road between the columns and under the arch. In the rear view mirror he watches the girl hold firmly to the hand of the rolling shape of what Paul figures must be her little brother. Ten and five, he guesses. The five-year-old in Oshkosh overalls—brilliant red hair and cheeks to match. The girl's shiny black ponytail bounces as she skips beside the churning feet of her brother. Every other skip she reaches with her free hand to push up the black-framed glasses that slide down her nose.

Paul drives half way around the fanned wheel of Airstream trailers. In the center of the wheel grows a vigorous patch of blooming marigolds, asters, zinnias, and daisies. Directly across the drive in the window of one of the trailers, Paul catches the movement of a curtain. Sun flashes off the curved loaf of one of the Airstream trailers and in the window he glimpses a smiling face. An older woman. Plump cheeks. The style of the trailer is as dated as the deco arch, but so clean the sun's reflection makes it appear to pulse. The woman waves. Paul returns the wave. Tentative. Not that he doesn't appreciate what he assumes is a friendly greeting, but he's not quite ready for it.

Cruisewell had sent a map with the last lesson. On the bottom of the map was written: PARSONAGE – HOUSE TRAILER C. By the time Paul stops in front of the post, with the curled plastic letter C, the two children stand by the side of his Jeep, faces up, sporting big smiles.

Paul hoists himself out of his vehicle, stands on the gravel, and rubs circulation back in his legs.

"Hi," the red-headed boy chirps.

"Hi."

"You must be Reverend Cruisewell's friend," the girl says, her head back, the saucer eyes studying him through her glasses.

"I'm the new minister," Paul answers.

"You're him, huh?" she asks.

The incredulous tone makes Paul repeat himself. "Right. Pastor Paul."

"Very interesting."

"And, who are you?" Paul asks, shifting his weight from leg to leg, still trying to ground himself to the gravelly earth.

"Susan Saunders. That's me, obviously. This is Sam. Reverend Cruisewell asked us to meet you." She hesitates and in a considered voice adds, "You can call me Suzie."

"Thank you."

"You're welcome."

Suzie steps back two steps as if to get Paul's image in full view. "You don't look like a minister."

"Probably not." Paul looks over the top of her head. His eyes take in the "C" marked structure: a slug-like form of a dust-streaked, partly rusted, grass encircled, certainly empty, slightly leaning house trailer. He notes it is not an Airstream.

"Maybe you could give me a hand," Paul suggests.

"To look like a minister?"

"No. I meant, show me around. You and Sam could give me a tour of the parsonage and the chapel."

"What's a chapel?" Sam asks.

Paul kneels to Sam's eye level. Before he can speak, Suzie interjects, "A church, dummy."

"And the parsonage is what I hope will be my home," Paul explains. "What'dya say we check it out?"

Sam's fat, sure fingers tuck themselves into Paul's hand—warm, alive, and inviting like a puppy's paw.

Suzie bounds down the path leading the way toward the empty trailer.

"There isn't any church," she calls.

"According to Reverend Cruisewell, it must be that building," Paul nods toward the metal building just to the right of the parsonage trailer. It appears to be a double-car garage.

"Yuk! The trailer is yucky and the other building is for storage. Not very appropriate."

"Appropriate?"

"Right. I'm very discerning," Suzie says with a push to her glasses.

"Discerning?"

"Don't mind Suzie. She likes to use big words. Learns a big word every day. Sometimes two! What'dya say?" Sam looks up at Paul, expectant, his face one big smile. "I rhyme rhymes." With that announcement, he re-takes Paul's hand and pulls him forward.

Up close the trailer grows worse: rusted, screen door askew, concrete blocks nestled in over-grown grass. With the toe of his boot Paul nudges open the floppy screen door and bends to insert the key Cruisewell sent with the last lesson. The keyhole is rusty and grime-filled as if minuscule animals had nested there for years. Paul wiggles the key unsuccessfully in the keyhole. With no luck, he turns the key upside down, holds the knob and tries a second time. Frustrated, he slams the key into the lock and the door opens, barely. The door binds against the edge of a curled rug.

The wet, moldy air pushes Paul two steps back. He squints and waits for the bad air from the inside to equalize with the fresh air from the outside.

"We'll wait out here," Suzie announces.

As the musty air slowly dissipates, Paul steps over the damp, swollen welcome mat. He steps over the loose rug edge and catches his boot on a curled slice of linoleum. He stumbles and his hand lands on damp corduroy. The back of a sofa splits like a rotten pumpkin. He pulls his hand back, shakes off the yellow crumbles of crud and coughs away the curdled air.

To his right he can make out a window and the vague outline of an eating nook. He cautiously steps one more step into the room and reaches for a ceiling light string. He pulls the string. The string drops into his hand.

Paul turns back for a bit of fresh air and sees Suzie and Sam waiting at the bottom step. He hates the fact they look sorry for him. He runs the palm of his hand up the paneled wall to find the light switch. He carefully flicks on the lights.

What catches his eye first is the blue mold etched along the wall base. The blue line continues up a wall and across the ceiling and down the other side of the room. It is as if someone had carefully blue-felt penned the trailer to designate manageable parts. Everywhere Paul looks he registers a need of repair: cleaning, airing, scrubbing, scouring. The windows above the eating nook hold yellowed plastic curtains. A faucet drips, making a soft plunking sound in a sink half-filled with water.

Paul yanks away the curtains and pushes open the sliding window. Below him the sink trembles with a luminescent oil slick. Paul plunges his hand into the sink, pulls the rubber plug, and the creamy water gurgles and swirls away in a dark funnel leaving a rim of grime. The satisfaction Paul feels at the fact that the sink drains surprises him. He knows it is the smallest ray of hope, but then it is a ray of hope.

Outside the children wait like small staunch statues and smile when Paul calls to them, "Well, not all is lost. Let's let this air. How about we check the other building?" Paul can hear his phony, chipper voice. "Suzie, I hope you aren't as discerning about the chapel as you were about the parsonage."

"What are you going to do with the garage?" Sam asks.

"The chapel?"

"No, honest, it's a garage." Suzie explains. "For junk. The ladies once used it for aerobics. That was a couple of months ago. They got discerning when they got sore. Everyone quit. The aerobics instructor left. He didn't last that much longer than the cooking instructor. Before the cooking classes, it was a garage that everybody put junk in. Now, it's been returned to its original intention!" Sally smiles a huge smile at her row of words.

As they walk through the grass, still dewy from the previous night, Paul asks, "The aerobics instructor and the cooking instructor, where did they live?"

"Who knows? It wasn't in that trailer, I'll tell you. That trailer is ready to implode!"

13

MAKING IT BETTER

Suzie pushes open the door to the garage. Paul leans over her slight body and sees that Suzie is right. Along the back wall stand floor-to-ceiling cardboard packing boxes. Directly in front of the boxes are sawhorses as if guarding the sheet of plywood that leans against them. Directly in front of the table-to-be-assembled, are three curved rows of dusty folding chairs as if the invited speaker stepped out and never returned. Along the sidewall, on its side, is a cardboard statue. It takes a second, but Paul finally realizes the cardboard statue is Bill Clinton, partially obscured by a matted green mohair over-stuffed couch, which in turn, is draped with an embroidered white tablecloth. Something inside Paul sighs with relief. It's nice to see another Democrat.

Next to the over-stuffed couch, a box spills with what appears to be jump ropes and weights, propped against slabs of workout mats.

The third side of the garage holds a pegboard of whisks and wooden spoons, metal colanders and nested measuring cups. At the base of the cooking display, a shelf holds four paperback copies of *Joy of Cooking* and the soft pastel glow of Tupperware containers.

Just then, Paul sees something move. In the center of the room in the center of the crescent of chairs sits two Tupperware shallow dishes, one reflecting a moon surface of pale milk, the other holding a crumbled mess of half eaten cat food.

Sam dashes behind Paul, pushes Suzie aside and heads toward a calico cat skulking under a folding chair. "Here, here Smuggins," Sam calls and his pudgy hands clasp the cat to his chest, its head buried under Sam's chin. Sam pushes the cat towards Paul and says, "The food's for Smuggins. She lives here. You want to give her a smooch?"

Paul accepts the cat, warm in his hands. The static halo of fur is sweet to his touch. One black eye surrounded with one black furry spot blinks and the rasp of cat tongue cleans his thumbnail.

"She's ours," Sam says, his voice full of pleasure and ownership.

Paul mutters into the head of the cat. "Smuggins, Sam, and Suzie. How is all of this in an Adult's Only No Pets Trailer Court?"

Suzie giggles. "Well, they think of us as visitors. Visitors are allowed." Suzie kneels to fill the saucer with new kibbles. Paul places Smuggins on the floor and they watch. Sam duck-walks around the cat and adds to Suzie's explanation, "But not for much longer." Sam stays glued to the magic circle created by the chairs and the soft purr of the cat. Suzie walks through the chairs, straightening each a fraction of an inch. She scoots an empty packing box in front of the half-circled chairs and stands behind it. "Pay attention! I have an announcement to make! Visitors are here through the generosity of Reverend Randi MacArthur Cruisewell! We are here not because he likes children and pets! We are here because he... likes...," and Suzie says with her finger in a "shhhh-this-is-a-secret" gesture, "He likes our mother. When he gets to see her!"

Sam claps his hands. "Bravo! Bravo! Sooooo true!"

"I'm not finished!" Suzie clears her throat. "I am pleased to announce we get to stay until things are settled. Until Saundra is hired. A steady job. This is a conundrum." She gives Paul a happy, gap-toothed smile. Paul waits. Then Suzie's spirits sag. She comes from behind the box, sits in a chair, her shoulders slump. She speaks as if talking to herself, "Saundra will never get a job. She'll never settle down. We'll never have a dad. Never, ever."

"Who's Saundra?" Paul asks.

Sam giggles, his hand over his mouth. "You're not s'posed to say that. That's what Suzie calls her." Sam looks at Paul as if they are about to share a huge secret. "She's our mom."

"Saundra." Suzie sits up straight and speaks directly to Paul, "She acts like *no* mother. Even Reverend Cruisewell can't get her to settle down."

"They do stuff in the car when she doesn't play her accordion. He pays her," Sam says as he retrieves the cat from Paul. Sam holds the cat close and with one stubby finger explores Smuggins' ear. The cat yowls and jumps and Paul catches it mid-air. He holds her until she purrs. He wipes food crumbs from her whiskers.

"What do you think about that?" Sam asks.

"Well, I'm sure whatever your mom and Reverend Cruisewell do, is, well, I'm sure it is..."

"It's not *that*!" Suzie stands in front of Paul, her hands on her hips, her chin extended. "Reverend Cruisewell does a lot of business in his big car and sometimes Saundra is his executive assistant!" Her voice has taken on an I-have-to-explain-everything tone.

Paul hands Smuggins to Sam's outstretched hands. "Gentle now." He turns to Suzie. Her magnified black, black eyes meet his and her mercurial face slips from silly to sincere. She radiates hope. "Everything's going to be okay. Honest. Wait 'till you meet Grandma Bella," Suzie says with authority.

"Grandma Bella is the best grandma in the whole world." Sam spreads his arms wide, the cat clings to the front of his overalls with its needle-like claws, and then slides paw under paw until it hits the floor and scurries behind the box of jump ropes.

"Grandma wins at bingo and gives us tons of prizes!" Sam holds up his thumb to show a bright blue plastic ring with a black and yellow Batman.

"Pretty great," Paul says. He watches Sam study his thumb. A long-forgotten tug of five-year-old joy seeps behind Paul's eyes. He remembers the time everything was on its way to wonderful. And then he remembers once, once when Bear rewarded him with a miniature "welcome bear" with ball-bearing eyes. Three-inches tall. Perfect. A gift before his father was either silent or angry. Paul blinks. He blinks again and doesn't wipe his eyes.

"It's okay," Suzie says. "Grandma Bella said to invite you for lunch. She's waiting. She will discern we're late."

14

GRANDMA BELLA

Paul closes the door to the mess in the garage and follows the children along the curve of the gravel drive toward the Airstream on the far side of the trailer court.

"Deduce. Or assume," Paul calls to Suzie as she walks ahead.

"What's that mean?" she calls back without turning.

"Deduce or assume work better than discern."

"Doesn't matter. I've said discern ten times today. I'm done with 'discern' practice." Suzie runs the last few steps, spraying bits of gravel, landing on the wooden steps that front the Airstream surrounded by an array of orange, pink, red, and yellow roses. Fat and joyous.

Through the screen door Paul sees the rounded shape of a stout woman, one hand lifted in greeting. The front door pops open and the woman with salt-and-pepper gray hair and skin the color of fresh peaches offers him her outstretched hand. Her grasp is warm, firm, and welcoming. She smells of melted chocolate. She wears a voluminous bright orange-pink muumuu that matches the color of her cheeks and the color of the roses.

"You must be Reverend Cruisewell's new recruit. Paul. Paul Whitinowsky?"

He nods and before he can answer she continues in a staccato voice, "I'm Bella Bostick. Grandma Bella! Welcome to our abode." She steps back to let Paul enter the sparkling clean, pristinely neat trailer.

"He's the minister," Suzie says.

"And, so you are," Grandma Bella looks Paul up and down.

"But no big hair like Reverend Cruisewell," Sam observes.

Grandma Bella smiles, "Sammy, my sweet, not all ministers have that kind of hair." She turns back to Paul, "Would you like a cup of coffee? Something to eat?"

The rich, dark smell of chicory sends Paul's appetite soaring. On the white Formica table, in the eating nook tucked into a corner, sits a red crockery bowl of blackberries. Next to it is a wooden platter heaped with cut squares of brownies, their insides bursting with walnuts. The brownies are the same size as the one-inch brownie cubes Paul's mother used to bake and place on a pedestal dish, as if on a throne. Paul is astounded at all of these memories. Where are they coming from? He shakes his head as if to shake away the feeling and he takes a brownie offered by Grandma Bella.

"You okay?" she asks.

"Delicious," Paul responds. "Thank you. Nothing that a brownie won't cure."

"And it's been a long journey, I'm sure."

Paul doesn't miss the implied meaning, or what he perceives as a second message. He finishes off the brownie as if he has nothing to say. At least not at this moment. But he realizes Grandma Bella will be a formidable friend and one of these days he promises himself to learn whatever it is to be learned about ministers, and widows, and children with a mother they call Saundra.

The children slip into the eating nook. Grandma Bella scoots a slat-backed chair into place for Paul.

"Lunch in two seconds," Grandma Bella announces and bustles about the four-foot-square kitchen. Before long, she pulls toasted cheese sandwiches from a toaster oven, pours milk into two cobalt blue glasses and then pops a cork from a half filled bottle of Chianti. Rich, red wine bubbles into two wine glasses. Paul hesitates to reach, unsure if Cruisewell has mentioned the liquor prohibition. It appears he hasn't.

Grandma Bella places the sandwiches on white crockery plates in front of each child and then there is silence. Sam and Suzie fold their hands and stare at Paul. Paul looks at each expectant face, including Grandma Bella's, until he realizes they are waiting for him.

"Would you like to say grace?" Grandma Bella asks.

Paul's mind blanks. His mouth turns dry. He can not remember one word of one prayer from one lesson.

Suzie narrows her eyes, without breaking her stare. "My turn!" and she bows her head to say, "Come Lord Jesus, be our guest, and let these gifts, to us be blessed. AMEN!"

Paul closes his eyes as if he might pass out and prays not for the food but for strength and forgiveness for hating this small, innocent girl who has, thankfully, upstaged him on his very first day as a minister.

In the moment of silence as they each take their first bites, and first sips of wine, a thrumb of a lawn mower, a persistent purr like a large contented cat, fills the kitchen nook.

"I'm going to have a lawn mower when I grow up," Sam announces.

Paul nods and smiles around the bite of the thick cheese sandwich. Unlike the Velveeta of his childhood, he is astounded at the ooze of cheese, the slender disks of tomatoes, the paper-thin slices of green peppers and the layer of something green and tasty that oozes at the edges of the multigrained bread.

Suzie pushes a crockery bowl toward Paul. "You can have more pesto if you want. It's because of the cooking instructor. The one that didn't last."

"Now Suzie. Alphonse introduced peppers, he did not create pesto. And he stayed just long enough until it was time for him to be on his way." Grandma Bella turns to Paul. "And, just how long will you be with us?"

"A long, long time, I hope," Paul says trying to make his answer convincing.

"Oh?" Grandma Bella says.

"Three months for sure," Paul can hear doubt, he can feel doubt. There is something about the intense gaze of Grandma Bella's coal-black eyes that has made the truth pop out.

The lawn mower passes close and for a few moments of silence, they eat. Then, as Paul watches, Sam meticulously dissects his sandwich. Along the edge of his plate he places the bread, the tomatoes, the peppers, and a small mess of pesto. Sam carefully rolls the melted mozzarella into a ball. Grandma Bella smiles benignly at his industrious destruction of the sandwich and shrugs a what-ya-going-to-do expression. Sam extends his hand with the cheese for Paul's approval.

Paul can feel the beginning of a small, piercing headache over his left eye. He must have looked in need, for Grandma Bella refills his wineglass. He begins to feel it would take more than wine to make the day's events smooth over.

"Drink up, Pastor Paul. I can see you've never had the pleasure of an extended conversation with children." Grandma Bella wipes the edge of Sam's mouth. "Suzie, Sam, finish up, and then would you be so kind as to pick a nice bouquet of flowers while our guest and I have a few minutes of adult conversation. Alone."

"Pastor Paul needs a whole lot more than flowers to fix up that par-son-age," Suzie says as she stands at the open door waiting for Sam to join her. "He needs a cleaning service."

"True." Grandma Bella answers. "In a few minutes we will be just that. His cleaning service. For now, pick a bouquet."

Sam tumbles over Paul's legs and follows Suzie out the door. Grandma Bella's face folds around a serious expression and Paul can see questions coming: "So, Paul, may I be so bold as to ask you about your relationship to Reverend Cruisewell?"

"Well, he calls me a recruit."

"For?"

"To be the minister. Here at the court. In the chapel. The New Dawn Is Breaking Adults-Only Chapel." Even to Paul it sounds like a bad joke and when he sees a smile tickle the sides of Grandma Bella's wrinkled mouth he feels as close to laughing as to crying and waits for a cue from her as to how the conversation will proceed.

"Paul. Let me tell you something. Before you, that garage was the New Dawn Is Breaking Aerobics Center and prior to that it was the New Dawn Is Breaking Culinary Building."

Paul groans and asks, "Compliments of The Reverend MacArthur Cruisewell?"

"The very one."

"Does anyone know I'm coming?"

"*Everyone* knows you're coming. They would have all been here to greet you, but today is bowling day. New Dawn Pin Busters. I volunteered to welcome you. Cruisewell was a bit vague about what your duties would be. He continues to have infinite faith in his recruits." Grandma Bella sips her wine. Then she chuckles, "Imagine that. Well, let's not imagine that. But I should explain to you your accommodations. We didn't clean the trailer because we thought you might choose to live off campus, as the aerobics instructor called it. The trailer has gotten so bad, we half expected Cruisewell would replace it, like he's replaced a couple of our trailers."

"He replaces your trailers?"

Grandma Bella raises her hands to indicate the trailer in which they sit. "He said this would be more convenient, as long as the children were visiting."

Perhaps it is the confusion, or perhaps he is just tired, or perhaps it is the wine, but Paul feels slightly dizzy.

"Are you okay?" asks Grandma Bella.

"It's the liquor. I've been abstaining. But then it's been a long drive, and the trailer, and the kids, it's all so new. And he actually *gave* you this trailer?"

Grandma Bella laughs. "It's been so strange since Reverend Cruisewell arrived. We're all kind of used to his gifts by now. Look at Big Bill's lawn mower!" Grandma Bella pulls back the curtain. She points as Sam rolls by on the lap of a man driving a green and yellow, brand new, John Deere mower. Sam waves two flowers in greeting and triumph!

Grandma Bella waves and blows a kiss out the window. And Paul wonders when the driver throws back a kiss.

"Now, about *your* trailer," Grandma Bella says.

Paul waits, thinking perhaps by some miracle she might say a new trailer would be delivered for him. Soon.

"We should have cleaned it as a welcome, but then we all have different ideas about how much we want a minister. I don't want to dampen your spirits or anything, but you might find some resistance. I think the aerobics instructor kind of put us over the edge."

The newly chewed cheese sandwich churns deep inside Paul's stomach. He glances up with a beseeching look. "Could I ask you a very straightforward question?"

"Shoot."

"What is it with Cruisewell? Exactly. Do you have a clue?"

"Haven't! But given the circumstances, here's what I would do if I were you. Make the best of it. We all have theories about the Reverend. We believe he's well intentioned. We don't think he's evil: a crook, a con-man, a charlatan. Nothing like that. What we don't know is what he is, exactly. We have all concluded that he likes us, we eight widows, the children, Big Bill. I've concluded he very much likes my daughter, Saundra, but I stay clear of that. Saundra appears to have confusion in the relationship department. I'll say no more. Being a man, yourself, I don't want to prejudice you."

Paul waits. This is no mother he has ever seen or heard.

Grandma Bella sips her wine. "There's a little tea planned for tomorrow morning. We'll get you introduced. Maybe what we've all been waiting for is a minister. Who knows? By the way, where was your last congregation?"

Paul can't bring himself to lie. Under Grandma Bella's stare a lie isn't even a consideration.

"No last congregation. I'm a logger. An ex-logger."

Grandma Bella laughs. Her five-foot frame rolls and shakes with laughter. "This calls for a toast. And it is a well earned, well needed, end to our meal." She lifts her glass to Paul's. "Here's to New Dawn's new minister!"

Paul drains the last of his wine. For a passing second he imagines a new dawn, sees himself sharing wisdom with eight widows. Then the image fades and Grandma Bella smiles and an ear worm of an idea crawls into his brain and he knows she doesn't need any of his wisdom, even if he had some.

"Open the door!" Suzie calls. She stands at the door clutching a large bouquet. She bangs the screen door with her foot. Paul reaches to push the door open.

Grandma Bella squeezes out of the eating nook, accepts the bouquet, and gives Suzie a hug of thanks. From the kitchen sink she waves and calls out to Bill and Sammy, "Come on, you two, time to work!" The John Deere keeps thrumbing, makes another turn, and pulls up to the trailer. "Suzie, tell Sam to get the bucket by the faucet. Tell Bill the minute he's done mowing that we could use him at the parsonage. We've got a few hours of work ahead of us."

From under the sink Grandma Bella pulls rags and sponges and lemon-scented soap. She fills Sam's bucket with containers of Windex and Brasso and Ajax and Pine Sol. Between the cleaners she stuffs paper towels and steel wool. She hands Paul a mop and a broom and a feather duster.

Suzie leads the parade waving the flowers and she sings as loud as she can, "We're goin' to the chapel and we're goin' do some cleaning." Even Paul joins in the singing as they all head to the derelict trailer and the stuffed garage.

Trailer first. Within minutes Suzie removes the scatter rugs and hangs them on a clothesline between the trailer and the garage. Grandma Bella hands Sam an old tennis racket. "Buddy. Beat the stuffin' out of those rugs. Stop when there's no more dust." Sam grabs the racket and heads for the rugs. In minutes he is beating them with a vengeance.

From his truck, Paul retrieves his toolbox. Within an hour every loose board and every curl of linoleum and rug edge is flat and secured.

Grandma Bella washes windows.

Suzie stands on a step stool and scrubs the sink.

Together the four of them push the bedroom mattress outside and drape it over a stump. Sam hammers it with his tennis racket.

When Big Bill arrives, they take a break for introductions and everyone steps back to admire their work.

Bill declares, "Let's move furniture!"

Outside, they bring a chair, the sofa, a bookcase, two lamps, the mattress, and a side table. Like a tornado's undoing, the pieces nestle about the grass.

The trailer windows, open and spotless, welcome the sweet afternoon air. Wax dries on the linoleum and the parquet floors and the newly washed wall-to-wall rug dries.

"Time for a break!" Grandma Bella calls. "I'll be right back." Within minutes, from across the court, Grandma Bella returns with a tray of glasses filled with milk and a plate piled high with brownies.

"Hooray! Grandma Bella saves the day!" Sam calls as he dances around his grandmother.

"I knew there would be treats worth all this work," Big Bill announces. "And, exactly why are we doing all this work? Why not ask for a new trailer?"

"Well, who knows. Maybe later," Grandma Bella says. "Got to see just how long the minister gig will last. Not to doubt you, Pastor Paul."

"Hear that Paul? Need to build some faith around here. These women been left high and dry by the last two. But there's me. I'm their best example. I tell you, it's worth it." Big Bill gives Grandma Bella a quick squeeze. "Isn't it?"

"You're right, my sweet." She turns to Paul, "A little love and a little faith work like glue."

Grandma Bella hands each person a glass of milk.

"And just how did you become a minister?" Big Bill asks, with a questioning brow, eyes wrinkled from sun, a look that Paul feels would accept just about anything. Seeing Paul hesitate, he's quick to cover the question, "Well, why not? Nice to have another man around the place."

In the late afternoon, starlings whirl above their heads as if in celebration. Behind the perimeter of the trailer court, large pines cast afternoon shadows. From Borealis Avenue, four blocks to the east, cars hum. Frogs call from the creek. Grandma Bella sits on the front steps of the parsonage trailer. Big Bill sits on a galvanized wash tub with Sam between his knees. Suzie pulls up a chair. Paul stretches out on the grass, his head propped with one arm. For the moment he relaxes.

Soon, Sam with a half-eaten brownie in his hand, is sound asleep, tucked against the bulk of Big Bill.

"I think Sam's got the right idea. A little nap before dinner would be just the thing," Grandma Bella announces, nodding to Suzie to gather the glasses.

Paul stands, leans over to whisper to Suzie, "I'll carry Sam if you finish his brownie."

Back at Grandma Bella's, the children tucked in for naps, Big Bill and Paul sit in the nook of the Airstream while Grandma Bella chops greens. Paul loves the sound of her knife pounding the wooden board and for a second he is back in the cabin, his mom busy cooking, and he remembers comfort and warmth and is pleased to have it near again. For the moment the three sit in silence as a rolling sun slips behind the Cascades leaving a jagged silhouette.

Grandma Bella slides thimble-sized glasses of limoncello and a plate of spiced almonds in front of the two men. "To hold you over until dinner is ready."

"Dinner? Are you sure? Twice in a day?" Paul asks.

"Pure bribery to keep you around!"

"Thanks. I'm flattered. But then, I'm an easy target."

Grandma Bella lifts her glass of limoncello, "And here's to you. May your life be long and prosperous."

Paul watches as Big Bill holds the delicate glass and sips it gently. He follows suit. All the time he wonders if Grandma Bella knows about the money. About his drinking? About his joblessness? Does she know about everything? Paul sips the sweet liquor and loves the bite of sweet lemon. He drinks with the same caution as Bill and wonders that he is drinking at all. Maybe the slow sips are the answer to his fear of falling off the wagon. A wagon he knows he still has one leg in.

"Here's to you! And here's to your new home. I'd never guess that trailer could look that good!" Big Bill says as he raises his glass. "We'll dump the sofa and the mattress. I've got stuff stored from Angelina's old trailer."

Paul wants to ask about "Angelina," but realizes it must be Grandma Bella, when Big Bill gives her a friendly tap on her backside as he speaks. The way he says her name, the way he touches her, the warmth between them makes Paul homesick for Twist, the bar, Elsie and Travesty.

"Let's make a dump run now. Stop at the storage shed. Be back in time for Sweet Angelina's dinner. What'dya say?"

On the way to unload Big Bill's beater—a Ford he affectionately calls Gator, Big Bill scrutinizes Paul, "You don't look like a minister."

"So I've been told." Paul is defeated, deflated, exhausted, done-in. Big Bill immediately adds, "Not that you have to! It's a God-awful look if you ask me," Big Bill's words carry an apology.

"It's okay. It's just that's twice today."

"Let me guess. Suzie?" he asks.

"The very one."

"She's a quotable child. But don't let it get you down. The children are pleased you're here. I could tell. Especially Sam."

"Don't underestimate Suzie. She's already asked if I'd ever thought when I was a kid of growing up to be a dad."

"That's our Suzie! That child. I love her dearly, but she never misses an opportunity. Pay no mind. What she doesn't know is that it's Saundra's attention she needs, not a nonexistent dad."

"And their dad?"

"There is no dad. Never was. Saundra's been going about finding herself. In the middle of which some fool sperm bank deemed Saundra worthy of a donation. Not once. Twice! The result is two beautiful children. The consequence is no time to see them. How, with such a solid mom, she got so crazy, I'll never figure out. Thank God for Angelina. Because of her, because of both of us, the children know about the Seattle Art Museum, Bumbershoot, The Folk Life Festival, the Azalea Grove at the arboretum. They've a good life."

Paul falls into a silence to digest all this additional information.

Back at Grandma Bella's, her trailer is full of the warmth of noodles boiling, meatballs simmering, bread rising. Paul and Big Bill squeeze into the eating nook.

"Few more minutes," Grandma Bella announces and comes to stand behind Big Bill, her hands gently kneading his neck. His head slowly sinks until his chin touches his chest and his eyes close and Paul can almost hear a soft snore as his breathing matches the slow methodical movement of her hands. "He's kind and good and steady and he's as curious as the children about the world outside this trailer court." Bella smoothes his eyebrows and leans her large bosom at ease and gentle against the back of Big Bill's head. Her arms slip around his broad shoulders and her hands clasp as his hands meet hers and she smiles at Paul across the table and Paul knows the children not only have the attention and warmth of Big Bill but they have the model of two people who care for each other and their warmth is palpable and spreads to anyone lucky enough to be in their company.

Soon, the children join them at the eating nook after each takes a turn to wash their hands. Big Bill and Paul follow suit. At the table, Big Bill says grace. Conversation is sprightly, recalling the work of the day. An hour slips by. A yawn overtakes Paul. He stretches his arms.

At the door, Grandma Bella reminds him, "See you in the morning. Don't forget you have a ten o'clock tea!"

"Like I could forget."

A few steps down the path, Paul hears the familiar, lovely sound of a screen door slamming.

Grandma Bella calls, "Don't forget your prayers!" Her laugh follows him as it melts into the early evening croak of frogs.

Before the sun has completely disappeared, Paul is on his porch taking in the circled trailers. He listens. In the half dark he hears the white silver leaves of the aspens shimmering as if a thousand tiny hands were applauding the day.

15

REX'S

Wagons circle.
Bears pull Airstream trailers at a crashing, galloping speed.
Screams clot in Paul's throat. He struggles to yell, "Stop!"
The Airstreams move faster and collide—explode in the sky, and fragments
of bear balloons float to the ground.

Paul snaps out of the dream. He can't remember where he is. Slowly the room comes into focus. Above his head the cool morning air squeezes through an inch of open window. Paul breathes deep and reaches to push open the slatted blinds. Out the window he can just make out the lumps of trailers. Dew reflects off metal surfaces. The trailers, tucked into the hazy morning fog, appear to snooze like satisfied hippos.

Paul's eye catches movement just past the center circle of the court. Through the tilted heads of roses, three trailers over, he watches two angular bodies with arms outsstretched, curling their hands back and forth like fledgling birds. He squints to see two women pivot and reach and he watches the hypnotic movements. Anxiety grips his gut. The image of docile, television watching, bingo playing, Wednesday bowling, little old ladies, dissolves like a slug under salt. He knows like he knows the grain in wood, women who practice Tai Chi at six-thirty in the morning will not be docile parishioners.

Showered and dressed, Paul nibbles the last of yesterday's chicken. The kettle is slow to boil. Halfway through pouring instant coffee crystals into a chipped, blue-flowered coffee cup, Paul turns off the kettle. He needs company. Good-old-boy company. Guys who like or don't like you and it doesn't matter, company. Paul grabs his jacket and knows exactly where he's headed. Rex's Diner.

As he pulls out of the drive, he thinks he sees the women wave. He waves back but realizes they've just finished another set of exercises. In the rear view mirror he watches them watch him drive away. They're talking. No question. They're talking about him.

Past the Mini-Mart, the red neon of Rex's diner glows through a hedge of laurel. Paul pulls in beside a 4 X 4, a Harley, and Big Bill's mowing machine. He leans over the wheel to peer into the restaurant. Inside, the warm yellow light reveals hunched forms at the counter. The backs of men at breakfast make Paul think of Twist. He recognizes the back of Big Bill.

As Paul enters the diner, Big Bill turns and welcomes him with a sweep of his arm. "Pastor Paul! Just like that. I conjured him here!" Big Bill laughs a huge laugh. The men, bent over large platters of pancakes and browned sausages, turn, nod their heads hello. "I was just telling the boys about you!" Bill adds with a slap to Paul's back.

The pear-shaped man behind the counter, with "Rex" stitched in red letters on his white pocket, greets Paul with, "Welcome! Whadayahave?"

"Three eggs over easy, a stack, and four strips of bacon. Coffee and juice. Large."

"A breakfast you'll need! Tough day ahead! Not everyone gets to meet all the widows at once!" Rex slides a mug of coffee to Paul. "You'll get used to it. It's like living in a small town. Everybody knows what everybody knows."

Rex slaps bacon on the griddle, talks over his shoulder, "So, you're Cruisewell's latest recruit? A minister." Whips eggs, and looks over the edge of his glasses. "That's different," he says. "Unique." Wipes his hands on the towel.

Paul puts out his hand. "Paul. Paul Whitinowsky."

"Everyone calls me Rex." Rex's hand is large, bone-gathering firm. "Meet your neighbors, Jake and Bud." The men shake hands, and as Rex cracks eggs, he keeps the conversation going, "Sometimes that group, were speaking of the ladies, here, they are interesting with just the tiniest bit of mean." He finishes up the breakfast, "and sometimes they're just fun." Rex slides a plate of toast toward Paul.

Paul doesn't answer. He'll wait and see where the conversation winds its way.

"And sometimes their neither!" Big Bill says with a big laugh.

"You haven't met the ladies yet?" Rex asks.

"Just Grandma Bella. And Suzie and Sam. Ten o'clock today, I'll meet the whole catastrophe, as they say."

"Right. The tea. Bill will be outside mowing the lawn. Even if it doesn't need it. He's out there keeping watch."

Big Bill flags for his tab and stands. "Gotta go. My second breakfast, my real breakfast is waiting." With a firm hand on Paul's shoulder, Bill admonishes, "You just hang in there and everything will be okay."

The door wheezes shut behind him and Paul watches Big Bill swing up onto his mower. Something about the tilt of his shoulders and the angle of his cap brings "The Duke" to mind. A hero riding into the morning sun. Paul would have changed roles in a minute, ridden that mower, and let Big Bill be the minister.

Jake and Bud stand at the counter counting out bills and coins. Paul concentrates on the pulp of the jam, the sharp toasted edge of the bread, the snap of the bacon between his teeth. He listens as the men talk of carburetors and the Seahawks and they leave together, as solid as friendships get.

Rex scrapes the grill with a hard metal brush. Paul tries to ignore the overwhelming reality that he is totally, completely, absolutely alone. With a fork he pushes the crumbling mess between puddles of syrup and bacon grease.

"Anything wrong?" Rex asks as he fills Paul's coffee mug.

"Not a thing. Food's great. Just not as hungry as I thought."

"Know just how you feel. You get up. You're hungry. Starving. You order just what you thought you wanted. And zowey, you think about everything that might go wrong and your appetite jumps ship."

Rex removes the half empty plate. "Don't worry about the ladies. They may be a little critical, but on the whole they're a nice bunch; most of 'em, that is."

"On the whole?"

"Well, Cruisewell is so damned well intentioned, but he doesn't think. Alphonse just wasn't that great a cook. And the aerobics instructor was too young to have a clue about old. The two of them probably wouldn't survive anywhere, let alone under the scrutiny of 'the widows.'"

Rex pours himself a coffee. Paul watches Rex tip his cup to avoid the toothpick that appears to be a permanent fixture in the right side of his mouth.

Rex asks, "You a real minister then?"

Paul lies, or maybe he doesn't. He nods 'yes' to the question.

"I'm not one to give advice, but here's just a little something that might help you out. Have lots of potlucks. I'm in the cooking business and I still say, have lots of potlucks. Then start a regular bingo night. Things get slow? Have them write their congressmen." Rex rolls the toothpick to the left side of his mouth. "Now, here's another great idea, have them take field trips to the state capitol. Invite in the local pols. These women, they have opinions, let me tell you. They ain't shy about letting you know exactly what they think."

Paul watches the toothpick travel across Rex's bumpy lip.

"Consider staying light on the preachin' part of things. Can't imagine them takin' to being told much of anything about what to do or what to be. Know what I mean?"

In a singular motion Paul finishes his coffee, lays out a five dollar bill. "Know just what you mean. Thanks for the advice."

"It'll be a good show! Keep us informed!" are the last words Paul hears as his boots crunch in the gravel of the parking strip. He doesn't think he heard a laugh.

Outside, the new morning sun, bright as gunshot, cuts through the aspens south of the diner. Speckled light shifts in dollar-sized spots over the gravel. Inside the Jeep, Paul lets his head fall against the cold of the steering wheel. He tries to remember the lesson on breathing. Paul lets air go high in his nose. He lets air flow out over his upper lip. He takes another breath. And another. He yearns for the oblivion of sleep. Sleep with no dreams. He closes his eyes and tries not to think about ten o'clock.

Paul's head snaps back. A sequence of doors slam as a family of four enters Rex's. Around him the parking lot has filled. Ten feet away a trucker sits in his cab. Paul lifts his hand to acknowledge the man's stare. The trucker jams his rig into reverse, shifts gears, and eases the Peterbilt into traffic. He heads east. He didn't wave. Paul lets out a deep breath and wishes the man had waved.

16

SAUNDRA COMES HOME

Checking his watch, fearful of the hour, Paul's pleased to see it is just after eight o'clock. He hasn't dozed that long. He puts the key in the ignition. At the edge of the road he waits for traffic to ease. Through a scrim of sunflowers with heavy heads, Paul can see the edge of the trailer court. Bright yellow catches his eye and he can make out Big Bill's mowing machine taking its course.

As he drives toward the white arch, Paul's surprised to see Sam and Suzie sitting on the curb of the Mini-Mart. They appear to be sorting penny candies. Suzie sucks on a Red Vine. Sam licks his hand. From where he sits Paul can see the stigmata-like stains in Sam's palm from a fist full of disintegrating Red Hots. Suzie counts change into her coin purse. Paul watches, unexplainably soothed by their intimacy.

Just as Suzie pulls at another bite of licorice she looks up. Her eyes wide. Paul follows her gaze. Down the street comes a blue and black, slightly rusted, Morris Minor panel truck. As the tiny truck passes the children, Sam's mouth flies open into a wide hoot of recognition. His red hand shoots up like a stop sign and jerks back and forth. From his lap spill Red Hots and Jaw Breakers. Sam thrusts his body up and off the curb. He stumbles, stops for an instant, and then runs across the Mini-Mart parking lot.

Without looking or stopping, Sam runs across the road as the Morris Minor turns into the trailer court. Paul's breath catches before he realizes Sam is already safe on the other side. His heart swells when he hears the plaintive call of Sam's clear, bright voice, "Mommy! Stop! Stop! I'm Sam. I'm Sam. Mom, I'm Sam!"

Suzie gathers the scattered candy, stuffs it into her paper bag, and runs after her brother. "Sam! Stop! Right now!" and she doesn't modulate her voice one bit. She yells, "You stupid, stupid boy!"

The Morris Minor stops in front of Grandma Bella's Airstream as Sam pounds his way down the gravel drive. Arms outstretched, Sam's precarious trajectory ends ten feet from the panel truck. His feet lose purchase. His body falls forward. His palms hit gravel.

Paul parks and jumps from his Jeep. Before he can get to Sam, Suzie's there. He's belly down, elbows braced, hands pocked, face puckered, calculating the hurt, caught between a whimper and a good cry. Sam tries to push himself up. Suzie tucks her hands under Sam's sprawled body and turns him to face her. She blows on the combination of red stain and scraped skin, which gives Sam enough time to forget to cry. He pulls away and reaches the Morris Minor just as his mom opens the door.

Two steps away from Paul, Suzie stops. She folds her arms in indignation. She glares. She stays her distance from the Morris Minor. She proclaims, loud enough for most everyone in the trailer court to hear, "I hope she doesn't think I was chasing that stupid Mickey Mouse car!"

"That must be Saundra," Paul says. "Your mom."

"Hardly," Suzie spits the word.

From where he stands Paul can just see into the back window of the miniature vehicle. Clothing and boxes, shopping bags, and an accordion case. His view of the driver is blocked. Then from out the front door protrudes a long leg, the foot of which is encased in a shoe with a stiletto heel held together with a criss-cross of red straps, topped with a red bow. Paul notices. He even notices two hugged-together toes, like tasty miniature sausages, protruding from the front of the red shoe. Purple toenails. The purple polish sparkles.

At the top of the leg is a swatch of red mini-skirt.

One hand grasps the edge of the door. The arm is tan and wrapped with a cascade of clanking silver bracelets. A woman appears. The filmy parachute white of her blouse gapes, revealing ripe, rounded breasts. The image of clear-cut hills fills Paul.

The top of the woman's head is a mix of soft and hard, dark and light. Streaks of blond hair spring from a dark center. Cascading hair is interlaced with a series of tiny braids bound with white glass beads and finished off with fluorescent pink ribbon.

As she unfolds herself, the leather of the car seat appears to catch and pulls the mini-skirt higher. Her ringed fingers push at the patch of skirt. Out of the car, she stands on one leg and with one hand, she braces herself against the roof of the Minor.

"Mommieee!" Sam calls.

The woman turns, flamingo-like, on one red heel. Sam's arms encircle his mother's legs and he anchors her with a full body press. They sway in a mismatched dance—sway and totter. A long high wail accompanies their timber-like fall, giving Paul time to grab Sam from being squashed by the angular mass of his mother.

Sam safe, Paul reaches to help the splayed body, only to be assaulted with a crescendo of "Damn, Damn, Damn!" Followed by, "Don't touch me! Don't you touch me!" Paul steps back at her words. Then she stops yelling and all of her energy and all of her attention focuses on a bright spot of red sticking out of the white gravel, and with great anguish she moans, "Oh, no! My shoe! My beautiful shoe!" The broken-off heel of the shoe protrudes from the gravel—a lone red totem in a clutch of white stones.

Paul's eyes go from the heel to her hand clutching her ankle where already the swelling flesh protrudes between the encircling straps. With disgust, she pulls her foot free of the heelless shoe.

Paul can feel the press of Sam's body into the back of his legs. Suzie stands her distance, her arms firmly crossed. Smuggins streams across the drive, slides under the trailer, bares her teeth, and hisses. Grandma Bella appears at the screen door, throws her towel over her shoulder, and hurries down the path to her daughter.

Paul gives Sam a lift and with tear-filled words Sam blubbers in Paul's ear, "I din't mean to. I din't mean to." Sam holds tight and Paul can feel the warm, wet pressure of the child's head curled tightly into his neck.

Ignoring the whimpers and yelps of Saundra, Grandma Bella helps hoist her daughter to a standing position. "Hush this minute," she scolds. She registers the scene in a second and says, "Either we drive to the emergency room or we call an ambulance which your nonexistent medical insurance won't pay for."

Saundra looks through smudged mascara to consider the reasoned, firm voice of her mother. "Okay. Give me a hand. But, damn it, be gentle." She holds her body as still as possible and waits for her mother.

"Pastor Paul, you take over," Grandma Bella says and heads for her Fairlane Ford.

Paul puts Sam down and steps forward. He offers an arm and Saundra stands upright on one leg. He can see she is fighting the pain, but not so that she doesn't have the energy or spirit to say, "Well, well, Pastor Paul. Isn't that nice."

Paul's body supports the curve of hers. He realizes she looks slender but her arms are strong and considering her pain and a bit of disorientedness, she seems to have no trouble fitting herself into him and giving him a good up and down look.

Grandma Bella backs her car into place and Paul scoots Saundra into the front seat. Saundra's eyes glisten and her eyelashes bat. She appears breathless and shaken to just the right degree of helplessness that is followed by a sweet smile and a fixed glance at Paul. "Thank you," she says softly. In all the professed pain and confusion, Paul feels the hike of her skirt, the extended length of her leg, the weight of her body—all are calculated. He thinks she even winked, but perhaps she had winced.

Grandma Bella turns the key in the ignition and Saundra rolls down her window. She commands, "And someone, please, save my precious shoe!"

17

A SHORT SERMON

Paul stands between the children, as they watch Grandma Bella drive slowly around the circle of trailers. At the entrance, to the immediate right of the arch, on the front steps of one of the Airstreams, two women watch, their heads a cloud of pink rollers. They stand with arms crossed, deep in conversation, watching the Fairlane disappear into traffic. Then they turn their eyes on Paul.

Suzie waves. "The twins," she explains. "Wave. They're in their analytical mode. Analyzing you."

It is then that Paul realizes he has an audience of more than just the twins. Four doors are open. Paul does not doubt that he is being analyzed—analyzed, scrutinized, examined, criticized, and dissected by the ladies.

Suzie reaches for Paul's wrist. "You don't have to wave to all of them, just nod your head. Acknowledge them. Just stop looking worried."

"What? Me? Worried? I'm not worried. Everything's fine. Just fine."

Suzie doesn't respond. Her hand tightens on Paul's wrist. He waits and finally after a huge sigh, Suzie says, "Things aren't usually fine when *she's* around."

"Don't you say that!" Sam says with a push at Suzie. "She's our mom!" Before he can give her another push, Paul picks Sam up and holds his wiggling. Paul demands, "Hold tough, little guy. We'll figure this out. Your hands okay?"

Sam's lower lip pushes into a well-rounded pout. His lashes are wet with tears.

Through his tough pout, a second layer of tears begins to build. His voice, all worry, asks, "She gonna be okay? She gonna come back?"

"Suzie, why don't you go pick-up your mom's shoe," Paul suggests. While Suzie is distracted, Paul looks directly into Sam's brimming eyes, and says with conviction, "What with a shoe like that, and you and Suzie waiting for her, of course she'll be back!"

"Oh, good," Sam says as his thumb finds his mouth and his body sighs with content.

Suzie sits on the trailer steps and jams the two parts of Saundra's shoe together. She stands to put her right foot into the shoe, teeters until the heel snaps again. With an over-hand throw, Suzie sends the heel flying into the rose bushes. "Just like her! How come, Pastor Paul?"

"How come what?"

"How come she wears stupid shoes? Anyone can see she's going to fall down, break her stupid neck."

"Ouch. Not much sympathy from the first born."

"Well, poop!"

"I'd guess she wears shoes like that for fun," Paul answers.

"Fun looking stupid? Falling over?" Suzie's voice is crisp and angry. Paul looks around the courtyard and he now can see everyone has taken notice. If not at an open door, at a window with the curtain pulled back.

"We have an attentive audience," Suzie states.

"Yep, I can see that. Back to the subject. Listen up. A bit old fashioned, perhaps boring. But true. I'm going to bestow on you ... did you get that? Bestow? A nice big word. I'm going to bestow on you a truth."

"Great. Just what I need. A big truth," Suzie sits down, plants her elbows on her knees, her head in her hands.

Paul speaks to the top of her head, "Judge not lest ye be judged."

Suzie looks up, her eyes wide and magnified, "Now you do sound like a dumb preacher and you haven't known her long enough to say whether she should be judged or not!"

Without answering, Paul puts Sam down, nudges Suzie so that he can get by her and opens the screen door. He pours three glasses of orange juice. He places the glasses on the kitchen nook table and watches Suzie through the scrim of the door. Suzie has rescued both parts of the shoe and twirls the top by the strap.

"Soups on!" he calls. "Well, orange juice. But there's a glass for you."

Suzie follows Sam inside. She bangs the door and slams the shoe into the nook's corner. She pushes her glasses up her nose. She reaches into her jacket pocket, opens her candy sack and takes out a Red Vine. She sticks the Red Vine into the orange juice. She slurps and then she nudges the sack of candy just short of the middle of the table.

"Ah, I'm taking that as a peace offering," Paul says and reaches inside the sack for a single Red Hot. He offers the sack to Sam. Sam searches until he finds a jaw breaker and then searches for another. He puts both in his mouth, his cheeks bulge in a chipmunk grin.

"Good choice," Paul says.

Sam grins around the two bumps that have turned his tiny teeth fluorescent pink.

"Well?" Paul neatly folds the sack and places it in front of Suzie.

"Well, what?" Suzie asks.

"We're candy conspirators together."

"Umm, nice word," Suzie acknowledges.

"So, tell me. Are you surprised to see her? Are you pleased to see her? Are you angry that she's back? None of the above? All of the above?"

Suzie sucks orange juice through the red vine. Sam follows her example. Orange juice dribbles down his chin. He lets the jawbreakers drop into the bottom of his glass.

After a large slurp, Suzie says, "None. I just never want to see her again."

Sam's foot bangs Suzie's leg. Paul stops a second kick.

"Let's start over. Fresh. Let's think about how we might help your mom."

"She needs help?" Suzie slams down her orange juice glass. Juice sprays the table. "What about us? She never helps us!"

Paul reaches behind his head to unroll a paper towel. He sops up the orange juice. "Somebody's got to start somewhere." He unrolls a second paper towel. "Here, wipe your face. You've got orange juice in your eyebrow."

Suzie ignores the paper towel. "Oh, yeah? Why would she? Start anywhere? She won't. That's what she does. Nothing. She comes. She goes. She's not gone to one teacher's conference! She doesn't know one word I know!"

Paul chews on a Red Vine. He chews and swallows, chews and swallows. "Okay, okay. Let's start over. How about this? You know when kids 'act out' at school?"

"Act out? You're using a very funny voice. Don't preach at us. Sam and I know more than you. Don't we Sam?"

"Stick with me," Paul says and reaches for Suzie's hand which she immediately pulls away. "Act out. When the teacher yells, 'Stop that acting out!' "

"Everybody knows that," Suzie answers with a sneer. "Roger Blaney is always acting out. So what?"

"Why? Why does Roger Blaney act out?"

"He's a dork."

"Why?"

"He just is. He breathes through his mouth. No one likes him."

"Maybe he wants you to like him. Everybody wants to be liked. You.

Me. Sam. Roger Blarney wants people to like him."

Suzie smacks her hand over her mouth, lets loose a huge laugh, "His name's not Blarney! It's Blaney!"

"Okay, so Roger Blaney, not Blarney, is a dork. If he can't get you to like him at least he's got you talking about him."

"So?"

"So, this has something to do with the red high heels."

"She's no kid."

"Right. Not being a kid doesn't keep people from acting out."

"You trying to say no one likes her?" Suzie leans back to give Paul an incredulous look, her sticky hands out, palms up, asking. "Not like her? What about all those stupid 'uncles' that like her? What about Grandma Bella? Even when she's mad at her, Grandma Bella *still* likes her!"

Sam interrupts, "Yeah, Reverend Cruisewell really likes her. Really, really likes her."

"That too!" Suzie is near shouting. "Everybody isn't..." her voice cracks.

"What about you?" Paul asks.

Suzie doesn't answer. She sticks out her chin. She stares at Paul.

"Do you like her?" Paul asks.

"No! I hate her! Besides! She's my mother! She's supposed to like *me!*"

"You're right, Suzie. But we're talking about 'acting out.'"

Suzie lays her head on the top of her arms, her glasses push against her smooth, rounded cheek. Paul reaches to rub the tiny bones of Suzie's neck. He says, "Let's make a deal. I'd guess your mom's going to be around for awhile. What with her ankle. Why don't we try to let her know we like her?"

Suzie peeks through her arm, raises an eyebrow. "Who's we?"

"You and Sam. Me, too. Pretend..." Paul pushes the word at Suzie. "Just pretend. For a little while."

"She's been like this forever."

"Try."

"I don't want to like her."

"She's your mother."

"I know *that.*"

"Then start right there. Try. We'll set a limit. Three and one-half days. We'll start when she gets back. How about it? Let's make a deal."

Barely whispering, Suzie answers into her folded arms, "Okay. But just for three days."

"Three and one-half days! That's a start." Paul leans back, hands behind his head and as he does he looks at the clock on the stove. "Oh, my G..." Paul swallows the word, "...goodness! It's nine o'clock! We've got a garage to transform! Right now!"

"A day for miracles," Suzie says with the slightest smile.

To the garage, Paul carries a tray with the tea and cups and saucers. Suzie carries a plate of cookies. Sam carries a dish of pink and green mints in one hand and his sack of candy in the other. Paul turns to see his troops behind him and has visions of a row of birds following Charlie Brown.

18

TEA WITH THE LADIES

Inside the chapel, Paul sets the teapot on top of a box. He rubs his hands down the sides of his jeans.

"Nervous?" Suzie asks.

"Hands itch."

"Means you're going to get money."

"Not likely. Truth is, I am nervous. Fifty minutes. There's not much time for miracles."

"It'll be okay. They're really not that mean." Suzie snitches a cookie. Through a mouth full of chewing she mumbles, "I'll be back." She wipes her mouth. Waves her hands, "I forgot to choose my word for today!"

"No! I need you!" Paul calls.

Suzie disappears out the door.

Sam comes to stand next to Paul—gives Paul's hand a squeeze in reassurance. They stand in a semi-dark room that smells of mold and everything old. Paul reaches for the light switch. The fluorescent lights sputter until they settle into cold illumination. In the light, the room looks worse.

Sam leans against Paul, looks up reassuringly and says, "I'll help."

"Allll right! Let's get at it." Paul circles the room, from a box grabs a towel. "Catch!" In a full frontal grasp, Sam's arms fly out. He runs to the chairs to whisk away the dust.

Suzie stands at the door. "What do you think of the word 'retribution?'"

"Well some of us have a tea in…" Paul looked at his watch, "…in forty-eight minutes." And it crosses his mind that Alice in Wonderland had nothing on him.

"What do you think it means?" Suzie quizzes.

"Something like, people get what they deserve."

"Very good! And it is a very good word," Suzie smiles and accepts the push broom Paul hands her.

"Get busy or we'll all get the congregation's retribution!" Paul says.

"That's funny. They know what this place is like. Let's clean half of the space and challenge them to clean the other half after they have their cup of tea!"

"Suzie you are brilliant. But not how I'd like this ministry thing to begin. Sam, my man, put the chairs in a circle."

Paul can't believe he remembers Chapter Ten of his lessons: *CIRCLES WORK BEST.*

While the children clear a space, arrange chairs, sweep the floor, Paul pulls open the top on a packing box marked, MISC. BOWLS, TABLE CLOTHS, KITCHEN STUFF. "Eureka!" he calls.

Together they pull two sawhorses and the large sheet of plywood to the front of the chairs. Paul flicks a large white table cloth into the air. The cloth billows over the plywood. With the chairs in a circle, the platters on the draped table, Paul's confidence has grown. "No retribution in sight!" Paul gives Suzie a high five. Sam walks up to get his.

"Falling down is retribution for someone who wears very tall, very skinny, red high heels."

"There will be retribution if we don't finish this up in thirty minutes!" Paul directs Suzie, "Hide the cat dishes and I'll be right back."

Paul runs to his trailer and retrieves the vase with the bouquet of flowers. He places it on the alter-like table between the mints and the tea pot.

"Everyone deserves retribution for their bad ways," Suzie continues, speaking to Paul from behind the cardboard cut out of Bill Clinton where she has hidden the cat's dishes.

"Keep trying. While you're at it figure out why Sam fell down this morning, why Smuggins ended up in a 'no pets allowed' place, and why I got chosen to be a minister. Figure that out and you'll unlock the meaning of 'retribution.'"

Suzie pushes her glasses into place. She squints. "Retribution *is* a hard word to use ten times."

"Try 'restore.' We've restored the garage. Or maybe revitalized. Or maybe revived." Paul walks around the garage, shoving boxes against the wall. "'Regenerate' or 'rejuvenate.'" Paul closes a gap in the chair circle. Sam flicks his dusting cloth at the cat and Smuggins grabs it with her front paws, holds on, and Sam pulls her across the floor. The cat's bottom collects missed dust bunnies. Miraculously, as Paul watches he catches sight of a perfect find. From a corner behind a pile of boxes he unrolls an Oriental rug and centers it in front of the cloth-covered table. "A transformation!" Paul exclaims.

Sam comes to lean against Paul to admire their work. Together, they relax. Paul is amazed at how great he feels. He finds himself full of smiles and good cheer. The room actually looks quite nice with the slender neck of the teapot pointing at the gathered flowers in their crockery vase on top of the white table in front of a maroon and cobalt blue Oriental rug on which the freshly dusted chairs sit in an inviting circle.

Smuggins darts through the chair legs, bounces off the seat of one, drops behind the row of boxes and stops behind Bill Clinton's feet.

"Suzie, I think you might want to put Smuggins in the parsonage."

"It's *her* garage. That isn't the right retribution for a cat."

"Suzie…"

"Good idea. The tea ladies can be mean." Suzie scoops up the cat. "Smuggins would get a retribution she doesn't deserve."

"Like what?" Paul asks.

"Who knows? Mean old ladies can think up just about anything."

"Mean?" Paul says as he re-stacks the aerobics mats into a neater pile.

Not giving an answer, Suzie, with cat in arms, stomps out the door.

"She just says stuff," Sam says and retrieves the cat's bowls from behind the cardboard figure. "Doesn't mean it. Much." With feeding bowls in hand he follows his sister.

Paul checks his watch. Fifteen minutes to go. He catches a breath and wishes this tea would get started. Even more, he wishes this tea was over. At just that moment, one whole side of the garage slowly opens. Boxes teeter. Paul jumps to avoid the falling-down mess.

Outside Sam stands with a garage door opener in his hand, his face beaming with pleasure and power. Dust motes sparkle in the sunlight.

"Sam!" Paul yells. The door stops halfway up. "Give that to me! Now!" Sam's face falls, fear brightens his eyes. Paul runs out the door and grabs the opener. Sam's eyes well with tears.

"Come on, little Buddy. No tears. I'm just a bit nervous. I didn't mean to yell." Paul bends to give Sam a hug. Sam hugs him back. Paul holds on wishing he didn't have so much to learn, so fast. "It's okay. I didn't mean to scare you. I had visions of all those boxes crashing down inside."

"I'll take that word!" Suzie say. From a back pocket she opens a small three-ring notepad with a stub of a pencil. She writes, "V-I-S-H-O-N-S."

Paul sighs just short of a groan. He holds the opener between his and Sam's hands and returns the garage door to its closed position.

"'Vish-ons' is going to be tomorrow's word."

"It's *my* word," Paul says surprised at how mean he feels and how he suddenly doesn't want to correct Suzie's spelling and he doesn't want to give up his word. It's his word.

"You can't own words," Suzie snaps. "Enough! Remember how you asked us to help you be a minister?" Suzie asks, arms crossed, lips tight.

"I asked you to help me be a minister?"

"Yes! You did. Here's how to do it." Suzie holds her pencil up like a conductor conducting. "One, don't repeat people's questions. Two, don't condescend!"

"Con-de…" Paul's head hurts and he yearns for a beer.

Suzie walks back and forth in front of the garage punctuating the air with her pencil. "Good. Stopping like that is a good start. And if I were you I wouldn't condescend to anyone at this tea." Suzie stops and closes her notepad and puts it into her back pocket and disappears inside the garage. Sam takes Paul's hand and leads him inside. "We're ready. Don't worry," he says and gives Paul's hand a tug.

Inside, Suzie finds a box marked "Christmas". She removes a strand of metallic stars and together she and Sam drape the stars across the table.

As they step back to take a final survey of the transformation, the sound of Grandma Bella's Ford pulling into the driveway cuts through the air.

Sam is out the door. Paul and Suzie follow. Sam abruptly stops six feet away from the car as if remembering the morning's catastrophe. Grandma Bella turns off the ignition, and exits the car to open the back door for Saundra. Saundra fills the backseat with an extended leg. As the door opens she demands, "Just get me out of this God damned car and watch out for that white gravel-shit."

"Saundra. You watch that tongue of yours. You're never too old to get your mouth washed."

"Well, if it hadn't been for this stupid white gravel, I wouldn't have broken my high heel!"

"Be glad you didn't break your neck!"

Grandma Bella steadies the crutches as Saundra pulls herself to stand. "Those shoes cost me three months' tips! Three months for the best damned heels in the whole damned country and…"

Grandma Bella lets go of one of the crutches. It clatters to the ground. She turns, leaving Saundra with one crutch and an audience of three. Well, truly, an expanded audience of the entire trailer court.

"Don't leave me! I don't know how to work these…things." Saundra's voice pleads.

At the door of her Airstream, Grandma Bella turns. "You need to earn help, Missy. You can jolly well stand there for the rest of the day until you clean up your mouth."

"Oh, Mommy. You don't understand."

"It's not the shoes. I understand shoes. It's your language. In front of the children. In front of all my friends. In front of the minister."

At the word 'minister,' Saundra looks up with a smile. "Oh, yes, I forgot. That minister. My deepest apologies." Her smile broadens.

Paul feels Suzie's hand slip into his as if to say, "Be Careful. Danger. Stay

Away." Paul gives Suzie's hand a squeeze and then he walks forward to pick up the crutch. "Sam, you get on your mother's other side," Paul instructs.

"Well, how nice. Someone who can help. A man of the cloth." Saundra reaches for the crutch Paul holds upright. She maneuvers her arm up and over the brace. For the second time that day Paul sees more cleavage than he's seen in years. Maybe ever. Saundra stands between the crutches, eye level with Paul. Sam at her other side.

"I'm Saundra Saunders."

"Yes, I've gathered that. I'm Paul Whitinowsky."

"He's our new minister," Sam says, his hand tentatively touching his mother.

"*The* Pastor Paul?" Saundra says in exaggerated wonder.

Paul doesn't answer.

"It *is* a pleasure to meet you." Her handshake is firm and warm and strong in his. Whether it is the tea gathering, or the closeness of Saundra, or the revealing maneuver of the crutches, Paul doesn't know which is making him the most uncomfortable.

Suzie watches, arms crossed, her head tilted in a watch-what-you're-doing, keep-your-distance angle.

By now, all around the trailer court, doors have opened and the widows are about to gather. It is time. Paul has no doubt that his congregation-to-be has seen the whole show.

"Better get over to the tea party Pastor Paul," Grandma Bella calls. "Suzie, get the door. Sam, hold your mom's purse. I'll be right there."

And so, the women arrive. All bearing gifts—a variety of plates covered with napkins. Paul stands at the door of the garage, with what he hopes is a welcoming smile and nod-of-the-head greeting as each woman says her name.

"Betty Bagley." Betty wears an aerobics outfit—bright pink with a purple stripe down the leg.

"Joan and Janice Wittenhouer." The two women are obviously twins. They have exactly the same smile, rounded chins, bright blue eyes, and short, permed hair. With that the similarities end. One wears a green and pink muumuu and the other wears tight jeans and a giant sweater and they both look great for what Paul figures must be sixty-some years. As they pass Paul, each lifts the edge of the napkin to reveal their offering: a chocolate layered cake and twenty tiny, tiny sandwiches.

"Olga Simmons." Olga carries a platter of lace cookies layered with neon pink frosting.

"Molly Entwhistle." Molly balances two plates. Sugar cookies with sprinks and a fruit cobbler.

"Call me Beenie." Beenie, one bottle of sparkling cider extends from each hand for Paul's approval. "I'm also representing Julia McBride who is visiting her grandchildren in Renton. Her apologies, but she has so many grandchildren, they keep her busy. However, she is very excited about meeting you. She used to be married to a minister. The third marriage of seven. You'll like her! Very feisty."

Paul takes a deep breath and follows the women into the garage. Everyone exclaims about the transformation of the room. The aerobics-woman beams and pours Paul a cup of tea. One of the twins, Janice, if he remembers right, hands him a plate filled with three sandwiches, peach cobbler, four cookies, and chocolate cake. Everyone waits with anticipation as he takes a bite. Paul umms and ahhhs at exactly the right moment. Satisfied, the women fill their plates and find places in the circle of chairs.

"Well..." and Paul stops speaking, wondering what to call these women. Women? Ladies? Certainly not widows. He decides on no greeting. "It's time we should begin."

Paul's prepared. All night, as sleep evaded him, he recalled the lesson on *Organization.*

"Beenie, we'll begin with you. Please introduce the woman on your left. Tell us, but mostly tell me, one interesting thing about her."

Beenie looks Janice Wittenhouer up and down. "Well, I can't tell you *that!*" she says with a full-throated laugh. "But I can tell you the obvious. She's a twin, with attitude!"

Each woman proceeds with an observation. Paul thinks the idea of the lesson was to get everyone to relax, laugh, and enjoy themselves. The lesson promised the group would ease and conversation would flow. What Paul hears is a slight edge of competition and nothing changes until Molly Entwhistle, who has already had her turn, waves her hand at Olga as Olga begins to speak, "Oh! I forgot! Most important. Very, very important. I have a new granddaughter!"

Beenie looks at her with skepticism. "New? Are you sure?"

"Newest."

"That's two years ago!"

"But now! Now she walks and can sing 'Old McDonald'. In French!" A few skeptical eyebrows arch.

It takes all of two seconds and Paul realizes grandmothering is the conversation sustainer. There's no stopping the women as they speak out of turn, open their purses, take out pictures, raise their voices. Paul is concerned that the twins seem not to be joining in. He pours them fresh tea as conversation flows around them. He asks how long they have been part of the group.

"We're not part of the group."

Joan nods and says, "We have no grandchildren because we have no children. We've never been married. Couldn't quite see the reason for it. Not that we haven't been asked, for we certainly have, but no one seems to be as good of company as we are." Joan grabs Janice's hand and they both smile in agreement. "No weddings. No deaths. No widows."

"Strange. Reverend Cruisewell speaks of you as 'the widows' so I was under the impression you were all widows."

"Oh, that Randi. He just doesn't want to embarrass us, so he includes us in the 'widows'. He also thinks if we haven't been married, we will be. One of these days. Sometimes we think he acts like we are trying to seduce him. Imagine that! Or…," Janice adds, "he is trying to convert us. We never can figure him out. Crazy and sweet!"

Janice bursts into laughter. Joan follows suit and catches her breath to say, "Which ignores the fact that he's twenty years younger than we are. We do love to tease him! Keeps him perky!"

The room has grown quiet as the ladies catch the tail end of the twins' conversation.

Paul sees they are waiting. He quickly runs through the last of his crazy lessons: Lesson 28, *ORIGINS AND ROOTS: WHERE YOU CAME FROM*, or Lesson 29, *KEEPING BUSY: HOBBIES AND SUCH*, or Lesson 30, *PAST AND PRESENT PROFESSIONS*.

Once the question of "where" is barely out of Paul's mouth, the women take over. They are from Idaho, Illinois, Maine, Kentucky, North Carolina, and Seattle by way of Colorado. They don't wait for Paul to ask another question, before they tell him about their past lives: librarian, nurse, ski instructor, travel agent, high school teacher in American History, linguist, fortune teller. To a person, they have chosen New Dawn for its flowers and greenness and because of Reverend Cruisewell's assurance of community involvement. And, of course, the trailers.

"And classes!" Betty Bagley comments. "I did like that aerobics instructor!"

Olga Simmons says she preferred the chef.

Molly Entwhistle comments, "That cook was no chef!"

The twins end each other's sentences and proclaim the New Dawn Is Breaking widow's group can do just about anything! And, Janice adds, to put a punctuation mark to the conversation, "We could sure use a little more politics to spice things up!"

Eventually, it feels to Paul as if the tea is winding down and he stands. Which Olga takes as an opportunity to proclaim, "Time for Questions and Answers!" All eyes focus on Paul.

Some questions feel just shy of gunshots and Paul follows Lesson 5: *BE THANKFUL, BE TRUTHFUL, BE DIRECT*. He tries to answer questions with precision and honesty.

"I'm a third generation logger."

"Yes, I did go to college. At Eastern." He does not mention he did not graduate.

"My religious training? Springton Seminary. Decatur, Illinois." His eye catches Olga and he wonders, being from Illinois, if there is such a seminary, and would she know, and will she expose him, now, this minute, as a fraud. She doesn't blink.

The questions continue.

"I've not been married."

"Yes, I would if the right woman happened along."

Finally, the questions end and the conversation drifts to the upcoming Sunday service. The women have ideas on just how to change the "clubhouse".

"Chairs should be in rows."

"We need a box for the lectern."

"Lectern?"

"What you, the minister, stands behind."

"Of course."

"Well then we need an altar."

"No, let's not have an altar. Let's just have flowers on the table. Then everyone can believe what they want to believe."

"Like in nature?"

"If you wish."

"I have another Oriental rug! A long, skinny runner. In one of those boxes, if we can just find it. It would be for an aisle. Every church needs an aisle!"

"That would be lovely."

Everyone agrees and the tea has come to an end.

However, Paul remembers another lesson and stands by the door to shake each woman's hand. With his two hands. *Parishioners will feel taken care of, protected, honored, should you shake his or her hand in two of yours. No kissing.*

The women all say "yes" or "absolutely" when Paul says he is looking forward to seeing them for the Sunday service at eleven o'clock.

Grandma Bella is the last to leave. "A wonderful tea, Pastor Paul. I've errands this afternoon and need to get the children to soccer practice. We'd love for you to join us for dinner. Six o'clockish?"

Paul thinks he has just received an invitation, but after the past hour, surrounded by the force of the women, it may have been a command.

As soon as the room is empty, Paul pushes away boxes and collapses into an overstuffed chair. It is not a slumping kind of chair. It has straight sides and a perpendicular back forcing him to sit up and when he does, his head slumps forward into his hands and for the hundredth time he wonders what he is doing.

He slowly replays the morning. He wonders just what the 'widows' expect of him. He's thought of them as widows for so long, there is no replacing the word. 'Widow' seems to him a word that is dark, heavy, and full of 'please help me-ness'. But not these women. Not only do they not fit a stereotype, they seem to be doing just fine without a minister. What could he possibly do for them and what could he possibly tell them in a sermon? Maybe by sermon-time he will have suffered a severe back spasm. He'll have to stay in bed for a few days. Maybe they'll want to take care of him. Maybe there are a dozen other solutions to Sunday that he hasn't even considered.

But then, as he thinks about the upcoming sermon, the women haven't seemed all that critical and they certainly haven't been mean. They talked a lot. They had been straight forward. They'd even described briefly but critically the other 'classes' Cruisewell had provided. Paul thinks they'd probably met secretly and voted the cook and the aerobics instructor out. He has the distinct impression, no, the distinct fear, they think of him as just another class of some kind. The women seem most ready to try anything. He is their next 'anything'. Paul rubs his eyes with his knuckles until black spots skip behind his eyelids. It has been a long, long morning. He turns the lights out, closes the door, and heads back to his trailer.

He falls into his too short bed.

He doesn't wake until Suzie bangs on the door and calls, "Pastor Paul! Dinner's ready!"

Grandma Bella pushes open her screen door. In her flour dusted hand she holds a jelly glass of wine. "Thought you might need this." Paul accepts gladly and lifts the glass in a salute, or a toast, or a thank you, or a greeting, or all of those things, to let Grandma Bella know he is pleased to be in the cocoon of her living room having survived the day. Grandma Bella lifts her glass in return. "You did well, and I think from all the good words I've heard this afternoon, everyone is pleased you have joined us."

Grandma Bella opens the door and calls, "Suzie! Sam! Dinner's ready!" At the counter she finishes cutting slices of handmade noodles and drops them in a large kettle of boiling water. She wipes her hands and says in a half-whisper, "My daughter is also pleased you're here. So ignore her fluff and bravado. Neither one means what she really means."

Paul hasn't enough courage to ask what Saundra might "really" mean. He asks, "Need help?"

"Set the table. Thank you."

She calls down the hall, "Children! Wash your hands. Wake your mom."

Grandma Bella continues her half-whispered words, "I know she's a bit chagrined. Her first impression was not her best." Grandma Bella slips sauce from an iron skillet into a spatter-ware bowl. "Nothing is quite what you expected, is it?" she chuckles. "I gather Reverend Cruisewell didn't tell you much. He thinks we widows need something or someone. He just hasn't figured out who or what it is yet. I'd say your chances for success are as good as any. Maybe even better, what with the children totally enamored of you!"

Maybe it is the wine, or maybe it is exhaustion, or maybe it is that everything is new and confusing, but Paul cannot make any sense of what Grandma Bella has just said. Is her observation about the trailer widows or about her daughter? Or him? Who needs what? And chances at what or with whom or…? Paul gives up trying to understand and places the knives, blade in, just like his mom taught him.

"Children!" Grandma Bella calls, "Come to the table."

The door to the bedroom opens and shuts. Suzie calls, "Just a sec!" Paul can hear her explain something to Sam about his shoes.

Paul rolls his wine glass between his hands and then asks Grandma Bella, "I have a question." He stops. He realizes he has a dozen questions. He decides to start with the simplest: "How is it, in this adults only trailer park, no one seems to have noticed the children are children."

"Visiting," Grandma Bella answers. "Probably an extended visit, but a visit."

Sam approaches with one shoe. Suzie is directly behind him.

Suzie speaks to Grandma Bella, but eyes Paul the entire time, "Sam says he's going to wear his tennis shoes."

"And?" Grandma Bella asks.

"For Sunday church? He should dress up."

"That's two days away."

"He should break in his new shoes."

"Just who is whose boss here?" Grandma Bella asks as she brings a crusty loaf of bread from the oven and cuts it into large slices. She grates flakes of Parmesan cheese over the sauce and waits for Suzie to answer.

Sam holds his tennis shoe in the air as if it were part of the answer, part of the question.

"What do you think, Sam?" Grandma Bella asks.

Sam squints first at his grandmother then at Paul. His eyes barely open, his lips clamped as if to make a major life decision.

The fuss over shoes makes Paul think he should come to the rescue. "It's okay, little buddy. You can wear…"

Suzie fixes Paul with a stare and says with bite-sized words, "Once upon a time at a *real* church, we dressed up."

"Sam, they're your feet. It's my church. You have my permission to wear whatever you want."

"But…" Suzie counters.

"Now, now, children. No squabbling."

By the encompassing look, Paul realizes he has been included in this admonition. Grandma Bella centers a platter of noodles covered with a steaming sauce of tomatoes and garlic cloves and anchovies and peppers and black olives and capers. "A glorious mess!" she exclaims. And then she calls, "Saundra, dinner's on the table!"

From down the hall, Saundra responds, "I could use some help with these damn crutches."

"You'll get no help with words like that!" Grandma Bella yells back.

Sam runs down the hall.

A yelp comes from the bedroom. "Best I help," Grandma Bella says. "Paul, would you do the honors and begin filling the plates?"

"Sammy!" Saundra's voice verges on the edge of irritation, exasperation, and thankfulness.

"I'll be right back," Grandma Bella leaves.

"Just wait," Suzie says. "She'll get you later."

And Paul wonders what in the world that means. And who will get whom.

19

PUTTANESCA

Everyone bows their head. Everyone folds their hands.

"My turn!" Sam calls. He waits a second and then says into his folded fingers, "Thank you. Dear God. We love puttanesca! Amen." He lifts his head and smiles a big smile at Paul.

"What kind of a prayer..." Suzie's chastisement is interrupted by Grandma Bella, "Paul, this dish is a special treat we serve for very special guests." She winks at her daughter and Paul realizes the yelling is forgotten, the children are eating, the room is wrapped in pleasure, and he finds himself at home and pleased at the aroma of such a lovely dish, ingredients of which he has never seen combined before.

Suzie chimes in, "What a great idea!"

Paul has the distinct impression he once again has missed something.

"So. What kind of a church are you bringing us?" Saundra asks, all smiles and a chipper, congenial voice.

Paul answers with words from some past lesson, "I think of it as a Johnny Appleseed kind of church. A church for everyone."

"Buddhists?" Suzie skewers the word in such a way that Paul knows she is trying to put him on the spot.

"Fine with me."

The screeching sound of fork against plate draws attention to Sam. He is industriously separating olives from peppers from anchovies from capers. He looks up. "I think a club would be fun. Or a fort. What if the chapel was a fort?"

"Or," Suzie adds, "Why not have a country club? You could serve drinks and people could dance. Then everyone would want to come."

Grandma Bella pulls a strand of hair away from Suzie's face. "Suzie, don't tease. Perhaps another subject?"

"Sure. How do you like the puttanesca?" Suzie asks beaming.

Saundra gives Suzie a mean-eyed look that Paul has no trouble reading. It is a 'Suzie-mind-what-you-say' stare. Sam slurps a noodle off of his plate. Grandma Bella offers to pour Paul more wine.

"Wellllll…"

"Child. Eat your dinner," Saundra corrects her daughter.

Suzie pulls her head back from her mother's look as if Saundra's words demanded ignoring.

"I'll bet you've never had puttanesca ever before!" Suzie says and without hesitation adds, "It's a seduction dish!"

Paul looks from Suzie to Grandma Bella to Saundra. He thinks better of saying anything and makes an appreciative 'umming' sound.

Saundra takes a deliberate bite. She drinks a delicate amount of wine and then she explains. "It's only Mother at work, doing what mother's do best. Puttanesca is what she served Big Bill the first night he came to dinner. The dinner was magic. Do you know Bill?"

"The grounds guy. Yes, I do."

"Right. You can bet within the hour he'll be around. But sometimes this dinner works and sometimes it doesn't."

Paul chews slowly enjoying the rich sour taste of the dish. "You've lost me."

"My mother, and before her, her mother, believe, believed, in spells. Not witches or demons."

Paul looks to see how Grandma Bella is absorbing this family story. She lifts her eyebrows as if to say, "What's a mother to do?"

Saundra continues, "Just certain womanly spells." Saundra looks up over her fork where she holds a tangle of noodles. "Now, that bit of information will make your ministry much more interesting—dealing with spells and brews and womanly concoctions."

"And how does that relate to this meal?" Paul asks and realizes Saundra's story, goofy as it is, told in a straight forward manner, allows him to ask the first straight forward question of the evening.

"So this is to seduce me? No problem. I'm seduced. I've spent a wonderful day and could not have asked for more. A wonderful meal. Thank you for including me."

Grandma Bella laughs, "Saundra's being very polite. Probably it's the "minister-thing". Let me tell you more. In Italy, the women of the street, looking to give up their trade, serve puttanesca to capture a permanent man. The women fearful their men may starve serve puttanesca. The women ready for babies serve puttanesca. I thought it wouldn't hurt, you being single!"

The children burst into laughter. Saundra bursts into laughter. Grandma Bella leans back with a large smile. "So that is the story of puttanesca."

When Saundra catches her breath, she tells Paul, "What you don't know is that the last two candidates, the aerobics guy and the cook, had this dinner and they disappeared. You just automatically got on the list. My mother never gives up trying. Even Randi Cruisewell! And with him?" Saundra rolls her eyes. "Well, with him, I got a job as a secretary! So, it worked for him, but not the way my mother keeps hoping."

Grandma Bella hands Paul the platter, "More, Paul? I think Saundra has elaborated a bit too much. But good cooking is good cooking, especially when it's mine!"

"Puttanesca has the taste and smell of..."

"Saundra! Enough! Watch your story telling in front of the children."

"What? My children? Remember who brought up this subject! And her vocabulary. Just who chooses Suzie's words?"

"I choose my words!" Suzie explodes. "If I had a parent around to help me, maybe I would choose better words like 'antiquated!'"

"She sure does choose those words! Too many!" Sammy exclaims.

Grandma Bella snaps smartly, "Children!"

And Paul is amazed how they all chuckle, return to eating as if some of the words weren't hard and demanding. It is as if the words are crisp and close to harsh, but are smothered in 'family'.

A moment of sweet silence descends. Paul relaxes. He loves the up and down craziness of the conversation. The food is delicious. No one will stomp away from the table. No one will use silence like a hammer. Paul thinks of Bear, sad silences, and minutes that became hours when no one said a word.

Saundra, head bent, says in a soft, controlled voice, "You know I'd be here more if I could find a real job. Full time work. Playing the accordion in small-time towns in small-time bars is not what I want to do. I really want to be here with you."

Suzie twirls her fork through the noodles on her plate. She rocks back and forth as if she is trying to digest her mother's words. Then she says with an edge of wisdom and wistfulness, "We need to have Reverend Cruisewell over more often."

"That will be the day, little miss. He's so busy dashing all around the state, but we certainly could try again," Saundra says and passes the bread plate to Paul. "Take this dinner as a compliment. We seem so at home with you, we've had one of our rare, but rather interesting, family 'discussions'. We're glad you've joined us. This trailer court could use some revving up. So, here's to you." Saundra raises her glass. "Welcome to New Dawn. When I'm around I even might attend your little church. But then, maybe I won't. Sleep on a Sunday morning is high on my list. Which says nothing of the fact that I'm rarely here on Sunday mornings."

Sam lets the pasta drop from his fork. He holds on to Saundra's arm. He begs, "You gotta stay. Your foot's gotta get well."

"Thank you sweetheart, but a twisted ankle is no excuse for not working."

Grandma Bella offers the last of the wine. Paul thinks twice, then decides this isn't the same as drowning his spirits at The Big Drinkers' Bar. He extends his glass. Grandma Bella pours and then says to Saundra, "For the children's sake, you might suggest to Reverend Cruisewell that he hire you full time."

"Mom, as long as I'm good at the accordion, I'm not going to spend any more time than I have to, in that limousine. Maybe, just maybe, if he had a real office or a real house, things could be different."

"What do you do exactly?" Paul asks.

"For Cruisewell? Between gigs he has me check charts to find towns in, excuse the stupid euphemism, 'financial transition'. Towns going bust. I get tired sitting in the back seat of his car sorting through faxes and books and pamphlets. Cruisewell's got a lot of energy. So much so he hasn't seemed to notice I'm indispensible to him. "

"Faxes? In his car?"

"Car's got everything. Computer. Fax. Refrigerator. Television. Whatever you want, it's there. I think Cruisewell has...what'd you call it? In school now, when kids can't concentrate?"

"Attention Deficit Disorder," Suzie snaps out the words.

"Right. Suzie, you are so bright! Attention Deficit Disorder. He never sits still. He's always on to something new. A Polka at double-time is one way to describe Reverend Cruisewell's energy. But, I must admit, there is something attractive about all that energy."

"And he pays well," Grandma Bella said.

"Yes. That he does." Saundra directs her attention to Paul. "Just what is it he thinks you're going to do?"

"It's a little un-defined. His instructions were to play it by ear. Come Sunday, assuming he's here, I hope to get some help. From him."

"If I don't play 'till dawn' I'll be around. It will be interesting to see what happens. Cruisewell is always interesting. Crazy. Fun. Intriguing. Don't you think so Mom?"

"Don't get your hopes up."

Sam snuggles against his mother. Saundra wraps her arms around her son and kisses the top of his head.

"Don't go," Sam pleads.

"Not for long, honey. We're talking Tacoma, I'll be back before you know it."

"That's what you always say."

In the silent moment that follows, Suzie twists in the nook so that her full attention is on Paul. "Pastor Paul?" He hears a slight plea. Her voice has lost its belligerent, demanding edge.

"Yes, Suzie," he answers, but as he looks at her magnified, 'asking' eyes, he tries to calculate in what manner she might be preparing an attack.

"Would you help us?"

Paul hesitates, wary. "If I can."

Sam pulls away from his mom, his eyes wide with hope, pleased to be part of the 'us'.

Suzie keeps her eyes on her target. Her voice is two beats short of begging, "Will you help us collect for Unified Ways Children's Walk? Take us somewhere to collect besides the trailer court?"

Grandma Bella reaches to wipe a dribble from Suzie's chin. "Suzie. We've discussed this."

"Yes, but that was before we had Pastor Paul. He's our minister! Besides, think of how much more money we could donate if we could go to more houses." Suzie's eyes grow large as she pleads. She turns to Paul, a beat closer to desperation she adds, "Would you? Would you please? Please?"

"It sounds like Grandma Bella's already said…"

"Yes, but people change their minds!" Suzie reaches behind her to grab the Unified Ways tin. She shakes it. One loan coin rattles. We could win! Sam and I could win and get the prize!"

"What's the prize?" Paul asks.

"Tickets! Free tickets to the County Fair! In Monroe! We've never, ever gone to a Fair. Please, oh, please."

Paul has watched the words pass back and forth. He can think of no reason not to take the children.

Grandma Bella asks, "Would you mind?"

From Suzie and Sam's bouncing in place, he knows there is only one answer. "Great! I'd love to. When?"

"Tomorrow night!" Sam explodes. "Hooray! Hooray! Hooray! Hooray!"

Grandma Bella's hand gently lands on Sam's head.

"Fan-tas-tic!" Suzie waves her arms in victory.

Sammy silently bounces up and down, his fork waving a noodle.

"Sammy!" Saundra says sternly but with a chuckle, "Enough already."

"I'll make a map! Ten houses? Twenty houses? How far do we get to go?" Suzie asks.

"The neighborhood, my sweet." Saundra answers. "One hour, two at the most. Cover as many houses as you can. Then home!" For the moment, Saundra and Suzie are in complete agreement.

Saundra requests, "Give me a hand. Time for the evening news. I've got to get my foot up." She pushes back her chair, uses Sam's shoulder as an anchor.

The television screen scrolls and stops on a couple screaming with joy over a newly acquired refrigerator. Saundra speaks to the screen: "Like you don't already have a refrigerator! What do you think?" she reaches to cuddle Sam next to her, "Can't have too many refrigerators huh?" She clicks the remote and the television stops as a news announcer warns, "Parents, remember, tomorrow night is the Unified Ways Children's Walk. Our goal this year is ten thousand dollars! Let's see if we can meet it! The walk begins at 4:00 tomorrow, late afternoon. Remember, we have free tickets to the Monroe County Fair. And this year, the county chainsaw competition will be the primary attraction. So, leave your lights on! Welcome the children for this single night of giving!"

Paul can't believe what he's heard. A chainsaw competition. At Monroe. And if the children win? And if he needs to take them to the fair? And if…

Sam leaves Saundra's side to put his elbow on Paul's knee, he cups his hand under his chin, and counsels Paul, "You would make a great dad."

Paul's eyes tear so unexpectedly he is pleased when a syncopated knock on the door takes Sammy's intense gaze away from him.

Grandma Bella calls, "Come on in! Door's open!"

"I could smell that puttanesca all the way down the block. It was calling me!" Big Bill steps inside the trailer. He touches the brim of his cap, "Ladies! Paul! Sammy, old buddy! Good to see you all." He gives Grandma Bella a smooch on the cheek, looks under the lid of the cast iron skillet, "Thank goodness you've left some for me!"

"Grab a plate. Scoot over, Paul."

Soon they are all hearing about the new mower. Bill pulls a catalog from his bib pocket and explains every detail of the T-Series Kubota tractor with a hydrostatic transmission and OHV engine.

Paul half listens. His head is full of the words CHAINSAW COMPETITION! He watches Saundra page a magazine. He watches the children spread Legos down the hall. He relaxes. What if? What if the children win the prize? What if he ends up at the county fair? What if, by some miracle, he was able to compete?

The spell is broken when Grandma Bella announces, "Children. Bedtime." Without grumbling they place their Lego tower in a corner, throw the loose pieces into a Tupperware box and disappear down the hall. Saundra appears to have fallen asleep in the recliner. Grandma Bella cleans up the dishes and Bill continues to study his brochure. The evening ends when Sam and Suzie, pajama clad, come out to give everyone goodnight kisses, including Paul. And Paul notices that Suzie gives her sleeping mom the gentlest of kisses.

Paul takes the moment of 'goodnight's to bid farewell.

Outside the evening is on the edge of cool. Above his head a breeze clatters leaves. A dog barks somewhere in the dark. All in all it has been a pretty good day. No, a pretty fine day. And possibilities? And possibilities.

20

SAUNDRA MAKES A CALL

The following morning, Paul wakes in a great mood. He drives the Jeep over to Rex's for breakfast with the boys. On the way back he stops at the Mini-Mart for Cheerios, Campbell Soup, and a six-pack of Red Hook. When he drives up to his trailer, it is only eight o'clock. The morning is young and bright and Paul is ready to transform a tea room into a chapel. He feels as if nothing can stop him.

He stores the groceries, grabs a beer, and heads towards the garage. Standing in front of the chapel, Paul surveys his little kingdom. Thinking everyone must certainly still be in bed, Paul is surprised when he sees the twins in their vegetable garden. They wave. Paul cups the beer in his right hand and waves with his left. Then Mrs. Entwhistle pulls back her curtain and waves. Paul nods 'good morning'. Just as he opens the door to the garage he sees the other widows through the white arch of the court. They are too occupied to see him. They jog in the direction of the Mini-Mart and disappear around the corner past the laurel hedge in the direction of Rex's diner.

Astounding! He feels the truth in Rex's proclamation this morning, "That bunch of women? You have a hand full."

Paul steps inside the garage and tries to imagine a church service with those women listening. He sips the cool, soothing beer as he pokes around the boxes they had pushed aside the day before. In a box marked 'Decorations' Paul finds a dozen squat candles. He places the candles in a row down the middle of the white-sheeted plywood and saw-horse table. Presto! Change-o! An alter.

Encouraged, Paul rummages through the next box: three table legs, a length of clothes line rope, a nested bunch of woven baskets, an assortment of old tools.

"Whatja doin?" Sam asks, his arms wrapped around the pushing body of Smuggins. Paul slips the beer into one of the baskets.

"Hi, Sam. Just messin' around."

"We're not supposed to bother you."

"You don't bother me. Where's Suzie?"

"Here!" Suzie calls, as she bumps past Sam. The cat flies from Sam's clutch and disappears behind a stack of boxes. Suzie walks around the altar checking out the candles. "We went to a *real* church once. It had pews, and an altar, and a big statue, and flowers."

"That's nice. Do you have a soccer game today?"

"Nope! It's library day and then swimming lessons. But, most important, today's the day we need to get the most money! I'm working on the map!" Suzie waves a piece of paper. "I've mapped out twenty houses! Twenty more would be great, don't you think?"

"Forty? Well, I guess we'll wait and watch our watches."

"Hey! That's a great rhyme!" Sam exclaims.

Suzie makes a face at Sam, like he's nuts. Turns back to Paul. "You didn't forget did you?"

"Of course not! But between now and then I've a church to create. Want to help?"

In minutes they have rows of chairs in front of the altar. Two empty boxes are stacked and covered with white tea towels stitched with red carnations.

"A pulpit!" Paul announces, to which Sammy bursts into laughter and through his giggles asks, "What's a pul-pit?"

"That, mister smarty-pants, is where I will stand to tell you what to do."

"You're not my boss!" Sam laughs and claps his hands.

Paul grabs Sammy and hugs his twisting, wiggling form. "Maybe not, but I am your official adult escort for tonight's gathering of the bucks!"

A figure fills the doorway and blocks the morning sun. "Sam! Suzie! Grandma said not to bother Pastor Paul. Besides, Grandma Bella's waiting. Time for the library and you need to get your suits and towels." Saundra maneuvers her crutches through the door.

Suzie picks up her map, stomps by her mother and calls over her shoulder, "We weren't a bother! We just turned this dumpy garage into a chapel. Sam, come!"

Sam reluctantly walks backwards toward the door. Suzie pokes her head back inside. "Pastor Paul, don't forget! Tonight!"

"That's right!" Sam runs back to give Paul's knees a hug and then heads towards his mom. Sam stops and looks up at his mother, "Promise? Sunday is our day together?" Saundra bends to push his hair back into place. "Promise, little guy. We'll all go to church and then a whole day together!"

Saundra winks at Paul. His stomach clenches at the realization that a real person will be sitting in this unreal church. A critical someone.

Paul watches Saundra watch her children get in the Fairlane with Grandma Bella. She looks tired and is wearing a sweat suit with one leg sliced to make room for her cast. She doesn't have yesterday's bristle and bluster and she certainly has none of the 'come-on' style she'd exhibited when she drove up in her Morris Minor.

"Kind of embarrassing when your daughter hates every bone in your body," Saundra says as she works her way into the center of the room and lowers herself in the first row of folding chairs. She looks around the room. "It's really crappy, isn't it?" she says.

"May I agree with you? Crappy hardly describes it." Paul hesitates and then adds, "Your relationship with Suzie is pretty crappy too. But, there's hope." Paul turns a chair to slide under Saundra's encased foot.

"You sure? You the childless one? You know about hope and children?"

"No question. There are moments."

"Moments? Rare moments." Saundra closes her eyes and rolls her head as if to loosen the muscles in her neck. "You have any advice? All that training. You know all about kids, marriage…what else? Death? Dying? Group therapy? I'm sure you are well prepared. Advice galore."

"Couldn't have said it better, myself," Paul says making his voice as even as possible, showing as little of the irritation he is feeling. He studies Saundra and wonders for the tenth time how someone who has the ability to look so good and who easily shows her affection for her son, remains clueless about winning love from her daughter.

"Don't start workin' on me. I ache. I'm broke. I slept on a sofa bed with my mother, so I didn't get any sleep. And I've only got two more pain killers."

"And you play tonight?"

"And I play tonight. The Crocodilian Bar."

Paul stretches his legs between two chairs. He crosses his ankles and sits in silence. He can't think of one good ministerial thing to say.

"Tell me, Mr. Minister, you're all about knowing stuff about life. I'll bet you don't know the answer to this question. Why does shit keep happening?"

"Ah, the big question. Realize I've only been a minister for two days, so I don't have all the answers. Yet."

Saundra's head falls back with a great laugh. "A two-day minister. Sounds par for the course. So tell me about before two days ago."

"I was getting ready."

"Getting ready?" Saundra folds her arms across her chest. "Oh, right, those stupid lessons."

"You know about the lessons?"

"Well, truth will come out eventually. So best I tell you up front. Who do you think graded those lessons? You did okay. Mostly. But here's my advice, don't go around thinking life is a multiple choice quiz."

"I never thought it was…" Paul is confused and for some reason hurt by another deception. He wishes Saundra would disappear. She doesn't. She keeps right on talking, "So I gave you a mix of grades. Didn't you notice the pattern? Two 'A's' then two 'D's?' And all my great words of encouragement? I have a list I choose from, 'Keep it up!', 'Almost got it'. 'Try again'. And oh, lots of smiley faces."

Paul is somewhere between being pissed and being astounded. And it seems to him, as Saundra spills secrets, that she pushes up her breasts without even thinking about it. She stares back at him. Maybe she did think about it.

"So now, you're here. You've finished the lessons. But did it ever dawn on you exactly how much getting ready it takes for a trailer court of widows and two children?"

There's no answer. "Why do you do that?" Paul asks.

"Do what?"

"Get pissy about everything."

"I don't get pissy at everything. I get pissy when it's appropriate."

"Like with the kids?"

"When was I pissy with the kids?"

"Which incident do you want to start with?"

Saundra doesn't answer.

"Let's take the first one. You're broken shoe…"

"An appropriate outburst."

"You made Suzie feel bad then…"

"Well…"

"You made Sam cry when you yelled at him not to touch you when you got back from the hospital."

"I hurt. Besides, they understand."

"You sure?" Paul feels his anger growing. "I doubt it. You think I'm not prepared. Who in hell prepared you?"

Tears well in Saundra's eyes. She turns her head as they spill and she wipes them away with her sleeve.

All the understanding and compassion Paul had been studying these past weeks disappears. He wants to verbally clobber Saundra. He doesn't want her to cry. But, he's angry and he feels mean. "You're worse than the kids when they are at their very worst! You make Suzie look like a grown-up, with how silly and mean you are." Paul's words surprise him. He's like a little kid on a roll. When Saundra hiccups with a stifled sob, he's slightly satisfied. Only a small part of him wants to take his words back. Then he sees her shoulders shake with sobbing.

"Truce. Let's stop. Your kids are great. That's something you must have done right. I apologize."

While Paul waits to see if there is any kind of an armistice, he thinks maybe these outbursts give explanation to how Suzie can be irritating—trying to be grown-up to protect herself from her mother's childishness. Before Paul can think more about admitting to his strange pleasure of hurting someone, he looks up to see Saundra rub her eyes, tip her head back, and take deep breaths. Angry, she demands, "So?" She pushes her hand into a side pocket and recovers a torn wad of Kleenex.

Paul thinks he wanted a fight. He pushed for a fight. Now he doesn't know what to do. He can't believe tough Saundra isn't that tough. She dissolves quickly and recovers quickly.

He decides to push the *truce* idea.

"I was indulging in an early morning beer. Would you like a swallow?"

Saundra twists her Kleenex. She tears off ends in little tufts. "I'm fine," she answers.

"Then I'll have one." Paul leans down to retrieve his beer. The slug of liquid brings relief.

"I'm so frustrated..." Saundra says barely holding back more tears.

"Geeze, Saundra, we're all frustrated."

Saundra pushes the tattered tissue to her eyes, wipes away black mascara that has begun to seep down her face. "You don't know frustration." she says.

Paul does not respond. He knows enough not to respond. A line from a lesson bounces in his head: "When counseling, remember to be spontaneous." In the box closest to him, the corn-yellow cover of a National Geographic catches his eye. The cover's right hand corner reads, "The Tattered Map of Chernobyl." Paul says in what he hopes is an understanding voice, "Life is a tattered map."

Saundra peeks from behind her Kleenex. She bursts out laughing. "When all else fails say something really, really stupid!"

"It was a try."

"That it was. Appreciated. Sometimes, not making sense, works."

"A 'what-a-ya-goin-to-do-when-all-else-fails' stance?" Paul asks lifting his beer to toast this pause in their back-and-forth harangue.

"Exactly. I think I'll have a taste of that beer."

Paul wipes the top with his shirt-tail and hands the can to Saundra. "Truce, then?"

"For awhile," Saundra says and takes a slow sip of beer. They sit in a companionable silence.

"I promised mom I'd try to spend more time with the kids."

Paul waits. Saundra hands Paul the beer, and continues speaking. Her voice drops so Paul has to lean forward to hear. "I get so tired. I feel like I haven't had a good night's sleep in weeks. I get a gig. I come home, late, to sleep on a sofa bed. I'm grogged-out and worried and I'm supposed to be a good mother. Kids are a scary proposition. Especially when I get so damn tired."

"Want an idea?" Paul checks to see if Saundra is ready to take any advice he might have. "I know I've not much experience to speak from, but it might be good just to remember they're kids."

"That's it? That's your pastorly advice?"

"Well, I think it helps to remember we're bigger than they are. There's a part of them that likes that. Having bigger people around. I also think we know more than they do."

"You're talking about Suzie, remember."

"I said I 'think' we know more. We can always pretend."

"You're so full of it. Pretend?"

"Yeah. Somewhere in those lessons, a piece of advice stood out."

"Which is?"

"Act like what you want to be. It'll happen."

"One of Randi's major insights. He does believe that. And, for him, things do happen."

"True? Amazing." Paul hesitates and then asks, "Like the limo? Like the gold chains? Like people like me doing his bidding?"

"Well, it's better than a kick in the ass."

"Thanks. You know how to give a guy hope."

Saundra stands and swings her crutches under her arms. "I do what I can do."

Paul reaches out a hand to steady her.

"Thanks for the so-so advice and the beer." She gives Paul a smile. "Truth be known, the foot isn't feeling that good. With mom gone with the kids, I think I'll go get some sleep."

Paul works to not make eye contact again. Saundra's use of the word 'sleep' makes him leery. He's never been good at figuring out women's words. He always wonders if women say or mean more than the words they say.

Saundra winces as she carefully swings her body out the door.

As he watches her make her way back to Grandma Bella's trailer he thinks: she probably did hurt, she probably does need a nap, and she probably meant exactly what she said.

"Many thanks for taking the kids tonight," Saundra calls.

"You're welcome," he answers.

She just keeps walking. Not one bit of a come-on.

The rest of the day Paul makes a dozen runs to the hardware store, the lumber yard, the dump, and the grocery store. At four o'clock Grandma Bella drives into the trailer court. Minutes later he hears the chirping sound of Suzie and Sam's muffled voices. Then they are at the chapel door. Each holds a donation tin.

"Stupendous!" Suzie cries as she turns to survey the finished work. "It's really stupendous!"

"Flattery always works," Paul answers. "You're pretty stupendous yourself! And it looks like you're ready to go."

"You've done a stupendous amount of work,"

"Enough already! Where's that brother of yours?"

"Here!" Sam pokes his head around the corner and rattles his donation tin.

"Sounds like you've already got a donation!"

"Grandma. Grandma gave us each four quarters."

"Priming the pump, she deemed it," Suzie explains.

"Deemed?"

"Yes, deemed. Nice word, huh?"

"Indeed, it is."

"Let's go! Let's go!" Sam calls from the door. "Too many words!"

Outside the sun streaks under the late afternoon clouds.

Paul hurries to catch up with his charges. "Hey you two, before we head out. I've a stupendous idea. Let's visit the widows. I'm sure they're all waiting.

Suzie says, "I'm not sure that's a stupendous idea, but it's a good idea. The stupendous evening begins!" She looks up at Paul. "There. That's 'stupendous' ten times. I'm done. Did you notice? Ten times!"

"How could I have missed. You were stupendous."

21

ALL AROUND THE NEIGHBORHOOD

"Our pleasure!" says the elderly couple in unison. "Bye, now! Bye! Keep up the good work!"

Paul takes Sam's hand, carries his collection tin.

"I think we've just about done it," Paul says.

Suzie shakes her can and heads toward the next house. "There are three more houses on this block!"

"There are no lights on."

"And I'm tired," Sam says, shuffling his feet to slow them down. Paul picks him up.

"Stop her," Sam demands, his finger pointing at Suzie as she reaches the walk to the dark, unlit house.

Suzie waits for Sam and Paul. "How can anyone not be home for United Ways! What kind of person is that anyway?" her voice is full of disgust.

Paul can't believe the evening is losing its wonder and charm. He pretends Sam's weight is dragging him down. He stumbles and staggers. He calls, "I can't take another step. Too much money! Too much Sam! My arms ache!"

Sam giggles, "Hooray. Boys win. Head for home."

Suzie stands on the steps in front of the dark house. "This house might not be excessive," she says.

"Accessible?"

"That's what I said."

"Close. No cigar."

Suzie walks to the front door. She cups her hand over her eye to see inside. "Geeze," she says in disgust. "Nobody's home."

"Next two houses are also dark. It's a sign. It's a sign they're not home. Let's call it a day," Paul calls.

Suzie reluctantly comes down the steps.

Sam mumbles into Paul's neck, "Think we're going to win?"

His words are drowned out by the brumming sound of a Honda scooter. A woman in wind-floppy overalls, a black leather jacket, a decaled and fluorescent pink helmet, comes around the corner. She turns down the driveway where they stand. As she passes she waves and yells, but her words are lost.

"What did she say?" Suzie asks.

"Didn't hear a word," Paul answers. "Gotta wait and see." He watches as the woman sets the kickstand and runs into the house. The porch lights come on along with an entire string of white twinkle lights. The door flies open.

The woman, her helmet and leather jacket gone, stands in the doorway. Across the front of an oversized sweatshirt are the words "Fly With Me! Do Aerobics!" At the end of a slender wrist she wears an oversized candy-pink plastic watch. She waves her hand in a circular motion beckoning Paul and Sam and Suzie to join her on the porch.

"Come in! I'm home!" She points to the watch and rolls her eyes as if to tell them why she was late. "Finally! I didn't mean to be late. Please, come in!"

Paul herds the children into the foyer of the turn-of-the-century house. They all stand in a small coved entryway. To Paul's left is a hall-tree covered in an assortment of hats: billed, straw, wool, plastic. The helmet she has just removed swings gently from its chin strap.

Behind her, the living room glows in a splash of color. The woman steps back and indicates they should come inside. Close now, Paul sees the wisps of her hair spring from matted curls from the pressure of the just-removed helmet. She has a face that reminds him of fresh milk—white and smooth. Her eyes are the shade of spring fiddler ferns. His breath catches. He wants a time out. He wants a space, a vacuum, a moment where he can just stare at her.

"Wait right there. I'll get my donation," she says.

She walks back to the kitchen and they hear a rattle of coins. Then Paul sees her trim form in the light of the refrigerator as she removes a platter. She returns to the front room. Paul takes it all in until he feels Suzie bump against him. "It's not nice to stare," she whispers.

The woman offers Suzie a jar full of quarters. "Here, all yours! Be sure to share what's there with your brother!"

Paul notices her toothy smile. Her center teeth don't quite meet and the irregularity makes her look wholesome. Fun. Inviting.

She offers a platter of Fig Newtons and peanut butter cups. "Help yourself! Take two! Take three! I always have a treat for this night, you guys working so hard, doing such a good job, for such a good cause!"

Her words spill around Paul like jelly beans. Rattley, hard, smooth, colorful, bouncing. He has an image of wanting to take each word and suck it for its sweetness. He wants to chomp into each and every sugary coat. Paul blinks. He realizes she is waiting for him to say something or do something. The platter is extended. He takes a Fig Newton. It is hard and cold. He doesn't even like Fig Newtons.

The woman kneels to Sam's height with the platter of treats. Suzie steps back and looks at Paul and makes a twirling circular motion at her temple and she rolls her eyes.

Paul pops the rest of the bar into his mouth and grabs Suzie's hand to stop her motion.

"Good choice!" Suzie says as Sam takes a peanut butter cup and then another.

The woman straightens. She is tall. Almost as tall as Paul. She smiles directly at him. "What a great night to be collecting with your children."

The Fig Newton becomes a gooey mess in his mouth. Paul can't speak. He chews and chews trying not to choke.

"Are you having success?" she asks Suzie and offers her the platter for a second time.

Paul watches the woman as she chatters, her eyes large and excited. Her lashes black and long. Her eyebrows arched and dark.

"Umm, it's been great...just wonderful!" he finally says, wanting her to quit speaking to the children. Wanting her to talk to him.

She turns to Paul. "I'm sorry I wasn't home when you got here. I came as fast as I could, but my class just finished." She nods her chin at her sweatshirt as if to explain where she's been.

"He's not our dad," Suzie says, her voice sour and tight.

"Right. I'm not their father."

"But he could be!" Sam says.

"Sam! You've been warned." Suzie pushes Sam.

"Well, he could be."

A pocket of silence holds the four of them. Paul watches slow warm color inch up the woman's long slender neck. She prattles, "Take two! Or three! Cookies. Candy. I've missed the other collectors and now it's getting dark and they've encouraged children not to be out late. I'm so glad I didn't miss you. I was going to dole out all my change, but all of it's yours! Hope you win the trip to the fair!"

"I'm their minister. We have permission...from their grandmother...to collect..."

"Well, that's so nice. Nice for children to have someone to take them out. And extra nice that you waited for me. Nice that they want to be with you."

Paul can't figure what she has just said and he wishes he hadn't mentioned the minister thing. She tips her head and turns slightly away. It helps him to breathe to think maybe her confusion matches his own. He waits for her to speak next, not wanting to take a chance that whatever he might say would be stupid.

She stumbles over her sentence. "You didn't…don't look familiar, not that I get to church that often, but not because I don't need it or wouldn't want to if…" She looks away from Paul to Suzie, as if to break the craziness between them.

"Have you lived in our neighborhood that long?" she asks Suzie.

"Pastor Paul's brand new," Sam says.

"We're from the next-door neighborhood and now I think it's time to go," Suzie says and turns toward the front door.

Paul puts out a hand to keep Suzie in place and with his other hand stops Sam's reach for another treat. "I'm the new minister at the trailer court off Borealis. Suzie and Sam are visiting their grandmother."

"Oh, the 'adults only' court. I've noticed it. It's so crisp and clean."

"You do aerobics?" Paul asks.

"I teach aerobics. But not just aerobics. I work at a studio, that's why I was late. I was late at the studio and late for the exercise class and then I just got here…"

"Help!" Sam exclaims, as he looks down the front of his shirt. A slide of chocolate covers his front. I lost my candy." He looks around to see if it is on the floor. "And I've got a slobber on my front."

"Wait. I'll be right back." The woman takes long strides as she heads for the kitchen and returns with a wet towel. She kneels and wipes Sam's hands and face.

"I think we'd better be going. It's late." Suzie says. She turns and walks towards the door.

Paul kneels beside Sam. The three of them, munchkin-height, focus their attention on Sam's front. Paul can smell an edge of mint, or wild rose. He breathes deep to take in more of the scent of her. His hand touches the bib of Sam's overalls, where her hand had just been. "Looks like you're good as new, little buddy," Paul says.

Sam looks down at his front and continues to chew on the last candy he's popped in his mouth.

Behind them Paul hears the front door open. He calls over his shoulder, "Suzie, wait."

Paul turns to his hostess and asks over Sam's head, "What kind of studio do you have?" Behind him the door opens further and Paul feels a rush of cold air. Impatient, he calls, "Suzie, just a sec. We're right on schedule. One more block, just like you asked."

"We don't have one more block," Suzie calls back and keeps on walking. Paul wants to yell at her, "Do so…"

"Oh, this kind of stuff," the woman stands as she answers. She gestures toward a square oak coffee table which holds an assortment of glass bowls in banded colors. From a basket by the door she pulls a mailer and hands it to Paul. "That's me," she says. "Annabelle Lee Fulsome."

The over-sized postcard has a picture of a single bowl in glowing bands of red, purple, and lemon yellow. He turns the card over and reads aloud: *ANNABELLE LEE FULSOME presents her fall work of BANDED BOWLS.* Along one side of the card is a long, narrow, black and white picture of Annabelle Lee in coveralls, her protective eye-ware pushed up on her head, and a glowing mass of glass at the end of a long pipe. She stands in front of an open furnace.

"I'll keep it…the card. May I keep the card?" Paul's words stumble.

"Show opened last Friday. Not far from here. Blast of Glass Gallery. If you have time, you should come by and see it…the show."

"Great. Sounds really great. Glass blowing…and the bowls…are pretty…I mean, they're beautiful." Paul takes a moment to look around the living room. For the first time he notices there are bowls everywhere. Some bowls nestle like Easter eggs. Some are filled with dried flowers and river rocks. Some stand alone. Each bowl is a rainbow of three or four colors.

Suzie stomps back up the front steps into the hall. "It's time! It's late! And Sam's asleep."

Sam is curled, asleep, by Paul's feet. His thumb is tucked securely in his mouth. Paul hoists him to his shoulder.

"Oh, goodness me, I'm sorry. I've been jabbering. Thanks for stopping by. Maybe I'll come by sometime and hear you preach."

"Well, sure. Do that. The chapel isn't quite ready. But, great. Someday, when it's done, that would be nice."

From the door, Suzie says in overly polite words, "Thank you for the treats. Especially the Fig Newtons."

"It's still more a garage than a chapel," Paul explains.

Suzie interrupts, "It *is* a chapel. And thanks to me and Sam, it's a lot better than yesterday." Her chin protrudes and her eyes blaze.

Paul turns away from the tyranny of Suzie. He thinks by making his voice low and calm he can soften the image of Suzie's attack on Annabelle Lee. "Well, we still have a bit of work ahead of us." Then with a stroke of brilliance, at least Paul feels it is brilliant, he recalls the whole chapter on the importance of volunteers. "We're trying to 'grow' the congregation. We're always looking for volunteers."

"Volunteers?" Annabelle Lee says with what Paul hears as interest. Paul registers her response as one full of possibilities, an invitation, a future.

"We can use all the help we can get. Any time."

"Well, tomorrow I have an assigned time at the furnace in the afternoon, but my morning's free."

"Great!" Paul tries to modulate the pleasure he's feeling.

Suzie's words are terse, "It's way, way past dinner time. Grandma Bella will be worried!"

"When you come over, you can't miss us. The chapel's right in the middle of the trailer court. Looks like a garage." Paul extends his free hand, "I'm Paul. Paul Whitinowsky."

Her hands are surprisingly small, but very strong. Paul reluctantly lets go.

"Thanks for your generosity and your time. You were more than generous."

"Lovely talking to you."

"Well, maybe we'll see you sometime? Soon."

"Yes, I think so."

Paul's smile muscles ache. Sam nestles softly into his shoulder. "It's time." Paul says.

The three of them walk down the walk. From the front door, Annabelle Lee calls, "G'night! See you soon!"

Paul turns and waves the fingers of his hand that hold Sam's back.

"Great," he calls, "Just great!"

At the end of the walk, Suzie waits. Her eyes are steely. "Fig Newtons! Yuck! And generous? Generosity? You repeated yourself! And she said lovely? Who ever says a word like lovely! You two are from another planet." Suzie's words are crisp and cold.

They walk home in silence.

At the arch, Suzie says, "Besides, she's skinny."

Paul doesn't answer.

"Grooow a church?" Suzie's voice is full of disbelief.

Paul picks up the pace, wondering if they'll ever get to Grandma Bella's trailer.

Grandma Bella opens the door. Paul hands her Sam's money tin. She exclaims, "Looks like you did all right!" Sam wakes up, rubs his eyes, "We did great! Didn't we Pastor Paul?"

"We did more than great!"

Suzie dumps the change on the kitchen-nook table. Begins counting coins. Without looking up she says, "The Fig Newton Lady was weird...but interesting."

Paul hears the tiniest note of apology in Suzie's voice. "Interesting. Good word. Maybe she really will come by."

"But we're doing pretty good without her."

"You're so right."

"But there's tomorrow."

"Yes, tomorrow. So, what's your word for tomorrow?"

"I don't know yet. I'll choose in the morning."

"I've got one. How about serendipitous?"

"What does it mean?"

"Let's look it up."

Suzie runs down the hall and returns with a large dictionary she can barely hold.

"Be quick!" Grandma Bella says. "Dinner's almost ready."

"Pastor Paul's got a new word. He's going to help me look it up."

Grandma Bella wraps her arms around Suzie. "You're sure he hasn't done his duty for the evening?"

"This will be quick," Paul says. "Starts with s-e-r-e..."

Suzie reads the definition. Writes it down in her book. Demands of Paul, "Were Sam and I serendipitous?"

"Twisting the definition just a bit, you could say that."

"And the Fig Newton Lady?"

"Annabelle Lee Fulsome. Miss Fulsome."

"Mssssss. Fulsome. Was she serendipitous?"

"What's this all about?" asks Grandma Bella as she makes room for bowls of soup between the coins and the dictionary.

"Oh, just someone we met. Someone who tried to seduce Pastor Paul."

"Suzie! Shame on you! I'm sure whoever she was, she was a very nice lady."

"We don't know for sure she's nice. Guess what she had for treats?" Suzie pulls back and looks up at her grandmother. Her voice grows around the word, "Fiiiggg Newtons...yuck!"

"I think we need to finish this story another time. Pastor Paul, I'm going to assume you would enjoy a nice quiet dinner, alone. My grandchildren are wonderful, but I know for a fact, they can exhaust one."

Paul couldn't agree more. He gladly accepts a thermos of soup and a plate piled high with buttered fresh bread.

"Say goodnight, Suzie."

"Night, Pastor Paul."

"And?" Grandma Bella added.

"And thanks for taking us."

"G'night. It was my pleasure. Thanks for going with me."

Paul walks towards his trailer.

"Pastor Paul?" Grandma Bella's voice calls from where she stands in the door of the Airstream. "Pretty good third day as a minister?"

"Better than pretty good!" Paul answers.

As he walks he considers the strangeness of life. From Twist, where single women were non-existent and where he couldn't remember speaking to a child, to a new life where his life is filled with both.

Dinner finished, totally exhausted, Paul studies the invitation to Annabelle Lee Fulsome's opening and savors the moment. Pretty good day? Yes, indeed.

22

TRANSFORMATION

The next morning Paul wakes to a Northwest miracle day. The sun sneaks under the remains of the low-slung fog. The weatherman predicts temperatures in the mid-sixties. Mysteriously, the dread over tomorrow has not appeared. Paul feels in his bones everything will be okay. Over a bowl of Cheerios, he pages through the book of sermons from his correspondence class. Even those topics don't seem as unusable as they had in Twist: *The New Spirit; Jump Around, Turn Around, Face the Day; Creating Your Own Life.* He just doesn't recall all of these 'up' ideas being there before.

Two hours later his spirits jump higher when Suzie runs into the chapel where Paul is rewiring a dimmer switch. She announces, "Guess who's coming? The serendipitous Fig Newton Lady!"

Paul steps outside to see Annabelle Lee Fulsome jog down the gravel road and under the arch. She waves and slows to a walk. As she moves towards them, Paul notices how compact her body is, wrapped in Lycra running shorts and top. She puts her hands on her knees, and bends to catch her breath.

"What a great run," she says all smiles. She unsnaps the pedometer from her ankle and checks it. "Just under two miles from home to here. Perfect distance." She looks skyward and adds, "Perfect day!"

Paul's gaze follows hers. Wisps of high clouds skitter across a crystalline sky. Paul lets the sky go to spend more time looking at Annabelle Lee. Curls of hair cling to her forehead. Dew soaks the edges of her running shoes. A streak of sweat blurs the fabric between her breasts.

"We were hoping you hadn't changed your mind."

Annabelle Lee unties a sweatshirt from her waist, pulls it over her head, and tucks the pedometer into her belly-bag. "I hope there's still work to do," she says with a smile that takes in Suzie as well as Paul.

"We're pretty much all done," Suzie says with authority.

"Great. Show me!"

Suzie leads the way. Inside the chapel Paul watches as Suzie explains everything they have done. Her voice holds a crisp edge, as if to dare Annabelle Lee to find fault.

"Very nice. The flowers add just the right touch," Annabelle Lee says as she walks around the room, checking out boxes, the chairs, the votive candles.

"That's Suzie's doing." Paul gives credit.

"She's got it right! It's all in the atmosphere. Suzie, the bouquet brings just what's needed to the room. Were the candles your idea, too?"

Suzie's smile disappears just as Paul looks to see if her coolness might melt. "No, Pastor Paul found them, I'd guess. The boxes are full of stuff and no one cares if we steal from them."

"Steal?" Paul feels a necessity to explain. "No, no, Suzie assured me that the boxes are Grandma Bella's, mostly, and that she gave her…that's you, Miss Suzie…permission to use anything we wanted." Paul feels like a fool in this I'm-back-in-fourth-grade explanation.

"Well, yes." Suzie gives an inch. Barely.

Sam's shadow spills into the garage. He stops with a look of surprise and exclaims, "Hey! Hey! Hey! It's the Fig…"

"It's Annabelle Lee Fulsome, Sam. Ms. Fulsome," Paul adds with a firm voice. "She's come to volunteer."

Annabelle Lee interrupts, "Annabelle Lee is good enough. And who's that you've got there?"

"Smuggins. She's our outlaw cat," Sam says gleefully, holding the cat up for Annabelle Lee to see. The cat exposes its belly to Annabelle Lee's fingers.

"So, what's next? What can I do to help?"

Sam holds the cat tight as he gives a thorough look at the garage. "It's kind of cold and scary in here, don't you think?" he asks Annabelle Lee.

Sam's words hit Paul with their truth. The chapel suddenly slips back to being a garage full of assorted junk.

Annabelle Lee walks to the side of the room where she peeks into the top two boxes. "Good observation, Sam, but I don't think it will take much to work a transformation." As she speaks she turns the cardboard statue around to see who it is. "Well, would you have ever guessed!" She leans Bill Clinton against the wall. She steps back to view it, turns it around to the blank side. "Suzie? Sam? There's cans of paint in one box. Do we need to ask permission to use them? If we can, I think we can create something rather special."

117

"We're free to use any of the stuff in the boxes. It's just all junk," Suzie answers. "We play house in here all the time. Nobody cares. Grandma and the 'aunts' like to see it being used."

"The aunts?"

Sam bursts into laughter. "The ants! The ants! They're not ants!"

"I think Suzie means all the widows here in the park. And their grandmother, Grandma Bella, previously mentioned. I have been led to believe they've given us permission."

"Sam, what are our chances of finding a hammer and a nail?" Annabelle Lee asks.

"Noooo, problem," Sam says. He drops Smuggins and heads for a toolbox in the corner of the garage.

"And here, more Christmas tree lights! We could put those to good use!" Annabelle Lee lays them on the altar, twisting them into the white lights from yesterday's tea. Then she holds the empty box up for all to see. "Got a knife?" Sam scoots a toolbox towards Annabelle Lee. She finds a box cutter, a file, and two butcher knives.

"An abundance!" Annabelle Lee says and deftly cuts a side out of the box in the shape of two diamonds. She peers through the hole and explains, "A stencil."

Two hours later Annabelle Lee plugs in the lights and they all stand back to admire their work. Annabelle Lee bows to Suzie and Suzie bows to Paul and Paul does a jig holding Sam's hands and exclaims in a sing-song voice, "We've done it! Yes indeed, we've done it!"

They stop to stand in silence.

"It's astounding. I'm not sure it's quite a chapel, but it is certainly no longer just a garage," Paul exclaims with a wide, relieved, sincere, and very grateful smile. He'd give most anything to give Annabelle Lee a big hug. Sam gets one instead.

The Christmas lights glow through swaths of tulle draped from the four corners of the ceiling. A dozen cans, in which Paul helped Sam pound holes, now hold candles and they glow in a line down each side of the room. A floor of diamond shapes glistens and marks the center aisle, alternating in color from maroon to dark green, to turquoise. Gem like. The Oriental runner drapes the altar table and the original white sheet serves as a skirt to the table in ecclesiastical elegance.

"That's the best," Suzie points to the cardboard figure that stands behind the altar. The painted backside of the Bill Clinton statue looks almost Christ-like.

"The outstretched arms make him look just like he's...what's the word...bestowing a benediction?" It's a question, but Suzie's words are full of satisfaction. She's pleased and she's past being pouty. "We did a stupendous job! It's something like a real church!"

"Kinda great!" Sam adds.

"No! Better than kinda!"

"Okay! Okay!" Sam goes to stand in front of the transformed Bill Clinton. "He's got good eyes."

"And! To add a final touch! Music!" exclaims Annabelle Lee as she pulls a cassette player from her belly-bag.

Harry Belafonte's voice flows out of the small machine: "Daylight come and ya wanna go home…Daaay-oh…"

Suzie grabs Sam and dances him around the altar.

Paul and Annabelle Lee sway and clap their hands to the children's dancing. Paul calls over the music to Suzie, "This calls for your new word!"

"It's serendipitous!" She calls back. "This morning has been completely serendipitous!" Suzie and Sam let their hands go and invite Annabelle Lee to dance with them. By the final chorus, they all snake around the room adding their voices to Belafonte's. When the music ends, they laugh and clap and Paul is close enough to Annabelle Lee that rather naturally, he thinks, his arm goes around her shoulder and he gives her a hug. Her arm circles his waist, she hugs him back and he exclaims, "God damn! It's a great day!"

Suzie gives him a look.

"Hello!" Grandma Bella's voice calls from outside the chapel. They turn to see her at the door with a tray stacked high with tuna fish sandwiches and slender slices of homemade pickles.

"My! Oh, my! This is some chapel!" Grandma Bella exclaims as she walks down the aisle and places the sandwich tray on the altar. Paul notices her eyes rest on the figure of Clinton. Grandma Bella doesn't flinch. She turns to her granddaughter, "Suzie, sweetheart, would you go back to the trailer for the lemonade." Suzie runs to the door. "Don't slam the screen door. Your mama is sleeping."

Paul brings chairs up to the altar table, pushes back the votive candles. "Our table!" he pronounces. "And, Grandma Bella, this is one of our volunteers, Annabelle Lee Fulsome." Annabelle Lee extends her hand to Grandma Bella.

"I'm grandmother to Suzie and Sam and one eighth of Pastor Paul's congregation."

Sam scoots a chair closer to the altar. He accepts the sandwich Grandma Bella hands him. He points the sandwich at Grandma Bella. "She's our mom's mom. Our mom plays an accordion," Sam says proudly.

Suzie enters the room with the pitcher of lemonade and plastic cups tucked under her arm. She mumbles, "She plays a squeaky squeeze box."

"Oh?" Annabelle Lee answers as she accepts her sandwich.

"Suzie! Please pour the lemonade." Grandma Bella hands Annabelle Lee a glass. Suzie carefully pours. In her most thoughtful voice she says, "It's a very large accordion. It makes our mother look like a…I'm working on just the right word. One of these days I'll figure out what it is." She fills Annabelle Lee's glass to the brim.

"That's enough, Suzie!" Grandma Bella rescues the pitcher from the hands of her granddaughter. "Suzie's mother is an exceptional accordion player. She was the National Accordion second runner-up three years in a row. In Nebraska. In fact she's staying with us here in the trailer court, right now. She'd have joined us but she had a, what she calls a 'gig' last night, in Tacoma. She got in very late, so she's taking a nap." Grandma Bella spreads her napkin across her lap and asks of Annabelle Lee, "And just what is it you do?"

"I'm a glass artist. I work at the studio at The Fine Art Center. I make bowls. When I'm not making bowls, I teach aerobics for the Parks Department. I trade out studio time. It's a very nice arrangement."

"Oh," Grandma Bella says, her face quizzical and wondering.

Paul sees Grandma Bella's confusion and her wish to be polite. He comes to her rescue. "She a glass blower. She makes beautiful bowls with bands of colors. Shows them at a gallery. Sells them at a gallery."

"Oh, really?"

"We met last night out collecting," Sam says, helping with the explanation.

"Oh! You're the Fig Newton Lady!" Grandma Bella exclaims.

Sam rocks in his chair with laughter. "You're not supposed to say that!" Sam says and laughs and laughs until he starts to choke and Paul picks him up and slaps him on his back. "That, little fellow is quite enough laughter."

Annabelle Lee is all smiles. "Paul. It's okay." Annabelle Lee turns to Grandma Bella. "Truth is, I really dislike Fig Newtons. I purchased them so I wouldn't end up eating the leftover treats. Seemed like a good idea at the time!"

Annabelle Lee checks her watch. She takes the last bite of her sandwich. "Hate to leave you all, but I've got to get going. I'm scheduled for the hot shop at one o'clock."

"I'll be glad to give you a lift," Paul offers.

"Can we come?" Suzie asks.

"Enough, my munchkins," Grandma Bella says. "You two help me clean up. Paul, take your nice friend to work. It was a pleasure meeting you, Annabelle Lee. Don't make yourself scarce."

Everyone stands. The children carry the empty sandwich platter and the lemonade pitcher. Grandma Bella gathers the used paper towels.

They leave and Paul is pleasantly aware he is alone with Annabelle Lee.

23

CHAINSAW JACK

"Well?" Paul asks.

"I really need to get to work. You sure you want to take me?"

The words make Paul's brain go dead. He can't think of what to say. *Take her? Yes, of course, he'd like to take her. Here. Now.* He wants to meditate on the moment. Like a lemon drop. Sweet. Sour.

"I need to stop by the house to change. It's on the way." Annabelle Lee walks out the chapel door. Paul follows, his mind buzzing.

At the jeep, he holds her elbow to help her in. He reaches for the safety belt but stops when she says, "Its okay. I can do it." The lesson is not lost on Paul. He walks around to the other side of the Jeep. Gets in. Puts the key into the ignition. He remembers to breathe.

They drive through the arch. Paul feels like he's just driven straight through the pearly gates.

"So, tell me..." Annabelle Lee asks, "...just how'd you find this trailer court church?"

Words come slowly to Paul. "It found me. Kind of a long story and sort of dumb."

As they drive Paul recounts the story of Cruisewell's arrival in Twist. He tells Annabelle Lee about the limo, about how Cruisewell was looking for help. How he, Cruisewell, was pretty impressive in his white suit and gold jewelry. Paul leaves out his buddy's phony application and the repossession of his car.

"Who is he, really?"

"I'm not quite sure. He's been generous. He doesn't make too many demands, kind of hands off. Don't get me wrong. I had to finish the correspondence course and everything." For a quick second, feeling over-energized, Paul considers reciting the books of the Bible as proof of his training. Then, he thinks, how stupid. He fills the void with the second thing that comes into his head, "I expect Cruisewell will show up sometime tomorrow morning."

"That's good. I was beginning to think he wasn't real. He sounds...dream like."

"He is dream like. An apparition. Once you meet him, I'd be interested in hearing what you think."

Annabelle Lee turns to get a better look at Paul. To study him. "Do you have any idea why he chose you? This strange, weird person?"

"Oh, he's not all that strange. He didn't just show up in Twist without a reason. Buddies of mine actually contacted him; they thought I needed some help. They sent my name..."

"Needed help?"

"Well, not help, help. A change of place. Pace. A new start..."

Paul stops talking and silence seeps around them. The traffic bunches up. Paul concentrates on driving.

He honks, at no one.

He changes lanes, for no reason.

He turns on the windshield wipers, it's not raining.

He turns on the heater, it's not cold.

"Not to be too personal or anything, but being an artist, I'm curious about the money-end of things. How's this whole thing financed? This ministry."

"Don't know, exactly."

"Isn't there a headquarters or something? A denomination? Someone's got to be in charge."

"Well, sure, there's something, someplace. A headquarters. In Illinois. They sent me a certificate." Paul is pleased to drive around the corner and see Annabelle Lee's driveway. "When you meet Cruisewell, you'll see. An interesting guy. He cares about people. Just a bit un-knowable. Not secret. Just a private kind of guy. Generous."

"Yes, but there are things like the Builders Without Borders, United Ways...dozens of places that care about people, but they don't just exist in space...in thin air...in a trailer court."

"Yeah, I know, but, he's for real. And like I said, he's involved. He likes a real 'hands-on' experience..."

"You just said he was a 'hands-off' kind of guy."

Paul stops the Jeep. Annabelle Lee touches his arm. She leans over and in a mock-whisper says, "Maybe you're a front. Maybe he's a drug dealer."

Paul laughs. His laughter rattles around his ears. His laugh doesn't sound like him. To change the subject he suggests, "Go change. I'll wait."

Annabelle Lee gathers together her belly-bag, pedometer, and sweat band. "Come on in. I'll be just a minute. No need for you to sit out here in the cold."

Paul looks around. He can't figure out what she's talking about. He's warm. He's sweating.

He follows her into the house.

Inside, Annabelle Lee takes the steps two at a time and disappears upstairs. Paul studies the blown glass pieces in the front room. He reaches for a small bowl. The heft surprises him. Three shades of yellow cast stripes over his hand. His hand glows warm. He turns to the clatter of Annabelle Lee's steps on the stairs. She is dressed in the overalls and the ribbed sweater from the night before. In her hand she carries a multi-pocketed bag.

"Amazing stuff. Did you make all this?" he asks as he returns the bowl to the coffee table.

"Stuff?" Annabelle Lee says with a smile.

"Oops, sorry. What do you call it?"

"When I'm generous, I call them 'bowls'. Lots of us call such stuff 'stuff'. But sometimes, at the point of a sale, we refer to our stuff as 'glass art'. There are some who care, and spend, and they tend to call glass art, sculpture. Sculpture costs more than bowls. 'Stuff' is a difficult sale."

"Do you do more than bowls? Other…stuff?"

"Nope. Bowls are what I do."

Paul holds the door as Annabelle Lee grabs her keys.

Inside the truck she points the way to the park.

"How'll you get home?"

"Oh, there's usually someone around. It's a real community over there. Not to worry. If all else fails, there's a short-cut through the park and I'm home in no time."

As they reach the corner of Ninety-fifth and Borealis, Paul stops for the light. He hears a familiar low rasping sound. His attention is drawn to a huge sign stretched over a grassy area in front of a low-slung brick and glass building. Between two posts flaps an oil-cloth banner that screams, "CHAINSAW JACK'S CHAINSAW ART COMPETITION. BIG PRIZES!"

Annabelle Lee groans. "I can't believe they do that! Makes no sense to destroy perfectly good trees! Making really stupid stuff. Decimates the forests! It's completely idiotic!"

"Oh?" Paul hesitates, but only for a second. He declares, "It's what loggers do when they don't work."

"Good. Less trees cut, the better. Think of the waste. Think of the owls."

"Owls! My God, woman, families are not eating. Besides, trees cut today are almost always second growth or farmed."

Behind him, a driver honks. The light has turned. Paul pulls forward and before he's crossed the intersection, he hears a bellow, "Paul! Preacher Paul! Wait up!"

Between Annabelle Lee's outburst, the honking driver, the unidentified (but familiar) voice, Paul freezes. Behind him the driver blasts his horn again and shakes his fist in the air.

Paul pulls over.

"Hey, man!" The voice calls again, and across the plant strip in front of Chainsaw Jack's, lopes Brummer. His son, Spindler, lags at a distance. Paul can't believe his eyes. Brummer waves his arm to a parking place around the corner. As Paul drives by, Brummer whacks the fender with a resounding thud. Brummer is all smiles.

In the parking space, Paul reaches over Annabelle Lee to call out the window, "Brummer! I can't believe it! Whadaya doin' here?"

"My two-foot bar went out. Easier to come to Seattle than wait for parts."

Annabelle Lee clears her throat.

"Oh, Brummer, 'scuse me. Meet Annabelle Lee. Annabelle Lee, this is Brummer. And behind him, that's Spindler. His son." Paul waves, "Hey! Spindler! Lookin' good!" Spindler unloops his thumbs from his front pockets to make a half-hearted wave. Paul stares and notices Spindler's hand self-consciously travels to cover his nose. A nose ring for God's sake! Paul looks at Brummer, looks back at Spindler, and decides not to comment.

"Amazing! I'm gone three days and it's old home week!"

"Dad, I'll be over at the competition." Spindler turns and shoves his hands back in his pockets, hunches his shoulders, and shuffles away.

Brummer calls to his son's retreating back, "Call me if they get ready to announce the winner." He turns back to Paul and Annabelle Lee, "Kids. It is not the best of times." Brummer pulls off his cap, pushes back his rumpled hair, and replaces his cap as if he'd just wiped away his 'kid worry'.

"So, back to saying hello. I'm an old fallin' buddy of Paul's," he explains to an unasked question of Annabelle Lee's.

"God damn, is it good to see you!" Brummer's big paw-of-a-hand covers his mouth. "Oops! Not supposed to talk that way around Paul any more."

Annabelle Lee looks at Paul. She looks at Brummer. "I'm sorry. I don't know what that means. A falling buddy."

Brummer slaps back his cap and exclaims, "Fallin! We logged together. Years. Before him, his dad. We go way back. Paul, he's one of the best. Well, was. The youngest, anyway. The young went first. But then, the old dogs are seeing the end of their days too."

Behind them a cheer goes up from the crowd under the chainsaw competition sign. Brummer turns his head toward the noise. "Drat. I'd guess that means I just got knocked out of first place." He turns back to Paul, eyes wide. "Paul! Go give it a try! No one here can beat you!"

Paul strains to see who's carving. "Don't recognize him," he says.

"It's a nobody. A backyard carver. Believe me. You'll win. Borrow my saw." Brummer adds, "It's a thirty-minute cut."

"What's the prize?"

"A new Stihl two-footer or two hundred bucks."

"And easy, you say."

"In the bag."

"Okay! I'll be right back. Got to drop off Annabelle Lee. Sign me up." Paul moves to put the Jeep in gear.

"Wait!" Annabelle Lee looks from Brummer to Paul. "You're actually going to cut up a tree?"

"Why wouldn't he? Paul's the best. Really the best. Brilliant, in fact. Cuts anything: Roosters in tutus. Like you couldn't imagine. Like no other rooster in the world!"

With teeth tight, Paul says, "Brummer, it's okay." He revs the motor. "Gotta go. Need to get to her studio. Be right back!"

"Now, wait a minute." Annabelle Lee interjects.

Paul yells out the window over Annabelle Lee's objection, "Annabelle Lee's a glass artist. A real artist!" Paul thinks Brummer will understand if he can get him to realize Annabelle Lee makes real art and if he can get him to understand, maybe Brummer will shut up about cutting trees.

Nope! Brummer is undaunted. He looks directly at Annabelle Lee, "Like he's not an artist? Well, let me tell you little missy, he's hiding his light under a bushel! Go on. Tell her how you were in *The Seattle Times!*"

Annabelle Lee turns to Paul and exclaims with an emphasis on disbelief, "You were in what? That rooster article was *you?*"

Paul nods, feeling chagrined, confused, confounded. And deep in his belly, somehow, ashamed.

"Himself! You'd be stupid not to see him heft a saw. Skip whatever you're doing and join us."

"Brummer. It's okay. She really doesn't want to stay. Reserve me a space. I'll be back."

Annabelle Lee puts up a hand. "Now wait just a minute. Maybe I want to see you...do...what do you call it?"

"Chainsaw art! That's what we call it!" Brummer booms.

Annabelle Lee's hand falls on Paul's arm. "You think I'd miss this? It isn't everyday I get to see chainsaw art. For that, I'll be late to the studio." Annabelle Lee unsnaps her seat belt.

Paul lets the motor die. The inside of the Jeep is hot. There doesn't seem to be enough air. "Your choice. But you're going to see one of those precious trees cut. Oh, by the way, it's not a tree. It's a log."

Brummer interrupts. He calls, "Follow me!" He points at the registration table. Before Paul can take the key from the ignition, Annabelle Lee is out the door.

At the sawdust-filled arena a freshly carved long-necked vulture stands center stage. As they near the stage, the weight of the head pulls the vulture over. The head lays, one eye exposed, smack on the ground. The crowd moans and cheers.

Brummer whacks Paul on the back. "That puts me back in the competition. Equal with that bear. The crowd votes. I should have kept my mouth shut about you competing."

"Too late," Paul says as he signs the registration form. "Get me your saw. I'm gonna whup your ass."

Brummer moves to the edge of the circle next to a winged eagle to pick up his saw. Paul recognizes the angle of the carved head. The eagle has a certain haughty toughness that identifies it as Brummer's. Paul accepts the set of earphones and the chaps Brummer hands him. While Paul pulls the Velcro tabs shut, Brummer wipes and oils the saw blade. Ready, they wait.

From where they stand, Paul watches a tall lanky guy in tight jeans take the stage. He wears a fluorescent pink shirt with silver tips on the collar and a huge buckle with CHAINSAW JACK emblazoned on it. With a portable microphone, he announces, "Friends! I want to thank you for coming today to our monthly competition. So far we've got this wonderful bear. As fine a bear as you'll ever see and we have over here, an eagle." He points in the direction of Paul and Brummer.

"Hey, Jack!" Brummer yells. "Got another competitor here!" Brummer waves the registration form in the air.

"Well, sure." Jack says and accepts the form from Brummer. "Sure enough. Another competitor. Boys, roll out another log. Looks like we have someone else with an eye on the prize. And I'd like to remind the crowd about that prize. It is a Stihl! The best chainsaw in the world! And you can buy one right here at Chainsaw Jack's!"

Chainsaw Jack hitches up his pants, drawing attention to the belt buckle. His voice echoes over the crowd. He continues his patter. "Anyone, you there sir, even your little boy, could do what these guys do. Rent a saw! Buy a saw! Everyone can be a chainsaw artist! Carve bears to your heart's content."

The crowd cheers as Paul walks into the center of the arena. A fresh log is rolled out. Through the cheers, Paul can hear Brummer's whoops and hand claps. He even thinks he hears the clear, high voice of Annabelle Lee calling, "Hooray, Paul!"

Chainsaw Jack's voice booms, "Everybody step back just a bit! Don't want no little ladies getting dust in their eyes. Back up and let's see what we have here." Chainsaw Jack checks the registration form. "Let's see. Need a bit more information here. Your name? Address? Need your address. And of course, your occupation. Need a complete application, here on this form, or we don't have any cutting."

Paul glances down the form. He glances at the bottom paragraph about Chainsaw Jack not being liable for injury or anything else. At the bottom of the form in large, bold letters Paul reads: CARVINGS ARE THE PROPERTY OF CHAINSAW JACK. Paul writes his name. Writes his new address. At 'occupation' he stops. Then he shakes the pen as if to dislodge the ink and a growing truth, he writes: Minister.

"Folks, this here is…" Chainsaw Jack squints and brings the form close to his eyes, "This here is Paul Whitinowsky! Goodness gracious, folks, you aren't going to believe this! Paul Whitinosky is a minister! Minister to the New Dawn is Breaking Trailer Court! Oh, my! Well, I'll be. That's a familiar name. Paul Whitinowsky. Whitinowsky," he repeats. Paul sees a look of recognition roll over his face. "Well, let's see what a minister can do with a little inspiration from a Stihl and a hunk of spruce."

Chainsaw Jack shouts into the microphone, "Even the righteous choose to carve at Chainsaw Jack's! ALLLL RIGHT!" He checks his watch. "Begin!"

Paul adjusts his earphones. He walks around the log checking for knots. He runs his hand over the wood. He checks the distance between the log's growth lines. He pulls the toggle and the engine catches. His arms grow warm with the sweet vibration. A fine spray of wood chips bursts from under the teeth of the saw. With sureness and care Paul pulls the wood away from a twisted sea creature. Halfway through the thirty minutes he signals Brummer for the twelve-incher. To the carving Paul adds scales, a forked tongue, and an eyebrow over a knot hole.

The crowd whistles and claps its approval.

In exactly twenty-eight minutes, Paul hands the saw back to Brummer, brushes off his arms. He wipes the sawdust from his face. He looks to see Annabelle Lee watching him with a half-smile and a quizzical brow.

Chainsaw Jack is back. "So, folks, this is all done democratically, as you know. We have four competitors today. Cheer and yell and clap. That's how you vote! Let's get us a winner!"

The crowd's decision is quick and decisive.

Paul, Brummer, and Annabelle Lee crowd into Chainsaw Jack's office while Paul waits to receive the winner's check. Spindler stays in the display area of the office, fingering the selection of new chainsaws.

Inside his office Chainsaw Jack clears a chair for Annabelle Lee, touches her shoulder as he indicates she should sit. And then he addresses Paul. "You're not bad. I could use someone like you. Need a sponsor?"

"Thanks. But no thanks. I've got a job, as you seem to know. How is it you seemed to recognize my name? And seemed to know about New Dawn is Breaking?"

"Well, there's Cruisewell. He gets around. He's an old poker buddy. Since he's given up poker, he's always trying to get me involved in one of his schemes. So, I recognized your name right away."

"His schemes?" Paul asks.

"Oh, you know. His latest 'thing'. He's always doin' something. Food. Aerobics. Hospitals. Translating dictionaries. Now the church thing. You should know."

The edge and sharpness of Chainsaw Jack's voice irritates Paul. He wants to get his money and leave. Mostly, he doesn't want Annabelle Lee hearing all this crazy stuff. She hasn't said much since he finished the carving, and now she has a look of disbelief that isn't all that pleasant.

"So! What will it be? One of my great saws, or two hundred bucks?"

"I'll take the cash."

"Sure you don't want some real work? Work for me? Few extra hours carving. Out front. Make you look good. Make me look good." Chainsaw Jack closes his eyes and pulls his hand across the space in front of him. "I can see it now. Pastor Paul Stihl Carving!" His eyes pop open. "Get it? Stihl carving! What do you think?"

"Like I said, I've got a job."

"I'm not offerin' you a full-time job. I'm asking you to compete once in awhile. Carve once in awhile. You've got potential."

Brummer steps up close to Chainsaw Jack. Brummer pushes his face close to Chainsaw Jack's face. "Lighten up, Jack. You're not talkin' potential here. Paul's the best!"

Chainsaw Jack is undaunted. "Well, if he's not carving, then he won't be the best. Besides, have you seen Henry Hightail? Steve Swampgrass? Now those guys are the pros!"

Irritation moves up through Paul's arms, into his shoulders. The only good thing that seems to be transpiring is that Annabelle Lee's look of concern for the trees has turned into a glare. She glares at Chainsaw Jack.

"Time to pay up, Jack," Brummer says.

Chainsaw Jack slowly counts twenty tens into Paul's hand.

"Well, if you ever change your mind…"

Paul turns to leave. Brummer and Annabelle Lee follow him into the display area where Brummer signals Spindler it's time to go. Outside, along the front of the office building, they are surrounded by twenty variations of the same black bear, one hand up, the other holding a board with 'welcome' carved on it.

"They really could use your imagination, Paul," Brummer says, nodding towards the bears. "Sometimes I think I'll gag if I see another one of those

God-awful 'welcome bears!' "

Annabelle Lee interrupts, "Hate to say it, guys, but I've got to get to the studio. It's been an interesting afternoon." She extends a hand to Brummer. "It's been a pleasure." She calls to Spindler who sits on a bench held up by two carved bears. "Spindler, nice to have met you!"

Spindler looks up surprised, as if he is pleased he's even been noticed, let alone remembered by someone he hasn't spoken to.

Brummer walks Paul and Annabelle Lee back to the Jeep. From behind the wheel, Paul leans over Annabelle Lee to extend his hand to Brummer. "If you have time, come by for a beer. See my new place. It's close. At the light and down six blocks. Drive by Rex's Diner, turn under the arch. You can't miss it."

"Love to. I'll get my gear. Half an hour?"

Paul waves goodbye. The warmth of Annabelle Lee's shoulder clings to his arm.

They ride in silence. Paul takes a deep breath and finally gets up enough courage to say, "You're not saying much. I gather you didn't like the competition."

"It's a new experience. And a surprise. I liked your carving." Annabelle Lee is quiet for a block and then she adds, "But did you see how many trees it must have taken to create that stupid herd of bears? And this is just one little place on one little street. Think of that multiplied all over the Northwest! All over the country. Dozens and dozens of poor trees given over to carving those stupid, stupid…," she shakes her head in disbelief, "…bears. And they call that art?" As Annabelle Lee speaks she points so Paul knows at which streets to turn. Paul tries to figure out how to answer without yelling at her.

"Then! I watch you handle that saw. You were brilliant! You know space and form. Paul, if you can carve that well, why not…"

"You think it's corny?" Paul's words are half question, half accusation, tight and neat and just on the edge of anger.

"Well, not the sea monster. It has a certain integrity. But that other stuff?" Annabelle Lee's words fly out, "My God, a headless vulture? Giving up a tree so some stupid idiot can carve a vulture whose head falls off?" Annabelle Lee is on a roll. Her words fly around Paul like a chainsaw gone mad. "And then Chainsaw Jack has his one in-house idiot carve another bear? Did you see the guy *he* wanted to win? Wears an idiot belt buckle just like Jack's! Not even discrete about who gets prizes! He thinks the crowd is too dumb to know anybody'd notice. And it doesn't cross his mind someone might show up who can really carve. Like you! He thinks the crowd will just go ahead and vote for his man…because it's a bear!"

Paul waits to see if she is finished. She isn't.

"At least the crowd knew what was best. Give them credit for that. But it's just, just, the whole idea is just…"

"Don't stop. I'm interested in what city ladies think of us country folks."

Annabelle Lee points down the block to a flat roofed brick building. "Stop here. This is the studio." Her words have become clipped, and angry.

"Sorry. Sorry about the city lady jab," Paul apologizes.

"Right!" Annabelle Lee jumps from the Jeep. "Thanks for the ride." Her voice is not thankful.

Paul watches her walk away. Her strides are long and angry. She doesn't look back. She doesn't wave goodbye.

24

NOT LOSING IT

Paul drives a block. Then he cranks on the steering wheel and pulls a U-turn. He brings the Jeep to a halt in a "Load Zone" in front of Annabelle Lee's building.

At the front door, the weight of the solid oak, the brass door handle in the shape of a growling lion, the wide expanse of empty hall through the lead-framed windows, gives Paul pause. Perhaps this isn't such a good idea.

Then, determined, he pushes on the door. Immediately to his right, a couple emerges from a classroom; they walk hip to hip. The guy, hair pulled back in a pony tail, and the girl with swirling tattoos around each arm are totally engrossed in each other. Paul steps back and lets them pass. They continue their intimate conversation, arms wrapped around each other, fingers tucked into the rear pockets of each, heads bent to exclude the world. Envy stirs in Paul. He moves down the hall, determined to find Annabelle Lee and explain to her that he is not a bad guy, not a tree killer, not an insensitive nobody. She needs to know. He needs to tell her.

Paul checks each empty classroom. He moves quickly down a wide hall ripe with the smell of newly waxed floors, his footsteps echoing in the cavernous building. At the end of the hall, in a room just right of the exit door, Paul sees a classroom of students, each at an easel. In the center of the group a table is cluttered with gourds and bowls and ostrich feathers. The room is filled with the scritching sound of charcoal on paper. No one looks up.

A tall skinny kid with an earring and a wisp of a beard sketches. He is creating a mess of scattered lines and no recognizable anything. The kid rubs frantically at the charcoal and abruptly jumps when Paul taps him on the shoulder.

"Hey!" he exclaims. "Careful. You'll mess up my drawing."

"It's great. Great." Paul lies. "Can you help me out? I'm looking for the glass studio."

The kid jabs the air with his charcoal. "Other side, down the hall, past the boiler room, in the basement."

Paul follows the pointing finger, hurries, and continues on his search for Annabelle Lee. In the furthest corner of the basement he hears a soft whooshing sound. Warm air bellows from the room. Orange light and a blast of heat stop Paul. The room is a pleasant inferno. Slow moving bodies are silhouetted against the bright white heat of what appears to him to be open-holed furnaces. Three teams work, their movements slow and sure. No one speaks over the hallow, soft roar. Each set of two glassblowers communicate with hand signals and head nods. One team works a glowing mass on the end of a pipe where the amorphous, blowing bubble barely wobbles as it turns into a near-perfect round shape. Another duo rolls a glass glob along a metal table where it gathers metal filings into itself.

Furthest from where he stands, Paul sees Annabelle Lee grasp a pipe on the end of which hangs a softball-sized mound of molten glass. Her partner, which Paul can't help noting is muscular and trim, jeaned, open-shirted, intense, is bronzed by the glowing light. Under his open shirt, the assistant wears an old-fashioned T-shirt, like the kind Paul used to see on older loggers, an undershirt which shows off muscles and sweat. Paul sucks in his gut.

The god-like partner works with a scoop-shaped wooden block. Burnt black from use, the wooden block tames the glass and the glass slowly shapes itself inside the scoop. Annabelle Lee leans forward and the subtle leathery apron she wears folds into her body as she bends to blow into the pipe. Sturdy, protective glasses hide her eyes. She is sure and deft. The outline of her in the furnace light accentuates the length of her body. Paul is mesmerized.

Then her assistant trades the block for a set of wooden paddles. The glass at the end of the pipe expands and slides as Annabelle Lee gently blows air, as delicate as a flutist. The assistant waits for her signal, paddles erect and ready. They are like dance partners. Paul can detect the respect with which the attendant waits for Annabelle Lee's direction. Annabelle Lee's concentration never wavers. The slowly moving globe of glass expands. With a long-nosed pair of U-shaped tongs, she opens the globe to make a bowl shape. Within minutes she prepares another cup of glass and together the bubbles join. She returns the joined pieces to the furnace, and she and her partner repeat the maneuver until Paul can see that the end result will somehow be a layered bowl.

It occurs to Paul that there is something similar about the sure way

Annabelle Lee works glass and how he carves wood. He is pleased at the comparison. No question the results are dissimilar, but he can't help thinking that he and Annabelle Lee share an approach. He knows he doesn't have words to put to it, but as he watches, the idea solidifies. He can hardly wait to tell her.

The assistant maneuvers a pair of metal clippers. He holds the tool against the connection point between the bowl and the pipe, Annabelle Lee strikes the pipe smartly with a wood paddle, severing the pipe from the bowl. Then without request or instruction, a third assistant, from one of the other teams is there to catch the bowl in padded mitts and takes it to an annealing oven. The bowl disappears deep inside. Both men signal Annabelle Lee with a wave of a glove, something resembling a thumbs-up, and turn to help another team.

When Paul looks around, Annabelle Lee has removed her single glove and pushes back her glasses. Paul realizes by her slight smile and direct look that she has been watching him and waiting for him to approach her.

"I'm impressed," Paul offers. "Amazing!"

"Well, thanks, It's not all that difficult."

"Sorry, I don't believe you. Didn't cross my mind that you were anything but a pro."

"Sorry to say, I don't think of it that way."

"Why not? You knocked my socks off!"

"Just your socks?" Annabelle Lee giggles.

Paul doesn't know what to say. He can feel himself blush. He waits her out.

"Truth is, at this stage of my career, I can do them with my eyes closed," she says.

"Still impressive."

"There was a time..."

"Yes?" Paul asks and then waits as if speaking to a skittish animal.

"The first bowl. I remember the first bowl that stayed round and on-center. Didn't wobble at all. Sheer pleasure. It's just been a few hundred bowls too many."

"But you keep at it."

"Some things you do because you do them well, long after..." Her sentence drifts away.

Paul follows her as she moves towards a wall of finished glass pieces.

On shelves of wooden planks stand cups and platters and twisted vases that appear not to be made to hold anything. Annabelle Lee points to the bowls along one shelf. "All mine." She says and then points to two more shelves. "And those. And those."

"May I?" Paul asks and touches a feathered red and white bowl. "May I pick it up?"

"Be my guest."

"I love the feel." Under his hands the bowl is solid and sure. The weight and smoothness are as opposite of wood as he can imagine.

"I do love glass, from the time it's silica, then sand, to when it's a molten mass, to the finished product. That I love."

"You're leaving out something?" Paul asks.

"The part I don't love?" A slight smile plays around Annabelle Lee's mouth. He knows he's erased some of the anger from when they were in the Jeep. He smiles. Maybe, just maybe, she'll keep talking.

"You're so damn…oops, darn good," he says and knows what he really wants to tell her is how good she looks, how beautiful in the glow of the furnace. He takes a deep breath.

"You okay?" Annabelle Lee asks.

He turns and doesn't answer. He places the bowl back on the shelf. "Tell me more."

"About what?"

And from the tiniest edge of panic in her voice, he rephrases his question. "Your work. Tell me about how you got here. Why you do what you do."

"Well, about glass. Let's see. Where to start. I know my material. With glass, I'm in charge. Otherwise…" Annabelle Lee wiggles her fingers in front of her and lifts her eyebrows, her lips tight together. Then she blushes and for a second Paul sees something he hasn't seen before. He sees her uncertainty. For a reason he can't grasp, the uncertainty gives him hope. Up until now, everything she did, she did with an abundance of precision. She has a way of making him feel like he is ten years old and she is wise and ancient. He is flummoxed and she is in control. He searches for words and she is never without. And then the wiggling fingers, the tight lips, the 'I'm not sure of myself' look, lets him know she just might be feeling some of the unease and excitement and hope that fills him.

"Let me show you," she says and starts walking. Paul follows.

In a long storage area next door to the furnace room, with shelves along one side, Annabelle Lee points to a dozen perfect bowls.

"My stuff. More of my stuff," she says.

Paul lets out a low whistle. "Lots." The word is all he can think to say. He hears in her voice an edge of self-disparagement. It surprises him. He expected her to be proud of her work. The bowls glow. They are beautiful. He doesn't get it. He wants to rave and tell her the bowls are like wondrous Easter eggs.

"You're right," she says. "Lots. I'm criticized regularly for being 'prolific'. What's meant is that I'm *too* prolific."

"That a problem?"

"Not if you have a thirty-year mortgage and four years of student loans.

While there's a market for bowls, I make bowls."

"Give them what they want."

"Exactly."

With a deft throw, her gloves land with a plop in one of the bowls. He wonders at how casual she is, so close to the edge of disrespect for her work.

"Well, I'm still impressed."

"Follow me. Let me show you."

In a long narrow closet-like room there are rows and rows of more bowls.

"I might as well be a factory."

"This all yours?"

"Most of it. See this?" Annabelle Lee picks up a small bowl. She drops it into a large steel barrel. The glass shatters, the blast of shards snap against metal, echoes through the room.

"What?" Paul cries. He watches as she drops a bigger green gem-like bowl into the barrel. "What are you doing?"

"Don't get excited. These are seconds." Her hand holds a third bowl. "This," as the third bowl explodes, "is quality control. Repetition calls for perfection."

Annabelle Lee reaches for a fourth bowl, grapefruit sized, the color of a perfectly ripe peach. "Here. You throw it. That exploding sound is so satisfying." She throws the bowl to Paul. He catches it just in time.

"What if I keep it?"

"Sorry," she says and pushes his hand so the bowl rolls into the barrel.

Paul groans. "I thought it looked..."

"It didn't."

"I'd like to have one. Where can I buy..."

"Forget it. Maybe someday..."

Paul doesn't answer. He lets the words float there in the air. He wants her to remember she has said 'someday'. A promise.

Annabelle Lee turns to run her fingers over the lip of five or six bowls in the same number of seconds. She appears to decide in a fraction of time if a bowl should be smashed or saved.

"If someday I do want to buy one, what would it cost?"

"More than they should."

"How much is that?"

"Couple hundred, under a thousand."

"A thousand?" Paul's voice betrays his surprise, his naiveté, his certain stupidity. He can't reel back the words.

"No. You're like the crazy public. I just said, under a thousand. So, my work grows in demand and value with every misheard word."

Annabelle Lee tosses a last bowl into the barrel. "Ker-splat," she calls.

"Aren't you being a little hard on yourself?"

"You would be, if you did nothing but make bowls for ten years."

"Let me get this straight. You're telling me, after watching you at the furnace, so carefully and beautifully creating those bowls, that you hate doing what you're doing? You come here every day, and you hate it?" This time Paul does not hide his feelings, he lets his disbelief roll out like a Mack truck.

"No," Annabelle Lee says. She crosses her arms, leans against the wall, one leg crossed over the other, her toe to the floor. "Don't get me wrong. I love the process. But when you're...I'm...an artist creating product for people who have my name on a list of glass makers to own, except they don't know why. Those collectors are caught in competitive buying with other collectors, and I'm one of their targets." Annabelle Lee's teeth clinch and the words spit out, "It's dreadful. Dreadful and stupid."

Paul looks over the rest of the shelves. A bright glint of green catches his eye. He kneels. In front of him on the bottom shelf stands an array of frolicking glass animals. He picks up a bowlegged frog with a yellow bowler. He holds it so Annabelle Lee can see what is in his hand.

"Prell! Perfect Prell. And hopping! Wow!"

"What?" Annabelle Lee laughs. "Prell? We call that 'intense emerald green'. It is almost as expensive as manganese red. Prell? You want to call it a shampoo? Fine with me!"

"I meant it as a compliment!" Paul cups the frog in his hand as if it might dance away. "It's the perfect color. There was this bottle. In our kitchen window. I always thought of it as the purest, most perfect color in the world. It was my mom's Prell Shampoo. And here it is in this great frog." Paul reaches for another animal. "What are these?"

"Nothing. End of the day stuff."

In his hand Paul holds a figure that is complex and stupefying: a yellow fish in a green vest with purple stripes. A gondolier's hat with a red ribbon droops over one eye at a rakish angle. One fin offers the tiniest bowl of velvet red raspberries and lime green kiwis.

Paul gently places the fish next to the frog and picks up another figure. This one is an apple on roller skates, a hobo bundle jauntily at his shoulder. Then an alligator on a skate board covered with metallic forget-me-nots. Sky-blue bubble-eyes.

"Guess that's all for today," Annabelle Lee says. She stands at the door to the storage room waiting, her hand ready to turn off the light. Paul looks up from where he sits on his haunches, lining up the glass animals.

"Why are these hidden here?" he asks.

"Not hidden. Just out of the way."

"Why are they 'out of the way?' Why aren't they displayed with all those expensive bowls?"

"They're throw-aways. My little stash of throw-aways."

"Not such 'throw-aways' that they're in the trash barrel."

"They're mine. Things not much wanted."

Paul places a dancing bear at the end of the line. It holds ten cherries, as if it were juggling them. The bear wears yellow rain boots with black snaps. "What do you do with them?" Paul asks marveling at the detail and craziness of each one.

"I don't do anything with them. After I've made my quota of bowls for the day, I reward myself. I take time to make one of them. And then I keep it. Down there with all the other rewards I've given myself."

Annabelle Lee comes from the door to kneel beside Paul. He can hear her breathe. She picks up the apple, holds it in her palm, where it nestles inside the curl of her fingers. Paul resists cupping his hand under hers. Annabelle Lee speaks as if she were speaking to the apple itself. "With these I can work by myself. I don't need an assistant. I can do what I want to do. It keeps me sane."

She gently places the apple back in its place. Then she lifts the skate board figure and lets it ride the flat of her hand. "Once I showed these to my gallery owner. He says they aren't quite what my 'niche' requires." Annabelle Lee wrinkles her nose. "Their clients wouldn't understand. Their clients like bowls."

She stands and wipes her hands on her overalls as if she were brushing away the idea. "So I keep them. One of these days when there are too many of them, I'll throw them in the break-up barrel. But not yet." Her voice carries wistfulness and a wedge of sadness. "That's that."

Paul holds the fish. He lets his fingers play over the surface of the fluted scales. He is afraid to say anything, afraid his interest and wanting is transparent.

"Now, don't get greedy," Annabelle Lee says, but with a smile as she reaches for the fish. "Someday, maybe, after awhile..."

"Like parents saying 'soon' to the question 'when will we be there?' "

Annabelle Lee laughs, "Kind of like that. Don't push it, Paul. Remember we weren't even speaking an hour ago." She takes the fish from Paul. Their fingers touch. She puts the fish on the shelf.

For a minute, Paul imagines...but the minute passes and Annabelle Lee walks out of the room and through the furnace room and down the hall and Paul follows.

At the front door they stop. "It's nice to think you like them. Nice to think someone likes them."

"How could I not like them? They're great! They remind me of my own work."

Annabelle Lee blinks, like the idea has just slapped her across the face. Paul thinks he sees an edge of indignation in her stance as her body shifts.

"Your work? But…" And he thinks he hears an edge of insult in her voice.

"But what?" Paul asks. He could have bit his tongue. The closeness he'd felt only seconds ago, vanishes. The comparison of his work to hers had just popped out. From up and out of his gut. There is something about her work he knows. He understands. Instinctively. He thinks of his assortment of animals back at the trailer. Animals he'll never show anyone. If she ever sees them, he knows she will understand.

Annabelle Lee stammers, answering his question, "Oh, ah…um…it's just that…they're glass, and well, chainsaw cutting is…well…I guess I can see why you might think that."

Words, unbidden fly from Paul's mouth, "But chainsaw art isn't real art? Right? And your throw-aways are less if I make the comparison, so what I do is crap and what you do is…"

Annabelle Lee turns away as if she had just been hit.

"What?" he demands.

She turns back, "I was pissed at you before and now I'm pissed at you again!"

"That was hours ago," Paul says and on an uptake of breath lets out a moan, "Oh, no! I forgot! I invited Brummer and Spindler to come by the trailer court!"

"I can't think of a better place to end this discussion." Annabelle Lee's words are sharp, but something in her eyes doesn't match her words and Paul snaps back to being crazy about the space between her teeth.

"Join us!" Paul pleads. "Please! Dinner?" He asks as if a meal were a bribe. He so much wants her to come back with him. If only he can show her his carved animals, everything will be close and warm and hopeful and he can concentrate on the mint-ness of her.

"Right! So we can continue to argue? No thanks." She looks down at her overalls and adds, "Besides, I'm in my work clothes." Paul knows she is on the very edge of saying yes. He can hear it. She wants to come back with him.

"Like loggers would care! Like Brummer would even notice! Come. I've got to go." Paul pushes open the heavy oak door, turns and asks, "Please?"

A slight smile crosses Annabelle Lee's face. "Why not? Haven't had a free meal forever and haven't had a good argument in days."

Paul grabs her hand and rubs his fingers over her smooth rounded fingernails, sweeter than the glass scales of a fish.

"Thanks," he says.

25

ANNABELLE LEE AND SAUNDRA MEET

Gravel flips from under his tires. Paul brings the Jeep to a halt in the drive next to his trailer. Brummer's truck is nowhere in sight. From the other side of the court, the children run, arms waving, voices calling, "You missed them! You missed them!"

The children's words tumble over each other, "We had milk and cookies without you! We heard all 'bout Twist!"

"And carving!"

"And bears!"

"And everything!"

"And you missed them!"

Sam reaches for Annabelle Lee's hand. Even from where Paul watches he can see the cookie remnants deep in the crevices of Sam's fingers. Sam's hand folds around Annabelle Lee's and he pulls. "Come meet our mom!"

Sam beams with the pleasure of bringing his mom a great, great prize.

With no ability to stop the determined child, Paul follows. Suzie walks beside him. What creates the most concern is Saundra, sitting in the sun, watching as they walk toward Grandma Bella's trailer.

"Serendipitous, huh?" Suzie asks.

Paul tries to figure out how to handle the introduction that is about to happen. Words and thoughts and confusion and too many women swirl around him. Suzie makes small skipping steps beside him. "Don't worry. Ministers have lots of members. We're all members!"

Paul can't digest the words. Warning? Assurance? He has no option but to follow Sam, Suzie, and Annabelle Lee towards disaster.

In front of the trailer in an aluminum folding chair, wrapped in a down jacket, her head tilted back to the last rays of sun, Saundra sits. Her leg rests on an overturned galvanized tub. Her toenails glitter. A new coat of gold sparkles on black, death-like purple.

As they draw close, Saundra slowly brings a cigarette to her lips and stares through exhaled smoke. To Paul the scene feels like the O.K. Corral. The tension grows exponentially with each step. Maybe it is the angle of the cigarette, or the arch of the eyebrow, or the bend of the toes. He can't figure. Saundra, who only hours ago barely recognized his existence, now looks as if she has territory to protect, and he's it. Or maybe it is imaginary. Maybe Saundra just has that look and it has nothing to do with him. Maybe this isn't the O.K. Corral. Maybe this is "Guess Who's Coming to Dinner?"

Paul clears his throat. He swallows twice. He adjusts his tongue. He'll just introduce Annabelle Lee and all will be well. The two women will say hello like any two normal people. The children will stop beaming as if they expect a whole lot of something. And whether Suzie's comment has anything to do with whether either woman becomes a member, he'll just have to think about that later, in the middle of the night, when he's taken to spending minute after minute chasing questions he understands even less than the answers he conjures.

For now, after the introductions, perhaps luck will be a lady and he will walk Annabelle Lee back to his trailer, and they'll have a wonderful dinner, and she'll be smitten with him, totally enthralled, and life will be full of all the right answers.

Paul steps between Annabelle Lee and the seated Saundra. He holds out both hands and sees himself like the Good Shepherd any normal minister would be. He says, "Annabelle Lee, meet Saundra, Suzie and Sam's mother, Grandma Bella's daughter. Saundra, this is Annabelle Lee Fulsome." Paul can hear himself say her last name and he swears Saundra checks out the tops of her own breasts and then looks to see how Annabelle Lee compares. Then Saundra, as if in slow motion, passes the cigarette from one hand to the other. She reaches out her long finger-nailed hand and for a dismissive moment shakes Annabelle Lee's fingers. "Nice to meet you."

Sam leans against the arm of his mother's chair. A smile of encouragement plays over his face as if all of his best friends should now have a good time. His head bobs 'yes' to all the unspoken words; like he can convince them how wonderful it is that they are all together. Saundra smooches his cheek and then rubs the lipstick away.

"Nice, huh?" Sam asks with a smile about as big a smile as he's ever smiled.

No one answers.

"You're nice," Saundra says and tips back her head to direct her large, perfectly polished lips in a smile towards Paul. "Your guests have come and gone."

"My guests?" Then Paul remembers. "Oh, my screw-up for today. Messed up, again. Had some important things I had to do. Got busy. Preoccupied. I think old buddies will understand."

The space around them once again fills with silence like everyone is considering Paul's excuses.

Suzie, with clipped bright words attempts to rescue the moment. "Brummer and Spindler had to get on home. They loved Grandma Bella's cookies. They took a bunch with them!" Then her eyes grow wide with adoring admiration, "Oh! And Pastor Paul, they said you're a carver. A chainsaw champion!"

Sam, encouraged by Suzie's enthusiasm, leaves his mother to twirl around Paul's legs, churning his arms in sawing motions making 'brumming' lip vibrations.

Annabelle Lee speaks as if to camouflage Sam's topic. "You've got great kids. Did they tell you they helped put the chapel together?"

Saundra squints at Annabelle Lee and takes a final drag from the remains of her cigarette. She lets her words fall slowly, "They talked of nothing else."

Paul's arms ache. His eyes grow squinty and his lids grow heavy. He yearns for a beer or better, a single blistering shot of whiskey, or a bed, or the dark, cool center of a forest. He yearns to be any place but here.

Saundra says, her words taut, as if each were pinned to a clothesline for Paul to see, "So! Ready then? For tomorrow? The Big Day?"

The words hang there. Paul yearns for ease, for good thoughts, for friendliness. The image in the correspondence lesson of smiling parishioners, the hub of devout up-lifted faces, the "Joyous Gathering" of hands joined, is nowhere to be seen. Where, oh where is the communal bliss?

Just then, Grandma Bella fills the door of the trailer. She comes down the stairs and stands in the final glow of the setting sun. Relief falls on Paul like manna.

Grandma Bella wipes her hands on her apron and begins the conversation where Suzie ended. "We made them feel right at home. That Spindler. He did have an appetite. I think he put away a quart of milk all by himself. And his father. A good man. They admire you so much, Paul. It was a pleasure having your friends with us, if just for a short time."

"Thanks for being here and taking care of them. Can't believe I...well, I got busy...forgot..." Paul stammers.

"They were just fine," Saundra says. "Just fine. Brummer wants you to know he expects to see you in a few weeks."

"How's that?"

"Didn't say. Parting words. 'Tell Paul we'll see him in a few weeks at the Nationals.'"

Now everyone does turn to Paul. Everyone waits for the minister to speak. With intuition and grace, Grandma Bella says as smooth as cream, "Children, dinner's almost ready."

Sam tugs at Grandma Bella's dress, "Can't we invite Paul and Annabelle Lee?" Encouragement and love spread across his face—a sweet sheen.

"I think maybe six people might be just a bit too much for the trailer and Pastor Paul, I'm sure, has already made plans for his guest." Grandma Bella reaches down for Sam. She cups his small body in her wide reach and hoists him to the edge of her ample hip. "But you certainly are thoughtful, Sam."

With her free hand, Grandma Bella tips the edge of Saundra's crutches. The crutches clatter into Saundra's lap. "It's getting chilly. Time for everyone to get inside. G'night, Pastor Paul. Annabelle Lee, nice to see you again."

As Annabelle Lee and Paul walk back towards his trailer, Annabelle Lee calls and waves, " 'Night everyone. See you tomorrow at church."

Paul winces. He doesn't think he'll ever get used to the idea that Sunday is going to come around every single week.

As he opens the trailer door, Paul asks Annabelle Lee, "Then, you're planning on being here tomorrow? Church? Here?"

"Thought so. You invited me."

They stand inside the confines of the trailer. Paul points to the curved dining nook. "Have a seat. There's only room for one at the stove."

"Would you rather I didn't come tomorrow?"

"I'm not sure I'm ready for tomorrow. I'd rather tomorrow never came."

"Don't worry. We can have a quick meal, you can run me home, and the whole evening's yours to get ready. To sweat it out."

Paul opens a beer for Annabelle Lee and hands it to her. "Such a delicate way to put it. Sweat it out."

"Little anxiety doesn't hurt."

"Believe me, this is not a little anxiety."

Paul bangs around the small kitchen. The few pots and pans, odd shaped and dented, miraculously hold enough water for pasta and enough tomato sauce for two. There is even a heavy black skillet, cast iron, primed and ready for sautéing. Paul spreads out the ingredients from Elsie's boot-box package. He breaks the dried sprigs of rosemary and deftly chops the onions and parsley. He thumps a clove of garlic on a board with the heel of his hand. He opens a small fragrant bottle of olive oil.

Onions first. They turn translucent. He adds the crushed garlic. Soon, a pungent aroma fills the small space. Paul pushes a window screen open. The cool evening air whirls through the kitchen and Paul feels the fun and excitement he used to feel cooking over a campfire with Bear, and his mom. Before things went sour. Paul smiles at Annabelle Lee who rests in the corner of the eating nook, her legs stretched out along the cushions. She smiles back. Lifts her beer to toast the moment.

"So, tell me about your life," Paul asks. It isn't the question that he wants to ask. He wants to know if there is a boyfriend, an ex-husband, anyone who might show up to claim her. Paul imagines a cast of thousands waiting to dash the tiny seed of hope that he realizes has grown in the last few hours. Her silence seems thoughtful. He fears the worst.

Paul shakes the frying pan to unlodge the onions. "Well?" he waits. He can't believe how he wants to beg her, plead with her to tell him she is single and free and waiting for an ex-logger who cuts down her precious trees, but has changed his life, and is now a minister, and is just the person she wants to fall in love with.

"My life? Mostly it's about glass. You saw most of what I do. I'm fairly successful. I've blown glass forever, it seems. Someday I'd like to study in Venice. There's an island there, Murano, where they blow the finest glass. That would be fun. But it takes money, and it's hard to save for living in Italy, and I don't even know if women ever, ever are allowed to blow glass there. Besides, when you're on your own, you just don't go running away to Italy."

Paul takes a long drink of beer. He feels so good. She's said, 'on your own'. His beer is ambrosia.

"You sure there's nothing I could be doing?" Annabelle Lee asks.

"No. Just keep talking. I'll be finished in a minute." Paul grates a chunk of Parmesan cheese into a small bowl.

Annabelle Lee reaches for one of the pretzels Paul has placed between them. She nibbles the edge and continues talking, "Well, my work supports me. The aerobics classes keep me in shape and add a few more dollars. Life's really okay. But, I wish…"

Paul has visions of her saying, "I wish you were just crazy about me," and he would answer, "I am. I'm already there. Now. And maybe we should just…" He listens to the tiny bites of pretzel breaking on Annabelle Lee's teeth. When he brings a platter of noodles, the pan of sauce, and the bowl of cheese to the table, Annabelle Lee has the round piece of pretzel up to her eye, monocle fashion.

"Enough about me," she says. "I'm Sherlock and I would like a clearer picture of you!" Annabelle Lee finishes the pretzel in a single bit. "You're a bit out of focus."

"Out of focus?"

"You tell me you're an ex-logger. That you loved cutting trees. Now you're a minister with a garage for a chapel and eight widows for a congregation. It's a rather unordinary life, if you haven't noticed."

"Right, I've noticed," Paul says and hands Annabelle Lee a plate. She holds it towards him as he serves the tumbling noodles.

"Almost Italian!" Paul lets the sauce run over the edge of the pan and it puddles around the steaming pasta. He smiles at Annabelle Lee and realizes he is overwhelmingly pleased that she is sitting there, with him.

"This is just great," Paul beams.

"Fun to be here."

"Well, good, because I'm a bit out of practice. Entertaining anyone."

"How's that?"

Paul sits kitty-corner from Annabelle Lee. He twirls the spaghetti onto his fork. "Well, Twist isn't the heart of society. It's back-country where people tend not to speak in full sentences. Loggers spend more time cutting than talking. Logging is loud and it can be dangerous." Paul stops. He wishes he'd kept quiet. She's bound to see, the longer he talks, that he is not smooth, not cool, not worth her time—and he cuts trees. Lots and lots of trees. She will see he is a rusty, going-on-middle-aged, out-of-it, logger.

"Somehow, you didn't answer the question," Annabelle Lee reminds him as she takes a perfectly twirled bite of spaghetti. In one bite she catches the small, sculpted mess.

He likes that she eats, not delicately, but with purpose. He realizes he is staring.

"Well?"

"What?" he asks.

"Finish your sentences. Tell me about how you got here."

"That's hard."

Annabelle Lee swirls a second twist of noodles against her spoon and waits.

"It's hard telling a woman, at least a woman who's got a thing about trees, about what I've done for most of my life."

With the mention of 'trees,' silence romps into the room and grabs Paul so he can't think what more to say or how to explain anything. He swallows and his swallow is loud. He wishes for a miracle. He wishes he'd thought to turn on the radio. He wishes for some old-timey sweet worded song to fill the silence. He wishes he could tell her how he is over his head and about to drown.

A rat-a-tat knock of knuckles on the aluminum screen door saves him.

"Pastor Paul! Pastor Paul! A telephone call for you."

Paul slips from behind the curved Formica table and opens the door. Grandma Bella stands in front of him. Through gasps, she says by way of explanation, "I ran. He said it was very important."

"Who? Who knows I'm here?"

"Someone named Jack. Says you know him."

"I don't know a Jack…"

"Says it's important. Real important…"

Paul turns, calls to Annabelle Lee, "I'll be right back. Don't go away. Grandma Bella, can you entertain my guest?"

At the Airstream, Paul cups the phone to his ear, turns his back to the television where Jeopardy has the intent interest of Saundra and Suzie. Sam, pajama clad, assembles a Ferris wheel of Legos.

"Paul Whitinowsky here."

"Paul. It's Jack."

"Jack who?"

"Jack for God's sake. Chainsaw Jack."

"Chainsaw Jack. How the hell…how'd you find me?"

There is silence on the other end of the line, then Chainsaw Jack says in a 'you're dumber than a stump' voice, "Your application? Today? The competition?"

Paul is sure he did not put down a phone number. He doesn't have a phone number.

"Randi told me how to get a hold of you."

"But…"

"No, buts…just listen to me. I've got this brilliant solution to our problem."

"We don't have a problem."

"I know! But I've solved it anyway!"

Paul looks at the phone like the words are coming from an alien.

"About the subject we talked about today," Chainsaw Jack says.

"What subject?"

"Of letting me be your sponsor. We could start tomorrow. Mountain Man Chainsaw Competition at Rainier."

"Jack. I've already told you. I've got a job and of all days, Sunday isn't one I can be taking off. Especially not tomorrow. Especially not to go carving."

"Randi said it would be okay."

"Randi? Randi Cruisewell? He told you I could go cut trees?"

"Not a problem. Said to tell you, just have a Sunrise Service. He won't be able to get there, but said he'd see you later in the day.

Paul wants to scream, "You idiot! You two stupid idiots! You don't take a guy and just jerk him around after all those stupid lessons, and worrying, and…" Paul rubs the space between his eyes, hard. He tries to think. Then, in a slow voice, like he is speaking to a four year old, he says, "My first service is tomorrow." It is all he can do not to say, "I don't have a sermon and moving the service one hour earlier will kill me!"

Jack's voice shouts over the line, "I've got it!"

"I…"

"Just listen, for Christ's sake." There is a deadly silence, like Chainsaw

Jack finally realizes who he is talking to. "Oh, sorry, didn't mean to offend you."

"Forget that! Your attitude offends me!"

"My attitude is my best feature. Now listen for a good, God-damned minute!"

Paul's hand clenches the receiver tighter. He wishes it was Jack's neck.

"You there?" Chainsaw Jack asks.

"I'm here. I've got company, so get on with it."

"Here's how it works. Just listen. Then you can say yes or no."

Paul waits.

"You listenin'?"

"Get on with it, man." Paul twists the telephone cord in his hand. He turns away from the wide-eyed stares of Suzie and Sam. He realizes Saundra has turned down the sound on the television.

"Okay. Here's how it works. You have a sunrise service. You sing."

"Sing?" Paul's gut clenches for the hundredth time and then un-clenches. He could sing. He did sing. He knows every gospel song from forever. He and his mother did dishes and harmonized every gospel song written. In high school, chorus had been the one thing he'd aced. In the woods, he led the crew in "Volga Boat Man" and "Swinging the Ax." At the bar, he's the one who most often got everyone singing the chorus of "Waltzing with Bears."

"Listen, damn it. You'll be done at eight-thirty. I'll drive. I'll provide the saws. I'll even pay your entry fee. We're there at ten o'clock. Cutting starts at ten-thirty. The prize is five hundred dollars for first place. Brummer says you're the best. I saw what you can do! I don't doubt your talent. When you win? You give me one hundred dollars. For being your sponsor."

"Jack, people are used to going to church at…"

"Your first Sunday, right?"

"Right."

"They aren't used to anything. Eight widows, right?"

"Yeah," Paul's fingers bunch the skin at his brow, "…eight."

"It seems to me it isn't going to take all that much time to tell eight widows the service is at seven-thirty. Start early. Sing. We'll be out of there. Did you hear how much the first prize is?"

"I heard."

"And it isn't the money, Paul. Though, it's not bad for two hours of work. And a little publicity. But what's most important, and I quote The Reverend Randi MacArthur Cruisewell himself, 'you'll be doing what you do best'. God's gift to you."

Before Paul can interrupt, he hears the edge of Jack's voice slip to smooth, hypnotic silk. "It's not that you've only been called to preach, you've been called to cut, something not enough people have witnessed."

"People here at this trailer court are depending on me."

"You will meet their needs. After they all enjoy a good sing, you tell them you'll be back in time. They can have their Ladies' Aid Meeting, or whatever they call it in the afternoon. Paul, this is your chance to do two things you really need to do. I wouldn't be tempting you like this if I weren't a religious man myself. I know when someone's called. Carving is a gift. A talent. You can't ignore your talent! And my gifts! I'm the best promoter you could ask for. Trust me. I'll take you to the moon!" His voice ends full of confidence. Full of faith.

"Let me think about it. What's your number. I'll call you back." Paul knows he's stalling, but he needs time. He needs to think.

"Paul, don't! Don't call me. I'll just be there. Eight-thirty. If you're going to cut, come out and get in my rig. If you decide to let everyone down, well, that's your choice. I'll see you in the morning."

The phone goes dead.

Paul places the receiver in the cradle. Suzie watches him. Sam comes over to take his hand.

"You gonna do some chainsaw stuff?" Sam asks, his eyes wide and full of five-year-old wonder.

Paul knows that whatever he does at least two people, small people, will support him.

Suzie asks, "Well?"

"Okay, okay." Paul says with resignation. "Let's think about this. Suzie, what would it take to tell everyone in the court that we're going to have a sunrise service tomorrow? Seven-thirty."

"About ten minutes!"

"I can help!" Sam chimes in.

Suzie is already pulling on her sneakers. Sam grabs his coat.

"It's done!" Suzie calls.

Saundra lets out a loud laugh, "Guess what! Those people on Jeopardy don't know diddly. They didn't know Ralph Lauren and they didn't know Karl Lagerfeld! Pastor Paul, you should get on this show. Give you something to do when you're not meeting people's needs!"

The sarcasm fits like Saran Wrap over Paul's guilt. He feels the cool night air push into the room as Suzie and Sam head out the door.

Shortly after they leave, Grandma Bella returns.

"The kids are making the rounds...they'll be right back," Paul explains.

"So they said. What a unique idea! A sing-along. I'm sure you can use my daughter's talents. There isn't a gospel song she doesn't know. Right, missy?"

"Yep!" She calls. "Thought you'd never ask. Wouldn't miss this first gathering of the needy for anything."

"And," Grandma Bella reaches out a reassuring hand to Paul and continues, "Your friend, Annabelle Lee? She probably hasn't had a chance to tell you, but she plays guitar. I'll bet she'd love to join us."

Paul, hearing Annabelle Lee's name, heads for the door.

"Get along with you. She's anxious to hear about Jack's phone call. She had no trouble remembering exactly who he was. Told me the whole story. I think she said, very politely, that Jack is a bit of an ass. Can hardly wait to meet him!"

Paul walks towards the trailer. He wonders what Annabelle Lee will think about an invitation to a sunrise service so that he can go cut trees.

26

PAUL TELLS HIS SECRET

"You're back!" Annabelle Lee sits in the large overstuffed chair; the knit bag that holds his carvings is draped over her lap. Along the arms of the chair she has placed the twelve animals. One follows the other in a whimsical parade. In her hand she holds a carved bear. Paul's eyes catch her eyes and then she turns from his gaze as if embarrassed and unsure.

"Hope you don't mind?" she says. She nervously pulls open the string bag and gently places each animal inside. "I was, well, waiting and looked for something to read and…found this bag stuffed between some magazines." She looks up, her face drained of its smile. "I know I shouldn't have been so nosy, but I opened it, and there they were. So inviting. So wonderful. Yours, I'd guess."

Paul slumps into the booth in the kitchenette. He pushes away the cold plate of spaghetti and breaks off an edge of the loaf of sourdough bread. He chews slowly and washes down the bread with the remains of his beer.

"Want another?" he asks lifting the empty beer can.

"No, thanks."

He knows once again, she is waiting him out.

He makes a long reach to the refrigerator door. He takes out a Red Hook. "That bag of stuff is all that's left. You sure you want to know?"

"Of course. Are you sure you want to tell?"

"No." Paul laughs nervously, "I mean yes." He hears his jittery laugh. He looks to see her watching him. No question, she is interested and concerned. He loves how her right eyebrow is just a bit thicker and higher than her left.

"Go on," she says.

"Honest. It's no big deal."

"When someone answers a question with 'it's no big deal'..."

"...you know it is."

"Right."

Paul reaches for the bag and removes one of the carvings. His thumb runs the length of the alligator's tail. His fingernail catches on one of the four boots on one of the four squat feet. He doesn't know where to start.

"Start with the bear," Annabelle Lee hands it to him. "Tell me about the bear."

Paul trades the alligator for the bear. "Why that one?"

"It's signed. It's different from the others."

Paul studies the round, rolly bear. "It is different. Not so crazy. It's the only one that isn't mine." He sits it down on the table, as if the bear might now rest its back on one of the beer cans. "Let me start with the goofy ones. The ones I carved."

Annabelle Lee tucks her legs under her, pulls the multi-colored afghan from the back of the chair and nestles it over her shoulders. Every gesture tells Paul, "I'm ready. I'm listening."

Paul releases all of the animals from the bag. His fingers play over them, barely touching the jutting limbs, the protruding snouts, the rounded bellies, the jaunty top hats, and flared bell-bottoms. It is a menagerie he loves. "There were more. I burned them."

"Too bad."

"It didn't seem so at the time. They were so personal. So, not to be shared." He looks up and she nods her head for him to continue.

"They're dreams. Creatures from dreams. My dreams. For awhile I'd carve an animal a night, a dream a night."

"When'd you do that?"

"*Where* I carved them is probably as important as when." Paul pushes the dirty dishes aside and carefully places each animal on the Formica table. He scoots them into a circle of dancing animals, circling the bear. "I did them sitting next to a Monarch, that's a cast iron stove, in a cabin a mile outside Twist—a cabin my dad built for my mom. There was a time she loved that place, a time *I* loved that place. It's where my dad died. He took some time to die. While he died, I carved most of these."

Paul makes his voice slow and easy. He tries to keep his voice free of emotion, fearful she'll hear his anger, more fearful he'll feel his anger and his sadness. He clears his throat. Annabelle Lee waits, her eyes steady on him.

She says, "Yes?" to ask him to continue. Paul is surprised he's said so much already. Never has he talked about Bear and those last days. "You really want to hear this?"

A second, almost imperceptible dip of her head is a 'go ahead' signal.

Paul closes his eyes, breathes deep and plunges into the words: "A logging accident. A widow maker. You know a widow maker? A widow maker is a limb that falls crazy. Or a tree you think is headed in one direction and it veers to another." Paul lets out a deep sigh. As he says the words he sees the branch fall, feels the air's push, sees his dad turn surprised, and fearful. "It caught his right leg, just at the kneecap. Near severed it. I was with him. I think my seeing him get caught was about as bad as getting caught. He was so damn proud. He'd taught me everything about the woods and how to survive there. Respectful. Cautious. And here he was, slammed to the ground, like any other idiot, done-in by the woods. We got him to the hospital. After a month, when he wasn't whole, he demanded I take him home. 'Escape' was how he saw it. He hated hospitals and doctors. Most of all he hated being weak and out of control. It was the loss of power. He was big into power."

The carved bear rests in the outstretched palm of Paul's hand. His words are for Annabelle Lee, but he speaks as if he is talking to the carving. "It wasn't long before things got worse. Gangrene ate into his leg. He gritted his teeth and made vows he'd tough it out. I'm not sure if it's considered tough or not when you die screaming. Here's the irony. I begged the doc to give him more morphine. The doctor tried to cut a deal: the hospital, for the morphine. Wrong call. Bear was not into making deals. When they saw they couldn't bribe him, they used the excuse he'd get addicted if the morphine wasn't hospital controlled." Paul bit his lips, then ended with, "He died by inches."

"Paul, that's horrible. Why didn't you… "

"I did. Believe me, I tried everything. In the end, my dad, Bear, wouldn't let anybody in the cabin. No doctors. No nobody. He slept with his shotgun. He meant it. Well, not everybody was told to get out. I was there. The doctors did the best they could short of a court order. It was left to me. I hated it. Even the doc relented…to a point…I did get more morphine. I gave Bear as much morphine as they gave me. It was never enough." Paul blinked his eyes, surprised at the stinging tears. "And then it was."

To stop the image he continues talking. "All that time, to block what was going to happen, I carved. I'd pick up a piece of wood, any piece, long as it fit my hand, and then I'd disappear into the world of that animal. The more complex, the better. The more it occupied me the less I heard Bear breathing. When it was over, I saved these few, and I burned down the cabin."

Annabelle Lee's eyes go wide. Paul doesn't know if it is disbelief, or concern, or shock.

He turns the bear over and shows the bottom to Annabelle Lee. "This. This was a surprise. For all we went through, you'd have thought we'd been close. Didn't happen. I saved this stupid bear…that's all he carved…bears. It was there with all the other carvings. I kept it. The one thing I didn't burn." Paul turns the bear around. He studies the bottom of the carving. He runs his finger over the letters. "The inscription knocked me over. I don't know when he carved it. Not the kind of thing he ever said."

A slight patter of rain begins to tap on the metal top of the trailer. The musical pings sound like a dozen tiny drums. Annabelle Lee puts her palm up as if she might catch the sounds. She speaks slowly and softly. Studied words: "Strange carvings from strange dreams. You burn down the cabin your parents built when you were a child. You just happen to save a bear that says your dad loves you."

Paul tries to stop his thoughts. Clamps his teeth. He hates that she sees him like this. He wishes she hadn't been poking around his place and he damn well wishes they weren't talking about Bear.

"I'd say you could make a psychiatrist rich on half that material." Annabelle Lee's words are half joking, half concerned. "If you wanted."

"I don't want," Paul says, startled at the anger in his words.

Annabelle Lee sits up. "Sorry. Forgive me." She slowly unwraps herself from the afghan. She reaches for her jacket. "Been a long day. Time to go." Annabelle Lee stands and Paul feels he has no option but to take her home. She speaks as she buttons her jacket. "Big day tomorrow. You've got that service staring you in the face. I didn't mean to upset you."

"It's okay. It's okay," Paul answers. "And it has been a long day." Once again, he is filled with confusion and sadness and hope. He wants her to go and he wants her to stay. All he can think to say is, "I don't want you going away thinking I'm crazy, burning down the cabin." Paul rubs his eyes; it seems such a long time ago. "At the time it seemed like the right thing to do."

Annabelle Lee turns, "We all do things that don't seem so brilliant later. Who knows? It probably was an absolutely rational, ordinary, perfect thing to do."

Paul hears her words for what they are: soft and caring.

"Someday I'll tell you the whole thing. It's no big…"

"Don't…it is," she says and smiles up at him. "Another time. We'll have lots of time. How about that ride?"

Her hand finds his as they walk to his Jeep.

Driving, he thinks about two things: the fading warmth left by her hand in his and her words, 'lots of time'. He pulls into her driveway, and before he can get out to open the door, Annabelle Lee has already jumped down to the curb. She turns and leans in the Jeep window, "See you tomorrow, then."

"Great!" Then he remembers tomorrow. "Seven-thirty."

"Seven thirty?"

Paul chooses his words carefully. He says them slowly. "It's going to be a sunrise service. A song service. We'll keep it light. Saundra will be there with her accordion. Gospel music."

"I wondered why you were so nonchalant about preparing a sermon. Sounds like a great idea." Annabelle Lee pushes the door to be sure it's closed tight. She takes a few steps and turns back to ask, "Would you like me to bring my guitar?"

Paul is momentarily overwhelmed. Pleased. He can't believe she brought up the idea! Just like that! "How great! You'll play? Gospel?"

"Just an old wanna-be hippy. I know them all. 'Bringing in the Sheaves,' 'Amazing Grace,' 'Abide With me'. You name it, I can play it."

"Miracle! Hot-damn!"

"Watch your expletives!" Annabelle Lee steps back from the curb. "I'll be there!" She waves goodnight as she walks backward up the path.

Paul watches until she is inside and then he heads home. He hums 'Amazing Grace' and checks through his memory to see how many verses are still there.

For the first night in weeks, Paul sleeps without dreams and wakes in the morning before the sun is up.

27

AMAZING GRACE

At seven o'clock Paul studies the Airstreams. From trailer windows, pinpoints of light shoot through the morning mist. Paul imagines women gathering hymn books and Bibles, Suzie and Sam waking sleepily, Maxwell House coffee burping its morning tune. He wonders if anyone else's stomach churns, if the hairs on their arms feverishly stand up, if they have ignored breakfast.

He pulls the new black turtleneck over his head, it grabs at his ears, and then it snugs so tightly around his throat it is hard to swallow. This is an irritation he could do without. He reaches for his suit jacket and at the last second opens the refrigerator door to grab the last, lone can of Red Hook. Beer in hand, he heads for the chapel.

Inside, the concrete floor seems to reach up and suck the heat from his heart. He lights a dozen of the votive candles. The ruby glass glitters an illusion of warmth.

For all yesterday's work, the room has the look of a high school drama class, a very beginning high school drama class at the very beginning of a production, where nothing is in place, nothing is ready, and where, were there any people there, no one would know their lines. Paul tries to relax, he breathes in and out, he swings his arms to loosen up his body, and he reaches for the beer. The beer helps. He finds a mint in his jacket pocket and hides the can of beer in the cardboard box, cloth-draped pulpit.

Paul spreads the candles in their tin cans around the room, first one place and then another. He turns on a dial of a small space heater that yesterday seemed fine and today is so small, it barely cuts the cool morning air. Nothing seems to help. The pleasure of yesterday's accomplishments is nowhere to be found. The chapel doesn't look like a chapel and Paul doesn't feel like a minister.

From across the court aluminum doors open and close.

Mrs. Bagley is the first to arrive. She peeks around the edge of the door. "Am I too early?"

"No, no. Welcome!" Paul's realizes his voice is unnaturally high. He swallows a couple of times, the mint disappears and he can feel it slowly slide down his throat, fearful he'll choke to death right then and there. Miraculously, the mint doesn't lodge and he is able to say, "Come in. Take any pew…chair. Sit where you want. Remind me again, you're…?"

"Mrs. Bagley." She offers him a gloved hand. Paul feels pleasure at this churchly appearance and the churchly greeting.

The room begins to fill. The women call 'hello' to each other, exclaim over the twins new outfits. All make a point of saying hello to Paul. They stand around nervously chatting, not quite sure what they should do next.

Outside, the mist breaks and sunshine inches through the single window. With the sun, Grandma Bella arrives and moves from woman to woman. "Good morning, Betty Bagley." "Lovely dress, Olga Simmons." "Isn't this promising, Beenie?" Her chipperness spreads warmth. As she works from woman to woman, Paul realizes the greetings are for his ears. Grandma Bella is refreshing his memory with each name. It pleases him, but the fear of not knowing names is now overshadowed by the fear of Annabelle Lee and Saundra not showing.

Then he hears the clank of crutches and in walks Big Bill with the accordion followed by Saundra. Grandma Bella scrambles to arrange a second chair for Saundra's leg. Suzie arrives behind her mother, Smuggins in one hand and Sam in the other. Still no Annabelle Lee.

Paul can stall no longer. Olga Simmons and the twins and Molly Entwhistle are already seated. Saundra runs her fingers over the keys and looks to Paul for direction. Paul, at the front of the room in front of the altar announces, "Ladies, it's that time. Please be seated." When everyone has found her place, Paul leans over the pulpit without squishing it. He looks at each woman as if to say 'good morning' again. He clears his throat, and begins: "Church protocol calls for a sermon," and is aware that his stomach burbles and bubbles. He should have eaten. He should have prepared a sermon. His head pounds. He clears his throat and plunges into words, like a cat after kibble on a slick floor.

"This morning, because we are just getting to know each other, well, I'm getting to know each of you, you all know each other," Paul clears his throat and continues, "I've chosen a special format for our introductory service. I'm calling it, well, we'll call it, 'Singing in the Day'. We'll begin with the gospel hymn 'Amazing Grace' and then we'll continue with, well how about we continue with your suggestions?" Then just as he thinks he can't stall another minute, Paul hears the sweet thrumb of a Honda scooter and then the 'thwack' as the kickstand slips into place.

Annabelle Lee comes through the door, all smiles, her guitar at her side. She heads directly to an empty chair next to Saundra. Paul feels the muscles in his arms relax. His headache vanishes.

"You all know Saundra and her gifts. And now we have a neighbor and friend to accompany her!" Paul can't contain his pleasure. His smile is broad. His heart is so happy it feels as if it will explode. "Everyone, meet Annabelle Lee Fulsome."

"Good morning, everybody!" Annabelle Lee's voice is sure and confident. The women return her smile. A few call 'good morning!'

Saundra gives her an "e" and Annabelle Lee plucks strings until they are a match. The two look like a sister team that has played together forever. Saundra whispers, "Amazing Grace," and her fingers run up and down the keys until there is a swooping chord.

Sam and Suzie inch up until they sit on the floor by Grandma Bella's feet, beside their mom. Smuggins pushes into the bend of Sam's folded legs. Everyone waits and then music fills the chapel and everyone sings. Lustily.

It is more than Paul could have dreamed or wished for.

Amongst the gathered widows, one voice stands out. Above the scratchy soprano of Beenie, loud and demanding, is the strong alto of Grandma Bella. The twins in fluty trills have every word of every verse. Sam and Suzie gather their voices on the chorus. But it is Saundra, with sureness and pleasure, who leads the congregation. Annabelle Lee's fingers carry the melody. Between Saundra and Grandma Bella, their robust power pulls everyone along. Even Suzie looks up with approval and amazement in her smile.

When they finish, to Paul's suggestion of a request, Suzie raises her hand and suggests, "This Little Gospel Light of Mine." She leans against Saundra's leg in a rare moment of intimacy. Saundra drops her hand to play with the curls that have escaped her daughter's ponytail. And then, accordion at the ready, Suzie leads, "All around the neighborhood," and everyone follows and their voices resonate off the walls with the chorus, "I'm going to let it shine, let it shine, all the time, let it shine." Big Bill leans back and listens, his foot keeping time. The last notes fade. Annabelle Lee fills the space between songs and then in unison she and Saundra hit three chords and everyone sings, "Swing Low, Sweet Chariot," and Bill takes a chance with the base refrain, "...swing low...swing low...swing low."

At the last, "...comin' for to carry me home," sweet silence fills the chapel. Everyone smiles and sighs with pleasure. Paul asks if there are any other requests. Saundra shifts her leg and without suggesting anything begins in a low, pure voice, "Sometimes I feel like a motherless child..." The moaning sweetness fills the room. Grandma Bella scoops Sam up on her lap and rocks him to the sweet sound of his mother's voice. Saundra pulls the final note out long and low.

"That was lovely," Mrs. Bagley says. Her words carry the gratefulness of everyone in the room.

Annabelle Lee's fingers walk over the strings of the guitar. She plays one verse of a slow rendition of "Jacob's Ladder." With a slight pause, she invites everyone to sing and everyone does. After five verses Annabelle Lee stops. The congregation breathes a communal sigh and enjoys the feeling of harmony and goodwill that swells around them.

Paul, in a calm, easy voice says, "Instead of a sermon, where I try to tell you something you probably already know, better than I know, what if each of us shares a good memory, something you've not told before, but something that we'd all love to hear."

Paul looks at all the faces of the women and, fearful they might not talk, he continues, "I'll start. I have a wonderful memory of my mother cooking huckleberry pancakes on our Monarch range up in the Methow Mountains. My dad and I had picked the berries that morning...a morning that felt very much like this morning. Cool air. A crisp, clean ending summer season. That's my good memory." Paul turns to one of the twins. They take his smile and the open gesture of his hands and never hesitate. "I bet you all wonder what it's like being a twin," Janice states, looking to see everyone shake heads in agreement. Joan adds on top of her sister's sentence, "Mostly it's wonderful, but sometimes it's burdensome. So one of my best memories is when…"

"We no longer wore matching clothes!," they say in unison.

"That's right!" Joan takes over. "We received a box of clothing from cousins in Minneapolis. We dove into that box and came out with different outfits."

"We've never dressed the same since," Janice says and looks down at her jean skirt and jacket by way of showing how it did not match Joan's flowered dress and flowered hat.

Molly Entwhistle is next. She sits demurely, her gloved hands holding her bag. Her hair is covered with a black lace handkerchief.

"Mrs. Entwhistle, do you have a memory you'd like to share?" Paul asks.

From her purse she produces a pack of photos. She chooses one and passes it to Mrs. Simmons on her left. "This is my new grandchild. Four months. Looks just like me!"

The ladies ooh and ahh over the photo and then each reaches for her purse and soon photos of grandchildren and nieces, dogs and cats, trips to the Italian Mediterranean and the Left Bank of Paris are circling the room. Everyone chatters and reaches across each other to pass a picture or retrieve a photo to say something that has not been said earlier. When Grandma Bella passes an entire envelope of photos of Sam and Suzie at the school picnic, Paul clears his throat in an attempt to regain control. It is eight-twenty.

Paul stands next to Annabelle Lee and reaches to pluck a guitar string. The women look up as if they have just remembered this was "church."

"It's time to end our first service together. Annabelle Lee, Saundra how about ending with, 'Abide with Me?' " And Saundra, if you would, give us the first verse. Saundra smiles. She begins to sing. At the chorus Paul signals everyone to join in. When they finish, Paul stands and with raised arms miraculously remembers every word of the Benediction.

While the women gather their photos and purses, Suzie jumps up. She disappears behind the altar and emerges with two baskets. She hands one basket to Sam. Sam walks up to Grandma Bella. Grandma Bella places a five-dollar bill in the basket. Paul watches as Suzie works the other side of the room. To Paul's astonishment, each woman follows Grandma Bella's example.

"Don't let anyone leave just yet," Grandma Bella says to Pastor Paul. "I'll be right back." In seconds Grandma Bella returns with an oversized thermos of coffee and paper cups. Joan and Janice Wittenhouer offer to drive to the Mini-Mart for sweet rolls.

The women discuss forming an "Aid Society," and what and whom they could aid. Suzie tells them they have fifty dollars to begin with and suggests they look into an after-school program where everyone plays Dodge Ball without getting mad.

Minutes later the "hooga-hooga" of an air horn makes the women stop talking. The horn blasts again.

"What is that?" Beenie demands.

"Who is that?" echoes Molly Entwhistle.

Everyone heads to the door. Outside, Paul turns to his congregation. He raises his arms. "Ladies, I'll explain later. I've got to go. Thank you for coming to this first service. Annabelle Lee, your playing was superb. Saundra, you were an inspiration. Sam and Suzie, thank you for getting the Ladies' Aid ladies grounded. Dear women, you were great!"

Before they can respond, there is a third blast.

Paul turns to wave at Jack to 'cool it'. He turns back to the questioning and slightly irritated ladies. "How about we meet this afternoon? Four o'clock? I'll be back and we can plan the next few months. Okay?"

The women nod but when Jack waves at them, they glare at the unmannered man who drives an irritating truck. Grandma Bella gestures, "Go, Pastor Paul, before he blasts that horn again."

"I'll explain...this afternoon," Paul calls and he covers the center yard at a run and pulls himself up into the cab of the truck. He leans out the window and waves. All the widows wave back—tentatively. The children run a few steps and stop, Sam's small white hand tick-tocks goodbye. One person who doesn't wave is Annabelle Lee. She stands next to Saundra.

It is the last image Paul has. Annabelle Lee holds a crutch as Saundra gets her balance. Neither of the women waved and Paul feels a slight sense of uneasiness. His congregation, all in all, seems to be a cohesive, singular body. Except this slight divergence and, Paul wonders, what happened to Cruisewell? Paul has the horrible dawning awareness that Reverend Cruisewell will probably show up at a normal time for a church service, say around eleven o'clock, and Paul won't be there. And then he remembers. This was all Cruisewell's idea. If not his idea, it did have his blessing.

Time to go! They drive under the arch, and Jack doesn't forget to give the horn a last, long "hooga!"

28

BACK AT IT!

As the truck swings out under the arch, Jack can't resist. He reaches up and yanks the air horn. The hollow blast of sound fills the cab. "Jack! Enough already! For someone who says he'll just drive away if I didn't come, you're being an asshole! Those are older women, for God's sake. You'll destroy their hearing!"

"Older? I dooon't think so! At least two of them aren't older. And you, taking God's name in vain. What kind of preacher talks like that! Right after your first Sunday service. Shame. Shame," Jack mocks. He sets the rig in gear and pulls onto the highway. Minutes later they head south on I-5 towards Mt. Rainier.

Over the churning wheels, Jack raises his voice and asks, "So, did you do what I said?"

"What did you say?"

"Have a sunrise service. Sing. I practically planned the whole service for you. And there was that good lookin' chick, two good lookin' chicks, so you must have done something right!" Jack laughs a laugh of deep, rolling, self-satisfaction.

Paul's irritation melts and gives Jack his due, "I must admit, it worked!"

"I knew it would."

"How's that?"

"Oh, I thought once of being a minister, myself. Before I sold chainsaws."

"You? A minister?"

"Don't sound so incredulous. Look at you! Anyway, I decided it wasn't my shtick."

"Not your shtick? Chainsaws are your shtick?"

"Right. Anybody can be a minister."

"Thanks. Just what I needed to hear."

Paul settles into a long silence.

A half-hour later Jack moves the rig to the far right lane to exit and they head east. A sign states Enumclaw is twenty-six more miles. Rainier, sixty-nine.

"You like it? Being a minister?"

"I hardly know. It hasn't been a week."

"Well, if you're as good as Brummer says, you can always make a living with a chainsaw."

"Real loggers don't make livings doing chainsaw art. No one makes a living doing chainsaw art."

"Oh, that must mean real loggers become ministers."

Paul ignores Jack. He watches as Enumclaw whips by and car dealerships give way to strip malls, which give way to RV parks, which give way to forests. Soon they maneuver wide bends in and out of the flickering shadows of tall Douglas firs. Paul relaxes and takes a snooze.

When Jack pulls the rig onto a bumpy gravel road, Paul wakes with a start. Out the window are rows of tents and campers. Around picnic tables, stacked with piles of baskets and blankets, thermos jugs and Frisbees, families gather. Jack wedges his rig into a space next to an empty swimming pool. Yellow tape blocks off a large parking strip where a dozen four-foot logs stand ready to cut.

Paul jumps from the cab. In a big stretch, he spreads his arms as if he could hold the crisp, cold air off the mountain snowpack. In the distance Mt. Rainier stands guard, whitewashed with new fallen snow. Under his boots, slick pine needles give off a tangy breath. Across the meadow the last of the morning fog reveals the black and white of gathered cows. Paul's body itches with the anticipation of cutting. He clenches and unclenches his hands, his whole body ready for the hours ahead.

Jack comes from behind the truck. He holds a canvas-wrapped saw under one arm and a large piece of cardboard under the other. "Grab the other two saws and the carry-all. We, my friend, have some cutting to do."

"We?" Paul calls as he retrieves the saws.

At the registration table, Jack flirts with the ladies in charge, unrolls a roll of bills, fills out the form, and pays the fee. To the women he winks a "I'd love to see you later" wink and hands two large safety pins to Paul. Paul waits for Jack to pin his number to his back. Instead, in front of the women, Jack takes out a black magic marker and writes on the cardboard over Paul's number: PASTOR PAUL. On the bottom he writes under the number, THE SAVING SAWYER.

"What are you doing?" Paul asks feeling like a fourth grader waiting for the teacher to do whatever teachers are thinking of doing.

"That's not all! Jack picks up the large piece of cardboard he's been carrying and shows it to Paul.

"Like it?"

"What the...?"

The words are in large block letters: PASTOR PAUL. NEW DAWN IS BREAKING CHURCH, SEATTLE.

Before Paul can complain, Jack heads toward the cutting area.

"We start in twenty minutes. Let's get you set up and I'll round up something to eat. Here are your chaps and earphones," Jack hands Paul a blue nylon bag and he leans the cardboard sign against the four-foot stump in the middle of Paul's cutting space. "I'll see if I can find something else to lean the sign against. It's an eye-catcher, don't you think?"

"Think? I think it's stupid. Bad form. For someone who questions my being a minister, you're sure using it."

"Well, you can count on the fact that I'm not stupid. While I'm getting food, I'll also see what media people are here. Oh, and next time, wear a collar." Jack walks away a few steps. He turns to say, "Although, there's something rather insouciant about the black turtleneck."

"Insouciant?" Paul throws the question at Jack's back.

Paul turns the sign face down and straps on his chaps. He studies his log. The growth lines are tight and except for a couple of minor knotholes he won't be fighting the grain. Paul picks up the twenty-four inch saw, balances it in both hands. He feels its heft. Nice. He smiles, pleased at the quality and condition of the Stihl. Jack might be an ass, but he has great saws.

Jack returns with corn-dogs and lemonade. "Here, these will get you going until the barbecue is ready."

Jack flips the sign, letters right side up. "Paul, you just don't get it. Listen to me. You've got a niche. You'll get a crowd just because you're a minister."

"Just? Just?" Paul moans. With as much sarcasm as he can twist into the words, he adds, "You know about such things, I gather."

Either Jack doesn't catch his tone or doesn't care. "I do," he says reasonably and with a smile. "Everyone loves a minister. They'll think you can't carve! Will they be surprised! Once word gets out...you'll see...each time..."

"What...each time?"

"Wait 'til you win. I know the psychology of winning. You win at my place, then you win this county, and then you take Monroe County. National's next. They're at Twist this year, you know? Wouldn't it be nice to go back and win right there, right in front of everybody in your hometown?"

"Jack, you don't seem to understand. I'm not free to go runnin' around the country carving."

"Work it out."

At which moment a voice calls, "Paul! Paul Whitinowsky!" and Paul looks up to see Hattie, pad and pencil in hand. "I can't believe it! Jesse said you had left Twist for a new career, and here you are!"

Paul steps up to accept Hattie's hug, and a kiss to both cheeks.

"Well, well, well, isn't this nice," Jack takes in Hattie. "I'd guess you, little lady, are a reporter."

Hattie pushes back the bill of her *Seattle Times* cap with her pencil, and says, "You're right. I *am* a reporter. And just who are you?"

Paul steps in. He can see Jack is about ready to bombard Hattie with a whole bunch of bullshit. "Hattie. Meet Chainsaw Jack. You're not to write one word about him or me being here at the contest. Everything is 'off the record.'"

"If you say so. But why?"

"How about a beer after the carving?"

"You've got a date. Meet you at the Silver Dollar in Enumclaw. And Jack, if you'll drop the 'little lady' crap, you're invited."

The one-minute warning bell rings. Hattie leaves to check out the other carvers.

"Amazing! A reporter and you've told her not to write about us! We'll discuss that later."

"You keep forgetting, I'm a minister, and I just don't need to remind the whole Northwest in *The Seattle Times* that I'm not. Get that? I'm not a chainsaw artist."

"An artist? Nobody said you were an artist."

Paul couldn't resist, "Only *The Seattle Times*."

"The *Times*. So I've been told. So? We've got to talk about this, after the competition is over. At the bar. With Hattie. Hot-damn!"

"Forget it, Jack. It's time to cut."

"Okay, okay. Do great! Remember a lot rides on this." Jack leans down to put a "Chainsaw Jack/Chainsaw Rentals" sticker in the corner of the sign. He steps back. He adds four more stickers.

The ten second bell clangs.

Paul adjusts his earphones. He's ready.

"Don't worry!" Jack yells. He gives Paul a thumbs up.

"Me, worry?" Paul grips the toggle to start the motor.

"I'll be praying for you!" Jack shouts over the sputter of the saw. He plants his feet and the minute the starting bell rings, his saw cuts wood. A large slice falls. He kicks the piece out of the way and bends to make a curved cut, the blade as sweet as a hot knife in butter.

Jack reaches to grab the free piece of wood. He sits it upright and places the PASTOR PAUL sign against it. Paul turns away from Jack, the sign, and the gathering crowd. All he can see or smell or feel is the saw cutting.

29

BRINGING BACK AN ALLIGATOR

Three hours later Paul thinks his arms will fall off. His hands are covered with sawdust and pitch. His hair is full of wood chips. Even with a half-hour break for barbeque, he's feeling the pain. His whole body thrums. Strangely, for all the aches, he feels great. He loves the low-slung animal he's cut. He isn't even angry that Jack's saw has blown a chain and he's had to finish most of the carving with a twelve-incher. Luckily, the chain missed him and sliced a lop-sided grin across the animal's face. A beguiling smile. And the chain is set aside. Paul has a great idea for the end of the cut.

Time passes. The final signal indicates cutting will end in one-half hour. Paul is already admiring his finished project.

"Somethin' else!" Jack yells approval as he studies Paul's alligator. He leans over the carving. He stops. He beats his fist against his head. He moans. He gasps, "Nooo!!" He bounds around the carving. "Paul! You'll be disqualified. Get that damn chain out of there."

Paul steps in front of the alligator in case Jack might reach down and pull the chain loose. "No way! That chain's the best part!"

"Fuckin'-H, Paul! You can't do that. You'll be disqualified."

Paul straddles the alligator, ready to keep Jack away.

Between Paul's feet lays the long, low crawling creature. Along its back is an inch-wide serpentine grove into which Paul had put the broken chain. Had he known the alligator was going to emerge, it would have been perfect to stick two of the church's red votive candleholders into the eye sockets. Paul smiles at the idea. Next time, he'll remember that.

Forty-five minutes later Paul sits on the ground, his back against the low profile of his carving. He watches Jack clean the saws.

"You probably didn't notice. The judge chose a bear," Jack grumbles.

"I don't carve bears."

"But you could have won first place with a bear. And that stupid spine-thing almost did you in! You might have won first place even then…except for that chain." Jack leans over Paul and glares. "If I'm your sponsor, I want first place! You think anyone remembers second? No! No one remembers and worse than that, we get two hundred and fifty dollars. We don't get five hundred dollars! You're lucky you even qualified for the county championship. Next time you wear a collar. Next time we figure out who's the judge and we carve to the judge."

"*We* carve? Jack, let's get something straight. You want me to carve? I carve. I carve what I want to carve and if the judge is too stupid to see what's best, that's his problem."

"You're telling me…" Jack sputters, "You're…damn…well…"

"I'm telling you *my* rules," Paul calmly replies.

"Well, good! That settles one thing. You'll carve again. Next week. I've already signed you up. I'd say we have a deal," Jack chortles.

"A deal?" Paul lowers his voice to a purr, "You want a deal? Here's a deal. You be my sponsor? Join my church."

"When hell freezes…"

"…that's when I wear a collar."

"This is not an equal trade."

"Your choice."

Jack doesn't say another word. Together they maneuver the alligator into the truck, pack the saws, and head for Enumclaw and The Silver Dollar.

Hattie waits with a beer and the minute Paul and Jack enter, she signals for two more.

"Hattie!" Paul slides into the booth.

Jack takes his seat and is all attention. He's full of smiles and head nods and solicitousness. He listens as the two of them catch up on what's happening. Jesse is fine and would have been carving but she had already qualified in Westport so she's ready for the nationals in Twist. And then Paul explains why his carving needs to be "off the record." He needs to make it clear that he is trying to establish himself as a minister. Paying back Cruisewell, which he will feel honor bound to do, is a frightening consideration.

"It's Sunday? You're a minister? You're carving? So, exactly what are you establishing?" Hattie asks with a chuckle. "Besides, I got some great pictures of that chain flying through the air and of you putting it into place. Great pictures!"

Jack nods his head in total agreement, his large toothy smile encouraging Hattie.

"And, if I can talk my editor into another story, there's the fair in Monroe!" Hattie turns to Jack, "You going to get him there?"

Hattie gives Jack a high-five. And for the first time since they've sat down, Jack joins the conversation with, "It's on the agenda. We'll be discussing that very fair at this afternoon's Ladies' Aid meeting. Right Paul?"

Paul doesn't answer.

"Well, that sounds like another great angle," Hattie says, her pencil poised, she and Jack acting like long-time conspirators. "The Ladies' Aid Society, an errant minister, a devil-takes-all chainsaw seller! Stories don't get much better than this. I'd like to be there this afternoon."

Jack pats her hand and says obsequiously, "We'd like you to be there."

Paul holds back, his comments like nails he'd like to pound into Jack's skull.

The beers arrive. Hattie interviews Jack about his business, his sponsorship. Jack's happy to oblige.

In silence, Paul tries to remember exactly what a minister does with a Ladies' Aid Society.

30

THE LADIES' AID SOCIETY

Jack's rig rumbles over the gravel drive of the trailer court at exactly four fifteen. The trailer court appears deserted. No curtains pull back. No children run to greet them. No one's pulling weeds. No one's mowing grass. As the rig grinds its wheels to a full stop, Paul realizes everyone must be in the chapel. Waiting. And yes, just then the women emerge, by one's and two's, until they are all assembled. Sam pulls Grandma Bella to the front of the group, his legs churning, his pudgy fingers returning Paul's wave. Suzie is right behind them.

"Guess what? Guess what?" she calls. "We got a stupendous phone call!"

Paul steps down and catches Sam in mid-jump. "We won! We won!"

Jack comes around the end of his rig. "What's up?" he asks Paul.

"Yes! What's up?" Paul asks, as Suzie does a victory dance around him.

"We won the tickets to the county fair! We get free rides! Every single ride is free!"

Jack gives Paul a whack on the back. "So there! The county fair, you say?"

Suzie nods her head.

Jack gloats, "That, dear friend, is a miracle if there ever was one."

Paul shakes his head, dumbfounded. And although the ladies are waiting with smiles at Suzie and Sam's great good fortune, they are waiting.

"We better perform another miracle," Paul whispers to Jack.

"Well, let's feed the Christians an alligator," Jack whispers back and laughs a ruffled, funny laugh. It helps. Paul calls, "Hi, ladies!" Sam grabs him around the legs as a reminder, "and gentleman." At which moment, Hattie pulls in behind Jack's rig.

"Let's do it!" Jack says as he jumps into the truck bed. Paul follows. They push and pull the alligator onto the tailgate.

Paul hears Jack call to the women, in a bright voice, as up-beat as an encyclopedia salesman, "Wait 'till you see what we've brought you!"

Paul sets Sam to the side, safely out of the way, and pulls himself into the bed of the truck. Paul pushes. Jack pulls. The carving protrudes. What the women see first is the silly grin and the protruding teeth of a very happy alligator.

Jack wraps both hands under the jaw of the carving. Paul guides the tail. At the moment the alligator rests in the arms of Paul and Jack, a bridge between them, Paul notes the looks on the women's faces: astonishment, interest, confusion, bewilderment. The face he dreads seeing most is Annabelle Lee's. He checks. Annabelle Lee is not there. Certainly she would have frowned at the loss of the tree, but he had hopes that she would understand the fresh, crazy edge of this carving.

"Watch it!" Jack calls. Paul wraps his arms more firmly under the body of the creature and they slowly walk it to the chapel. The women part like the Red Sea, not quite sure how to graciously accept such a strange gift.

"Trust me, they'll learn to love it. Recognize it as 'public art'. Welcome you as their leader. Be totally supportive."

Paul is not all that confident and his confidence slips even further when Jack continues to whisper, "If they don't start cheering like right now, we're going to reload this thing. And, it has just crossed my mind this bunch of old women ain't never going to buy chainsaws."

As they place the creature at the front of the chapel, Paul hears the screen door of the Airstream make a metallic slam. Paul can see, just over his shoulder, Saundra swinging her body on her crutches towards them.

"OOO-weee," Jack whistles under his breath as Saundra makes her not-unbecoming approach. The pressure of the crutches makes the round tops of her breasts mound above the 'V' of her loosely knit orange sweater. The sweater is as bright as neon and as effective. No one would miss Saundra, especially not Jack. Saundra stops at a short distance to admire the alligator.

"Pastor Paul!" she says, her lips glistening with orange as bright and demanding as her sweater. "We've been waiting for you! And an alligator! Who would have ever guessed you'd return with an alligator?" She leans on her crutches. She studies it. "I think it is rather wonderful!"

"Now, isn't that nice..." Jack says. "So discerning!"

It's all Paul can do to not yell at Jack, "Stop leering!"

Hattie moves about taking pictures. She even gets a shot of Saundra leaning over the alligator. She snaps Jack looking very interested.

As the women hesitantly move closer, Paul has a brilliant idea. He'll introduce Jack to Suzie. "Suzie, my friend, come meet Jack." Suzie gives Jack a look-over with the wondrous sneer only a ten-year-old girl could produce. Being a good minister, Paul proceeds with introductions. He starts with Saundra, the one introduction he can see Jack is waiting for. "Jack, this is Saundra. Saundra, this is Jack."

Jack lifts his white baseball cap with Chainsaw Jack embroidered in neon green, which matches the neon of Saundra's sweater. He pushes his hand through his thinning hair and then secures the cap at a bit of an angle. "Well, well, well, that was you who answered my phone call. Helped me find this genius," he says as he slaps Paul's sore back. "Such a lovely voice," he coos.

An image of a creepy, crawling lizard flashes through Paul's mind. Before Jack can ooze any more words at Saundra, Paul says, "And this is Grandma Bella, Saundra's mother. And of course," Paul reaches down to hoist Sam into the crook of his arm, "This is the great Samuel. Suzie and Sam are Saundra's children. Children, meet Chainsaw Jack!" Paul repeats the introductions for Hattie, interjecting, so all the women hear, "Hattie is here to get a story about New Dawn. New Dawn and its unique ministry." Paul looks to see smiles and a few raised eyebrows. "In a minute we'll all head inside and get that meeting going. "

Before they have a chance to head for the chapel, Sam exclaims, "I like this a lot!" He kneels and places one finger tentatively against the metal spine of the alligator.

Jack takes over. He explains, "That, my lad, is the latest addition to your church. It is called, a 'Welcome Alligator.'"

Suzie walks back and forth in front of the animal as if to judge it from every angle. "An alligator? For the chapel?" She sniffs her disapproval. Only days before Paul would have heard the sniff and the tone of Suzie's comment being directed at his alligator. Today, there is no question. The disapproval is aimed at Jack. Even a ten year old can see Jack is worthy of skepticism.

"Well, think of it this way. It's a friendly alligator," Paul says. He feels his role as the minister requires a bit of an explanation. "Everyone! Ladies! If you will give me your attention just for a moment. Where carvers come from, there is a tradition of 'Welcome Bears'. A 'greeter' as it were. And not to be outdone in any way, we've brought you 'Ally the Alligator'. Right, Sam?"

"Yes! It rhymes!"

"Just what I was thinking!" Paul can't help but laugh. "I'll need to cut a 'welcome' sign. Nothing like a little tradition for a church."

Mrs. McBride pushes to the front of the gathered women. She ignores the alligator and addresses Jack in a scolding tone, "Well, young man. You at least returned our minister for the meeting. We've been waiting now for..." she squints at the small numbers of her 'Sunday-go-to-meeting' watch, diamonds glistening, "...for some time." She gives Jack a look full of consternation, "Join us, Mr…"

"Jack. Just call me Jack," he smiles a saccharine smile.

Herding the women into the chapel, Mrs. McBride calls, "It is time, past time, for the Ladies' Aid meeting."

Everyone enters the chapel. Paul watches as Jack maneuvers his hand under Saundra's elbow as she works her crutches through the door. Jack turns to wink. His eyebrows lifting up and down in a Groucho Marx imitation and he says, so only Paul and Saundra can hear, "Can't imagine missing a Ladies' Aid meeting."

Paul is not amused. He feels bad about being late. He feels self-conscious about Jack's glaring interest in Saundra. He wonders how he's going to explain he just spent a Sunday, most of a Sunday, doing chainsaw art.

The chairs are now arranged in a circle and the altar is covered with plates and napkins. Teacups sit on delicate flowered saucers and a cut-glass plate is heaped with lace cookies. Someone has brought pink and pale green mints and a small silver bowl filled with assorted nuts. It all looks so "church-like" and orderly. At which moment, Paul remembers the beer can! Inside the podium! He steps back to try to get a glimpse of the bright red label. He can't see it and he dare not look as if he is looking for it.

Mrs. McBride pours Paul a cup of tea. He nods a thank you and tries not to look worried, or concerned, or like he's lost something. Like a beer. He'll just have to wait until after the meeting is finished, after everyone has left, and if it isn't there? A problem to be faced later.

All the women fill their plates, balance their cups of tea, and seat themselves. Their upturned faces reveal degrees of anticipation. Mrs. Simmons, the twins, and Molly Entwhistle even seem to relax a bit now that everyone is inside and seated. When asked, the women put their heads together and smile for the camera.

Paul wipes his hands on the legs of his jeans and takes one last swallow of the bitter tea. He tries to remember what his notebooks said about Ladies' Aid Societies or Parish Planning. He stumbles into the words, "Ladies, children, everybody, it is nice of you to take this afternoon to meet. Some of you haven't officially met our guest, Jack."

The women's heads turn their attention to Jack. Jack stands. He tips the edge of his cap and his smile takes in the circle of women. "It's such a pleasure to be here. I want you to know how much both your pastor and I appreciate being so flexible with your Sunday program. And I think you will be overwhelmed with what this morning has wrought…brought." Jack makes a slight bow, almost shy, not quite. He points to himself, "…brought to you, to your congregation. What you need to know and what you need to appreciate is that your minister, already, never misses a chance to build your congregation. Believe me. Because? Because I'm here. As your newest member!" And when he repeats the, "It's a pleasure," Paul notices that Jack takes a second to stare at Saundra, lest she miss his emphasis on the word, 'pleasure'.

Perhaps it is the extension of Janice's little finger, or the tap of a napkin at the edge of Beenie's smile, or the slight angle of Olga Simmons head, but Paul knows: these women have not been fooled. They are polite, but in no way have they been taken in. They are waiting.

Jack doesn't give up. He continues, "On the way back from our little adventure today, Pastor Paul and I had this discussion about how he can best minister to you. Right, Pastor Paul?" Jack does not wait for Paul to answer. He continues, more boldly now, "Pastor Paul would like to represent you. He'd like to represent you as a way of recruiting more members for this wonderful little congregation. You could always use more members, right?"

Mrs. Entwhistle points to each chair and silently counts, "We'll have to get more chairs...," her voice has the tiniest bite.

"Of course," Jack barely hides his look of disbelief at her comment. But, then no one has challenged the meaning of 'represent you'. Jack takes a deep breath, and continues.

Paul considers stopping Jack, but there seems nothing to lose in letting him keep talking. This is not an easily deceived bunch and Jack will learn that in due time. Paul notices Saundra check a smile and she gives Paul a wink that he thinks sends a message: Saundra is no fool.

Jack reaches for a chair. He turns it and straddles it backwards. He extends his arms as if to encircle the women. He speaks as if he speaks to each, "You see the County Chainsaw Art Competition is next Sunday. Paul qualified today. He more than qualified. He won second place! He should have won first place. The judge was inexperienced. Not up to the sophistication of Paul's carving. Winning second place was like winning first place! In fact," and Jack pauses to be sure everyone is paying close attention, "your minister will likely be in *The Seattle Times*, thanks to Hattie here. She is very interested in the world of 'outsider art,' wonderful art created by artisans with no formal training. Paul qualifies! He more than qualifies! He's a genius at what he does. Right, Pastor Paul?" And before Paul can say anything, Jack continues, his words a rush. "Already people are going to wonder where he preaches. So next Sunday, at the competition we'll have a large sign." Jack's arms spread wider and his voice has a 'wow, aren't we lucky' tone to it. "And, we'll explain exactly where your wonderful chapel is located!"

Paul's head fills with images of snake oil, used cars, and underwater land for sale in Puget Sound. Jack ends with arms outstretched as if he were a conductor, they his orchestra. "Why, with the likes of your minister, my sponsorship, your prayers, I'll take you to the moon!"

It is an expression Paul already hates. He wonders that the women don't turn on Jack, slap him with swinging purses, and make him cower from shame and stupidity. But as he watches the chorus of nodding heads, there is a part of him that wants what Jack is saying to be entirely true. Even as Jack talks, Paul's arms begin to remember the feel of the saw and the anticipation of the competition. As he checks to see how the women are taking this all in, he is astounded to see their faces glowing with the anticipated glory on which Jack has just expounded. Even Saundra's face has softened and her head ever so slightly follows the nodding of the other women.

Jack is not to be stopped. "And with more members, you'll be able to make more improvements. Better lighting! Real pews! With kneelers! A piano, or even an organ. Great, huh?" Now the women shake their heads with assurance and pat each other's hands. Their voices break into small murmurs of pleasure. Paul is amazed.

At just the point where they have finished agreeing with him, Jack stands and pulls Paul up and into the middle of this puddle of good feelings. "Here's what Pastor Paul and I discussed. Are you ready for this? Since next week's competition is near, we thought that all of you, all of us, should go to the fair at Monroe. Kind of like a Sunday service that celebrates the community of believers wherever those believers find themselves! Isn't that right, Paul?"

Paul can't believe he is nodding 'yes'.

Mrs. Bagley pats her hat into place and in the process raises her hand, indicating she has something to say. "Mr. Chain...Jack...this is quite unusual. What will Reverend Cruisewell say?"

Paul's heart feels like it has stopped. Not once all day has he thought of Reverend Cruisewell.

"Reverend Cruisewell...," Paul answers as if he were giving the idea of his boss a great deal of consideration, which at this very moment, he is. Hasn't Jack said he'd cleared today's competition with Cruisewell? Wouldn't Jack have told Cruisewell about the early service? Where was Cruisewell, anyway?

Mrs. McBride's voice stops the answer Paul doesn't have. "He joined us for breakfast, just this morning. He asked about you. We assured him our first service was very...light-hearted...he said he knew all about it and that he would try to get back for this meeting, this very meeting.

Undaunted, Jack interrupts, avoiding Paul's attempt to be in charge. "I'm sure he will think, I *know* he will think, the carving competition is not only unique, but a great, perfect idea for the church."

"The idea *is* unique," exclaims a familiar voice. All eyes turn toward the door. The Reverend Randi Cruisewell continues talking as he walks into the room. He extends a hand to Jack and Jack offers Reverend Cruisewll his chair (which Cruisewell ignores). "Jack, it's good to see you again. Here. In a church. Miracles happen every day." Cruisewell turns to Paul, "My man, my good man, a pleasure to see you with your congregation. He's a peach, isn't he ladies?" The women's heads nod, all smiles, and the room perceptibly loosens, as if they all know Reverend Cruisewell will play things easy and they trust whatever he brings them will be interesting, if not entertaining, if not bright and shiny new, and they have learned to be ready for a mighty fine time. No matter how long a project lasts!

Reverend Cruisewell signals Jack to sit and the Reverend becomes the center of attention. He is dressed in a cream-colored suit with a cream-colored vest. His starched collar is butter yellow and he holds his head erect. His hair still has loft, but Paul notices the high crown of hair is not quite so high or quite so 'airy' as it had looked in Twist. Or maybe it just seems so.

Reverend Cruisewell casts a benign smile around the room. He loosens his yellow-striped tie and spreads the stiff cardboard-like collar. "If you don't mind," he says as if they, like him, would enjoy his comfort, free from the tight constraints of his elegant, unusual attire, "we're like family here, aren't we now?" The ladies murmur 'yes' and Mrs. McBride hands Reverend Cruisewell a brimming cup of tea with two mints.

Holding the cup high as if to draw all eyes to the hand that holds it, Reverend Cruisewell smiles his thanks, and speaks with a voice full of syrup and fine enunciation. "Truth is, we do what's best for the congregation, for everybody. I've chosen Pastor Paul because I trust he is going to do what's best." He looks directly at Paul and says, "For all of us."

Reverend Cruisewell's presence is like glue. The slide of his voice, the manner in which his body leans into the circle of women, the soft edge of his words, the delicate way he sips his tea, his direct stare at Paul and Chainsaw Jack; all these movements and expressions bring the group together. Cruisewell sits the teacup on the altar. He turns to face Paul. He opens his palms as if giving Paul a gift. Paul realizes he's just been handed the reins and he should now take charge. Cruisewell hasn't had to say the words, "All yours," but he has said them. The gift of relinquishing leadership is made clear by the very way he half bows to Paul.

Paul comes to stand in front of his congregation and the day's soreness disappears. He rocks back on his heels, a gesture he remembers from so many weeks ago when Cruisewell entered The Big Drinkers' Bar. Something about the weight on his heels makes him feel as if he's just stepped into a dance and there is no question he will lead.

"If we all agree to the idea of spending the day together next Sunday…as a community…at the county fair, then, Jack, you will take care of transportation. Right?" Paul demands, more than he asks.

Jack nods a slow nod of agreement.

"Once we're at the fair, I will ask that you, dear women…," Paul searches for the next word, "…become buddies. Each of you will choose a partner, create a 'buddy system' like when you were children, each taking care of the other, and…," Paul closes his eyes, he feels sure and confident as he continues, "…take time to look at prize horses and chickens, even the cows, then take time to look at the grange displays and the canned fruits and vegetables."

Paul is on a roll, he feels a little like he feels when he carves. His voice grows in strength. "Your buddy and you will take note of this county fair celebration. The fair is a microcosm of the world. Watch the kids on the rides. Watch the dads and moms glory in the fun of their children. Notice the amount and quality of food that abounds at a fair. Think about this world where people come to share and celebrate what it is to get a blue ribbon for their efforts." Paul thinks the words have slid out with ease. Then he looks up and sees Saundra staring at him. Her eyebrows are raised in wonderment and the roundness of her eyes seems to say, "I can't believe this shit." Paul hurries to finish. "All things for which we are thankful."

Paul holds his breath. Everyone except Saundra smiles encouragement. The odds are in his favor. For the first time he feels like he's come close to doing that for which Criuswell has hired him. He is the real Pastor Paul. He's delivered a sermon and the congregation has returned to him a whole spectrum of responses: belief and pleasure all the way to the unuttered cry of 'bullshit'. Paul thinks this is probably what being a minister must be all about. It doesn't feel all that bad. Except for the one obvious nonbeliever.

Jack stands. He steps beside Paul, just as Reverend Cruisewell walks to Paul's other side. Jack says, "And of course, most important, we all need to give Pastor Paul our full support. At the chainsaw competition you'll see something beyond unusual. You'll see magnificence! Your minister has a gift. A rare gift and, given that gift, I have no doubt he will win first prize. A metaphor for life, I'm sure."

"Amazing," Reverend Cruisewell says as if he's just said, 'amen'. But, being Reverend Cruisewell, he continues to speak, "I think you both have convinced us of the rightness of next Sunday. I plan on joining you for the day. What with my limo and Grandma Bella's Fairlane, Paul's Jeep, and your rig, Jack, we won't have to worry about additional transportation."

"Loaves and fishes," Jack intones.

"Loaves and fishes," Reverend Cruisewell echoes. Cruisewell lays a hand on Jack's shoulder. The Reverend says in a confident tone, "I always knew you could have been a minister, Jack. But I think the right choice has been made. You stick to selling saws."

The room grows silent. A huge smile plays across Saundra's face. Paul tries to figure out what has pleased her, taken her from skeptic to just short of being a participant in all of this craziness. It surprises him to see her smile directed more at the diminutive form of Cruisewell rather than at the leering, interested Jack.

All in all, it appears any hesitation about the appropriateness of next Sunday's service/outing/whatever one wants to call it, has disappeared. Questions have settled as silently and sure as dust motes.

Except Sam. Sam runs up to Paul, grabs a leg, and with wide eyes inquires, "You never 'splained about the 'welcome alligator.'"

"Well, my boy, the explanation about a 'welcome alligator' is directly related to the 'welcome bear'. So, next Sunday, I'll not just tell you the answer. I'll show you the answer. Next Sunday you will see all the welcome bears you'll ever want to see in your whole life and you will understand what a unique and wonderful thing a 'welcome alligator' can be. Is."

"And," Jack adds, "You will appreciate this alligator even more because Pastor Paul carved it. He carved it and he has my permission to donate it to your chapel."

Sam's face puckers as if he is trying to sort out what has just been 'splained'. Suzie stage whispers in Sam's ear, "It's okay, Sam. Have faith. What's happening all depends on faith." She looks up at Paul. "Right, Pastor Paul?" All Paul hears is Suzie channeling Saundra's sarcasm. He shakes his head, but it seems to him everything is back to crazy and he hasn't an inkling how everything has happened, or will happen. But, everyone seems to be in good spirits, the widows are all a-flutter about next Sunday's trip, and Reverend Cruisewell seems pleased with what has transpired. The twins pass more tea and lace cookies and Mrs. McBride stacks used plates while Jack slips around the group of women to help Saundra stand. With that, the meeting seems to have adjourned itself.

Jack and Saundra leave together. Over the tops of the chattering women Paul catches, with surprise, Reverend Cruisewell standing alone, his eyes soulful, staring at the open door where Jack and Saundra have just left. Paul thinks he sees on Cruisewell's face a frown, or a flash of sadness, or envy, or doubt, or at the very least, wistfulness.

Grandma Bella interrupts his speculation. "Your sponsor? Jack? Do you think my daughter and he just might deserve each other?"

Paul, so taken with the unexpected droop in Cruisewell's usually manic demeanor, hasn't an answer for Grandma Bella. He follows her gaze and sees; she too, is watching the slightly forlorn Reverend Cruisewell.

"I think those two deserve each other," says Grandma Bella and before he can ask, "Which two?" Mrs. McBride, has come to Paul to offer the last two cookies. Paul looks for Sam or Suzie to send Mrs. McBride to offer the children these last two goodies. He erases the idea, when he sees Suzie stuffing the empty beer can deep inside a sack she is using to collect the paper napkins the women have left with their empty tea cups. With enthusiasm and no appetite Paul accepts the cookies. He chews and can't shake the sadness he's just seen on the face of the usually jovial, upbeat Cruisewell. It is not lost on Paul that this day is beginning to feel like a day everyone is hiding things: the beer can, the sadness, the lack of a real service, choices Saundra appears to be making. The only blatant, unhidden actions are Jack's—lustful, greedy, and intent on a buck. If ministering is about truth, if his life's about being a minister, who in this crowd is doing the better job? There is no doubt in Paul's mind. Jack is blatantly the better minister.

As if the Reverend has become aware of Paul's scrutiny and confusion, Cruisewell strides across the room, his face, once again, bright with good cheer. His hand extends to Paul. "Congratulations. It's been one great day."

Paul winces at the handshake. He knows he should say something. He should explain the trajectory of the day. Why there was no service. No real service.

Reverend Cruisewell speaks as if he's read Paul's mind. "No need to explain. Everything works for the best. We have a unique ministry here and you just might have found a unique way to serve it." Cruisewell turns to Grandma Bella, "I'd better get going, Bella, it's been a pleasure seeing you again. Always a pleasure seeing your...," again Paul thinks he hears a sliver of sadness in Cruisewell's voice, "...family." Cruisewell tucks his arm in the crook of Grandma Bella's arm and walks her towards the door. "I think the women are making a nice transition from aerobics, don't you think?" he asks.

Grandma Bella chuckles and pats Cruisewell's hand, "Reverend Cruisewell, I think we need to make this project a little more permanent than the last."

"I try..."

"I know you try. We're all going to try a little harder."

As they leave Paul thinks he hears Grandma Bella say, "I'd like you to try a little harder with that daughter of mine," but the more he thinks that's what she said, the more he can't quite remember her words. Paul is having a hard time patching the day together and placing the right feelings with the right people.

Jack bounds through the door. "Paul! Thanks for the great day!" He beams. "I think I'm going to like this church thing."

"Such a change of heart," Paul says, sarcasm unchecked.

"Well, not only is your congregation interesting, but it dawned on me that by leaving the alligator here, I'm better off."

"How's that?"

"A donation. A charitable donation. From my business to your church!"

With that Jack waves a carefree goodbye and he is out the door. "Taxes!" and he pumps his arm.

Jack lopes across the trailer court and swings up into his rig. He waves to Paul. He waves to Saundra. Paul didn't miss the fact that Jack sucked in his gut from the chapel door to the door of his rig.

31

A CONVERSATION WITH SAUNDRA

Paul stretches out, corner to corner in his bed, half asleep, half awake. His muscles jump. In the dark, the clock glows two-thirty. He replays the day. Not a huge success, but not a huge failure, either. Next Sunday rolls back and forth in his brain. He lets images of what he might carve flip through his head: birds, whales, mice, griffins. The longer he contemplates a menagerie of images, the more they double on top of each other until he has ostriches with four legs in hip boots, raccoons with top hats and walking canes, snakes with silver spurs. The images jump around and the more awake he becomes the more his mind buzzes and the more his arms ache. A pinging pain shoots down his hips and into his legs. He rubs the arch of his right foot against the calf of his left leg. He rubs his arms. His hands hurt. His whole body reminds him how out of shape he is.

Paul flips back the curtain above his head. Outside a silent fog cups the trailers. Using elbows for support, Paul watches the silence, lets the animal images drift away. The fog glows white in filtered moonlight.

A rattle of gravel pulls his attention to the path. Through the bent flower heads, a squirrel scurries, pulling a branch twice its size. The branch catches on some invisible thing. The squirrel tugs and pulls and yanks and, at that moment Paul begins to wonder if he shouldn't pull himself out of bed to help the little guy. Just then half of the branch breaks loose and the squirrel slips out of sight. Half of his treasure is left behind. Half of the treasure is his reward. Paul laughs out-loud, aware of the comparison between him and that tough little squirrel. Half of a treasure isn't all that bad. But by now, sleep has entirely disappeared.

Paul pulls on his pants and a sweatshirt, opens the new six-pack, and with beer can in hand heads to the chapel. Inside he rummages until he finds a number ten tin can and a pair of scissors. In the semi-dark, Paul cuts a cluster of asters and geraniums. Back inside the chapel he places the flowers on the altar, lights the votive candles, and then plays with the newly installed dimmer switch. Less light makes the worst of everything fade: stacked boxes in corners, the gardening tools along one wall, assorted clay pots, and half-filled bags of potting soil.

Paul pulls up a chair for his feet. With legs stretched, the cold beer in one hand, Paul looks around the room. There is something sweet about the incongruity of the chapel, garage, shed, storehouse. He closes his eyes. The slight scent of cinnamon from the burning candles makes him think of his mom at the Monarch baking snicker-doodles. For the moment, Paul slips into a rummy sleep, feeling blessed, and mellow.

"Hi! Want some company?" a voice punches into his reverie.

Paul jumps, knocking the chair over. Saundra stands at the door. She has traded her crutches for a black cane with a gold top. She is wearing a black satin jumpsuit. The sleeves are like huge loopy balloons gathered at the wrist. Her waist is encircled with a red, sparkly belt. She hoists her leg over the doorsill and Paul can see how the full-legged material helps to hide her cast. The satin materials slither, making a sexy sound as she maneuvers into the room.

"Be my guest," Paul says and places two chairs for her. When she's seated he leans towards her, the beer extended, "Be glad to share."

"Thanks, I'll pass. I've just had all the lutefisk and cider I could consume. It was part of the payment for playing at the Scandinavian Brotherhood." Saundra stretches her arms over her head, the black of her sleeves silhouettes the curled braids of her hair. She opens and closes her fingers. "It's been a long night. I didn't think people would request the 'Beer Barrel Polka' that many times." Saundra sighs and lets her arms drop. "It's a hell of a way to make a living."

"You make a living?"

"It's an expression. Things could be worse."

"But, you manage?"

"With the help of my friends. My mother, precisely. Thank God." She looks up to see if she has offended Paul. "Sorry, that just slipped out."

"What?"

"The expression. Thank God. I didn't want to offend you, so I said, excuse me."

Paul laughs, "Geeze, I'll never get used to this idea of being a minister. I didn't even hear you say 'God.'" Paul sips his beer. "You've got to realize, I've just come from the woods and a crew of loggers that compost the air with worse words."

Saundra chuckles as she stretches her leg on the empty chair. She pushes her braids loose from her hair and lets her head fall back. Her neck is long and glows white in the light of the candles. When she sits up, she reaches for the beer, "Just one little sip. Then, I've got to get some sleep." She hands the beer back to Paul. "You are the strangest thing Cruisewell has come up with, you know. He's crazy, but you must be crazier to have agreed to whatever it is he's had you agree to." Saundra laughs and a large braid falls into her hand. "God, that feels good. These folks demand big wigs and big boobs. Ooops. Sorry. It sure doesn't feel like I'm sitting here in a church talking to a minister."

Paul asks, "You know Cruisewell…well…then?"

"Randi? Sure. Randi has offered to save me from 'all of this'. A couple of times."

"Meaning?"

"Well, I thought he meant marriage, but we never pursue the subject. He gets all shy and crazy around me and we never seem get to the heart of the matter. He never gets explicit. I'm a bit gun-shy myself and part of me worries I'd just be another one of his hair-brained projects and…"

Paul finishes the beer and knows he's just been included in Saundra's description.

She looks up. "Oh, sorry. Again. Didn't mean to group you with all the rest. But Cruisewell's Cruisewell. It's hard not to get caught up in his 'smiley face' kind of schemes. He is one crazy fuck…er. Oh, god, there I go again. I've got some work to do on my language."

"You've never taken him up on his offer…or his almost offer?"

"Lord, no. One, he dresses like a drag queen. Two, he's crazy. And three, mostly, I don't think he means it. The proposals. The almost proposals. It's hard to figure out what he does mean."

"You're not building my confidence. He's my boss, remember."

Saundra winks a slow, smiling wink, "You want I should build your confidence?"

Paul tries not to blush. Tries to look cool. Nonchalant. Like ladies say things like that to him all of the time. He fidgets with the beer bottle. Rolls it back and forth in his hands. Coughs. Pulls at the leg of his jeans. Stands. Walks over to the light switch like he needed to do something to it. With the edge of a dime he begins to unscrew the light plate on the wall like it needed unscrewing. He has the distinct wish that Grandma Bella might come checking on her daughter.

The silence is making him nuts. "You've got a great mom."

Saundra pushes herself up with her cane. She laughs, twirling the braid wig, "Paul, don't worry. That 'come-on' was a joke. I like the fact you're a minister. Ministers are always a challenge. Besides, I'm exhausted. Got to go." She gives Paul's arm a pinch, a little tweak. "I didn't mean to embarrass you."

Paul pulls out the wires he'd just wired yesterday and reworks the electrician's tape. "No. I really did have to finish this job."

"Finish? At three o'clock in the morning?" Saundra asks, her voice with an edge of unease. "Don't take my come-ons for come-ons. It's residual stuff from playing to a group of crazed old men all evening…people say things they don't mean and I was just…"

"…and I'm just another crazy old man."

Saundra bursts out laughing. "Don't try that, 'oh poor me' stuff! You don't seem to have much trouble keeping the ladies away. All in all, I'd say you've had a pretty good first week. I can't think of anyone who isn't pleased you're here. Even Jack. Maybe, especially Jack."

Paul leans against the wall. Saundra leans against the doorjamb. For a minute, a fraction of a minute, Paul feels at ease with Saundra. No come-on. No come-hither anything. Just two friends talking.

Paul decides to take a chance. "Given everything, it has been a good week. There's one serious thing I want to tell you. Something I think you need to hear." Paul waits until he's sure Saundra is listening then he says, "You've got great kids."

"You've had more time with them lately than I have."

"Yeah, that's too bad. Good for me. Not so good for you. Suzie and Sam miss you. A lot."

Saundra steps out into the night as they talk. She stops, her head thrust back. Paul looks up at the sky, clear now with a spray of stars just visible through the feathered fog.

"Sammy's such a baby, still. I try to be a good mother. Now, Suzie. She quit needing a mom about ten years ago."

"She's only ten."

Saundra sighs, a small catch in her voice, "I know. I'm her mom, remember. A fact that does not please Suzie."

"You've not got it right. She thinks you don't like her."

"Love her. She thinks I don't love her. She tells me a dozen times in a dozen ways. Primarily, she won't let me touch her. Once, she was as cuddly and sweet as Sam. No more."

"She's an interesting child," Paul says.

"That's a unique way of putting it. It isn't like I want to be on the road ten months of the year." Saundra turns to Paul and says, "Think of it this way. When was the last time you went to hear an accordion player?"

Paul can't think of a good response.

Saundra takes a few steps toward her mom's trailer. She says to the sky, or to Paul, or to the night, "There isn't a whole lot of demand for accordion players."

"I'll walk you back to your trailer."

Saundra laughs a hooty laugh, "Ten more steps and I'll be there. When I get there, I'll wave and you'll know I'm safe."

Paul ignores her words and walks beside her. "Suzie can't be angry for her whole life."

"Oh? Look at me and my mom," Saundra says.

"Doesn't look that bad."

Saundra shrugs. "Comes and goes. Hard when you have to share the same pull-out bed."

Their feet crunch through the gravel. Frogs croak, crickets chirp. Saundra stops. Paul holds his breath. He looks down at Saundra's mouth. She does have a nice mouth. And just at that second Annabelle Lee fills his head and he feels like a juggler or a trapeze artist or a...

Saundra is in the middle of saying something, "...I pushed myself to the edge of the bed. I let out this long wail as I lost hold. Then I let out this rosary of words. Something like, 'Oh, shit, oh shit, oh shit.'"

"Your mom was not pleased."

"Right. My mother told me, no way, no how, would that kind of language be used in her house. She threatened to wash my mouth out with soap."

"Sounds like a mother."

"I looked at her, she looked at me, and we both burst out laughing. Then she said I was probably a little old for that, and I said she was a little old for that too. The next thing, she's into a long diatribe about how she isn't old at all! Her vehemence gave me pause."

"Which meant what?"

"She asked me to guess where she went the night before while I was at work. Guess where she was?"

"With Big Bill Dumpster playing Bingo."

"You know!"

"Just one of those things the kids mentioned."

Saundra groans. "This is not easy having a mother who's having more dates than I am. Anyhow, then she said it would be nice if I didn't call him Big Bill Dumpster, but called him by his real name. I asked just what that might be and she said, 'William Grosse'. I got the giggles so hard I almost peed. I asked if there was something she'd soon be announcing."

"You're thinking it's getting serious?"

"No one should eat that many meals at someone's table without being serious. So I asked her, 'Like an engagement? Like a big party?' She got all fidgety. All concerned. She suggested we drop the subject."

"Concerned?"

"Well, when I say party, she hears 'drinking' and no matter how I try to tell her I haven't got a problem anymore, she doesn't believe me."

"I shouldn't have offered you the beer?"

"Oh, I can handle it. Most times. But she then mused how the trailer court seemed to attract people with drinking problems."

"Who's that?" Paul asks.

Saundra looks down at the beer can in Paul's hand.

Incredulous, he asks, "Me?"

"Right. You. She's worried about you."

"No, no way!" Paul exclaims. He thinks how good he's been since The Big Drinkers' Bar. He hasn't had any whiskey in weeks. A few beers, but not that many. A little wine with Grandma Bella.

"She does notice such things. Maybe we could start our own twelve-step program. Another activity for the trailer court."

"Saundra, no way. First, I haven't got a problem. Second, I've got lots of things on my mind, like this crazy ministry thing. Beer helps. But not a lot of beer. Whatever your mother thinks, I don't have a problem."

"Whatever you say, Pastor Paul. But I did not miss the fact that Suzie found the beer can in the pulpit. Generously gave it to her brother. He turns them in for pennies at the Mini-Mart. You've increased his stash. Dramatically."

They stand in front of Grandma Bella's Airstream. Saundra swings herself up on the first step. Eye-level with Paul she leans over and kisses him on the cheek. "You're a good man, Charlie Brown."

Paul waits until the door closes and the light inside is turned off. He places the beer can on the step for Sam. Last one. At least for awhile. He can stop drinking any time.

32

MOVING RIGHT ALONG

The next morning Paul wakes sore. Every muscle aches. His arms feel like sprung rubber bands. He drifts back to sleep and wakes to a persistent bang of small knocks at his door.

"Pastor Paul? Pastor Paul?" Sam calls.

Paul turns over, drags the covers over his head.

"I need to talk to you!"

Paul moans.

"It's important, Pastor Paul," he begs.

"Sure, sure," Paul mumbles and pulls on his jeans. His hands fumble under the bed for his boots. "Come on in, buddy."

Sam's head peaks around the half open door. His eyes appear serious and his usual smile is set in a grim 'we need to talk' expression.

"Important, huh?"

Sam holds his finger out to help Paul tie the bow at the top of his boot. "Grandma Bella is 'set'," Sam's voice disappears into the collar of his jean jacket.

Paul put his head down next to Sam's. "Want to repeat that?"

"…Upset…"

"Want to take a walk? Talk about it?"

Paul closes the door behind them and takes Sam's hand. The air is crisp. A sheet of dew on the grass gives way to their footprints as they cross the grass circle in the center of the court. Sam steps slowly. Paul matches his pace.

"Well, why don't you tell me about it."

From inside his coat pocket, Sam pulls a crumpled beer can. He hands it to Paul.

The sharp edges of the aluminum are both cold and cruel while at the same time the surface soothes Paul's tender hands. He cups the can wishing somehow, magician-like, he could make it disappear. He can guess what Sam is going to say. He knows what Grandma Bella must have said. He can even hear Saundra trying to explain that it was 'only a swallow' and Grandma Bella having none of it.

"Want to tell me the whole catastrophe?" Paul asks not realizing how much he doesn't want to hear the sadness and concern of a five-year-old. This is worse than any 'talkin' to' Elsie had ever bestowed upon him.

"Your big trouble, Pastor Paul?"

Paul kneels beside Sam and decides to hit this problem straight on. "Grandma Bella said I was trouble?"

"Not 'sactly. She said Mommy had better not ever, never ever, ever come into our trailer again with liquor on her voice and when Mom said it was just a swallow and Grandma Bella asked where did one get just one swallow and she said in the chapel and then she said she was going to give you a talkin' to and you better change your ways. Or else."

They walk a few more steps. Close to the arched entrance of the trailer court Paul can see Suzie waiting for the school bus. She does not turn to acknowledge their voices.

Sam, face up, the small space between his eyes a gathered bump of concern, asks, "What you gonna do, Pastor Paul?"

"Change my ways, I'd guess."

"Better tell Grandma Bella."

"That, too."

Sam's face dissolves into a radiant smile. "Good!"

The school bus pulls around the bend and stops.

"We'll need to tell your sister," Paul says.

"Oh, sure!" Sam says and he reaches up for a hug.

Paul feels the soft curl of Sam's hands on his back and he breathes hard to keep the tears back.

"Time to go eat my breakfast," Sam says. He leaves Paul's arms, runs backwards and waves his hands shouting, "Hey! Hey! Hey!" to Paul.

Paul waves back. "Hey, hey, hey!"

As the bus pulls away, Paul looks to see Suzie's face. She watches from the window. She doesn't wave. She turns away.

In need of succor, Paul heads for Rex's.

33

WITH THE BOYS

The walk does its stuff. The air is fall-crisp. In the distance the Cascades cut a white jigsaw silhouette in the bleached blue sky. Across the road a dog barks and is answered by Canadian geese slapping wings overhead. As Paul walks into the parking lot of Rex's, Big Bill Dumpster pulls up in his Dodge Dart.

He calls, "Pastor Paul! Hear you came in second with your alligator!" He joins Paul at the door. "Saw that mean lookin' thing in the grass. Didn't run over it."

"Better not. It's Jack's tax write-off."

Paul holds the door for Bill and accepts the outstretched paw of a handshake. "Good job." A half-dozen regulars call greetings. Paul and Big Bill swing legs over the stools at the counter. Rex pushes the bristle brush over the grill one last time, wipes his hands on his apron, and slaps menus in front of Paul and Bill. "What'll it be?" Rex asks.

"Usual for me," Bill answers.

Paul checks the menu. He is surprised to see the first item offered is in fact, 'The Usual: Rex's own pie of the day'.

"Me, too. The Usual."

"Rex does make it easy," Bill says and stirs cream into the coffee.

"So, how did your first service go? I hear there was a lusty amount of singing. Lusty, in the best of meanings! If I'd known you were just going to sing, I'd have shown up," Rex says wiping the counter.

"And if we hadn't *just* sung?"

"I've spent a whole life of people telling me what to do, and not to offend you, you seem a little young to know much about what's to be done with the likes of me."

Paul, coffee spoon in hand, palms up, makes a gesture of surrender.

"You're right. Maybe, if I can keep things on the track we're headed, I'll never have to preach."

Rex places slabs of rhubarb and apricot pie in front of them. "Sounds like my kind of church," he says with a pleased chuckle and pushes the napkin dispenser between the two men. "You sound like my kind of minister," he adds. "That is, if I was looking for one."

Bill leans back to look at Paul. Paul doesn't flinch under Bill's disbelieving gaze. "If you don't ever preach, what is it you're going to do?"

"Beats me. I'm figuring it out as I go."

"When you've got it figured out, let me know. I hate passing up an opportunity to keep company with those ladies." Bill rubs his hands energetically. He picks up his fork. "Especially Grandma B. Ummm. Ummm. So good."

Paul wonders, but doesn't ask, if the compliment is for Grandma Bella or the pie.

"Rex? What about you?" Bill asks.

"I'm too old. For both ladies and preaching."

"Never too old. Just look at me."

"That's exactly what I mean. I look at you. I look at that bunch...great bunch...don't get me wrong. I just don't want to be a wife to any one of them. They see you can cook, they want you to cook all the time. I know. I've been there. I'll stay single."

A huge explosion of laughter escapes Bill. "Rex! I didn't say you should go over there and get yourself a bride! You go over there for a little company. A little socializing. It'd do you good." Bill raises his empty cup to Rex. "Don't know what you're missin'. For instance, next Sunday we're all going to the county fair. You should come along."

Paul pushes the edge of his fork through the pie. He doesn't blink. He doesn't look away from the pie to let Bill see his unexpected pleasure at the additional invitation. His pleasure is interrupted when Big Bill nudges Paul and announces, "Oh, I got a message for you. Grandma Bella wants to see you. This morning. Didn't say what. Maybe the kids. She sounded serious."

Paul swallows and something slips down wrong and he begins to choke. Bill pounds his back. Rex hands him a glass of water. A few swallows later, a few thuds on his back later, Paul recovers. While he finishes his pie, all he can think is that if he doesn't get back to the trailer court to talk to Grandma Bella, sometime soon, there might not be Bill's company or Rex's company or anybody's company at the fair. He knows he has to come up with an extraordinary drinking promise for Grandma Bella. He lifts his cup to Rex's full pot of coffee.

Bill continues to work on Rex to join them at the fair. "You're closed, right? Nothing to do. Sit around here and pick your nose. Get fat. Fatter. Watch television. Drink beer." Bill looks at Paul, then back to Rex. "Come on along."

Paul rubs his belly. He feels an inch of fat. And the beer remark? Was the beer remark meant just for Rex or for both of them? Had Grandma Bella already talked to Bill about last night?

Rex removes the pie plates, offers more coffee. He looks as if he is giving Bill's invitation consideration. He looks at Paul.

Paul answers Rex's stare. "Come! The more, the better. Especially more guys. Even Cruisewell's going."

"Randi Cruisewell? That's right. I forgot you're another one of his screwy ideas!" Rex cuts himself a piece of pie, leans back against the cooler, talks with his fork, "Now, the one that worried me the most was that cooking instructor. I thought my Friday night business might never come back."

"And?" Paul asks.

"He didn't last. Alphonse was a bit too much for everyone. The week after he left, the women were back for the Friday night waffle's group. All eight of them. They come here to eat. And to flirt." Rex chews contemplatively. "So, yeah, a day at the fair. I can handle that."

Bill slaps Paul on the back. "All right! Add another to your list. Does it cost to go?"

"Cost?" Paul asks.

"You know, like a registration fee?"

"Well, there's a ticket to buy to get in and then whatever corn-dogs and stuff you eat."

"You're missing a bet here, Paul. Think of a registration fee. How're you going to finance this 'ministry' thing if you don't get back some money? Unless Cruisewell picks up the tab indefinitely. Doubt that. He never sets these things for 'indefinitely.'"

Paul's shoulders slump. "No one should pay for what I'm doing. Suzie and Sam passed a basket yesterday. It was embarrassing. Nothing I've done, so far, warrants money. And you're right. Cruisewell assumes at some point this project will get off the ground."

"That's what he says. But everything dies before it gets a chance to even see the cusp of 'off the ground.'" Rex wiggles his fork, a few pie crumbs cling to the end of it. "Maybe Cruisewell doesn't mean it. The way he throws money at things, my guess is he'd throw more money if you asked."

"Be thankful you've got Cruisewell, and Rex is right. For now, just ride it out."

"Tell me what you know about Cruisewell," Paul asks. "About his money."

"If you don't know, then you know about as much as we know. We all speculate. No one seems to know where he gets it. No one knows why he's focused on this trailer court. We don't fight him...we sit and watch. It's been going on for a couple of years. It's a great mystery. My theory is I think he's got more money than sense and he's lonesome."

"Has anyone got stung?" Paul asks.

"Not yet! But then there's always a first time!" Bill laughs. Then he swallows wrong and the three of them go through the water and back pounding routine again.

"Before we all choke to death, I better head out." Paul places a five-dollar bill on the counter. "I'll see you...Sunday morning. For sure?"

"Ab-so-lute-ly. See you, Pastor Paul," Rex calls as the door closes behind him.

It sounds to Paul that Bill might have laughed, or maybe it was Rex, but he feels too good to take it other than being with guys again, having a place to be. A place where things feel easy.

And now? Now he's stalled long enough. Grandma Bella waits.

34

THE TALK

Outside, Paul stretches and breathes in the ripe coming-on-fall air as he walks to the trailer court. The curled dusty leaves of a twisted crab apple tree give off a sour cider smell so pungent it hits the back of his throat. Above him jet contrails bisect the sky. A cottonwood drops curled brown tendrils in a slow, sloppy fashion. He walks, kicking leaves, his fingers tucked into his belt and he's aware of the slightest tummy bulge. He worries about going soft and tries not to think about what waits for him at Grandma Bella's. He passes the arch. Continues his walk. For exercise. For time. To think. A half-mile later he's better. Feels he can face most anything.

When he gets back to the trailer court, his ease vanishes. Grandma Bella, in the center of the circle, pulls dead flowers. Beside her a plastic bag bulges with throwaways. A few fluorescent orange pompom dahlias stand as reminders that summer has passed.

Slowly, Paul walks the edge of the curved flowerbed. Grandma Bella looks up. She doesn't smile. She doesn't raise her clawed digging tool in greeting. She pushes her gloved hands against her knees. She stands and waits for him to walk to her. The slap of the gloves against each other causes dust puffs to explode. This is business.

"Hi," he says and waits.

Grandma Bella looks him up and down. Paul sucks in air, pulls in his gut, stands tall, tries to appear ready for whatever she has to give.

Grandma Bella slaps the gloves for a second time.

"About last night…" Paul begins.

"Yes. About last night." Her words are terse.

"It was just a swallow. Honest. Saundra took just a swallow."

"That's been covered. Settled. But, another problem…." Grandma Bella picks up the plastic garbage bag and twists a plastic tie around its neck, swift and sure and tight. "Saundra is not the only problem." She hands the bag to Paul, which he takes for some reason as a good sign. He follows her to the garbage cans by the arch. Grandma Bella continues to speak, "Saundra will do what she will do. But she has rules for living with me. She knows the liquor rule. There's no further discussion needed. For her."

Grandma Bella lifts the garbage lid. Paul drops the bag inside.

"My concern is Sammy."

Paul is taken back by the words. Grandma Bella's tack is not what he thought it would be. Grandma Bella's fingers rest lightly on Paul's shirt front. "While you're about capturing hearts…Sammy's I'm speaking of…I'm going to tell you just once. By him you do the right thing. You keep his heart whole. You figure that out. You do the right thing. You be honorable and you do good by him!"

Paul holds the words. He wonders not just what she means, but whom she means. Were her words a secret message about Saundra? Was 'doing the right thing' code for 'being honorable', which was code for 'becoming Sam's father?' Paul's eyes hurt. Something in what has just been said frightens him so much his kneecaps feel disconnected.

"Okay?" she asks.

Paul nods. He's agreed to something but he doesn't know what.

"Now, how about some lunch?" Grandma Bella reaches over and pats Paul's middle. "You going to do something about attracting women, like that sweet Annabelle Lee, you better not let that middle get any bigger! I've got a good healthy soup simmering. Follow me." And then she turns and says, words like bullets, "My suggestion? No more liquor."

"Sure."

"No I mean it. No more liquor."

That's it! Lecture over. Her last words have hit him hard. The rhubarb apricot pie is still rattling around in his gut. He understands it is not Saundra. He understands it is no more liquor. The rest is code.

In the trailer, Saundra works at the dinette table, a pile of brochures and scribbled notes in front of her. She is wrapped in peach colored sweats, her hair pulled back with a huge tortoise comb, its tines trace furrows through her hair. She looks like a luscious fresh fruit. Cantaloupe. Or mango, maybe. If Annabelle Lee weren't forever interrupting his thoughts, Saundra would be more than interesting.

"Hi!" she calls and raises her arms to her mother. Grandma Bella gives her a hug. "My little girl. How're you doin'? How'd you sleep?"

And Paul watches, astounded. What about the concern over last night? What happened to the lecture? The penance? This was no family confrontation he could have imagined. Paul looks from one woman to the other. He's filled with awe. Where is the edge? Where is the sulk? The anger? He thinks of Bear. Every blow-up in the cabin had gone on for hours, sometimes days. Silence was a battering ram that slammed against walls and dishes and bodies. Silence consumed air. Silence made his throat ache and his eyes heavy. As Paul watches the two women, he has a great urge to ask, "Hey? What's going on? You're supposed to have a knock-down drag-out verbal battle and everyone feels bad and pledges to do better and asks forgiveness."

Instead, Grandma Bella has given Saundra a hug and a kiss on the cheek and is now busy stirring an enormous pot of soup and Saundra has pushed aside the papers she's been working on to make room for Paul at the eating nook. "Welcome!" she says. "You okay?"

Grandma Bella heads down the hall. She calls back to Saundra, "Don't let the soup boil, sweetie! I'll be right back."

"Woodshed that bad?" Saundra asks and gives Paul a conspiratorial smile.

Paul must have looked even more confused.

"The woodshed talk. Mom had her little talk with you, didn't she?"

"She did."

"You okay?"

"Yeah...sure...," Paul feels like a bad swimmer in a very deep swimming hole with steep, slippery sides.

"Don't worry. She won't bring it up again."

"She won't have to."

"Good." Saundra stands at the stove, turns the dial, and blue flames recede from the bottom of the cast iron pot. She points to the loaf of French bread. Paul takes the cue. He stands and pulls a knife from the rack, brings the cutting board back to the table, and he slices the bread into flat ovals. He is pleased the dreaded conversation has come and gone. He needs to figure out what "it" is, that is not going to be brought up again.

Sam brings a pile of books and Paul becomes the designated reader. He can think of nothing more that he would rather do. He wonders if this is part of being the minister. Whatever, he reads from *Big Dump Truck*. Reading fills time and the snuggled body of Sam feels great.

Over lunch, Saundra pushes her brochures and charts to the side and fills out a calendar for Grandma Bella, noting her 'gigs,' her times, her bars. Three days she schedules RMC.

"Randi McArthur Cruisewell?" Paul asks.

To answer his curious stare, Saundra explains she is helping Cruisewell do a study of sites in Washington State. Loss of jobs. Increase in taverns. Number of religious organizations. Active social services. Timber. "And, I'll be looking into summer camps. For families. Are there any? And if not, what are the possibilities? And…"

Paul's thinks Saundra's list will go on forever. His head begins to pound. His eyes feel like the light is too bright. He must have squinted, because Grandma Bella insists he drink a thimble-size glass of plum brandy. Paul hopes it isn't some kind of 'liquor' test, but the size of the glass and the swallow of liquor are definitely in the 'medicinal' category. Before the tiny amount of liquor eases the tiniest number of his neck muscles, Grandma Bella assures him the liquor 'this time,' is an antidote. She explains, "The primary reason for having a bottle of home-made plum brandy around is for situations like this: headaches or toasting." Paul couldn't have agreed more.

Lunch ends. Sammy takes a nap. Grandma Bella turns her laser attention on Paul. She asks, "And this afternoon? What have you planned for this afternoon?"

"I thought I'd review those lessons. Follow your daughter's example— make some lists. Later I thought I might try to find a health club. Any place near?" Grandma Bella hands Paul the yellow pages. "Go. Go do your homework!"

And so the week passes. Paul studies. Twice he has dinner with Grandma Bella, Big Bill, and the kids. Early morning at Rex's becomes a routine. He takes long walks and gets to know clerks in grocery stores, mini marts, and coffee houses. He finds a local YMCA, but no aerobic classes. On telephone poles he checks advertisements. It's all a stall. Finally he goes by the hot house and the gallery where Annabelle Lee has her show. He never finds her there. He stands outside her house, but not for long, fearful neighbors will think he's up to no good. Finally, on Friday he leaves a note on her front door to remind her about Sunday morning. And then he hopes.

That night, after a dessert of tiramisu, he and Big Bill list the women and who each will ride with Sunday morning. He includes Annabelle Lee's name and he continues to hope.

Dinner over, Saundra offers to walk Paul half way home to be sure he's safe.

"Safe?" Paul asks before he realizes it's a companionable joke.

Outside, half way across the court Paul states, "Your Mom said something and I haven't a clue what she means. Maybe you know."

"Sure, give it a try. I'm not always sure what Mom means."

"She said, 'keep Sammy's heart whole'. Sounds more like she's warning me about you!"

Saundra gives a hooting laugh. "That's my mom. She thinks every man is after me. Or that I'm after every man. She worries that someone nice like you comes along, and she can see you're not just flipping over me, and she worries that Sammy will fall in love with you, not me, and he'll get his heart broken. So, dear friend, if you can, become his very best uncle. That'll do it."

"That's it?"

"That's it. You'll see. Grandma Bella protects us all. Particularly Sammy. But, you'll see. When the moment comes, she'll also be protecting you. She'll tell me, 'Keep Paul's heart whole.'"

"Does it feel strange to you? That saying? I thought maybe it meant more."

"More? Like what?"

"Like, I don't know. Marrying you or something."

"Oh, Paul. She's a mom. She's just there to protect. Everyone. Like moms do. I'm freezing! Got to run. It's just a sign she loves you, already! Enjoy it. She's a great mom!"

Paul thinks about it as he walks the last few steps to his door. His whole heart envies Saundra, Sammy, and Suzie.

35

AN EPISODE AT THE PARK

Saturday morning, there is a persistent pint-sized knocking on the door. Paul gladly pushes away his pile of lessons.

Suzie and Sam are all smiles, all energy. "It's a no-school day!" Sam explains holding Suzie's hand up by way of explanation. "Grandma said we can go to the park! Wanna come?"

"It's just on the other side of the alders," Suzie points to the row of trees to the east of the arch.

"Swing the swings!" Sam adds.

Paul grabs his jean jacket. "Lead the way!"

Each child grabs a hand and pulls Paul down the path on the backside of the trailer court.

"It's good you agreed," says Sam. "We couldn't go unless you said yes." His fingers wrap around Paul's and his face turns up to give Paul a break-your-heart smile.

"I'm pleased you thought to ask me," Paul responds. He can't remember being happier. His hand gives Sam's an extra squeeze. Sam telegraphs back and skips beside Paul, scuffing rocks in front of them.

Three blocks further Paul, Suzie, and Sam scramble through a patch of faded blackberries and come out on the edge of a baseball diamond. On the far side of the long narrow park, Paul is surprised to see the red brick of Annabelle Lee's studio. The close proximity amazes and pleases him. Aware of the short cut, maybe later he'll walk over to see if she is there.

But, for the moment, there is swinging to do.

"Push me!" Suzie calls and slips onto the smoothly worn seat of the swing. Paul stands behind Suzie, each swing pushing her a bit higher. Suzie's legs stretch in front of her, her body almost parallel to the ground. Her ponytail hangs straight as a plumb bob.

With each return, Suzie folds her legs back and then pushes again, gaining height with each scoop. She pushes again. She goes higher.

"That's enough!" Paul yells, "…high enough!"

Suzie calls back, the wind catches her voice, makes it hollow, "S'never high eee-nough!"

Sam sits in the sand box to the right of the swing set. He pats the sand with a shovel he's found, beats the sand flat, echoes Suzie's call, "…high eeee-nough!"

Suzie pushes one more time. Paul watches the chain jump as it collapses on itself. Suzie's head snaps. Her ponytail jerks. Her eyes and mouth make a startled "O". Paul runs. He grabs the chains and makes quick hopping steps backward to keep from being hit by the swing seat. Paul steadies the chain and his voice is as taut as the chain had been seconds before. "Suzie! Don't do that again." Paul's heart pounds, his voice shakes. "You scared both of us."

"Sam?" she asks looking around Paul to see Sam. Sam's eyes are wide, his hand holds his shovel up as if to say "Stop!"

"Probably Sam, too. I meant both of us. You and me. You were as scared as I was."

"You were scared?"

"Of course I was scared. You could have fallen. Out. Crashed."

Suzie looks up at Paul, challenging him, "And if I'd fallen, if I'd crashed," she begins to twist the swing, her voice following the motion of her body, "If my head and my brains had fallen out, like disgorged, and I was just a mess of bones, what would you have done?"

"Well if it was all of your brains, disgorged? And your bones? All broken?"

"Every bit. The front. The back. A big watermelon crack of brains. And a pile of bones, would you have been plaintive?" Suzie's swing unwinds.

Paul moans, "All this to say 'disgorged' and 'plaintive'? Two words in one day?"

"Yes," Suzie twirls the swing seat back, barber-polls the twist of chain. Paul gets his hands out just in time. "Pretty good words, huh?" she asks.

"Not bad. Maybe a little too much for one day, but nothing wrong with over-achieving," Paul continues to play the game. "Sometimes your efforts resonate with purpose."

"Resonate?"

"That's my word," Paul says. "My word for today."

"You're jokin' me. You don't do words," Suzie squints up at Paul as she twirls in the swing, her legs straight out so they just bump his knees.

"I do as of today."

"Why?"

"Something to share."

"I don't do it to share."

"I know. *I've* decided to do it to share," Paul steps back as she twirls past him. "I think you do words to help you grow up."

"You think that's why I do words?"

"Not sure. Just crossed my mind," Paul answers.

"I *would* like to be grown up."

"My turn. Why?"

"So I can take care of Sam and me."

"Grandma Bella takes care of you. Now that I'm here, I can help take care of you. Your mom takes care of you when she's here and she thinks of taking care of you when she's not."

Suzie tucks the chains of the swing in the crook of her elbows, leaving her fingers free to count. "One, Grandma Bella is very, very old. Two, you're not for sure. Three, just like you said, Saundra does the best she can. Ain't much."

"You're hard on your mom, Suzie."

Suzie stops turning. She looks up at Paul. "Well...yeah...but..."

"And Grandma Bella isn't that old. She might seem old to you, but believe me, she's not that old." Paul sits in the swing next to Suzie, his feet extended over the mud puddle underneath. "And I'm planning on being around for a good while."

"Because of the Fig Newton Lady?"

"We should call her Annabelle Lee or Miss Fulsome, now that we know her name."

"Msssss Fulsome? Is that why you might stick around?"

Paul twists in the swing a quarter turn so that he faces Suzie. "First, one 'S' in Ms. Fulsome is plenty enough if you're going to use that slightly sneering voice. And, second, I'll probably stick around because it seems there's stuff for me to do."

"You're not very good at running a church, you know."

"I'm on the steep side of the learning curve." Paul's legs cramp in the twisted position and the too-small board of the swing pinches him. He steps out of the swing and lowers himself to the grass. From where he sits he can see Sam curled up in the corner of the sandbox, fast asleep. "Sam okay?"

"Sure. Just napping. So, finish telling me about all the stuff you're going to do!"

"Slowly, we'll get people interested in things, projects…get them talking to each other. Discussion groups? Maybe a book group? Whaddaya think?"

"Maybe you could get them to form a group that appreciates children."

"Brilliant idea! For God's sake child, you are thinking!"

"I don't think ministers say 'for God's sake' like that."

Paul stands. Holds out his hand. "Okay, let's make a deal. You be respectful of Annabelle Lee Fulsome and I'll be respectful of God. Deal?"

Suzie's palm slaps his, "Okay, but it's a weird deal since your side of the deal is job related."

"Your's is child related!"

"Okay. Deal's a deal. Now, tell me more reasons why you're going to stay."

"Well, there's you and Sam. Maybe we could start a Sunday school? Start a youth group?"

"With two kids? One who can't even talk that much?"

"True. We'll need to get some more kids. But I'm going to work on that. I could do a talk on 'suffer the little children.'"

"They already think they suffer enough with us."

"I'll end by talking about what great kids you are and how you could help them carry groceries, take out their garbage, feed their cats."

Suzie frowns.

"For a fee, of course," Paul adds.

"You'll do that?" Suzie leans forward in the swing, her arms protruding like baby robin wings.

"Why not? It seems I can use this job just about any way I want."

"Like to make big eyes at the Fig…Ms. Fulsome?"

"I didn't make big eyes."

"Oh, yes, you did! Right before you had that ben-eee-diction! I saw you." Suzie leans far to one side and looks past Paul. "And here she comes!"

Annabelle Lee takes long striding steps across the park. She wears a soft pleated dress that falls to her ankles. She is wrapped in an oversized belted sweater. The sun shines through the flowered fabric, silhouettes her long legs as she comes toward them.

She raises an arm and calls, "Hi, everybody! I thought maybe it was you three! Hoped it was!"

"What a nice surprise," Paul says and stands, brushing his jeans clean of grass. He tucks his shirt in and tightens his stomach muscles. He holds out both hands as she draws near. He thinks he can get away with this 'preacher' kind of greeting. Nice, to fold his hands around her fingers.

"Guess what?" she asks tilting her head to one side, her eyes on his.

"What?" he asks and his hands feel empty as she pulls away and sits on the edge of the sand box. Her dress pillows around her. Sam wakes and comes to sit next to her. Paul watches with envy as Annabelle Lee reaches out to bring Sam to snuggle close.

"I've been gone all week. To Chicago. I've won a huge grant! A big, big grant! Until the official announcement, there's no talking about it. I got in late last night. You're the first to know!"

"Great. What does that mean? What do you have to do?"

"Well, it's a bit mysterious. It's called a Junior MacArthur award. You know about MacArthur awards?"

Paul answers yes, but only has a vague recollection of reading something about MacArthur awards once. Remembers the 'big money' part.

"The awards are given anonymously. They don't tell us where the money comes from and they don't care how the money's used. I can spend it anyway I want. No strings. No guidelines. Totally unbelievable!"

"Amazing! So, what will you do?"

Annabelle Lee runs a hand through her hair, shakes her head as if she is trying to dispel the disbelief. "I don't know! I haven't had time to think about it. It must be like when people win the lottery. Do they go crazy and buy castles in Spain or do they go back to their job and just feel nice and secure?"

"Castles in Spain?"

"No, no. It's not that much. It's not the lottery. I'm pretty sure it comes from an interest in glass blowing. I think that's how they found me, so I'll probably want to use the money to do something special with glass."

"I thought what you really did was teach aerobics!" Suzie's voice is crisp and full of doubt.

"You're right, Suzie. I do teach aerobics. I do that to keep myself in shape. But what I do mostly is blow glass. I'll take you down to the studio some time. I think you'd like it."

"Why?" Suzie's word pops out like an arrow. She sits stiff and tall, like she thinks it might make her look more grown up, even if she is sitting in a swing.

Annabelle Lee answers, her voice gathered and soft, "You'd understand if you saw it. I promise I will take you to the studio soon." Then Annabelle Lee's face brightens and she looks from Suzie to Paul. "How about right now? You want to go? It's just at the end of the field over there." Annabelle Lee points at the buildings across from them on the far side of the playground.

Suzie swings herself back and forth. She makes no effort to leave the swing. Annabelle Lee asks Paul, "What do you think?"

"Well, I'd like that."

Sam has come to stand next to Paul. His eyes focus on Annabelle Lee. "I'll go. Leave Suzie here."

Paul scoops up Sam, holds out a hand to Annabelle Lee and the three of them start to walk away.

Suzie jumps from the swing, "I'm supposed to babysit Sam. Wait for me!"

Suzie squeezes into the space between Annabelle Lee and Paul, her hand finds Paul's.

As they walk, Paul asks, "Why's Sam so sleepy?"

"Who knows?" Suzie answers. "But then we did watch Citizen Kane last night after David Letterman."

"You did what? Where was Grandma Bella? Why weren't you in bed?"

"Grandma Bella had a date. We waited up for her."

"Maybe we better skip this little side trip here and get you home for a nap."

Suzie doesn't let go of Paul's hand, but turns to walk backwards as she speaks. "No! No. We're fine! I'm not sleepy. Besides," she stops at the curb, turns around to face forward, "we're almost there." They head up the brick walk to the double doors of the studio building. Suzie pulls Paul forward. Annabelle Lee brings up the rear. Had he turned, Paul would have seen smiles to melt his soul.

36

A LITTLE BIT OF AWE

On a wooden bleacher in front of the glass furnace, Suzie sits next to Paul. Sam sits between Paul's legs, one step below. All three faces glow with the warmth of a single furnace. Annabelle has changed into overalls and a long sleeved t-shirt. She wears heavy boots. And for the last half hour she has transformed a glowing glob of molten glass into what will soon be a shimmering bowl.

Paul is aware that Suzie's eyes never leave the dance-like partnership of Annabelle Lee and her assistant. Annabelle Lee makes the slightest nod with her head and her assistant moves with her to a wooden bench. Annabelle Lee eases herself to sit while she rolls the pipe back and forth, back and forth, hitting the molten sides with a torch shooting a narrow band of blue flame. The bowl grows and then it is snipped to form a cup and a second bubble of glass is prepared to fit into the first. Three bubbles of glass later, the dance ends. The bowl is cut from the pipe, as if it were taffy. The assistant, with Kevlar-gloved hands, carries the bowl to the open door of the annealing oven.

Annabelle Lee comes to sit with them on the bench. She stretches out her legs over two rows of the bleachers and mops her brow. She is all smiles and exhaustion. Her skin shimmers in the light of the furnace. 'Lush' is the word that comes to Paul's mind.

Suzie leans against a guardrail, as if studying Annabelle Lee.

Sam yawns and slips up to sit in Paul's lap.

"Whaddaya think, little guy?"

"Pretty."

"Exactly my thoughts," said Paul.

"I've got some cleaning up to do and in ten minutes I get to assist someone else. It's a tradeoff. I'll walk you to the door," Annabelle Lee offers a hand to Sam. Suzie joins them and they walk down the hall together. Suzie keeps turning to look at Annabelle Lee. She doesn't say anything, but a look of wonder has replaced all of her skepticism.

At the front of the building, the sky is alive—a 'V' formation of birds slithers in circles overhead and catches the updraft, flying happy.

"We should get going. Grandma Bella might be wondering where we are," Paul says, his voice carrying his reluctance to leave. The warmth of good feelings keeps them standing close to one another. Paul wants to touch Annabelle, but he can't figure a casual way to do it. Instead, he boosts Sam up in his arms and Sam gives Annabelle Lee's cheek a kiss goodbye. Suzie shields her eyes with one hand and looks up at Annabelle Lee. She says 'thank you'. Twice.

The three of them walk down the front walk. Paul turns to wave. Annabelle Lee leans against the push-bar of the open door and calls, "Paul, dinner later? My place?" Paul almost stumbles, catches himself, yells, "Great! Yes! Thanks!" He fears his voice might have sounded too pleased, too anxious, too excited. Too late. He smiles to himself. He swings Suzie's hand. He *is* pleased, anxious and excited.

A ten-year-old voice cheeps, "Got yourself a date!"

"Grandma Bella, we're home!" Suzie calls as they run down the path to the Airstream.

Grandma Bella stands waiting at the screen door. "I was getting worried about you two. Well, three."

Before Paul can answer, Suzie chatters, excitement pushing her words into each other, "We just saw the most beautiful thing, the most beautiful glass! It was magnificent! I've never seen anything so wonderful…" Suzie's arms fly wide "…in my whole life!"

Grandma Bella opens the door for them. She wears a pink ribbed chenille robe. Her head is tied with a purple and gold metallic scarf over curlers.

They bundle inside. The children pull off jackets and sweaters and hang them on hooks by the door.

"I'll hear about it over lunch. Wash up!"

Grandma Bella pats her curlers and says, "Excuse my appearance. I took a little nap. Catching up after last night. Kind of late."

"So I heard," Paul says, surprised at the edge in his voice.

"And, just what did you hear?" Grandma Bella asks.

"Suzie explained they needed to wait up for you. Late."

"She needed to wait up for me?" Grandma Bella calls down the hall. "Suzie! Suzie, you better get out here. Right this minute."

Suzie emerges from the bathroom. She walks slowly towards them, drying her hands on the front of her sweatshirt.

"Suzie, you told me you were in bed at nine o'clock last night. Just what did you tell Pastor Paul?"

"Sorry, Suzie," Paul wishes back his words. He looks into Suzie's accusing eyes. "It's just that I was concerned when I heard you had...I'm going to blow your story here...had watched David Letterman last night. I *was* concerned."

Grandma Bella's eyebrows touch the edge of her metallic scarf. "Suzie! I think you might tell Pastor Paul about our agreement."

Suzie shifts her feet and stammers, "Well...we...well we...we *were* in bed. We watched TV in bed."

"In bed?"

"Well, we brought our blankets and pillows out to the TV. And we watched."

"The agreement is what needs explaining, not where you watched television." Grandma Bella turns to Paul, "I think her exact words were that she was 'exceptionally' responsible. That she was old enough to babysit. That she would, in fact, donate half of her babysitting money to the new church."

"But Saundra... Mom...she was..." Suzie whines.

"This has nothing to do with your mother."

Sam hangs an arm around Grandma Bella's knees, pushes his way into the middle of the discussion, "Boy, everybody's been in trouble lately."

Suzie is undaunted. With hands on her hips she continues, "What the problem is...it's like a movie where there's two women, and the guy can't make up his..."

"Suzie! I think we don't need to hear anymore and I notice your hands are not quite clean. Back to the bathroom." Grandma Bella points and Suzie turns. "You too, Samuel." Sam follows Suzie. Paul would have sworn he saw the pleased expression of a very cagey minx on Suzie's face. Suzie has a way of obeying and escaping at the same time. And something about the interchange, the whole mess has a solid edge of pleasure for Paul. It feels like blame is being passed around and it all feels rather friendly.

"I want to hear that water running!" Grandma Bella's voice is not irritated or angry or blaming. There is no question she is in control. Paul smiles and hopes somehow Grandma Bella will find a reason to offer him another plum brandy.

"I'm only explaining." Suzie's voice is barely audible from the bathroom and the sentence dribbles off in the rush of water as Sam demands, "Move over."

Paul feels the need to explain. "It was told to me in confidence."

"Paul, ten-year-old confidences are not quite binding."

"I'm embarrassed. I accuse you of neglecting your grandchildren, and you think I'm seducing your daughter, and all the time…"

"Worse things could happen to that daughter of mine."

Paul feels his entire body groan. In desperate need to change the subject, as Grandma Bella opens the refrigerator, he offers, "How about I prepare lunch?" He looks over Grandma Bella's shoulder into the refrigerator. "Got eggs?"

"Sure. What a pleasure!" she says and passes a carton of eggs over her shoulder to Paul. She reaches for two Italian tomatoes and a bunch of slim green onions. Paul pulls out the chopping board and begins a rhythmic chopping. It's nice not to have to talk.

Eggs whipped, onions chopped, tomatoes sliced, cheese grated, Tabasco sauce ready, Paul waits until the butter has turned creamy brown before he begins the omelets. The children lay in front of the television watching reruns of Mouseketeers.

"If I'd known this was going to happen, I'd never have accepted that date with Bill," Grandma Bella says as if during the time Paul had been preparing the dinner, she's been worrying about last night.

Suzie speaks over Annette Funicello singing *Friendship*. "I thought you and Bill went to play Bingo. Old people don't date.

"Missy, you are asking for trouble if you don't watch your tongue."

Suzie comes to sit in the eating nook. Paul catches her eye. "Suzie, it's not like you to look so plaintive," he says, handing her the silverware to set the table.

Suzie doesn't take the bait. She asks, "Grandma, where's Saundra?"

"Your mother? Your mother is playing at a polka contest. She'll be home later."

"Polkas are so dumb."

"Suzie. That is uncalled for. Your mother is trying. It wouldn't hurt if you tried. You could begin by not calling her Saundra."

Suzie's voice almost sounds contrite, "I'll think about it."

"That's a start."

Paul slips the first omelet onto a plate. He begins the second. He remembers to toast the toast. He thinks through the morning. He tallies up the good and the bad. The 'good' column is filling up!

"Good eggs," Suzie says. "Extraordinary. Quite extraordinary."

Paul smiles his thanks and places her compliment in the 'good' column.

37

DINNER AT ANNABELLE LEE'S

"Roasted Bell Pepper Soup," Annabelle Lee explains.

"You cook like this often?" Paul asks.

"Not often. But well." Annabelle Lee lifts the soup spoon over the kettle and leans into the smell, sipping the taste.

"You look a thousand miles away," Paul says.

"Home to Idaho. Summer days. Mom's cooking. Here, try it," Annabelle Lee offers Paul the spoon.

Paul holds the hand that holds the spoon. Her fingers are cool to his touch. He notices a small burn scar, the size of a Junior Mint. He yearns to touch it with his tongue.

"What's it taste like to you?" Annabelle Lee asks.

Paul holds the taste in his mouth. Slurries it around. Catches the red and yellowness of it, and answers, "Sunshine."

"Ah. A poet. A pastor *and* a poet."

Paul blushes to be called more or less what he, not often, but once in awhile, feels about himself.

Annabelle Lee stirs the soup. "I think of summer days in McCall. When I make this soup I can feel the hot wind off the wheat fields. Mom grew peppers along one side of the concrete block wall of the garage. Everything was like that—the ugly and the beautiful hugging each other."

"Like your work?"

Annabelle Lee hands Paul a slender carafe of oil. "Here, dress the salad. Don't stop talking. You see my 'work' differently than I do."

"Well, that bowl, for instance," Paul says and points to the large bowl in which Annabelle Lee has dropped the leaves of butter lettuce. "The burnt orange rim. Smooth. The next band is crazed, blackened. But where you capture the ugly and the beautiful best is…," Paul nods towards a bowl of figures framed in the pass-through between Annabelle Lee's kitchen and dining room.

"Oh, those. That stuff really interests you, doesn't it? Believe me, they're nothing more than bits and pieces of leftover glass. Nothing."

"I think thee protests too much!" Paul says and walks to the other room. He returns with a glass figure balanced on the palm of his hand. "This is nothing?" He holds out to her a seated clown juggling three fish. One fish has a star in one eye. One fish sports an earring. The third fish smiles around two protruding teeth. On the juggler's head is a tri-corner hat from which protrude daffodils. One stem is broken. "It's happy and scary at the same time."

"Dinner's ready. Let's eat."

Annabelle Lee takes the figure from Paul's hand, places it back in the bowl.

"You don't like that I think they're great?"

"They're toys. Whimsy."

Paul lets the subject drop. He enjoys the soup, the crusty bread, the fresh scramble of greens in the salad. He can't remember a meal or a companion so beautiful.

Annabelle Lee refills her glass and stands to pour Paul more. He places his hand over his wine glass. "Thanks, I'll pass."

"Oh, I'm sorry about the wine. Not quite right for this dinner?" she asks.

"No! It's fine wine. This minister thing is keeping me at a limit."

"How so?"

"Well, I've promised the children's grandmother, Grandma Bella, I won't drink. So already I've broken my promise. One glass. That's my limit. Don't think badly of your choice."

"Thanks for telling me."

"Truth? Everything lately is a new experience. So this one-glass-a-day limit is just part of the newness." He lifts his empty glass in a toast. "And here's to you. One of the best new things that's happened."

Annabelle Lee blushes. He can see his words are too early. He lifts his empty glass as if to salute her and although he wants to tell her how beautiful she is, how charming, he says, "So. Here's to you and your grant. That's what you call it? Right?" Paul asks.

She is quick to answer. "Well, since I saw you, it's better than I thought. It's a princely sum. Even the director at the art center is amazed. No amount of begging made him tell me who the donor is or how they found me."

"Meerac!" Paul raises his glass again and responds to Annabelle Lee's quizzical look, "We had a French logger work with us. Any excuse, he'd cry, 'meerac!' Someone would get the tree to fall just right. 'Meerac!' Someone would survive a 'widow maker'. 'Meerac!' It's one of those 'fits-everything' words. It means 'miracle!' He used the word with not a lot of discrimination." Paul leans back in his chair, full, and content. "So go on…"

"Well, 'meerac' it is. I get an initial amount of money and then for the next three years, I get enough to let me work and then some."

"What will 'then some' do?"

"I'm not sure. But there isn't a single person at the studio that doesn't have a dream of owning their own building. We'd like to get land. Out somewhere. Build a major facility for glass blowing. Have a place to get away from the city. Get inspired. Refreshed. Like summer camp but for grownups. I'll be on the lookout for some land. It is truly a miracle, to have this much money."

They eat in silence. The warmth of the evening surrounds them. Paul has the slightest worry that somehow the 'miracle' might take Annabelle Lee away just when he's found her.

"What's it like where you come from?" Annabelle Lee asks.

"Twist?"

Annabelle Lee nods her head.

"For land?" Paul asks, surprised that he knew she was not asking to just make conversation. He could hear her intent. What she had just asked was a 'real estate' question.

"Have you been to Twist?" Paul asks.

"No. Friends have. Cross-country skiers."

"The Methow Mountains…they're as beautiful as a place gets. Some old growth still survives. Never touched."

"Thank God!"

Paul ignores the vehemence of Annabelle Lee's remark and finishes, "But word was out as I left that some old growth land would be up for bid."

"Bid?"

"Well, even in the beautiful forests, especially forests with big trees, money talks."

"You mean some idiot might cut down an old growth forest?"

"Yes and no. Almost all the old wood is on U.S. Government land. They decide what can or can't be cut. Not everyone agrees with their decisions."

"Well, that's obvious."

"Annabelle Lee. You just asked about land. A camp? You think no trees are going to get cut if you want to consider land where trees grow?" Paul tries not to be irritated. He can't stop his words. "You don't know. Besides, guys are dying for work up there."

"Yeah, and hundred-year-old trees, who've been there a lot longer than humans, are dying."

"Now you're comparing trees and humans!"

"Time to drop the subject."

Paul sits silent. The softness he'd felt from the wine has disappeared. The soup is cold. The air is like ice.

"Well, then I guess you're right." He folds his napkin and places it beside his plate. The silence grows like a monster—huge, ugly, and undeniable.

"I think I'll say goodnight." Paul stands. He feels like he is eight years old. He is angrier and sadder than he can ever remember. He wants her to say, "Don't go." He wants her to say, "Come lie down in my bed." He can see by the line of her lips she isn't going to say anything of the sort. Paul knows silence. He has no idea how to make it disappear.

He walks to the front door and takes his coat from the hall tree. "Well, thank you for the wonderful evening." Annabelle Lee stands at the table. He thinks he hears her say, "Good night."

In a final effort to rescue something, anything, Paul, with all the effort he can muster says, "The congregation is going to the Monroe County Fair tomorrow morning. Suzie and Sam asked that you join us." Paul opens the door. He stands with his head down; he can't bring himself to look at her in case she says 'no'.

She says nothing.

"We leave at eight o'clock."

Paul closes the door. Outside it is cold. The rain slaps against him and the wind rips leaves from the trees.

38

AT THE FAIR

Jack's rig follows Paul's Jeep, which follows Cruisewell's limousine into the dusty parking lot at the county fairgrounds. In the Jeep, the Wittenhouer twins and Mrs. Simmons have filled the hour's drive with chatter about their European trips. Each time they ask, "Pastor Paul, have you been to Venice?" or "Pastor Paul did you ever swim in the Mediterranean or hike in the Black Forest?" Paul replies, "No" and he feels horrible. He is so not cultured. He is so not interesting. Why would any woman want to spend time with him? Especially Annabelle Lee. So damn sophisticated. And probably charming the entire limousine bunch, because that is where she chose to ride. With the kids. With other chatty women who probably are talking about opera and ballet and everything he knows nothing about. Thank God he will be carving so he won't have to worry about who will or will not speak to him about things he knows nothing.

At the parking lot in Monroe, Paul tries not to pay attention to the limo parked next to his Jeep. Inside, as Cruisewell checks his hair in the rear-view mirror, the women gather their purses and their scarves and Suzie squeezes past their knees to be the first out. Rex and Big Bill emerge from the front seat. Rex opens the door for the ladies. Paul can see the back seat where the television flickers white and Sam bounces with pleasure. His hand holds tight to Annabelle Lee to keep her with him.

Paul tries to appear nonchalant, like he is waiting no more and no less than anyone else. He looks at the Ferris wheel in the distance as if it mattered. He checks his watch to see the time and pays attention to the line at the gate to see if it has started to move. He steals looks at Annabelle Lee's graceful exit with Sam in tow.

He hopes she might turn to look at him, give him a clue as to how or what she is thinking—about him, about them, about last night, about the stupid argument. Her attention is on Sam, who's pulling her toward the gate until he slips and falls on a shoelace. She kneels. All of her attention on Sam. It appears she has absolutely no interest in Paul.

Paul's sure everyone notices. Earlier, Annabelle Lee, in the most cursory manner, had said, "Good morning, Pastor Paul," and immediately took a seat in Cruisewell's limousine. And that was that.

Now, Paul watches her help Sam while Suzie waits with a barrette in hand. When Annabelle Lee's attention is on his sister, Sam heads for Paul, grabs his hand, and pulls him towards the girls. A little disconcerted, but not totally reluctant, Paul follows Sam's lead. They arrive as Annabelle Lee finishes snapping the pink plastic bow into Suzie's hair.

Ecstatic at his ploy of reuniting his two favorite people, Sam reaches for Paul to pick him up, and once in place, leverages his feet against Paul's side and gives a mighty push against Paul's ribs. He yells, "Catch me!" Just in time, Annabelle Lee folds her arms around Sam. At the catch, Paul's arms encircle Sam and Annabelle Lee. They both hold Sam.

"Blind faith," Paul says, his heart thumping, one arm firmly holding the weight of Sam and his other arm firmly holding Annabelle Lee. A smile crosses Annabelle Lee's face.

"Today's first lesson," Annabelle Lee says not avoiding Paul's direct gaze. Relieved, Paul takes the smile, the words, her not moving away, as a 'truce'.

Just at this sublime moment, the gates open, the lines begin to move, and Sam slides to the ground. He grabs Annabelle Lee's right hand. Suzie grabs her left. The moment slips away and so do Annabelle Lee, Sam, and Suzie.

Paul stands with Rex and Bill. They watch as Cruisewell ushers members of the New Dawn is Breaking Church into the fenced grounds for a day of 'worship'.

Rex whops Paul on the back, "You've got one fine looking lady in your corner."

"Well, for a few seconds anyway."

"Where's your guy?"

"Jack? Who knows. Given Saundra, he's probably taken the long way around."

At which moment, the three men look down the long row of parked cars to see Jack's rig lumber towards them and take up a double parking space. Jack swings out of his cab and hurries around the front of the truck, opens the door, and extends a hand. He gives Saundra a lift down. Rex, Bill, and Paul watch. All noticing, Jack's help lasts a bit too long and his hand slips from her arm to her curved bottom. The only thing that stops him is Saundra herself. She is more sure and quick with her crutches than one could have guessed and is out of Jack's reach before Jack's hand hits home.

She waves to the guys with a 'toodly-do' wave and is gone to join the other ladies in line.

Jack beams at the waiting men as if they were fellow conspirators. "Even limping she looks great," Jack says.

Paul doesn't answer and signals for Rex and Bill to help him gather together gear and the canvas-wrapped saws.

Jack continues to stare, transfixed. He says, "That's real pause for Sunday worship, don't you think? Any time you want me to escort that piece of your congregation—you just let me know…heh, heh."

Rex and Bill roll their eyes in disgust, pick up the saws, and signal Paul they'll meet him inside.

Paul confronts Jack, "You don't look good when you leer, Jack."

"Did you know she's something else? She plays an accordion. Did you know that?"

"Jack. It's nice to see you so enthusiastic, but…," Paul hopes the oozing sarcasm will not be lost on Jack. He has little hope, "…how about we get the rest of the stuff and head over to the cutting yard?"

Paul waits as Jack rummages behind the front seat of his truck. When he reappears, he holds a three-foot by four-foot sign.

"Whaddaya think?" Jack asks, all smiles.

Paul reads the clumsy block letters:

PASTOR PAUL
INSPIRATIONAL CARVING
SPONSORED BY CHAINSAW JACK—RENTER AND SELLER OF THE WORLD'S FINEST CHAINSAWS! YOU CAN LEARN TO CARVE! FREE TWO-HOUR LESSONS AT CHAINSAW JACK'S! INQUIRE HERE! GOD BLESS.

Before Paul can protest, Jack slams the door, locks the truck, and begins walking.

Paul picks up the duffel and hurries to catch up with Jack. Jack just keeps talking. "Surprises me you aren't interested in her yourself, or…," he turns to look at Paul, "…or maybe you are? Did I miss something?"

"Yeah, you missed something. She's one of my parishioners."

"And Annabelle Lee? The skinny one?" Jack raises an eyebrow.

Paul doesn't answer and Jack keeps talking, "It's okay. If you want the skinny one. I like them a little more rounded, myself, especially…"

They get in line with the other carvers. Mostly men, mostly in coveralls and if not coveralls, in jeans and jean jackets. To Paul, they don't seem all that pleased when Jack walks up. No 'hellos' or 'howyadoin' greetings. And then there is dead silence when Jack finishes his sentence, "…boobs." The three women competitors waiting in line turn their backs.

Not missing the slight, Jack demands of Paul, "What was that all about?"

"You, you idiot." Paul's words are brittle. He drops the duffel inches from Jack's feet.

"Hey, watch it! That's damned expensive stuff in there."

Paul unzips the bag. It is stuffed with gloves and chaps. Nothing is hurt. Nothing would have been hurt if he'd thrown it at a brick wall.

Paul lowers his voice, "Jack. Keep your stupid comments to yourself. These women aren't saws. They aren't for rent. They aren't for sale. So, don't talk about them like they are!"

"What are you talking about?"

"Just think before you open your mouth. Just once, try to think how you'd feel if they'd say," Paul twists his voice into a sneer, "Jack. The skinny old fart! He might take care of my rent."

"No way! They wouldn't talk like that and…"

"Right! So just shut up!"

Just then, Rex and Bill head toward them. Big Bill waves the papers.

Bill announces, "We're set. Our carving space is assigned."

Jack picks up his sign. He demands as if he's in charge, "Follow me."

As he walks away, Bill asks, "What's that all about?"

"Just giving him some ministerial advice."

"And the sign?"

"It looks like a maniac wrote it."

"You noticed," Paul says and doesn't hide his total disdain.

Inside the fairgrounds, everyone from New Dawn Is Breaking gathers at the edge of the roped-off area which is sprouting logs like Stonehenge. Inside the field, carvers file their saws, set out their models, adjust earphones and gloves, joke with one another.

"Nice spot you got there, Pastor Paul," Reverend Cruisewell says from behind the rope. "Good number!"

Paul walks over to where Cruisewell stands surrounded by the widows. Paul asks, "What about it?"

"Well, in case you didn't notice, it reads: 316."

"And?"

"I did that, you know." Reverend Cruisewell says with great pride.

"Three hundred sixteen?" Paul doesn't get it.

"Took a little bribe. But that's what money's for." He gestures to Paul to come closer. "Turn around."

From inside his vest pocket, Cruisewell pulls out a magic marker. He marks the bib. "Now it reads, 3:16. Get it? 'God so loved the world…' " Paul groans. Reverend Cruisewell laughs, "Must admit, that's not as blatant as your sign!"

Paul can't bear to look at Jack's sign.

Mrs. McBride sidles up beside Reverend Cruisewell. She holds her cupped hand out to Paul. Into Paul's hand drops a small braid of embroidery strings. Red, orange and purple, like a tiny braided ponytail. On the end of the strings is tied, what appears to Paul to be a set of jaws. A one-inch set of jaws that open and close.

"What is it?" he asks, trying not to recoil.

"Good luck!" she says. "My late deceased husband kept it with him right up to the grave. He'd been lucky right up to that minute!"

Paul ignores the basic contradiction, asks again, "Yes, but what is it?"

"Jaws of a lesser weasel!" she says proudly. "I know a beaver or something that chews wood would have been more appropriate but then it would have been too big and I don't have those anyway!" Her smile is as sunny as the day is becoming. Paul has nothing to say. He puts the strange little talisman inside his pocket. Mrs. McBride steps back, now shy and glowing with the pleasure of having given such a gift. Paul is afraid to acknowledge any of the gathered, fearful at what else might be waiting to be bestowed. He empties the duffel, fastens straps, and buttons buttons. He finds his gloves.

Being busy is no help. Each woman wants to touch him, shake his hand, kiss his cheek. He allows their blessings, but is pleased that no other woman thought to bring a good luck charm. As he ties a bandanna around his head, Annabelle Lee appears at the rope barrier. The children stand beside her. Sam munches a corn-dog. Suzie pulls wisps of cotton candy into the air before licking the pink web from her fingers.

He's pleased when Annabelle smiles and says, "I've been watching! Nothing like a little encouragement." She points to his pocket, "Nothing like a little pagan charm!" She extends her hand. Paul steps closer, pleased to hold her hand, pleased she's there, pleased she's acknowledging the fact that in a few minutes he will take on the eight-foot log standing in the center of his area. He'll be competing against twenty-five other carvers.

Annabelle Lee pulls him forward. She plants a kiss on his cheek. "For good luck," she says. "Not that you'll need it. The word is out, no one else has a chance!"

Paul knits his eyebrows. He has no understanding of who or how she knows.

Annabelle Lee nods to the sign. "You've got them spooked! Or, we might say, Jack does. He's no dummy. Hard to compete against God!" Annabelle Lee laughs and as she does, Cruisewell appears beside her from out of the crowd. "You must be Annabelle Lee!" he says as if he's been waiting to meet her all his life. "Welcome! Welcome! I've heard so much about you!"

The slightest frown of doubt slides over Annabelle Lee's face. Paul watches the two of them as they size each other up. A single thought crosses Paul's mind: he did not remember mentioning Annabelle Lee to

Cruisewell. Ever. He'll ask later. How is it Cruisewell knows everything and everyone, and if he doesn't know them, he knows about them? How is it Cruisewell seems to have access to more than the normal walking-around bloke? How is it this ministry thing is totally nuts and has brought with it such a strange (but interesting, if not out-right enjoyable) bunch of people?

Paul puts the questions aside. The ten-minute warning horn cuts the air. He concentrates on the log. Eight-footers are a lot of cutting. He rolls his arms. Studies the grain, the knots, the girth of the tree. He knows the minute the saw starts, everything in the world except the saw and the log will disappear. Everything will be gone except the sheer brute pleasure of cutting.

And then his calm is pierced by the chatter of Jack and Cruisewell.

39

A GOOD CUT

"Can't miss chances to remind people who we are!" Cruisewell admires Jack's sign.

"Reminds them about what they need. At least a good hobby!" Jack says as if to agree.

"Right! Admiration will attract new members."

"A minister with very specific talents! Multiple talents. That's the best!"

"And a trailer court full of wonderful widows isn't so bad."

"Have you noticed on television how the evangelists are multi-everything? They sing! They dance! They do karate!"

"Much more caring, wouldn't you say?"

"Even got baseball players and wrestlers!"

"And here *we* are with a chainsaw artist minister! Young. Well, youngish. What more could you ask for?"

"I think we need to win. I think we will win!"

"Exactly! What a marvelous day! What a marvelous experience!"

Paul takes deep breaths. He is not going to let anything interrupt this day, especially not the insane chatter of Cruisewell and Jack.

"Five minutes to go. How'd you like a corndog, Paul? Or chili? Big Orange Drink? Name it. My treat." Cruisewell's voice drives spikes into Paul's head.

At least Jack is smart enough, this time, to give Paul time and space. And miracle of miracles, Jack is also smart enough to be gentlemanly when he asks the women to step back from the tape line.

Alone, in his cutting area, Paul unwraps the saws from their canvas covers. Against a corner pallet he rests the saws in order of size: six-foot, then four, then two, and then the sweet twelve-incher. He checks the gas level in each tank. He adjusts the tightness of the chain and gives each a test start. From the duffel he pulls four chisels, sanding blocks, and three different sizes of rasps. He runs his finger over the blade of each chisel. Knocks a wood fiber from one of the rasps. His tools are ready.

Then he adjusts his chaps, finds his earphones, and pulls on his gloves. As he finishes checking each detail, he takes a deep breath. How strange that Cruisewell's lesson on breathing fits. Puts him at ease. He becomes aware of the smell of fresh laid sawdust, the animals in the barns to his right, and filtering in from a distance, the sweet smell of corn-dogs, caramel corn, and frying onions. He's reminded of every fair and every cutting he's ever attended. All in all he can hardly believe how lucky he is to be here today. Be here. Competing and cutting.

Annabelle Lee stands at a distance. When Cruisewell takes the hands of the children to one of the many rides, she approaches Paul. "So that's the amazing Reverend Cruisewell."

"Amazing is right. His enthusiasm sometimes…well…"

"Don't have to say it. He's got more energy than Sam. What's interesting is that he bought everyone tickets for rides. Of course, the children already had theirs, but it was very generous of him. He made a point of suggesting everyone ride with their buddy to have a shared experience. The guy's goofy!"

"Does he seem more than strange to you? More than goofy?"

"Strange is probably enough," Annabelle Lee says with a laugh. "Everyone needs a little 'strange' in their life. So, my advice? Relax and enjoy it." Her smile is totally reassuring.

Her presence is as good as breathing. Better.

"Oh, one other characteristic I've noticed," she says. "Rich. He seems very, very rich. If all that gold chain around his neck is real, and the little finger ring, and the white suits…have you ever worn a white suit? Do you know what it costs to clean a white suit? So, I'd add 'rich' to the 'strange' list."

Paul looks down at his black washed-out jeans. He wonders what people think when they see the small, dynamic Cruisewell all in white sponsoring a minister who acts nothing like a minister and dresses in faded black.

The one-minute warning fills the air.

"Do this for me, would you?" Paul asks. "Watch him during the day. See if you can get any clue as to what he's about."

The warning horn blows. Fifteen seconds. Paul picks up the largest saw. Then he happens to notice Saundra. She is on the other side of the field, deep in conversation with one of the carvers. Jack notices Paul's gaze and calls, "Be back in just a minute!"

Jack lopes off in Saundra's direction.

And then the low hoot announces the beginning of the competition. It's time!

Annabelle Lee gives Paul a thumbs-up and turns to join Cruisewell and the children. They walk toward The Tunnel of Love. The congregation follows, ticket books at the ready. Jack comes running with Saundra. Grandma Bella holds Big Bill's hand. Annabelle Lee and the children enter together. Cruisewell comes last. Paul wonders at the slope of Reverend Cruisewell's shoulders. Is he sad? Or is he relaxing, enjoying the pleasure of his 'family?'

Molly Entwhistle is the only person left watching the cut. She yells with hands, as if a megaphone is at her mouth, "You better start carving!"

Paul pretends he hasn't heard. He waves a hand and begins his ritual. He studies the log. What he could never have told her, or told anyone, is that his best carving happens when he doesn't know what he'll carve. At those times, Paul waits for the wood to tell him what to do. With the saw running, Paul takes a last walk around the log, his eye takes in every burl, every knot, each growth line. Paul raises the saw with both hands. The thrumming works its way into his body, up his arms, settles in the muscles across his shoulders. He breathes in the fumes of the gas, the resin of the pealed surface of the log. He twists his heels into the soft earth under the freshly spread sawdust and braces himself. He closes his eyes, takes a last long, deep breath and when he opens his eyes, the blade is just over the hard, fresh plane of wood where it descends into the giving surface. And then, he knows what will come.

40

A GALLOPING OSTRICH IN GO-GO BOOTS

Two hours later, with appreciative 'oohs' and 'ahhhs' over the chatter of the raucous, cutting saws, the New Dawn Is Breaking members move the length of the field checking the competition. Periodically, when they return to see how Paul's doing, they smile, they nod approval, they give a thumbs-up. Paul is encouraged. He's never had such a loyal audience. Especially, Annabelle Lee and the children. But especially, Annabelle Lee. She claps her hands, which he can't hear, but he sees that she is not displeased and he wonders if she can make out the love in his eye. He's slightly distracted, but not so much that the work doesn't progress. Paul finds himself full of smiles.

As the cut proceeds, out of the log emerges a bird on long jutting legs encased in stubby, flat-soled boots. Soon, on its head, at a jaunty angle, a top hat sits. Later a billowing bow tie wraps its neck. Then, under one wing protrudes a bouquet of roses and one eye is closed in a wink.

Paul can tell the carving is making Jack nervous. Jack bends to take in every detail. He raises and lowers his shoulders as if to dispel tension. He shifts from foot to foot. He cracks his knuckles. He sets and resets his namesake cap. He leans forward over the yellow tape trying to figure out what in hell Paul is doing. Paul is glad that cutting and talking don't mix. He knows Jack would be full of suggestions. Paul doesn't break his stride. He stays with his ever more wonderful ostrich.

Toward the end of the afternoon, Paul eases the twelve-incher around the curve of the roses and strokes the stems into relief. He considers thorns, but too late, the stems are clean and long— protruding from under the feathers of one wing.

Paul is hyper-aware each time Annabelle Lee visits. He wishes equally that she would go away and that she would never leave. She gives signals of support, pleasure, approval, but she is with the children and it crosses Paul's mind she may be showing her enthusiasm for the children's sake. He can hardly bear to think she might think his carving is stupid or silly.

The children love everything! They drag Annabelle Lee from one competitor to another. They secure autographs during breaks and collect souvenir chips of wood from each carver. They occasionally take time for rides and eats, but their greatest attention is paid to the chainsaw art and their hero, Paul.

Rex drifts from one widow to another, the 'on-call' escort. No woman feels neglected.

Grandma Bella and Big Bill hold hands. Their fingers entwined. Their eyes are for each other. Even the children cannot separate them with requests for rides and treats and visits to the petting zoo.

Saundra appears to be staked out by Jack, his hand more often then not tucked under her elbow. Cruisewell occasionally accompanies them, but he takes his role as minister seriously, and finds time, energy, and interest to talk to all of the widows and anyone who notices the Pastor Paul sign. All in all, Cruisewell farms the farm, but should Jack loiter or get distracted, Cruisewell never misses a chance to engage Saundra.

During a break, as Paul removes the earphones to rub his pinched ears, he thinks he hears Jack mention to Saundra something about a bet, about betting on a winner. It's a strange conversation, words said at an angle, behind a cupped hand. Paul can't connect the words to the competition. No one, as far as he knows, has ever bet on a chainsaw competition. What would prompt the subject even to come up? Who would lose money that way? Win money that way? As Paul adds details to the feathers, he puts the betting remarks out of his mind. He decides he must have misunderstood.

At the five-and-one-half-hour mark, everyone takes a fifteen-minute break. The silence brings dozens of fair-goers to admire and comment on the near-finished carvings.

Paul steps back to study his ostrich. He is pleased. The legs are bent at a cocky angle as if the bird might start clogging at any moment. Having checked the feathers, the roses, the angled legs, Paul takes a spool of thick malleable wire from his duffel. With a deft twist, he eases the wire into a ridge he's carved at the top of each boot. He encircles the boot with the wire. At the join in the front he bends the wire back and forth, back and forth, until he has a pompom that protrudes quite smartly at the top of each boot.

"Oh, no!" Jack groans. "Paul, don't. It's great without the doolies on the boots. Please. Please!"

Paul ignores Jack. Time to finish, he runs a sanding block over the surface and smoothes out the last of the rough edges. When the final horn blows, he is finished. He steps back and studies his creation. Enough and good. He leans to grab the rope attached to the pallet under his carving and Rex and Big Bill join him to steady the carving as he pulls his entry to the judging arena. In the process, as each of the competitors pull their creations forward, two topple, and the crowd groans. The tradition at the county level of bringing the carvings into an arena seems insane to Paul. He's heard of the accidents and wonders if it is to reduce the number of contestants.

"Paul, that falls and you'll get your due." Jack stands back, no room between Bill and Rex made for him.

"Jack, everything is okay. Take a deep breath and back-off," Paul demands and Jack steps back looking like a rejected ten-year-old child.

The three men bring the carving to the designated area. Jack rebounds and runs to pick up his sign and he stands, holding it, behind Paul's carving, lest anyone had not previously seen his message.

Three judges sit on a raised platform, clipboards and pencils at the ready.

Once the pallets are in place, Rex and Bill maneuver Jack to stand between them and as best they can, they block the sign. Meantime, Paul talks to other carvers, making small talk, speaking of slipped chains, past winners, the great weather. Everyone avoids discussing the carvings. Everyone knows to speak of the finished work before winners are announced is bad luck and bad form.

Paul searches out Jesse on the far side of the field.

"Hey, lady!"

Jessie joins him with a hardy handshake. "I saw you over there. You looked very intent. And surrounded. What is it with older women keeping an eye on you? Hate to tell you this, but your admirers were the talk of the day."

"My congregation," Paul says, wondering how Jesse could have possibly not known.

"Oh, that's what that sign's all about! Hattie was waiting to talk to you during the breaks, but she couldn't get close." Jesse looks around as if to find her partner. "Shall I tell her you're up for it?"

Paul runs his fingers through his hair. Sawdust falls. He tries to think what an article would mean or do to his new life.

"I'll find her after we finish. I owe her a beer if nothing else."

"Ooops, here comes the judge! Start looking like you don't care!" Jesse says and gives Paul a half push, a half hug, and she leaves to go stand by her creation.

The judges descend into the forest of carvings. They score and discuss. They analyze for sturdiness and finish. They make note of the dimensionality. They score for originality.

- Jesse's angel toots a horn
- a sailor in northeasters faces unseen rain and squalls
- an eagle flies
- a mermaid preens
- a pack of wolves howl
- a litter of puppies cuddle
- a sculpture of tortuous leaf-like shapes defies definition
- Paul's ostrich waits for a down-beat so it can dance
- and the rest are bears

Paul watches as the judges return to each carving. He thinks he has a fighting chance. His bird is deftly carved and he knows for certain, no one has ever carved an ostrich. Such a carving would never have entered a carver's mind. Whether the judges will like the top hat and large bow tie is questionable. Of course, the pompoms are a concern, but Paul feels they are absolutely necessary—a trademark.

The judges reassemble. They discuss. They check their notes. They add up their scores. The judges circle Paul's ostrich three times. They share notes. They nod as they make their decision. They return to the platform and take their seats.

The microphone squeaks and howls. A gravelly voice announces, "Ladies and gentlemen! It's time to honor the winners! Gather round!" The crowd moves closer. Sam and Suzie come to stand next to Paul. Paul does not turn to see if Annabelle Lee is behind them, so uncertain of her response if he wins or if he doesn't.

Paul waits, arms folded, hands tucked tensely. The judge bellows, "This has been a very difficult judging. As you know, we judge on originality and skill of carving."

For the moment, Paul's confidence grows.

"But we need to remind you guys...and gal...we are looking for wood...tradition says you can burn the wood and you can oil the wood...but tradition does not allow for metal. Here are the winners! First place is Hugh Hightop for his pyramid of bears! And now for a first in the county competition, second place goes to Jesse Ann Henderson. A woman! For her angel! Let's hear it for Jesse! And, now third place! We're breaking all the rules here! Remember what we just said about metal? Well, we've made an exception! Third place goes to Paul Whitinowsky. Pastor Paul Whitinowsky for those of you who missed the sign! Third place for the one and only ostrich in chainsaw history! Let's hear it for the winners! And don't forget we want to see everyone in Twist! For the Nationals! Today's winners are qualified to compete!" And then as an afterthought, the judge announces, "It is appropriate and welcome at this time for you to approach the carvers for purchase. You like it? Buy it! Support this ever-growing art form." And then the judge stops, as if to acknowledge that word has spread about the identity of the hand on top of a rooster's head in *The Seattle Times*. He looks directly at Paul. "We are on the edge, heading for the center of the art world! Buy now, while chainsaw art is cheap!"

The judge comes down from the podium to hand the checks to each of the winners. He yells, "Let's hear it ONE MORE TIME FOR THE WINNERS!" The crowd applauds, whistles, and cheers. Everyone swarms around the carvings and tries to be first in line to buy the winners. Paul gets slaps on the back and praise, but no one asks the price of his ostrich. Even Annabelle Lee isn't there to let him know…what? That cutting trees to make a crazy bird is okay? He doubts it.

Paul smiles and shakes hands and accepts hugs from women he's never seen before. As best he can, he contains his disappointment. He'd been so sure his ostrich would win. Now he has to eat crow. He knows the first thing Jack will say is, "I told you so!" Or worse. Paul looks around for Hattie. He considers avoiding her should she approach him. But why should she even look for him? Third place is not a story.

Paul accepts the hundred-dollar-prize check and stuffs it in his pocket. He thought for a minute the judge had a question, but he, the judge, shook his head and went to find Jesse to give her the check. Paul nods a thank-you to those who call out congratulations. And then, what he's been waiting for, but dare not admit to himself, he sees Annabelle Lee striding towards him. She is full of indignation.

"How could they? How could they not give you first place! Nothing touched what you did!" Annabelle Lee's voice explodes. Heads turn. Paul grabs her hand and brings her close to his side, "Shush, the whole fair is listening."

"As well they should!" Annabelle is undaunted. "First place was yours, hands down! They made up that stupid no-extraneous-stuff rule because they didn't know what to do with something so original! So fresh!"

Paul wants her to go on forever. At the same time he's a bit embarrassed by the ruckus she is making. Small puffs of dust escape from the sawdust as her foot hits the ground in anger.

"Calm down. That's how it is. Isn't the first time. Won't be the last." Paul lays out a canvas bag, places a saw inside it, zippers it up. "They expect certain things. They get what they expect. The judges are the judges. It's their job." Paul wraps another chainsaw. He can't think of any more words to defend the judges. She's right. They're wrong.

"I'll bet they don't even say you have to carve wood! I'll bet all they require is a chainsaw! They probably don't even have written rules. They probably just make up what they make up! Such stupidity!"

Paul stands, rubbing his aching back and notices Annabelle Lee's arm is covered with sawdust from when he pulled her to him. He reaches out and brushes the wood chips away. It stops her tirade. He takes the opportunity to stay close to her. He can smell mint, or a rare, unknown flower. Whatever it is, it works. It makes him yearn. He says, his voice even and soft, "Consider this. They could have disqualified me if they wanted. They didn't." Paul finds sawdust to brush off her shoulder. He lets his hand slide down her arm.

Annabelle Lee is not so quickly dissuaded. She looks at him, her voice more quiet now, but insistent, "What about the guys who used sanders and blow torches and cans of spray paint? Nobody said anything about them."

Paul is in heaven. His fingers can feel the strength and length of her arm. "Annabelle, you're right. And I'm thinking of doing the Nationals just to continue to confuse the judges."

Annabelle Lee steps back. "You're going to the Nationals? In Twist? Isn't it for three days? Friday, Saturday, and another Sunday? What about your...?" Annabelle Lee gestures to the members of Paul's congregation who have begun to gather around them. "You going to take the entire congregation to Twist? For a weekend?"

Just then Cruisewell walks up waving his arms in the air. "Paul! Pastor Paul! You did it! Our champion!" The members of the congregation hoot and holler and clap. "And! Guess what?" He waves a check. "I...we...sold it!" The clapping and cheering explode!

Annabelle Lee says so only Paul can hear, "At least there was someone smarter than those stupid judges."

Paul doesn't answer. He's still trying to believe that the ostrich sold. A price was never discussed. No one even indicated interest.

"Cruisewell, what happened? How? Who?"

"Well, it's going into a major collection. The buyer said she was sorry to have missed you, but she had to get back to Seattle. She's on deadline."

"Hattie? Hattie was here?"

"Yep."

"And she bought it?"

"Yep."

Cruisewell hands the check to Paul. "Truth is she left for two reasons. Because she bought your piece, she can't write about you. She also thought you'd not accept the check. So here you go! Oh, and she did suggest you might want to give ten percent to New Dawn, not that I suggested it, well, I did suggest it." Paul studies the number. He's beginning to think Hattie is as crazy as Cruisewell.

"This is crazy! Five thousand dollars? Who came up with a number like that?"

"Hattie did. She thought it was appropriate."

"Nobody pays that much for chainsaw art."

"Well, guess what. She did." Cruisewell turns and waves at Rex and Bill. "When you've stowed the saws, be sure to join us!" Cruisewell ignores Paul and addresses the women who stand preening and exclaiming over their winner. "Ladies, let's go celebrate! Dinner's on me! See you in the Barbecue Beef House! Everyone, forward!" And as if he were leading troops to battle, everyone follows Reverend Cruisewell as he waves them forward. He sings 'Bringing in the Sheaves' and the women join in.

It's a party! Even the crowd that watches joins in the singing.

Paul hesitates. He still has not been able to accept the idea that he's five thousand dollars richer. Well, less ten percent. And he knows Jack will expect some kind of cut. How much? Paul hasn't a clue.

"You heard the man, Paul. Come along." Paul doesn't resist. He stuffs the five thousand dollar check with the one hundred dollar check in his pocket and lets Annabelle Lee take his hand.

As they walk Paul can't help thinking, 'meerac!' How had all of this happened? Winning, but not winning. Annabelle Lee by his side. Not only by his side, but her hand in his! Why has she forgotten ideas about 'tree slaughtering?' Why is she so defensive of him? As they walk he revels in all her words, replays them, feels so damn good! Everything is going so well, he can hardly believe it.

Inside the Beef House everyone gets in line. Cruisewell heads to the cashier and in a not so quiet voice, he informs her that the New Dawn is Breaking Church of the Living Lord and their minister, Pastor Paul, are all on his tab.

Paul stands in line behind Annabelle Lee. Suzie and Sam wiggle their way in front of them. Annabelle Lee's hands rest on the shoulders of the two children. Paul thinks of placing his hands on the back of her shoulders, but resists, realizing that the Wittenhouer twins are directly behind him chatting about some teenagers with purple hair and nose rings who certainly must cause their parents pain. "Totally out of control!" Paul does not touch Annabelle Lee. He is in control. He does lean forward, however, just to where he can see the light shining through her ear, shell-like and kissable. He takes a good-sized breath and asks, "What did you do when you weren't watching the carving?"

She turns slightly as she moves down the line, "Everything! You name it and the three of us did it. Saundra joined us most of the time. We rode every ride, except I begged off the Rocketship. Bill took Suzie. Sam and I rode a bucking dinosaur thing. Great wasn't it, Sam?" Sam swivels under Annabelle Lee's hands to give her a big smile. She continues, "I've eaten an elephant ear, a corndog, a caramel apple. I can't believe I'm in line to eat again!"

"And Saundra? When she wasn't with you?"

"Who knows. I was pleased with the time she did spend with us. And Suzie? Suzie let her pleasure show almost all the time. Right, little Suzie?"

Suzie, says with a smile, "Yes, it's been a wonderful day!"

As they approach the display of food, Sam and Suzie point to choices and soon their plates are brimming. Paul savors the feeling of 'family'. He realizes he is also confused. He wonders how long it will be before the 'tree' problem slips back into their conversation. Annabelle Lee has not said one word all day about the destruction of forests, and there has been ample opportunity. All those cutters. All those stripped logs. The Nationals will be worse. Bigger trees. More cutters. Paul can't believe it when Annabelle Lee turns and sneaks a quick kiss on Paul's cheek. "You are such a winner!"

Paul can feel himself teetering on the edge of word-disaster. Did she mean he was a 'winner' generically, totally, or did she mean his carving, and if she meant the carving, what about the disaster of a conversation at her house? He fears if he responds wrong, another discussion will blow the whole afternoon away. Swallowing hard, he changes the subject, "Too bad we all can't go to Twist. You'd love it up there..." Paul stops. He'd almost said, "...there's lots of mountains. And trees."

"And just how is it you can go and leave your congregation behind? Again?"

Paul's spirits drop. She's right. In the excitement, the reality of the situation folds around him. "Can't, I guess. No way I can."

"Hey! Paul!" Chainsaw Jack is moving down the line of people. "I need to talk to you! Now!"

Suzie's eyes grow large. Sam murmurs, "Uh oh," and Annabelle Lee says, "We'll be right over there. I'll take your tray. Join us when you're done. "

Paul follows Jack. Before they are even out the back door of the building, Jack is grinding his teeth and when they are out the door, Jack explodes. "You idiot! You did it again! I can't believe it. You broke the rules. You must want to embarrass me!" Jack flings his arms in the air. He bangs the barn boards on the side of the building. Paul fears the noise will carry inside and soon everyone will be privy to this idiotic exchange.

Angry over Jack's loud outburst, Paul demands, "What rules? You read any rules? Nothing, anywhere, says I can't add anything I want!"

"Written! Schmitten! You know those judges. You've done this so many damn times! I learned all about your shenanigans today! You've got a reputation for doing this stuff! A bad reputation!"

"Then get yourself another carver! Better yet! Carve yourself! I carve what I carve. I'm the best you've got! If the judges can't see it? That's their problem!"

Jack raises his hand wide open and he bangs the wall again. His hand snaps back. "Damn!" A large sliver protrudes from his palm. "Now look what you've made me do!" He pulls out the sliver, sucks on the wound. "We've got a deal!" He spits. "You're my carver! Just get it straight next time!"

"Okay, today I'm your carver." Paul pulls the check out of his pocket. "See this? See this, you idiot?" Paul makes a decision at that very moment. "Half of it is yours. Well, half of it less ten percent. I'm tithing. So ten percent goes to the church. The remainder we split evenly."

Jack stops cold. "Really?" he asks in a totally shocked voice. "Really?"

"Yes, now I'm going to go eat dinner."

Jack walks away. Like he needs a time out. Paul is glad to give it to him.

Inside the Beef House everyone is busy chatting, eating, congratulating each other over the day's success. Paul slips onto a bench next to Annabelle Lee and the children. They look up expectantly. Paul realizes they must have heard some of the yelling, they look so sorry for him. He shrugs his shoulders and reaches for one of the cobs of corn. "Just Jack. Hollerin'. Not to worry. He's about as happy as a man can get. Let's eat."

Sam scoots around the end of the table. He looks up at Paul with wide eyes, "You're the best!" He gives Paul a big hug. Chocolate and cotton candy in Sam's hair attracts sawdust off Paul like a magnet.

"And you're my best supporter," Paul says and kisses the gooey mess.

"I don't know about that!" Annabelle Lee exclaims. Directly behind her Cruisewell appears. "I don't know about that, either!" he chimes in.

Sam slips back to his place. Cruisewell sidles in next to Suzie. He leans over to speak to Paul, "We're on our way, you know! Nationals next!" he exclaims.

"How's that?" Paul asks, wipes his mouth, trying not to choke.

"We'll work it out!" Cruisewell answers. "Everything works out!"

The words are like ambrosia.

41

NOTHING HAPPENS AS PLANNED OR IMAGINED

Cruisewell stands. He signals one of the waiters to bring a pitcher of lemonade and paper cups. When everyone has received their allotment, Reverend Cruisewell turns to Paul and cups are held in tribute.

"Here's to Pastor Paul, chainsaw artist extraordinaire, and the New Dawn Is Breaking Church of the Living Lord Outreach Program!" The women cheer. Bill slams his hand on the table. Rex out does him, brings his huge hands together to make echoing, hollow claps that draws the attention of the entire room. The room breaks into applause and Cruisewell urges Paul to stand and accept the accolades.

As he stands blushing and absorbing the attention, Paul thinks, "So, this is an outreach program."

Cruisewell drains his cup and makes room for Paul to sit next to him. In a confidential hunch, he leans his arms on the table, but pulls back when he sees bits and pieces of food embedded in the wood. For the moment, words are forgotten and his attention is totally on the elbows of his perfectly clean suit.

Paul waits. He'll wait Cruisewell out. As long as it takes. If there's a miracle in the works, Cruisewell is in charge. Then as if he's changed his mind, Cruisewell turns to Annabelle Lee on his other side and says, "Did you know he had this hidden talent?"

"More hidden than you'd ever guess," she answers. "What are you going to do about it?"

Paul hears a challenge in her voice and wonders what happened to the angry woman. The woman who from one moment to another appears to like him and hate him. Paul listens to the interchange between Annabelle

Lee and Cruisewell and accepts the fact that sometimes you just don't know.

"Well, it's time we got this light, meaning Paul's cutting ability, out from under a bushel! The Nationals! We've just got to figure it out!"

"I trust you mean you'll figure it out?"

"Indeed!" Cruisewell points his finger heavenward. "Nothin' we can't figure out. I figure more things out than you'd ever dream."

Paul feels compelled to object. "This is crazy. The Nationals are in Twist. It takes a day to get there. A day to get back. And the carving days in between."

"Pay no attention to him, Annabelle Lee. We're in the miracle business. Somehow. Some way. We'll get there," Cruisewell says with authority. "Watch out, Twist, here we come!"

"Well, one of us will already be there!" Annabelle Lee says.

Paul turns to her, "Who do you mean?"

"Me! I'll be in Twist. Tomorrow."

"You will?" Paul asks, incredulous. "That's my hometown," he stutters, as if everyone didn't know by now.

"Of course. It was your idea. A perfect location."

"Location for what? What idea?"

"Paul, there's just no reason," Cruisewell interrupts, "if everyone pitches in, we can't just have a little caravan to Twist for the Nationals. A service! A celebration! Further our outreach program. There's even an empty log cabin church there. We can figure it out!"

"Take the entire congregation…to Twist?" Paul asks.

"Place does not determine when or how we worship. And there is that church…" Cruisewell seems to drift off.

"You sure? I thought that log cabin church was a museum," Paul states knowing for sure that that church has been a museum for years.

"No, no. It's a historical monument. I'm sure we can get it for a service at some odd hour when it's not busy and you're not cutting. Anyone who can make a garage into a chapel can certainly borrow a real log cabin church for a service or two. Or we'll rent it. If I have to I'll buy it!"

"Buy a historical monument?"

"Well, right. Maybe not buy it. We'll borrow it. Settled."

Cruisewell's beaming smile takes in the whole room as if the whole room is part and parcel to the church, or the congregation. More people are listening, and heads are nodding, and calendars are being marked in the crowded fair eatery, where believers and non-believers have in common the love of a fair, and the growing love of chainsaw art.

Paul looks around at the widows, most of whom have been too busy eating or visiting to have heard every word, but he can see the announcement circling the room like a game of 'telephone'. As each woman hears the announcement, she turns to smile at Paul and wave at Reverend Cruisewell as if to say, "Count me in!"

What astounds Paul is that Cruisewell seems to know so much about Twist. Not everyone knows the small log cabin church even exists.

Cruisewell continues, "I know these women. Take note, Paul. Watch as they hear the news. They're keen for new ideas. Let's have a planning meeting the minute we get back to New Dawn. They'll need time to pack and buy toothpaste and a new outfit." Cruisewell beams his energy at Suzie, "You too, little miss. Toothpaste and a new outfit!" Suzie looks dubious.

"Don't you worry, missy. Your mom is going to get a big chunk of overtime next week, and I have work for her to do in Twist, so no question, you'll both need new outfits."

Cruisewell places his hand on Paul's arm, speaks at him with a sureness that is pure tele-evangelist, pure Randi MacArthur Cruisewell, "I guarantee you, this will work! It's a sin to pass up opportunities given by the Lord. Besides, think of the headline it will make! 'Hometown Boy Comes Home!'"

Paul moans, "I've only been gone three weeks. Not even!"

"Just shows how quickly we work." Before Paul can respond, Cruisewell waves his arms in the air. "Ladies of New Dawn! Time we should be getting home. Suzie, Sam, time to watch Sixty Minutes in the limo."

In the lot, Paul finds his ostrich and Jack's saws loaded and ready to go. Extra hands had joined Jack to load the truck. Saundra's presence helped. Four of the competitors stand near her joking and talking. Jack looks at Paul and says, "We're ready to go! Packed and secured. I'll deliver the art."

When did Jack start using the word 'art?'

"I offered. To your patron, Hattie."

"Patron?" Paul can't believe it. Who is this Jack, anyway?

"With that, we're out of here!" Jack hoists Saundra into the passenger seat.

Next to them, the limo fills. Everyone cheers as the ostrich heads west.

"How'd he know all that?"

"I told him," answers Cruisewell. "And he didn't hesitate when I mentioned that Hattie is a reporter. I think his words were, 'I already know her! She's my kind of woman'. That Jack, he knows an opportunity when he sees one!"

The women rearrange themselves and when all is done, Paul doesn't know how, but the Wittenhouer twins had already left with Jack, and Olga Simmons has squeezed into the limo. Paul is pleased; Annabelle Lee sits next to him. They're alone. Another miracle.

"You've had a day of it, would you like me to drive?" Annabelle Lee offers.

"That'd be great," Paul rubs his sore arms and registers his exhaustion.

Once on the highway, Paul leans back into the corner of the seat to better look at Annabelle Lee.

"Did you enjoy the day?"

"Perfect. Very, very exciting, in fact."

"How's that?"

"I got an appointment in Twist. Tomorrow."

Paul sits up, totally curious. "With?"

"Well, I can't talk about it much. It's with a realtor. So, whether you end up in Twist or not for the Nationals, I'll be there!"

"You said that earlier. I can't believe it!"

"Well, it's not so serendipitous as it looks," Annabelle Lee continues, "You knew I won the money—the grant?"

"Yes."

"And remember I told you how all of the glass blowers have dreamed of a place to work, a kind of retreat? Well, you talked so lovingly of Twist, I called a realtor. Meerac! As you would say. There's a piece of land...," the excitement in her voice is palpable. Paul can almost see the tall trees. He can almost smell the clean mountain air.

"Just like that?"

"Just like that."

"What piece of land?" he asks, certain he'll be able to identify every tree and blade of grass in the parcel.

"I can't tell you."

"Why not?" Paul sits up. Attentive.

"It's complicated. Semi-secret. It's a hot piece of land."

"Someone else making a bid against you?"

"Something like that."

It is clear she isn't going to tell him. Paul really wants to know. "I promise not to tell. Cross my heart."

"No. I really can't tell. I'll be there through the Nationals. But before that, I hope to have secured the land and have everything in writing."

"My God, you are serious!"

"God has nothing to do with it...maybe...but I don't want to jinx the deal by talking about it. So enough. The minute I've secured the land, you'll be the first to know."

Paul can see by the set of her shoulders, the way she holds the wheel, there is no way Annabelle Lee is going to tell him more. They drive out of Monroe and ease onto the freeway headed to Seattle.

A mile or two later, the silence makes Paul want to discuss the subject they have been avoiding all day.

"So what did you *really* think of the competition?"

"I told you. You know what I think of your carving. It's fabulous."

"Yes. I like it that you were pleased. But what about…"

"The trees?"

The tension snaps back between them.

"Maybe there are certain things on which we should agree to disagree," Annabelle Lee says, her voice cool and firm.

Paul does not want to disagree. He wants to be together with this woman. He wants the warmth back. He wants her in every way. Screw the trees.

Annabelle Lee's fingers curl around the steering wheel. He can see she is containing herself. Not saying what she feels.

"Like I said…" he began.

"Let it go, Paul. Don't preach to me. It's just too bad you carve…trees…"

"Yeah, right. Too bad for the trees." He hasn't meant to, but his voice carries a 'you are really wrong' tone to it. He can't stop, "Do you know how much energy it takes to fuel one of your furnaces? For an hour? For a day? One log wouldn't touch what glass blowers use in natural resources!"

That does it. The silence is back. Like ice. Paul pulls the collar of his jacket tight around his neck. He turns to the window.

Outside the dividing lines on the freeway click past. Late afternoon clouds slump down over the jagged hills. Rain spits and then slaps at the windshield. The windshield wipers wipe and pause. Wipe and pause. Then the wipers move into high gear. Slap. Slap. Slap.

Paul wakes when Annabelle Lee pulls in front of her house.

"It's been a day," she says. She is clearly still brewing about the trees and unforgiving about his outburst.

"That it has," Paul answers, trying to pull her back to the 'couples' feeling he'd been dreaming about.

Annabelle Lee hands him the keys to the Jeep as she opens the door. "See you then. Sometime."

"Sure. We'll do that," he answers, totally bewildered over the huge gulf that spreads between them.

Annabelle Lee gathers her jacket and her bag from the back seat. She rummages for her keys. For one second they could bridge the gap, but neither speaks and Paul watches as Annabelle Lee walks to her front door. He watches as she puts the key in the lock. The front door closes and the lock snaps into place.

He knows he should have gotten out, walked her to the front door. Been gentlemanly. He didn't. He just didn't think she wanted him to. And he isn't sure he wanted to, either.

42

A PLANNING SESSION

Back at the trailer court, the widows are seated in the chapel. An urn of coffee percolates and chocolate chip cookies are at the ready. Everyone listens with surprise and pleasure as Randi Cruisewell lays out the plans to attend the Nationals at Twist.

"We can caravan very much like we did the other day. Rex can't join us until Sunday, he's got a business to run, but I've got a friend with an airplane. We'll get Rex there." Cruisewell looks at his check-off list. "Grandma Bella and Big Bill can take two in their car. Paul, I'd like you to drive the limo with the rest of the congregation. I think Jack is the best person to assist Saundra with her bum leg and he can bring all the gear. I'll fly up early to make arrangements." Reverend Cruisewell rocks on his heels, smiles with satisfaction. "So! There we go! It will be a nice little vacation for everybody. We'll worship. We'll play. We'll rest. What more could God want?"

Paul shakes his head in wonderment. He does not point out to Reverend Cruisewell that 'rest' was supposed to be a one-day-in-seven proposition. But, if Cruisewell is willing, Paul is excited at the chance to carve at the Nationals. He's never had so many fans to cheer him on. And this time, he plans to win.

The women break into groups of two and three discussing with their neighbors the 'new outfit' they might need to get, as well as treats for the road. Paul watches and as they speak he begins to wonder if by some fluke he won the Nationals' one-thousand-dollar prize, he might consider paying Cruisewell a first payment. If he sells his carving, a second payment. He's barely touched the ten-thousand Cruisewell has deposited in his checking account, he could pay off the balance. He could put a stop to this charade and have a small nest egg to...and then Paul stops the thought process. If he's not a minister, what else could he be?

"Now, is there any other business?" Cruisewell asks.

"Not to put a damper on anything," Saundra's voice cuts through the buzz of excitement. "But, this is Twist. It is the Nationals. Where will we all stay?"

"Saundra, you know I plan better than that." Cruisewell chastises her. "This afternoon, I made a call. There's a new bed and breakfast under construction. Not quite ready, but I've offered some assistance, and they will be finished and waiting for us! It's ours. I'll leave tomorrow to be sure everything's in place. A small private plane can get me there. That's the same plane for you, Rex." Rex smiles his thanks. "Don't anyone worry. I've put things in good hands. Mine!" Cruisewell chuckles at his own joke.

"What about school?" Suzie asks, her voice full of hope.

"This is an educational trip if there ever was one. I'll write you your teacher's note." Cruisewell's answers no longer surprise Paul. Contingencies are covered.

"That's it?" Suzie asks, pleased and incredulous.

"We work in wondrous ways!"

Suzie's face glows. It is the most content Paul has seen her. The tiny bumps of displeasure that so often lodge in a ridge between her eyes are no longer there. He thinks back over the past few days and cannot recall one scowl or one bit of sarcasm. Sam's remained his happy self.

"Oh, one more piece of glory," Cruisewell comes to stand next to Grandma Bella and Big Bill Dumpster. "These two lovely folks have an announcement to make. Bill? Bella? Do us the pleasure."

The two of them stand. They hold hands. Grandma Bella blushes. Big Bill Dumpster clears his throat. "Well, some of you might have guessed, but it's time to share the good news with everyone. Grandma Bella and I decided to have a little celebration of our own. Reverend Cruisewell made arrangements. For those of you who might have guessed, we've secured a little chapel for a wedding ceremony in Twist. After Pastor Paul wins the Nationals, you're all invited to join us at the Log Cabin Chapel." Bill beams and gives Bella a hug.

Suzie and Sam explode with cheers and hops and hugs. They hug Grandma Bella and they hug Big Bill. Suzie bestows hugs around the room and even hugs her mother. The women smile and not a few get teary. Paul is so pleased for the two of them. Now, if only.

Everyone is pleased. But, before a moment of awareness hits Suzie, a moment that Paul can see coming as Suzie finishes her last hug, there is a dawning awareness that they will not all be able to fit in Grandma Bella's trailer.

"Where will we all live?" she calls, her voice desperate.

Cruisewell reaches for Suzie's hand, gives it a reassuring squeeze and announces, as he looks directly at Suzie, "We want you all here at New Dawn. Grandma Bella is so important to our family. And Big Bill has agreed to accept my wedding gift. A brand new Airstream to fit right next to your current home! You, Saundra and Sam will have your own home!"

From her carry-all, Grandma Bella pulls a large bottle of Chianti. She pulls out another bottle of sparkling cider. Drinks all around!

Saundra stands and raises her cup, "To my mother and to my brand new Dad!"

Everyone cheers and calls, "Here! Here!" and most have a cup of wine. Except for Saundra and Paul, who, with the children, finish off the sparkling cider.

Before the evening ends, Paul has a moment alone with Cruisewell, and makes an observation: "What is it with you pairing up Saundra and Jack. I see you sneaking longing looks at her."

"That obvious, huh?"

"I'd say so."

"I think of it as the Lord's work…" Paul can hear the indecision in Cruisewell's voice. "Or, think of it this way. Maybe she'll just get tired of him, but I'm betting on the Lord."

43

BACK HOME TO TWIST

Paul stretches his arms as if to embrace all of Main Street in downtown Twist. It is one o'clock. He's left his congregation checking into the B & B and has come straight to Travesty John's Big Drinkers' Bar. Elsie is occupied with a four-ßtop and busy directing two high school girls who maneuver trays and take orders.

Paul waits on the front porch and when Elsie has a free moment he pops inside and she opens her arms to give him a big smooch hello. "We've been waiting for you! Welcome home. We're crazy busy, but give me a minute to let the girls take over and I'll join you on the front porch. I can hardly wait to hear more about your life in the big city.

"More?"

"Well, your friend Annabelle Lee has filled us in. She is very, very interesting!" Elsie pats Paul on the back. "Talk to you in a minute." Elsie heads to the kitchen calling out Paul's arrival to Travesty John who is busy finishing up the lunch orders.

Paul hears Travesty yell, "Heh! Heh! Be right there!"

Paul pours himself a crockery mug with coffee and heads for the front porch. Being home is perfect.

The September sun is warm and the shadow-sides of all the buildings have lost their white morning frost. Paul leans back on the steps to take in Twist. Up and down the street booths are being assembled, goods are being unpacked. People call 'hello' and reacquaint themselves. Paul can't believe he is here. Everything so familiar. Everyone so ready to be greeted and he so welcomed back.

The air is pungent with the smell of sun-warmed spicy pines. Behind him is the familiar clink and clatter of customers. Above him, an eagle dips high overhead catching a thermal. Paul sips the rich black coffee and breathes in the cool, crisp air that surrounds him. Even his big rooster beside the front door looks great. He hasn't heard it crow, so maybe Travesty John forgot his threat of adding a recording.

Paul waves to a couple of old-timers, loggers, hanging out at the post office. He tries not to look as if he is looking for anyone particular. In the crowd of workers and gawkers he sees no one with short, black curly hair and a smile that shows a space between her teeth. Annabelle Lee is not to be seen. Paul wonders where she is. Twist isn't that big. He knows they'll run into each other sooner than later. He hasn't a clue what he will say.

Main Street continues to transform itself—almost medieval in presentation: flags flying, banners flapping, canopies sheltering, tent tops pointing skyward. Crews assemble booths, trucks make deliveries, electricians hang wires, vendors arrange pottery and tie-dyed shirts, dried flowers, and wooden toys. At the far end of the street an oilcloth banner slaps in the breeze and the words appear to dance: The Nationals – The World's Best Chainsaw Art.

"Paul! Paul, how the hell!" Travesty John slaps his back with a resounding thud. He pulls up a wooden stool and sits next to Paul. "Man, it's great to see you! How goes it? How's being a minister?"

Paul smiles. He doesn't have an answer.

"That good, huh? Well, it's great to have you back. Brummer should be here any minute. He wants to talk to you, first thing."

"What's up?"

Paul feels Elsie's arm slip over his shoulder. She eases herself down on the step next to him. Paul is overcome with smiles. He's so darn happy to be sitting between Elsie and John.

"Let me get a look at you," Elsie says, pulling back from Paul.

"It's not been that long." Paul is pleased, but he wonders, as she scrutinizes him, at the intensity of her look.

"You're right. Everything about you looks the same, right down to the boots."

"Can't find anything that feels as good as these boots."

"You'll never get this ministry thing down 'till you get the hair right," Travesty says as he reaches to muss Paul's hair.

Paul ducks away from Travesty's outstretched hand and then runs his fingers through his hair to give it a reasonable patting down.

"Just trying to give you a little loft there. Make you more ministerish," Travesty says with a chuckle. "Now tell us more about what's up. Exactly."

"Well, I'd say what's most interesting is that Cruisewell seems more normal to me all the time. I hardly even notice his hair. Or his white suits, or the clank of his gold chains. That's how bad it's gotten. By the way, have you seen him?"

"He's around. Not that we've seen him that much. He's on the go. In and out. Gets take-out and then he's gone. Do you know anything about what he's up to? We're all very curious."

"It confounds me. He confounds me. Money everywhere. But…speak of the devil." He points. As if parting the Red Sea, Cruisewell walks down the center of Main Street. The crowd makes way. "Here he comes. Let's ask him. Straight out, just who in the hell are you, masked man?"

"That would be an interesting question. But I would guess you need to show some respect. What with his supporting you," Elsie says, and then hesitates to ask, "but if we did prod him, what would he say?"

"No question, it's hard in the face of his continuous generosity to ask him anything tough. I know nothing more than I knew before. Except he seems to be involved in everybody's life. And you seem to think something's going on here. Right?"

"Right. You won't believe this, but he told John that because 'his people' would be taking over the bar so many times during the Nationals, he'd like to pay our mortgage for the month. Right, John?"

"Well, right, but I was surprised he didn't know, we don't have a mortgage. Haven't had one in years."

"So?"

"Cruisewell rolled out three hundred-dollar bills and insisted John take them. No argument. That was that!"

They watch as Cruisewell approaches. Behind him, like ducklings, follow the troop of widows. Sam and Suzie slip in and out of the growing number of booths in a game of tag. Grandma Bella and Big Bill bring up the rear, accepting congratulations. The pageant-like procession has a regal feeling to it. Animation and excitement surround The New Dawn congregation. No question people are curious about The Reverend.

"Reverend Cruisewell! Come say hello to Elsie and Travesty John," Paul calls. "They say you haven't had much time to spend with them! Been so busy."

Reverend Cruisewell skips up the steps, his hand extended to Paul. "Glad you made it. Hello, dear folks. And let it be known that I've not had much time with you, not because I didn't want to. We've just got things happening!" He winks at Paul. "All will be revealed. Soon! All very interesting. A few problems here and there, but nothing we can't handle. Little faith. Little money. Give some. Take some." Reverend Cruisewell rattles on. Paul can't keep up with the innuendos, the half-messages, the veiled bits of information. What he wants, and it doesn't happen, is for Cruisewell to mention Annabelle Lee. No luck.

"You're becoming quite a regular around these parts," Travesty John addresses Reverend Cruisewell. Paul hears the wide open sentence. Cruisewell answers with a wide open exclamation. "Love this country! Love being with all of you. Elsie, John, forgive me. Let me introduce Paul's parishioners." As each woman steps forward, Reverend Cruisewell performs the introductions. When he finishes, Elsie ushers everyone inside. "We're ready for you!" she exclaims. "Treats courtesy of Reverend Cruisewell!"

Out of earshot of the women, Paul says to Travesty John, "Can you believe it? My entire congregation in The Big Drinkers' Bar!"

Two round oak tables are filled with bagels, cream cheese, lox, and capers, peanut butter and sliced Granny Smiths. Elsie passes coffee and encourages the women to make themselves welcome to the snacks. Before anyone has taken a bite, Cruisewell announces, "Well, if you'll excuse me, I've a meeting. Enjoy yourselves. Here are quarters for the juke box. I'll see you at dinner!"

Elsie offers the plate of bagels to Cruisewell. He tips his head to say 'thank you,' wraps a single bagel inside a napkin and hurries out the door. He disappears into the crowd, and Paul strains to see which direction he's headed. How he'd love to follow. He's sure Cruisewell would lead him to Annabelle Lee.

The door opens and six of the concessionaires fill a corner table. Elsie grabs Paul's arm and whispers, "How would you like to earn a couple hours wages? What with the Reverend, the congregation, and the regulars, we could really, really use you." Elsie hands him a towel to tie around his waist and Paul immediately resorts to not being a minister. Or maybe, feeding the flock is just that. The thought makes him smile. It's so damn good to be home.

Over the chatter in the bar, Paul can just make out the rumble of a Harley threading its way along River Road. The grumble of the engine grows closer and then stops at the back of The Big Drinkers' Bar.

"Got to be Brummer!" Paul calls to Travesty John.

"Be quick! But go let him know you're here!"

Paul heads to the back door and Brummer, coming up the stairs two at a time, almost collides with Paul.

"Paul! Hot Damn! Spindler, say hi to Paul!" Brummer turns as if he expects Spindler to be right behind him. Next to his Harley is Spindler's Vespa. Spindler has already disappeared. "That kid! Thought he'd hang around, but no, he's gone. Again. Like that!" Brummer snaps his fingers. "If I'd known you'd be right out, I would have chained him to the bike. Damn. Maybe he needs some pastoral counseling! Or a good whop up-side the head. Something!"

"Oh, great idea! Me advising Spindler. Besides, why would Spindler need advice?"

Brummer groans and wipes his face with his bandanna, "Be glad you don't have kids!"

"He couldn't have changed that much in three weeks."

"Wrong."

The back screen door bangs and Travesty John joins them.

"You tell him, John. Tell him about my bird-brained son."

"Started with that nose ring, if you ask me," Travesty John answers. "Spindler is a mess. His nose all full of scabs, blood, and snot. Brummer, I thought you had more control."

"Right. Me, control Spindler? Let's get a beer. Take my mind off of him, it, whatever he's up to."

Paul holds the door for his two friends. Inside they fill the back booth.

"Brummer, what's going on? He's always been such a good kid. What's up?"

"Who knows? It's a long story. A crazy, long story. Let's get that beer."

At the bar, Paul can see the grill is hot and Travesty can use some help.

"Brummer, so sorry. The kitchen needs help. Go join the guys. Later, we'll sit down to a nice long talk…if no customers come in." Paul points to the apron by way of explaining that he has been rehired.

Paul cooks. Travesty pulls beers.

Grandma Bella finds Brummer in the back booth and gives him a big hug, hello. She calls all the women over. Pretty soon Paul and Travesty have served beer to all of the widows. Finally, things settle down and Paul heads back to the kitchen. As he pushes through the swinging doors, he stops. Across the room, at the window, Elsie holds Spindler's head turned to the light. Paul overhears her say, "Sweetie, it's going to heal. Just leave it alone. The least of your worries." Elsie dabs a cotton swab at Spindler's red nose.

Paul waits as Elsie's eye catches his. Spindler's voice, full of childish need of reassurance asks, "You sure?"

"Sure, I'm sure. Later, you come talk to me." Elsie pats Spindler on the back. "For now, get on with you. You aren't going to lose your nose. At least not today. And, sweetie, take care of yourself." Elsie gave Spindler a loving push on the shoulder.

Spindler turns around. His eyes go wide at the sight of Paul.

"What you starin' at?" Spindler's words are meant to sting. The teenager stomps past Paul. Elsie comes to stand next to Paul as they listen to the thud of Spindler's motorcycle boots echo on the wood floor. The back door slams.

"What was that all about?" Paul asks. He watches with Elsie at the window as Spindler cranks the engine of his Vespa and disappears out of sight.

Elsie shakes her head and sighs, "He's not at his best, lately, that's for sure. You'll hear about it."

Paul wrinkles his nose and makes snuffling noises. "Before we get into any bad news, let me get a smell of you. Why Elsie, you smell like sweet fried onions!"

"Is that an order?"

"Well, about a half hour ago I was going to hustle up a burger for Brummer, but…"

"Let me get at that. While I cook, catch me up on everything that's happened since you left."

Paul counts on his fingers, "Well, I haven't preached. I haven't recruited. I haven't married anybody. I haven't buried anybody. What else haven't I done?"

"How about spending Cruisewell's money. How does that go?" Elsie asks as she slaps hamburgers on the grill.

"Don't remind me. I haven't spent much, but anything I have spent is his money. It's crazy, Elsie. I don't know what this ministry-thing is about. I'm starting to feel trapped. I *am* trapped!" Paul accepts a glass of cold milk from Elsie. "And what's bizarre, is that I've done more cutting in the last three weeks then I did the last three years."

"That's good news! It's got to be a sign." Elsie grabs a Walla Walla Sweet and soon under a glob of butter the slices curl and turn translucent. The kitchen fills with the smell of caramelized onions. Paul closes his eyes and breathes deep.

Elsie brings him back. "Paul! Tell me more! If you're not a logger and you're not a minister, and you've been spending Cruisewell's money, how are you ever going to come home?"

Travesty John stands at the door. "He'll win the Nationals!"

Paul sighs. He accepts the plates Elsie hands him. "Money I've got for hamburgers. Buying my freedom I haven't got. Yet. Should I win? Well, I haven't bowled them over the last two weekends."

"So we've heard," Travesty John says.

"How's that?" Paul asks.

"Annabelle Lee. She told us you weren't picking up first place ribbons. She did say you were a spectacular carver, however. A little excitement in the eyes, I'd say. I half expected her to be here to meet you."

"She said that? To you? I can't believe it." Paul stutters. Then he decides to shut up. He realizes he sounds too earnest, too excited, too wanting, and he guesses he is probably a deep shade of red.

Whether Elsie and Travesty John notice, or whether they just don't want to embarrass Paul further, he can see them ignore his confusion.

Elsie scoots them out of the kitchen. "Take a breather. Go join Brummer. You guys need to talk."

Travesty John keeps talking as if the conversation hasn't ended. "That woman friend of yours has been here for the last three days. She chums with Cruisewell, on and off. So we don't see much of them. Between those two, I don't know which one is the busiest." He raises his eyebrows, as if he expects Paul to explain.

"Wait! I don't get it!" Paul exclaims. "You think the two of them are here together?"

"Nah, I don't think they're here together, together. They're just together a lot. Everyone's talking. Some kind of a deal. Craziness, if you ask me. It seems whatever happens they're in it together."

"What business deal?"

"She told us that she told you all about it," Travesty John says.

"All about what?"

"The land she's looking at. The art center?"

Brummer listens, follows the conversation like a ping-pong game.

Paul shakes his head as if he's just walked through a patch of cobwebs. "The center? The art center?"

Elsie arrives with two beers and another glass of milk. "John would you check on the girls. They look like they could use some help. Brummer, why don't you entertain the congregation. They could use some manly attention. Paul, I could use your help again."

Travesty leaves. Brummer strolls over toward the widows, hesitancy in his stride, but a smile on his face.

"Come with me Paul." In the kitchen Elsie throws an onion to Paul. She grabs three tomatoes. "Slice and listen to me."

"What's this all about?" Paul asks.

"First, tell me about Annabelle Lee."

"About her being here? I don't know that much about her being here. You two seem to know a whole lot more than I know about anything."

Elsie finishes the tomatoes. She peels carrots, chops them until there's a pile of orange disks under her knife.

Paul can't handle the silence. "She did say she has this idea about a center. An art center. That she is looking at some land. Wouldn't tell me much about it. Big secret. Competition, I think. Fearful she might not get it. I honestly don't know more than that. What do you know?"

"Let me tell *you* something. I've served breakfast to Annabelle Lee every morning for the last three mornings. We talk. I can tell you this. This is no dreamin' woman. This is a woman with a goal. She's the kind of woman…well, I've never said anything to you like this before, but if I were you, I'd find out what she's *really* doing."

"Like what? What are you talking about?" Paul doesn't wait for Elsie to answer. He says, "What you need to understand is, she isn't going to tell me any big secrets. She thinks I'm a tree butcherer."

"Well, it would help if you got her alone and found out about the trees."

"The trees? What trees? And getting her alone? I haven't even seen her."

Paul would love to get her alone. "I'm afraid I haven't much of a chance with her, in any way. Our last words weren't all that pleasant."

"A few words. Pay no mind. Everyone has a few words. John and I have our words. But, that's not what I hear in her voice. Not wanting to see you. Let me give you some womanly advice. When you see her…"

Travesty John comes through the door to fill the coffee pot. He gives them a look, shrugs his shoulders and leaves.

"You look like a deer in headlights," Elsie says.

"I just had a horrible idea. What if Cruisewell…what if Cruisewell and Annabelle Lee…could it happen? Oh, God, Elsie, what if he's worked his stupid magic on her. Geeze, I didn't even think of that. Look at the people he corrals and you say you've seen them together…and…"

Brummer bounds into the kitchen, an empty beer mug in hand. "Now, for some dessert!" He pulls up a kitchen stool. "Elsie, love of my life, well, love of my best friend's wife, how about you add me to the list of those demanding scrambled eggs. Something to top off that hamburger?"

"List of one," Elsie says.

"Great. Puts me first," Brummer says and makes kissy sounds to Elsie. Elsie throws a towel at him and she reaches with two hands for four eggs.

Brummer turns to Paul, "Being so preoccupied with Spindler, I haven't had a chance to tell you the most important thing. We've got a problem!"

Paul looks up from his chopping, relieved he doesn't have to pursue the dizzy, nauseous, stupid idea of Cruisewell and Annabelle Lee. Any problem was better than that problem. "What's up?" Paul asks.

"You didn't notice anything strange about the set-up for carving?" Brummer asks.

"I haven't been all the way down Main Street. Saw the sign. Looks like everything's under control."

At that moment Travesty John returns to the kitchen, places the coffee pot on the back of the stove. "Finished my job. All the women have gone back to their rooms to 'freshen up'. Mind if I join you?"

Brummer demands of Travesty John, "Tell Paul. Tell him the whole catastrophe."

"About the problem?"

Brummer nods and Travesty plows into the next sentence. "Yep. Indeed. We do have a problem. A big, big problem."

Brummer checks his watch. "And we've got exactly sixteen hours to fix it."

"I was hoping I had an answer to tell you, but guess it's time…," Elsie says as she hands Brummer his eggs and speaks to Paul, "…we've got us a mess…"

"Would all of you quit walking around whatever it is. Spit it out, for Christ's sake." Paul feels a gentle slap on his cheek. "Sorry, Elsie." He catches her hand to give it a gentle squeeze. "A problem? Can't be that bad."

Travesty John explains, "Well, indeed it is. In a nutshell, this Miss Annabelle Lee made a bid on the trees they were going to use for the cut."

"What? She...?" Paul asks.

"Annabelle Lee. Your friend Annabelle Lee."

"How can that be? The trees always come from Woodhouse's Timber. Besides, she's all about protecting trees. Not cutting trees."

"Not exactly." Travesty rubs his knuckles against his eyes, growls and answers, "It appears we screwed up. Instead of working with Woodhouse as usual, we decided to go for some big trees. Really big. We heard there was some clearing on National Park land. A fire lane. Not first growth, but some pretty amazing second growth. We checked out the area. Appears they were cut over a year ago. On the edge of the park. Spectacular trees and certainly bigger trees than we've ever had before. And then along comes Annabelle Lee. She makes some kind of offer, or she and Cruisewell did, because the offer was big enough to create a lot of government paperwork and she buys up the entire cut. In addition she's bidding on both the cleared land and the cleared logs...something about second growth needs permits from the government and can only be used for public buildings. All of this demands another environmental study. Slows the process way, way down. Which we think was her way of stopping everything and she oiled the state wheels with her money and her suggestions and that was that. Well, almost."

"So? No logs?"

"Right. No logs. And in the meantime, Woodhouse Timber is pissed because we ignored them. After their name was on everything all these years."

"Yes, Elsie, 'pissed' may be a crude word, but it's the correct word, and now we have no trees."

Brummer interjects, "Not having trees didn't cross our minds. Everything has moved so fast. The state's hard up for money, and here comes a piss-pot full. All we wanted was more attention on the competition and we were sure it would come with those really big trees." He clears his throat and rubs his hands as if to loosen the story from deep inside him. "We figured it's the Nationals. The Nationals! Here in Twist! The committee decided we should go for the biggest trees we could find. We told Woodhouse we didn't need their trees this time. And guess what? They don't like being turned down. In a bit of a snit!"

Travesty groans and continues his story, "Then Annabelle Lee shows up. Makes an offer, and everything comes to a roaring halt. She wants the land, the very land, the very trees, and her conditions are, 'don't use those trees for other than an art center!' So now, we're shit out of luck. She's not too popular right now with some people."

"And that's where Spindler comes in. He's passing out brochures. People taking sides." Brummer's whole body slumps. He looks like he's been sledge-hammered.

Elsie adds her explanation, "Yeah, the poor kid. You saw his mood. Well, someone paid him a few bucks…let me see…," Elsie pushes a phone book aside, and finds the flyer. "Here. Take a look for yourself."

Paul can't believe it! On the front of the flyer is a photo of Annabelle Lee. His heart stops. It is a picture he's seen on one of her aerobics flyers— all Spandex and long legs. Below her picture are large black capital letters: STOP THIS WOMAN. The pamphlet reads: *Outsiders have come to town. This woman has disrupted the National Chainsaw Art Competition. Stop her from buying our trees! Stop the Extremists! Stop this environmental hogwash! This is your competition! This is your chance to bring attention to Twist. Bring more business! Bring more jobs! Let your officials know! You cannot be bought! Stop her now!*"

"What the…" Paul whistles a soft sad whistle.

"It is a bit strange. The logs under dispute are from that stretch near Stewart Peak. Between Reynolds Road and Hinter Land Creek," Brummer explains.

"But there's no question that's national forest!" Paul exclaims, his voice full of doubt. "How can it be under dispute? The trees must have been cut for fire lanes. Fire Lanes are what save the forests."

"According to whoever put this flyer out," Brummer points to the name at the bottom of the flyer, The Save Our Jobs Foundation, "That outfit thinks she needs to be stopped."

"What you don't know is that there's been surveyors everywhere. Even before all this getting trees and not getting trees. The feds have been surveying and the privates been surveying and these foundation guys been surveying. Some mighty big differences of opinion. In the middle of it is your lady friend. Last Monday, out of the blue there's a town meeting and she puts her nose in it. Tells everyone about her offer and that she's hoping to build a school here, and bring artists and tourists and collectors. All hell breaks loose. Because you see, there's a second foundation. Kind of."

"And it appears the boundaries on the land aren't quite clear," Elsie adds. "Bids and counter bids have been flying. Well, only two to be truthful. But given both, everything has come to a stand still and in the end, there are no logs for the Nationals."

"What you're saying is, we have nothing to cut?" Paul asks, still not believing it's possible.

"And we have some really angry folks," Brummer adds nodding.

Paul re-reads the flyer. "This makes no sense. We should just call the Woodhouse folks and say we made a mistake."

"We've tried. We get on some stupid phone tree and we can't get a real human being to talk to us. We can't find anybody to apologize to!"

"Well," Brummer said hesitantly, "It seems someone wrote," Brummer clears his throat, "a committee here at Twist. Another foundation. This one is called A Foundation for The Preservation of Loggers. They heard the news and re-approached Woodhouse. Being a Foundation, and everything, they thought Woodhouse would be a bit forgiving. Real looking stationary and everything. Not just some dumb loggers. Didn't help. So that idea didn't go anywhere."

"Then out of the blue we see the flyers about Annabelle Lee, and someone does call. Offers us bigger logs than we've ever had before. Ten feet, eleven feet tall. Huge logs. It all looked very, very legit. And this second foundation undercut Woodhouse's price by a huge amount."

Travesty can hardly wait to add his two cents. "Extra large logs sounded like a miracle. Good economics...," his voice trails off.

"From the sound of it, let me guess. You two are the first Loggers Foundation?" Paul asks.

Elsie stands next to John, puts her arm around his shoulder. "Paul," she says, "you know John and Brummer love this community. They'd do anything to keep things moving. Twist wouldn't even have the Nationals if it weren't for their efforts. They had no idea we'd run into trouble. That second foundation seemed like a legitimate, if not great, deal."

"Why? Because they had stationary?" Paul asks.

"Don't be mean. It's not becoming a minister."

Travesty John can hardly speak. "Woodhouse is out. Annabelle Lee's made this crazy bid so her logs are out. We talked to someone who promises logs and all we have to do is make a down payment."

"How much?" Paul asks.

"All we had. We sent him five thousand dollars."

"Gone?"

"Yeah, we guess it's gone."

"But the second foundation put out flyers against Annabelle Lee."

"Things are so confused. The only reason Annabelle Lee and, we think, Cruisewell are the front-runners, is they've the most money. But who knows? Everybody snipping at everybody else. It just isn't like us."

"When the flyers showed up being so mean to Annabelle Lee, we knew there was a big problem," Elsie explains, "except for breakfast, we haven't seen that much of her. She seems so nice. Mostly she's been holed up in the office above the Methow Mountains News with the real estate agent."

Brummer interrupts, "It kind of doesn't matter who's to blame. We're running out of time. No one knows what's going on. What we do know is there are no logs and tomorrow morning's going to be here real soon. There's always a chance the mysterious crook who has our five thousand dollars might still come through, but I don't think so. We sent the money and then nothing. Absolutely nothing."

"You don't have any idea who they are? The one with the flyers? The one that called you?" Paul asks.

Brummer groans and says, "Here's how it happened. This guy calls. Sinzano. Says he hears we're having troubles. He promises to outbid everyone. Claims he has connections. Claims he'd get us the best trees. It was all done with letters, phone calls, faxes. Everything was being taken care of with so little hassle, we didn't take time to figure out exactly who he is or his foundation was…is…" Brummer falls silent.

"Except maybe your son," Travesty John says.

"Ooooh, ugh, my stupid son. But he won't say. I've told him to tell me or else. That's done a lot of good. He's more silent and hang-dog than ever. Silent. I couldn't beat it out of him with a stick."

"As well you shouldn't," adds Elsie.

"But there's got to be some one person behind it somewhere, isn't there?" Paul asks.

"The person? Well, we've got a name, but that's about all. Sinzano. Jackson Sinzano. No one's ever seen him. He just seems to know all about competitions. He never hinted at any troubles. He'd take care of previous offers. For us, not to worry. He'd take care of us. He knew just what to say. And he was giving us such a deal."

"None of this makes sense," Paul tries not to sound disgusted. It seems to him his friends have been screwed. Out of stupidity. "And if we find out who he is, so what? Maybe he didn't know the logs were National Forest logs. Maybe this is all a surprise to him too?"

"You'd think if the guy talked as good as he talked, he'd know for sure if trees were legal or not," Elsie argues. "This was no dummy."

"Elsie's right. The guy's smooth. He talks the language. He even suggested he might bring his own business to Twist. Has some development ideas, but says he isn't free to talk about them yet. We bought him. Hook. Line. The whole smush. But of course, we've never seen him. We should have been suspicious when he used the phrase, 'I promise you the moon'. Who talks like that, for God's sake?" Travesty John hits the side of his head with his wrists as if he might pound some sense into his skull.

Paul sits stone still. He can't believe what Travesty's just said.

Elsie pats her husband's back, and finishes with the final, frightening details, "Our money's gone. The contract guarantees him the base amount no matter what. We were to get the gate, plus registration fees. We couldn't lose. He offered a prize of ten thousand dollars. The price would draw the best chainsaw cutters in the country. He did state, for that big a prize, that the winning piece in the competition would be his. We agreed. We couldn't believe the deal we were getting. And he did ask that when he brings his business here, we give him a deal on the Car Repair/Sales Building. That building's been empty for years. Wasn't hard to get him that for almost nothing. So we were to win all the way around. Good buy on logs. The gate. The registration fees. And a prize!"

Paul wipes his face with a paper napkin, wads it up and pushes away the empty milk glass. "I think I'd better find Annabelle Lee," Paul says. "Above the Methow News?" he asks.

Elsie and Travesty John nod their heads, 'Yes'.

"I'll go with you," Brummer offers.

Paul and Brummer hurry from the kitchen and stop next to the customers staring out the window looking down Main Street. Paul looks where they look. He hopes he might, miraculously, see a truck delivering logs. Great big logs! He looks and hopes that all he's heard will be a bad dream and all problems will be solved. Instead, what he sees at the end of Main Street is what everyone is staring at. There is now a second sign, hoisted under the first. It snaps in the breeze. Paul points as if Brummer can't already see what he sees. Paul says in a low, sharp whisper, "It's Jack. Why the newest member of our congregation got to be a major sponsor for the competition I have no idea…well, I do. I have one idea and I'm going to kill him."

At the end of Main Street stretching from one light post to the other flaps a bright yellow banner: CHAINSAW JACK - OFFICAL SPONSOR OF THE NATIONAL CHAINSAW ART COMPETITION. "Chainsaw Jack" is in florescent pink. And Paul knows with absolute certainty the identity of Jackson Sinzano.

Paul stomps back into The Big Drinkers' Bar. Travesty John and Elsie look up, surprised to hear Paul announce, "Well, you've not lost your money! But heaven knows if you'll have any logs. I'll keep you informed." Paul rushes out the door and heads down Main Street. Brummer is right behind him.

44

TAKE YOU TO THE MOON

"Wait! Wait!" Brummer calls as he catches up to Paul. "It's him, isn't it?"

"None other!"

"Oh, my God," Brummer hits his head with the palm of his hand.

"You got it. Old Jackson Sinzano is none other than that asshole sponsor of mine. Why didn't you tell me?"

"Honest, Paul. Never dawned on me."

Paul and Brummer make their way through the booths. "Geeze, I can't believe it." Brummer says and cracks his knuckles. "Remember three weeks ago when I was down to get the saw fixed?"

"Sure," Paul answers.

"I didn't put this together. I was in the can there at Jack's place. You know Jack's voice. He's got a foghorn that carries, and he's talkin' to someone on the phone, and I hear him complaining about business. He's got plans. He says, 'We'll make it the best competition ever! With the biggest logs ever!' I figure he's talkin' about the idiot competitions he has in front of his place. He ends the conversation with, 'I'll provide the logs and...' he laughs his stupid laugh, like he's making a joke, but he isn't, and ends with, 'I'll be sure my guy wins'. And his last words, 'Sure, no problem, that road hasn't been used in years.'"

"Gyppo operation." Paul says with certainty.

"Worse. It just hit me. Trees the size we were promised? Every last damn one of them is going to be illegal. Night logging. National Forest Land. It happens. Not often, but it happens."

Paul moans and shakes his head, "I'll have to pull out. I can't compete."

"I can't believe that conversation was about us. Here. Twist. His guy winning."

"That's why I have to pull out. I *am* his guy."

"Cripes, Paul. This whole thing. I can't believe…"

They get to the banner. Look around to see if they can see Jack.

"Believe it. It's him. It's me. And now I've got to find that idiot and tell him to find someone else to front his stupid business."

As he speaks, Chainsaw Jack appears on the other side of the cutting area. Jack looks their way as if he's looking for Paul. Jack waves. Waves as if he hasn't a care in the world. He yells, "Paul! My Man! Got to talk to you!"

Paul hisses under his breath. "Great. Here he comes…the walking, talking asshole."

Paul pushes Brummer ever so slightly, "While I talk to him, would you go back and explain to Elsie and Travesty what we've just figured out. Tell them I won't be cutting. Somehow, some way, after I've smashed his face in, we'll tackle this problem."

"Which?"

"The logs. I can't compete. But for the next sixteen, well, fifteen hours, we've got a huge problem to solve. There's got to be logs somewhere."

"Good luck."

"No, no I've begun to believe in miracles. We've got to figure this out."

"Well, look there. If there ever was a woman who could figure something out…" Brummer points, "Look behind you." His head tilts toward the middle of Main Street. Annabelle Lee is winding her way through the crowd. She's so intent, she strides right by Paul and Brummer. She's headed toward Jack. Then Jack sees her. He stops mid-stride on his way towards Paul and abruptly changes his forward motion. He disappears behind parked RV's. He comes around up behind her. Taps her on the shoulder. Jack's arms spread wide, his fists pump the air. His anger shows a full block away. Annabelle Lee steps back. The feint of Annabelle Lee from the pumping arms, the forward lean of Jack, the animation of his mouth: there is no question he is screaming at her. Two inches from her face, he yells, "You, Bitch!"

Paul leaps over the yellow tape of the cutting area and breaks into a run.

Two older women making their way to Main Street, comment, "Well, if it isn't little Paul Whitinowsky."

Paul keeps running. Jack and Annabelle Lee's voices are drawing attention like a sponge in water. With only a few feet to go, Paul sees Annabelle Lee push a closed fist near Jack's face. Her hand stays in the air, her words, brittle and angry, carry to Paul, "You're not welcome here, Jack! Don't you dare get in the way of my business! And I'm letting all of Twist know, those logs of yours are illegal!"

Paul can hear hollow hooting sounds from three teenage boys behind him as they respond to her look, her voice, her stance. They call, "Atta girl!" "Bite his Ass!" "Get him!" "Lady's the boss!"

Annabelle Lee enunciates words as if she were shooting arrows. The arrows fly sure and straight and bulls-eye bound. "Don't insult me Jack, just take your greed and shove it! Last time, get out of town! That permission you got? It's bogus! And remember this! We don't need you!" Annabelle Lee throws up her hands as if to dismiss him. She turns and walks behind the booths. Her head high, her stride long and quick, teenagers clapping to her every step.

At the Methow Mountains News and Real Estate office, she takes the outside steps two at a time to the second floor. Her hair bounces with the rhythm of each step. She walks past Paul without even seeing him.

Jack laughs a mean, angry laugh and thrusts a finger into the air, "You'll see who needs who!" he calls to her back.

The two older women have stayed to look as Paul takes two giant steps and stiff-arms Jack with both hands. One woman asks the other, "Isn't he a minister now?"

Too late, Jack flies backward. Paul charges at Jack again. Three guys appear, drawn by the yelling. They wear canvas jackets with dozens of pockets for assorted ammunition. They are not to be ignored. They bully their way between Paul and Jack. One pulls Paul away. Two others hold a flailing Jack.

"Don't you ever..." Paul explodes.

"You're on the wrong side of this mess, you jerk!" Jack yells. "Wait till you see what that stupid broad has planned!" Jack half-wrestles as if he would get away from the men's grip, but it is apparent, at least to Paul, that Jack is going nowhere, but he has the last words, "Go on! Go on! Find out what that stupid...whatever you want to call her...has planned! It's nuts!"

Brummer arrives, the gathered crowd steps back, as if it isn't the first time Brummer has settled a dispute in Twist. "Okay. That's it. Everyone back to work. Paul, come with me. Jack, get lost." The crowd is reluctant to go, but it's obvious nothing more exciting is going to happen.

Brummer pulls Paul further down the sidewalk. "I'll go talk to Elsie and Travesty John. I know Twist. Word will spread. They'll think you and Jack killed each other and be worried about you," he said. "Don't waste time on Jack. Find out what's going on in the Real Estate office. I'll catch up with you in a few minutes." Brummer gives Paul a gentle push toward the news building and heads back to The Big Drinkers' Bar. "And forget about getting Jack's logs. That little scene? The whole town knows they're illegal."

Paul turns at the corner and takes the steps up to the second floor of the Methow Mountains News and Real Estate Office. On the second floor landing in front of a door with a frosted window he reads black block letters: LANDOWN REAL ESTATE.

Strange. Paul has never heard of them. Confusing. How can so much have changed in three weeks?

Through puddled scallops of the obscure glass, Paul can see the blurred shapes of three people. One figure is the shape and size of Cruisewell. One person, tall and slender, definitely female, holds a cane in the air as if she is making an important point. The third is the slender form of Annabelle Lee. Just as he knocks, he hears his name.

"Paul! Now is later! I'm not finished with you!"

Paul looks down to see Chainsaw Jack yelling at him, a fist raised.

"Stop right there!" Jack's voice is full of venom and anger. "You better listen to me!"

Paul stands above Jack. A single spectacular memory floods him. He is ten. He stands on a train trestle. His mouth fills with saliva. He looks down. Paul is not ten, but his mouth is full of spit. Good judgment or chicken-heartedness prevails. He doesn't spit. He swallows and walks slowly, one step resounding on the wooden board before he takes another step. When he's three steps above Jack, Paul takes a deep breath and suddenly feels inspired. He hammers his words, "No, you listen to me! You've got sixteen hours to grovel on your knees before Woodhouse and get trees for this competition. And you've got sixteen hours to find yourself a new cutter. And the permission to use National Forest trees? I trust Annabelle Lee. The papers are phony. Woodhouse is it, or there's nothing. Now get out of my sight!"

"You can't do that! You're my man!" Jack's voice makes a slight shift. He starts to whine. "Get Annabelle Lee off my back. Stop her and everything will be okay. The trees are there. They're cut...," Jack's voice begins to plead. "All these weeks of planning. You don't know what's at stake. I've got plans. Big plans. I can save Twist."

Paul spits out the words, "You couldn't save a Thanksgiving turkey! Get lost! Now!"

"But everything's all set," Jack is near weepy.

"No, I think the word is 'fixed,' " Paul snaps.

Paul is not two feet from Jack. In that second, Paul can see certainty and energy slowly leaking out of Jack. Jack's eyes narrow for one last thrust. A weak thrust, but a thrust. "That bitch friend of yours screwed up everything. This was going to be a clean sweep. I was going to open a branch here. Bring jobs. Bring money to this dump." Jack gets a second breath. "I don't need you! I don't need any of you. My name's on this competition and no one's going to take that banner down."

Jack turns away, then takes a final shot and yells, "I'll take my ideas somewhere else! Twist will be a joke. A party and no games! A circus with no acts! Nothing! You'll have nothing!" Jack stops as if he's lost track of where he was going. "But, if you side with me. There'll be a competition! You'll win!" He is back to pleading, "I need you, man!"

Paul is on ground level. He grabs Jack's arm. He's tempted to twist it off. "I'd suggest you head up these stairs and tell Annabelle Lee you're sorry and then tell the National's committee you've made a huge stupid mistake. Then get on the phone. Call Woodhouse. Beg. Fifteen hours."

Paul loosens his grip. Jack says, "It was supposed to be my competition."

"Well, it looks like it isn't. And National Forest trees are not your trees," Paul sneers and pushes Jack away. "Get up there and tell her you're sorry."

Jack almost trips, grabs the stair rail and hisses, "I've friends here."

"Well, good. If Woodhouse Timber won't come through, you'll need those friends."

Jack pulls back, a banty hen ready for a last peck. "You're nothing but a stupid jerk preacher! I don't need you! Logs? There are plenty of logs. There just won't be any logs for you!"

"Don't threaten me," Paul pushes Jack. Jack raises a fist.

"Stop it! Both of you!" Annabelle Lee demands. She stands directly above them. She leans over the rail, points a finger at Jack, "You listen up! For the sake of the community, we're going to let you keep your stupid banner. For that privilege, you stay nice. Real nice! Beginning right now!" Annabelle takes a couple steps down the stairs and continues lecturing Jack. "We won't even let the town know you didn't help solve this problem! If you just keep your mouth closed, we'll make everyone look good." Annabelle Lee eases back, leans against the rail. Her final words are weary and show exhaustion. Paul notices circles under her eyes and a weary slump in her shoulders. She says with a sigh, "There's been enough hardship in this town, nobody needs more."

Saundra and Cruisewell appear beside Annabelle Lee at the rail.

Paul looks from one to the other. They look like a team, they exude the power of a team. Paul is having a hard time fitting the puzzle-pieces together. He studies the three of them: Cruisewell looks as if he is enjoying the whole mess; Annabelle Lee looks as if she's had enough; and Saundra shakes her head as if she can't believe whatever has come to pass has come to pass.

Jack stammers, "I didn't do anything that wasn't legal. Much."

"Oh? We'll find out. Legal and moral are two different issues," Cruisewell interjects.

Paul barely hears Jack's words as he sees Cruisewell's fingers appear around Saundra's waist. Paul focuses. He can't believe what he's seeing. Reverend Cruisewell has his arm around Saundra's waist and Saundra isn't pulling away. Her hip snuggles up against Cruisewell's side.

Jack looks with hound-dog eyes at Saundra. "I thought you were on my side," Jack says with such plaintiveness it makes Paul feel just the littlest bit sorry. Jack looks as defeated as a school-boy bully.

Cruisewell leans over the railing. "Jack, I've given you chance after chance. Too many chances. How do you think Annabelle Lee knew which parcel of land to look at? To bid on? You always underestimate me Jack! You forget I was here months ago. I've studied this town. I know the logging business. You didn't have a chance. Those sixteen you cut? They're ours. Well, they're really Annabelle Lee's. She's not supporting the chainsaw competition, however, given her moral position on tree cutting, but since they have been downed, thank you, Jack, very much, they will be the base for the main building on the campus she is donating to Twist! And I'll be expecting a five-thousand-dollar donation from you! Or else."

Saundra's arm slips over Reverend Cruisewell's shoulder. The blatant sign of solidarity is more than Jack can take. His body bends, his head hangs. He is crushed.

Annabelle Lee stands tall. She slaps the dust from off her jeans and calls, "Goodbye Jack." She addresses Cruisewell and Saundra, "We've got some major work to get to before the day is done, right? Paul. Join us." She flicks her fingers at Chainsaw Jack as if she'd just removed a bug from her coat. "Goodbye, Jack!" Annabelle Lee calls with complete disdain. Paul is sure he's heard a dozen tones in Annabelle Lee's voice: warmth, forgiveness, invitation, hope, contrition. Disdain is a new one.

Paul is astonished. He isn't going anywhere but up these steps, behind the lovely, long-legged, jean-tight body of Annabelle Lee Fulsome.

At just that second, Suzie and Sam bound around the corner of the building and run up the stairs. They take in the scene at a glance. Sam tucks one foot into the second-floor railing and leans out making faces at Jack. Suzie stands next to Sam. Paul watches Suzie work her jaw and he knows in a minute what is on her mind. Before he can stop her, before he realizes he doesn't want to stop her, she lets a large glob of spit fall. It lands just in front of the toe of Chainsaw Jack's new Tony Llamas. Sam looks up with admiration at his big sister and then follows her example. He is more accurate.

Jack wipes his hand over his new red leather boots. In total disbelief, he steps back, his hand outstretched. The moisture on his fingers glistens. He slaps his fingers in the air trying to rid himself of the spit. Having no luck, he wipes his hand down the back of his jeans and stomps away.

Sam is oh, so, proud.

45

SOLVING PROBLEMS

Inside the real estate office, Annabelle Lee suggests to Paul, "You might want to find Brummer and Travesty John. It's time to bring everyone up to date."

"Give me ten minutes," Paul heads out the door, down the steps and almost collides with his two friends.

"Hey! Hey!" Travesty John puts out his arm to catch Paul. "What's the excitement?"

"I was on my way to find you."

"Well, we just saw Jack. He was past pissed. So, here we are!" Brummer says. "What's happening? Jack's one unhappy dude! Didn't even shake hands!"

"Be glad," Paul says. "Come on up. Annabelle Lee is going to fill us in on what's happening."

"Is there hope?"

"If Cruisewell's involved, there's always hope," Paul answers as they climb the stairs.

When Paul, Brummer, and Travesty John walk into the office they are met with the pumping sound of Saundra's accordion. Cruisewell sits next to her on a large wooden desk, beaming and patting the top of her leg in time with the music. Their voices blend in the words, "There'll be a hot time in the old town tonight."

Saundra's smile takes in everyone in the room. She pulls a long, final chord from the accordion and runs her thumb up the keyboard with a flourish. Cruisewell throws his arm over her shoulder and attempts to give her a squeeze. His arm is too short and the accordion is too big, so he leans toward her and she adjusts herself to receive his kiss on her cheek.

"Saundra? And Cruisewell?" Paul asks one and then the other, totally incredulous but pleased at the match. It feels right. It looks right. And two people couldn't be happier.

"We've kept it a pretty good secret, huh?" Cruisewell says with glee.

"So good, I can hardly believe it," Paul answers trying to remember who said what about whom these past days.

"Saundra's been working for me the whole time. Well, pretty much the whole time. She's a sleuth; she is, huh, sweetheart?" Cruisewell grins and pats her leg.

Paul recalls Cruisewell's look that first Sunday when Jack came-on to Saundra. Then last Sunday, Cruisewell looked so worried. It couldn't have been easy. Paul has seen the slick side of Jack. There was a tempting devil in Jack. Paul knew. Knew well.

Cruisewell probably needn't have worried. Because now Saundra sits next to him, close to him, and she beams. She reaches a hand out to shake Paul's. "Sorry, I couldn't let on. When you and Jack teamed up together, we, well, Randi, mostly, thought the church might turn Jack around. Save his soul. Instead, it looked like he might turn you around. Then Annabelle Lee got interested in land here at Twist and I knew from all those charts I'd made for Randi how he felt about the land, so we called Annabelle Lee. And, well, here we are!" Saundra's arms spread from behind her accordion to take in the room.

With pride and amusement in his voice, Cruisewell says, "I loved Annabelle Lee's idea of a campus for the glass studio and I absolutely could not abide the idea that Jack had cut down even second growth trees. As per the government's requirements, those trees will be used and honored. Annabelle Lee's center will do them proud."

Travesty John's face fills with awe. Brummer shakes his head in wonder.

Annabelle Lee picks up the story line and continues the explanation. "Thanks to Randi, we had money that talked. It didn't hurt that Jack's such an ass. And it didn't hurt that I could use my grant money free and clear. We learned of Jack's cutting…with a little money. Given all that has happened, and what might have happened, everything is turning out pretty well."

"Meerac!" Paul echoes. "A great project, but aren't we still in a twit over tomorrow? If the trees can only be used for building schools, what about tomorrow? The competition?" Paul looks from Cruisewell to Saundra to Annabelle Lee. "Unless Jack is taking care of it right now."

"Believe me," Cruisewell says. "Jack's not taking care of anything. He's burned his bridges. Nobody wants to talk to him, especially not the people at Woodhouse or at the National Forest office. They've thrown up their hands in disgust. We've had to do some creative teamwork of our own to keep him out of the slammer. And we've created a solution!" Cruisewell sits up as tall as his small frame allows. He beams, "Yes, indeed, we have!"

"What now?" Paul asks.

"Except for a few more small hitches, we'll be ready for tomorrow!" Cruisewell answers. Paul can't read from his voice if Cruisewell is being smug or mysterious. But Cruisewell's head remains high, his eyes shine brightly, and his hair positively glows in the light that cuts through the window.

"I don't get it," Brummer says in bewilderment. "With no trees, we've got no competition!"

"And there'll be a couple of thousand people here tomorrow wanting more than just caramel apples and cotton candy and a promise of an art school!" Travesty John chimes in.

"And our five thousand dollars…" Brummer groans. "We're stuck. We're the organizers. I can't see how you or anybody else is going to pull this off."

Annabelle Lee smiles. She comes to stand beside Paul. A pool of silence fills the room. She speaks to Paul, but the words are for everyone, "Trust us. It's going to be okay."

Paul doesn't know why, but when he hears her words and gazes into those black eyes, he relaxes. Everything *will* be okay. He just doesn't know how. He certainly doesn't know why.

"Let's toast to our imminent success!" Reverend Cruisewell produces a huge jug of raspberry lemonade with a Methow Mountains label. He passes out paper cups. Saundra scrunches around in a bag and comes up with a huge box of animal crackers, farm animal crackers, with a Methow Mountain label.

While the lemonade is poured and everyone chooses their animal crackers, Annabelle Lee sidles closer to Paul. She whispers sweetly to Paul in a voice so small he has to lean to hear her, "Sorry I haven't had a chance to explain all that's been going on. I had to move fast. I thought I'd see you when you arrived…so I could tell you everything, and let you know what a prissy purist I'd been, but things have been moving at such a pace…"

"I gather," Paul says patiently, hoping there is more to the explanation. He could continue standing here with her soft breath on his ear forever. And he wants to hear more about the 'prissy purist' part.

Reverend Cruisewell hands the last two cups of lemonade to the two of them. They step apart and he fills their glasses. "To us!" Cruisewell toasts. Everyone raises a cup.

"To miracles," Suzie adds.

"Well, of course! What else." Paul says and downs the cold sweet liquid.

"Course," Sam adds and lifts his cup for more.

Cruisewell walks to the center of the room. He makes small circling gestures with his hands as if he were rounding everyone up. "There are a few items left on our agenda. Believe me, everything's in good hands.

Annabelle Lee has a spectacular solution. It's not a sure thing yet, but we're very, very close."

These are words Paul didn't want to hear. Somehow in the toasting, in the good feelings, he'd assumed the log problem was somehow truly taken care of. Pretty near a 'sure thing' is not certainty. Paul wants certainty.

"With help from Randi, things do become possible," Annabelle Lee chimes in. "Not much left to do."

"Come on, you guys," Travesty's voice shatters the moment. "Let's get realistic. I've got a hundred pounds of hamburger thawing!"

Reverend Cruisewell beams, "I'm not the founder of World Wide Ministries for nothing. It's 'big leap of faith' time! Travesty, you keep unfreezing that hamburger. Annabelle Lee, you finish up that flyer we've been working on. Suzie and Sam, get out your magic markers to help Annabelle Lee. Brummer, you tell Spindler I'll need him in about an hour, and tell him I'll pay more than the competition. Saundra, you keep practicing your accordion and looking beautiful. Me? I've got a few more problems to solve."

Cruisewell takes Paul by the arm and walks him to the door. The room behind them grows busy with activity. Saundra plays a version of 'Waltzing with Bears' Paul has never heard before.

It appears faith is maintaining this crew and nothing is stopping their success. It also appears Paul will have to maintain a bit of faith himself, because no one, seems to be willing to let him be privy to the solution.

Outside on the balcony, Cruisewell ushers Paul to the top of the stairway, then walks behind Paul as they go down the stairs. He continues talking, "Hopefully, I won't be giving you directions much longer. But for now, trust me, and just do what I ask." They stop when they reach the bottom of the stairs. Cruisewell nudges Paul so that he faces the end of Main Street. "Go back to The Big Drinkers' Bar. Get a bite. Schmooze with your competitors. Tell them, no matter what rumors they might hear, not to worry. Then, get to bed early. You've got a big competition tomorrow, and I must say I would like you to win since I'm your new sponsor. Saws will be at your cutting area in the morning."

Paul is stunned. He starts to protest, but Cruisewell waves his words away, clearly not willing to tell him more. "Have faith," are Cruisewell's parting words.

Cruisewell turns and walks back up the stairs, as if his hair lifts him as he walks. From the balcony railing above he raises his hand as if in benediction. "That's it for now. So, don't just stand there. Go. Spread the word!"

Annabelle Lee appears behind Cruisewell. "I think he needs a little more than that." She shoos Cruisewell inside and comes down the steps. Her hand reaches out to Paul. "Soon enough, it will be clear," Annabelle Lee says. She stands close. He can smell the cinnamonness of her. Sometimes you just have to have faith." She smiles beatifically.

"But, everybody's busy, but me. Why am I out of the loop? Why can't you tell me what's going on?"

"Yes, I know it sounds nuts, but consider the source: Reverend Cruisewell. He's a little suspicious for a religious man, but an impresario at heart. He's made Saundra and I pledge to keep 'our solution' a secret. He says it's a little like tearing off the page of a day-calendar before the day begins. Very bad luck. He believes if we tell others what's going to happen, like magic, we'll screw it up." Annabelle Lee's hands go up in a defensive gesture, "I know. It's nuts. But then, think of what a wonderful surprise it's going to be."

"So, I get to go back to the bar. Alone. Eat. Alone. Go to bed. Alone. While everyone else makes magic?"

"Why, Paul, trust me. Magic will happen," Annabelle Lee says with a giggle.

Paul squeezes her hands. He loves the touch of her. His hand moves up to her elbow. He's used up all his words. He just wants to touch her.

"Hey, you two!" Saundra calls above them. "Annabelle Lee, we need your help!"

Annabelle Lee kisses Paul very, very near his lower lip. If he'd been paying better attention, it would have been his mouth. "Trust us, Paul. For now, just hang in there." Paul likes to think he heard yearning in her voice. He likes to think the kiss was off base because he'd moved his head at the wrong moment. He likes to think the idea of much, much more is on her mind as much as it is on his.

"I'll see you tomorrow," she says. "In the cutting area. And…a promise…I'll save tomorrow evening for you."

Tomorrow? Paul can't believe she said 'tomorrow'. She has! He can hardly think for the overwhelming feeling of good fortune! He smiles to himself. He is too pleased to ask if she meant what he hopes she meant. "Okay," he manages to say. He takes a step to close the space between them and takes her shoulders in his hands. He kisses her. He doesn't miss her mouth. He is light-headed but he knows when the kiss ends, there will be a tomorrow.

"Thanks," she says all smiles. "I hoped you'd do that. See you tomorrow."

Paul can barely walk for the clouds that are under his feet. Finding out about being a 'prissy purist' would just have to wait.

46

THE NIGHT BEFORE THE COMPETITION

Paul sits in the back booth at The Big Drinkers' Bar. Before him is a curved T-bone, the meat gone. French fries seep in the juice of the plate. Brummer slides into the other side of the booth and signals Elsie for a beer. Burps waits for the bone.

"How you doin?" Brummer asks.

"I'm trying not to think." Paul pushes the plate towards Brummer. "Help yourself."

"Thanks," Brummer takes the remaining fries. "Don't mind if I do."

"What do you think they're up to?" Brummer asks.

Paul rubs his eyes, tired and confused, he answers Brummer, "Who knows?" He looks through his fingers, "Does Spindler know?"

"Not that I'm aware. I sent him over there and haven't seen him since. Why are they keeping us in the dark?"

"Superstition. Just another part of The Reverend Randi MacArthur Cruisewell of World Wide Ministries belief system."

"Why are you sticking with him? You know you're no minister. You know he's crazy. Except for money, why are you hanging in there?"

"Don't underestimate money." The minute the words are out of his mouth, Paul wants them back. He hates sounding cynical. Absolutely nothing Cruisewell has done has been cynical. Brummer is right. He isn't a good minister. He's cynical. He's not even that good a carver. And he doesn't know how long he can go on in this charade. And if he doesn't win tomorrow, he's stuck.

"What ya thinking?"

Paul sighs. "I'm such a pawn in this stupid game. I drift along. Miraculously, for a very few days, I got to be a so-called minister. At the same time, I've cut more trees in the last three weeks than I have in three years. I pick up the saw and it's the only time I feel like anything."

"How's it going to end?"

"Who knows? I'm as much in the dark as you are. Taking one day at a time. Got to figure out the money. Got to figure out this silly ministry thing. But tonight I'm going to do what they want. Have faith. Get some sleep. Be ready to cut in the morning."

Brummer reaches out for the beer on Elsie's tray and orders a hamburger. He pushes his legs in front of him under the booth, folds his hands over the expanse of his belly. "Well, if you're not worried, I'm not either."

Together they listen to "King of the Road" and Brummer sings along to the music in an off-key growl. "That's you, Paul. King of the road. Carving again. No question. It's what you should be doing. Full time. It's in your blood. Father to son."

"Oh? I'm a great carver because of Bear? When do I get to be considered a great carver because I'm a great carver?" Paul totally fails at making the question light-hearted.

"Lighten up, Paul. Don't be so sensitive. You *are* your dad's son. He wasn't all bad, you know."

"I try not to think about Bear." Paul's words snap. Here, with his best friend, he feels like he's on the edge of an argument.

"That right? Bear loved you, you know," Brummer says, his voice almost soft.

"Had strange ways of showing it," Paul's voice loses its punch. He's strangely touched by Brummer's words. He stares across the room. He realizes Elsie is watching him. So as not to show how hard Brummer's words hit him, he signals Elsie with a drinking motion, bringing his hand in a fist to his mouth.

Elsie smiles, nods her head, 'yes' and brings Paul a tall glass with a head of foam. Foam curled around ice cream.

"Sweets for the sweet," she says. "You look like you could use this…Dad's Old Fashioned Root Beer and Carnation's best." Paul sips the float. Just like his mom used to make.

"Thanks, Elsie," Paul says, surprised at how close he is to tears. He can't believe all this emotion. Maybe it's nerves over the dispute with Jack. Maybe it's Annabelle Lee's kiss. Her promise. Tomorrow's competition.

"It's on the house!" Elsie says and turns to wait on the foursome at the next table.

Brummer leans across the table and says, "I was on your dad's crew all those years. There was a side to him I don't think he let you see: funny, crazy, full of it. That's why when he went down it was so hard. He'd just started getting over your mom's…"

"He drove her away," Paul tries to hide the anger in his words.

"Didn't mean he wasn't crazy about her. Same way he was crazy about you."

Paul turns the long-handled spoon around and around the tall glass. He looks up to study Brummer. He wonders what Spindler thinks of his dad. Spindler and Brummer. Paul and Bear. Matched sets. If only Spindler knew that Brummer was someone Paul would give his life for. Maybe he'll learn. Maybe, some day. Why don't fathers and sons ever get it straight?

"He was a great carver, Paul. Maybe he screwed up sometimes, but I can tell you, he loved being your dad. He was so proud of you."

Paul can see Brummer is waiting for him to respond. He just doesn't know what to say. A part of him knows there's some truth in Brummer's words. A part of him still hates the weapon of silence Bear used like a knife. A part of him will never forget the emotional explosions that came from nowhere and cut Paul to ribbons. A part of him will never forget the fact, the hard, horrid fact that his mom left.

"He wanted you to grow up and carve like him."

"Yeah, well, I carve. I don't know if I'll ever carve like him, or if I want to." Even Paul can hear the defensiveness in his voice.

"Geeze, Paul. Give the guy a break."

Something in Brummer's tone pleads with Paul and gets to him. Brummer rolls the beer mug between his hands, speaks as if he is speaking to empty space, "You don't know. It's tough being a dad."

Paul sees Brummer's eyes are moist. This is too much. He pushes back his chair and gets up abruptly. "Got to go. Strict orders. See you in the morning." As he leaves he gives Brummer a solid slap on the shoulder but he can't look at him. Paul's hand holds where it lands for a second and then he is out the back door and up the stairs to his old apartment.

Stretched out on the bed, Paul can hear below him, the clog of boots and the muted sound of pool balls snapping against each other. Just before he sleeps, he thinks and then he knows he hears the wheeze of Saundra's accordion.

He wakes from a half-dream of the last carved bear his father had done, the one with the inscription on the bottom, the one Annabelle Lee had handed him. Somewhere, somehow, he's stopped dreaming of crashing trees. This dream was full of dancing animals, lots of dancing bears. One bear danced, and kicked up a foot. On the bottom of the foot was an inscription. The bear danced and slammed its foot into the ground. The words pushed into the dirt. Paul peered at the words, tried to read them. The words twirled out of sequence. The words demanded a mirror to read them. Coming fully awake, Paul knows what the words say. The words say, "I love you."

Paul sleeps. When he wakes it is dawn and he knows exactly what he will carve. If there is really something to carve.

47

PART IS REVEALED

Outside the window of Paul's apartment, vendors call greetings to each other. The banners flap, 'Good morning!' and as hard as Paul strains to see the cutting area behind the banners, the view is blocked. Below, from inside the bar, Paul can hear the clatter of dishes and the smell of breakfast cooking.

He dresses and hurries down the stairs. The bar is already full of cutters. Four carvers from Florida call greetings. Jesse Ann Henderson looks up from the cup of coffee she holds in both hands and smiles. Next to her Hattie sits, already taking notes. Brummer is deep into a game of pool with three of the East Coast guys.

Most of the cutters already have numbers pinned to their backs and those who don't wait in line at the bar where Travesty John accepts registration forms. Paul recognizes most of the men. A couple of the women in line to register are new competitors. The new faces leave him no clue as to what his chances are of winning.

Paul heads toward the kitchen. The smell of bacon frying draws him in and he sneaks behind Elsie to give her a good morning smooch on the cheek.

"You ready?" she asks flipping a line of pancakes on the griddle.

"Ready as I'll ever be. Did the logs get here?"

"Wait till you see," she says in a voice calm, yet amused. He wonders at the tone and her sly smile. She hands him a crockery plate stacked high with pancakes. "Eat first. Then off with you! It's going to be a great day. Interesting, but great!"

"Faith. Have faith! Saundra, Cruisewell and Annabelle Lee said everything is under control."

"Great attitude! Keep it up, and here's some more to fuel you." Elsie places a tray under his plate. To the tray she adds slices of bacon, hash browns, and two eggs, over easy. Lots of new faces out there," she says nodding toward Travesty taking applications. "What're your odds?"

"Hard to say. Probably more important who's judging than who's cutting."

Paul pulls up a stool and places his plates on the chopping table in the kitchen. "Mind if I eat here? Keep you company."

"Oh, please! Be my guest. But, back to the 'winning' question."

"My winning hangs on the humor of the judges. I haven't been doing so well lately." He digs into his breakfast.

Elsie laughs, "Oh, yeah. Word's around you've been doing some crazy cutting. And you can't resist going the extra mile. What you got planned for today? Or should I ask?"

"You shouldn't. Bad luck. Besides, it's secret. My secret!" Paul mock-whispers. "Truth be known…"

"…you haven't a clue!" Elsie laughs as she pours another row of pancakes on the griddle.

Paul doesn't contradict her. Today is different than other days. He's always waited until the wood tells him what to do. This time, he knows the carving is going to be different. "You'll be surprised, Elsie. We all change."

"Spitzky is here. Ace, too. They're out front. Told me to tell you."

"Great!" Paul heads out the kitchen door. "See you at the judging! Keep your fingers crossed!"

As Paul heads into the bar he hears Elsie's parting shot, "Thought the expression was, 'pray for me!' " Paul knows he'll never make it as a minister.

He holds his tray high and maneuvers through the tight, packed tables to join Brummer, Ace, and Spitzky where they sit in the corner by the front window.

"Well, you ready?" Brummer asks. Brummer's usually laconic voice seems a bit nervous. On edge.

"Soon as I finish this," Paul says and takes another bite.

"It's crazy," Brummer nods toward the front window.

"Everyone's saying that, but everybody's in a pretty good mood, considering." Spitzky says and pulls back the curtain, "You won't believe this, Paul. Take a look."

Paul stands and scoots in front of Spitzky. Spitzky steps away so Paul can get a better look. The sun is bright. Everything glows with a sheen from the just melting frost. All Paul can make out is the jumble of booths, streamers, and signs. Paul watches as small groups of vendors congregate. Everyone seems to be talking with a great deal of animation—arms waving, hands pointing toward the cutting area. Paul's eyes follow their lifted arms, their outstretched hands. The cutting area behind the booths and banners has its usual bright yellow "Keep Out" tape around the perimeter. Bright light appears to glow from behind the yellow tape. Paul can't figure out what he is looking at.

"What is it?" he asks.

"I got a surprise for you!"

"What?" Paul asks and follows Spitzky down the center of the booths. Concessionaires call, clap their hands, hoot and holler. Paul thinks he hears in their greetings excitement and laughter. What is going on?

Many of the cutters follow. Hattie is in the front of the crowd. Camera ready.

"Can't wait 'till you see this!" Ace says.

"I don't see any logs," Paul squints. What's in front of him is a bright white mass. The cutting area makes no sense to him.

"You ready?" Brummer asks, right at Paul's shoulder. "Wait until you see!"

And then they are there. It takes a minute, more than a minute, for Paul to slowly, oh so slowly, take in what he sees. He can't believe it! He honest to God, can't believe it. "What the....what the...what's going on?"

"You got it, kid!" Brummer rolls a fist and pops Paul a good hard one on the arm. "I think I'm going to be able to give you a run for your money. This kind of evens the playing field! You better watch out!"

Paul walks past the "Keep Out" tape. He goes to the center of the circle that contains all of the cutting areas. His breath clouds in the crisp air.

Paul stares, mouth open. Stunned. "I'll be... ice?"

In the cutting area stands twenty huge blocks of ice. Like pictures he's seen of Stonehenge in his fourth grade social studies book, Paul looks at the huge monoliths. In wonder. The pillars glisten and glow bright in the morning light.

"Here," Brummer comes up to Paul and hands him a flyer. "After you left last night, this is what Saundra and Annabelle Lee wrote, and Suzie and Sam colored."

Paul takes the flyer and reads:

NATIONAL CHAINSAW ART COMPETITION!
FIRST EVER IN THE NORTHWEST!
TWENTY CARVERS OF NATIONAL RENOWN!
JOIN YOUR FRIENDS AND NEIGHBORS
FOR THE FIRST EVER NORTHWEST
ICE SCULPTURE COMPETITION!
$10,000.00 FIRST PRIZE!
SPONSORS:
CHAINSAW JACK AND WORLD WIDE MINISTRIES

Paul reads the flyer twice. He doesn't trust his eyes.

"This is too much! What's crazier? The ice? The ten-thousand-dollar prize or Chainsaw Jack and Cruisewell as sponsors? I don't believe it!"

Brummer roars with laughter. "It's great, isn't it?"

Hattie snaps a picture. Brummer exclaims. Paul doubts.

Brummer continues, "Everyone's saying...ice...no problem. Like they've all cut ice."

"Loggers cutting ice? Why aren't they all pissed?" Paul asks in disbelief.

"Well, this for starters," Spitzky says and flicks a fresh fifty-dollar bill in front of Paul's face.

"What's that?"

"You know the registration fee? The fifty dollars? We *get* fifty dollars! We don't have to pay. Logs or ice...who cares. Look around you...everyone's feeling a hundred dollars richer...the fifty they didn't have to pay, the fifty they got! Some here would cut bundles of hay if you paid them."

"And," Brummer adds, "The first prize is ten thousand dollars! Can you believe that?"

"I can't believe any of it...and Chainsaw Jack and Cruisewell? How'd that ever happen? They were ready to eat each other alive last night!"

"Who knows?" Spitzky asks and slips the fifty into his overall bib pocket. "I know we've got thirty minutes before the carving begins, so you better get your number."

Spitzky pulls the bill of his cap around to the back of his head. "I'm going to beat your butt out there today, son. I could use me a sweet ten thousand dollars."

Back in the bar, competitors gather their gear, pull on sweatshirts and zip up jackets. They fit the Velcro of their chaps and find their gloves. Their movements are quick. Voices chatter. The decibel level is high. Everyone is energized. Everyone is ready to win.

Paul heads towards Travesty John's registration table at the end of the bar. He's the last in line.

"Hey Paul, you're my man. I'm bettin' on you." Paul is pleased and honored. But three steps away, as he pins the number to his jacket, Travesty John's words stop him. His hands tremble and he pokes his finger trying to close the pin. He recalls an almost forgotten conversation. He turns back to Travesty, leans over the table and half-whispers, "You don't mean it do you? You're not betting?"

Travesty John rocks back on the legs of his chair. "Me? Betting? Like in money? Do I look crazy?" Travesty John sits forward. "Are you crazy? Asking me a question like that?"

"No. Forget it." Paul shakes his head to flick away the idea. "It was something I overheard. No big deal."

"You sure? You look…I don't know. Stricken."

"You ever hear of bets being made on competitions?"

"No. Never." Travesty John's eyes widen. "You don't think…yes, I can see you do. The conversation Brummer heard at Jack's. His man winning. Geeze. Well, it's going to be interesting to see what happens next. I can tell you certain. No one is going to buy off those judges. Besides, if Jack was going to bet on you…going to pay someone else not to cut so good…" Travesty shakes his head in disbelief. This was so beyond Twist mentality. "It's impossible. I think Jack isn't going to lose anything he might have put money on…now, I wouldn't put it past someone to take his money with an 'oh sure, I'll do that,' but when it comes to the actual cutting. Doesn't matter. You'll win. Jack's out of here."

"But that flyer. Cruisewell and Jack patched things up, I'd guess. Otherwise, how'd their names end up there? Together?"

"Guess you'll have to ask Cruisewell." Travesty John glances at his watch. "You better get moving. Ten minutes and that buzzer's going to sound off."

Travesty John hands Paul his fifty-dollar bill. The bill is crisp and new and stiff. Paul studies it. It is real.

"Nice, huh?" Travesty asks. "That's the last fifty!"

"The good Reverend?"

"You got it! Don't question our good fortune."

"That's exactly what I'd like to do…if I win, I'll buy myself out of this crazy predicament and then I'll take my chainsaw after him 'till he tells me what he's about."

Brummer beckons Paul from the front door. It's time to go.

"Right. Forget everything! Just go do it! Carve! Win!" Travesty calls as Paul waves a gloved hand and walks out the door with Brummer.

"Sleep good?" Brummer asks.

"Yeah, your words helped. Good words. About you and Spindler. Me and Bear. Thanks for last night."

"Last night? T'was nothing. Two buddies talkin' is all."

Before they are two steps into Main Street, Paul is surrounded by his own personal cheering squad: all the widows, Big Bill, Rex, Suzie and Sam. The children tag along behind Brummer and Paul waving small flags that say, "Hooray for Chainsaw Art!" It is then Paul realizes everyone in the crowd seems to have the small triangular flags. As they parade, there is no want for news reporters and television crews. Suzie and Sam hold opposite ends of a banner in front of their small personal parade that reads, WE'RE WINNERS! NEW DAWN IS BREAKING CHEERING SECTION FOR CHAINSAW ART. Everyone's name is signed in various spots all over the banner. It crosses Paul's mind that Hattie is going to have some stiff media competition. Somewhere, behind all of this, he imagines Annabelle Lee has been busy at work. He hasn't caught sight of her yet, and it is just as well. He's afraid seeing her would take his mind off carving.

Paul and Brummer step over the yellow 'Keep Out' tape. They leave the cheering section behind. "Last night's conversation? No big deal." Brummer says.

"Yeah. No big deal," Paul says and does not shy from giving Brummer a straight-on look of appreciation. They shake hands.

"Now I'm going to beat your hide!" Brummer proclaims. And Paul can hear he's in for some heavy competition.

"The hell you are!"

"Tsk, tsk." Brummer yells over his shoulder as he finds his cutting area. "Such minister talk!"

Paul finds his site. It's going to be a tough cut, no matter how easy the ice gives way to the saws. Probably, because the ice *will* give way under the saws, everyone is going to be challenged. On top of which, the prize money has put everyone on edge. Ten thousand for most is salvation. Paul isn't the only one who wants to win.

Ace's cutting area is next to Paul's. He has tied a scarf over the backward cap and pulls it tight under his chin. He looks like the Big Bad Wolf. Ace rubs his hands back and forth. Paul can't tell if it's from the cold or from nerves. Still, Spitzky, for as silly as he looks, Paul knows he is an honorable contender.

"Spitz!" Paul calls. "You hear how this all happened?"

"Who knows? Cruisewell's not saying. Jack's disappeared. Saundra is handling the television crew from Seattle. Annabelle Lee is everywhere, like a mother hen. You just missed her. She's a woman on a mission." Spitzky pulls on fingerless leather gloves. "It's crazy, wouldn't you say? Crazy nice. What do *you* think?"

"Yeah. A mission." Paul avoids Spitzky's question as he pulls back a tarp by the side of his block of ice. Just like Cruisewell promised, four Stihls gleam in the cold morning light. Paul checks each. He's ready.

"Five minutes," Spitzky says looking at his watch. "I'm so damn ready. Wish they'd get going. It's cold out here!"

Paul tightens his chaps, adjusts his earphones. He is as calm as Spitzky is wired.

"Isn't it strange that Cruisewell paid you ten thousand and the prize money is exactly the same?" Spitzky shouts.

Ignoring Spitzky and his remark, Paul shrugs a non-committal answer and pulls his earphones snug. There are just too many coincidences to be thinking about now. What he has to think about is what he knows he will carve. He just hopes the carving in his head lays buried inside this magnificent, glowing block of ice.

Gem like, the ice reflects the morning sun back at him, a cold heat that catches his eye, makes him wonder what care this frozen fluid demands. He's excited and nervous in equal parts and knows the playing field has been leveled like no other competition he's entered. Who here has ever carved iced before?

Paul's fingers wrap around a three-inch carving inside his coat pocket. Of all the miracles of the last three weeks, the miracle of tucking this bear into his jacket pocket was the biggest one. He'd wanted time alone to look at that bear, study it, think about his dad. After Annabelle Lee had found the bear, demanded he pay attention to it, Paul had tucked it inside his jean jacket. It wasn't that he'd forgotten it was there. He knew it was there all the time. His hand would brush over it; he'd feel it bump against his side. He'd just never had the courage to take it out and confront the powerful little guy.

Now, Paul removes it from his pocket. He places the tiny, dancing bear on top of the block of ice. He's never noticed before that the bear is smiling.

48

CUTTING ICE

Paul walks around the block of ice. His gloved hand reaches across the wide expanse of it. Taller than he is tall. Huge. He brushes the frosted skin off the enormous cube. He stands back to study the bulk and breadth of it, shot through with frosted seams of light. The tiny bear sits on top, looking down at Paul, challenging Paul.

Paul checks the level of the gas in each tank. He tugs at his gloves. He runs his fingers over the Velcro buckles of his chaps. He takes a deep breath and waits for the starting signal.

"Paul, something for you. I hope it gives you courage and satisfaction and inspiration."

Reverend Cruisewell hands Paul a letter. Paul reads:

My dearest son,

Out of absolutely nowhere, Reverend Randi Cruisewell has found me. Found me with the news that you are his protégé. He has not explained that yet, but he has offered me a flight home to Twist. He says you are about to marry a dear wonderful woman, and that I should not miss this event in your life.

I've missed so much. For that there are no words that will fill the space in our lives where I should have been with you. I left because I thought you were strong enough to live with Bear. I wasn't. Now that I am older and wiser, I can only ask for your forgiveness.

I'd also like to know you would want me at your wedding. I pray for that. I hope for that.

Until I hear back from Reverend Cruisewell that you wish me to join you in the Northwest, I will not make any plans.

Reverend Cruisewell has offered me residence at New Dawn. Close enough to see you often, but not so close should you need space and time to reacquaint yourself with the idea

of a mother. What I wish more than anything else in life is to be your mom.
I'll wait to hear,
Maria, your Mother

The shrill whistle slashes the morning air. One minute to go.

"Your answer?"

Paul brushes the tears from his eyes. He nods, "Yes."

The rumble of twenty saws rubs and pulses the air.

"And, share with Annabelle Lee?"

"Yes! And yes!" Paul yells over the roar.

"That's great! Start cutting!" Cruisewell yells at him with a big, big smile.

Paul reaches for his two-foot Stihl and with a quick tug the saw vibrates in his hands. The blast of an air horn simultaneously brings all of the saws to the ice.

Paul feels the virgin surface give way to the blade. Ice crystals shoot up, out, and away from the carvers. A rainbow of color surrounds them. Paul steps back from the pillow of floating light and wipes his glasses clean. The word 'caress' crosses his mind. He slows down. He is awed by the beauty of all that surrounds him.

Paul works the center first. He moves around the block with each pull of the saw. Slowly the shape in the ice grows curved and the bottom three quarters begins to match the bear outline of his dad's carving. He relaxes into the rhythm of the cuts and the sweet temperament of the ice. Gentleness is what the ice demands, as if it breathes, and Paul breathes with it.

Around him the tone and timing of the cutters slows. The stroke and slice of each saw responds to the fragility of the ice. Cutting is more languorous, more thoughtful, and potentially more catastrophic. Cutters work as if in slow motion.

A spray of shavings cascade over Paul's gloves and catches in the fine hair of his wrists. Out of the ice grow two spread feet, one foot more forward than the other, one knee slightly bent, the bear at an angle of movement and contained action. A round belly takes shape above the cocked legs. One arm shoots up in the air, the other arm stays cupped around the bulge of belly.

Time passes. The sun's cold warmth barely changes the temperature, and each carving glistens with the sheerest skin of melting ice. The crowd comes and goes, each observer bundled against the chill. Paul is barely aware. All of his attention focuses on the carving.

He changes to the twelve-inch blade. He now diverts from his model. He uses the rounded end of the saw and under its cutting edge, a salmon appears in the curve of the bear's arm. Above the bear's head the other arm stretches and holds a large block of ice waiting to be carved. Paul twists and turns the churning saw and a chainsaw emerges in the overhead paw. The ice chainsaw matches the one with which Paul now cuts. The bear holds a saw high. Triumphant.

Paul steps back and a small chuckle wedges itself deep in the back of his throat. He loves this guy, this bear, this polar beauty, this echo of his father.

There is only one hour left for details. Paul defines the snout. He makes heavy brows over the vacant space of eyes. He adds teeth to the wide-open, grinning mouth. Paul maneuvers the delicate blade of the saw around the extended foot, the bent knee. He gives the paw claws and a floppy growth of hair between the toes.

A fifteen-minute-to-finish warning blast brings crowds around favorite carvers. Paul's friends and parishioners gather round. They clap and cheer.

Paul frees his hands from his gloves. He reaches up and rescues the tiny bear stranded on top of the raised ice chainsaw. He tucks the bear back in his pocket. Secure and safe. Then from his other pocket he takes two black marbles. He rolls them in his hand and warms them with his breath. With a twist, he plants the marbles deep into the bear's eye sockets.

The crowd applauds with uncharacteristic whistles and shouts.

With ten minutes to finish, Paul picks up a one-inch gouge. With deft controlled taps he drives the chisel blade with a wood mallet. His hand has learned how much the ice will give. He turns this way and that, carving on the side of the bear's saw. He carves letters with deliberation.

The crowd watches. The loggers who stop to watch speculate. What is the word growing from the letters? Will it be DIETZ or STIHL?

Paul steps back. His hands fall at his side. In front of him is a raucous bear, ready to bound into a dance, its mouth open in a triumphant roar that ends in a smile. The bear's one arm cuddles a salmon, like it was kin. The other paw holds high a chainsaw on which is carved a single word. The block letters spell "BEAR."

As the final buzzer bleats, Paul rubs his gloved hand over the letters. The friction melts a fraction of the ice and the name glows. He steps back. He feels a hand on his arm.

He turns to see Cruisewell beaming. Next to him stands a small and slight, hesitant but happy, gray-haired, but perfectly coifed woman.

"Paul? Paulie?" she asks her voice questioning. Her voice inviting.

Paul studies the person in front of him. So familiar. So remembered. He opens his arms and engulfs his mom. And he cries.

They are surrounded by all of his friends and church members. Half the town. Half the competitors. Everyone is smiling. Everyone is cheering. Everyone is near tears.

Cruisewell announces, "All and sundry! Back to the bar! Drinks on me!"

Paul takes his mom's hand and tucks it in to the crook of his arm.

Before he leads the walk back to The Big Drinkers' Bar he studies the crowd. Annabelle Lee is nowhere to be seen. He's torn between waiting for her to appear, and triumphantly walking his mother down the aisle of the concessionaires. In the end, without Annabelle Lee, he leads the parade back to the bar.

Brummer meets them at the top of the steps. He reaches for Maria to give her a full embrace. He steps back and asks, "Remember me?"

"And how could I forget you?" she says with a chuckle. He joins them and escorts Paul and Maria to the back booth he has reserved.

For the moment, waiting for the judges' decision, Brummer, Cruisewell, Paul, and Maria sit in the back reminiscing and remembering and catching up. When Maria starts to apologize, Paul takes both of her hands in his and says, "Your letter is enough. You're here. That's what counts more than anything." At which moment he sees Annabelle Lee and signals her to join them.

"And right up there with 'more than anything' is this woman. Mom, I want you to meet Annabelle Lee. My friend. My confidant. My love. She doesn't know it formally, but she's also going to be my fiancée— if she says yes."

"Yes!! What else would I say?" Paul scoots so Annabelle Lee can join them and he gives her a big bear hug. He thinks his mouth will break from all the smiling.

The conversation slowly gets to this day. The carvings outside.

Brummer gives Paul a double-handed high-five and exclaims, "Well buddy, what can I say. You out-did yourself. Your carving is perfect. Whether you win or not, don't matter. This is the most perfect bear ever carved."

Paul can't think of a response. Winning the prize has disappeared in the hours of carving. He hasn't thought of anything but his bear, and then his mom, and now, Annabelle Lee.

Brummer's unconditional praise floats around him. He remembers all the things he has ever heard about bear carvings: no one but Bear ever carved a bear and won; bears are clichés; bears, no matter what, don't deserve to win. Paul lets the negative thoughts run through his mind. It's hard to hold them knowing that he has just finished the best carving he's ever done. And in ice! When he thinks about his carving being judged, he nails the thought that some things are worth losing for. Today's carving, whatever happens, is one of them.

The air-horn blasts and interrupts the conversation.

"That's it!" Brummer says. "Let's go hear what those judges have to say!"

As they walk between the booths to the cutting area, Paul asks Brummer how his carving turned out. In all the excitement about his mom being home, and Annabelle Lee saying "yes," Paul had totally forgotten to ask or even look at his friend's carving or any of his competitors.

Brummer groans. "Forget it. It's a pile of ice. I just didn't get it. I had a damn good time, but I ended up with slush. I had a great audience. What more could I ask for! You winning, perhaps. Let's go see."

As they walk Paul takes Maria's hand in his and takes Annabelle Lee's hand in his other.

Each carver goes to stand next to his or her creation. The townsfolk fill the center space.

Annabelle Lee squeezes Paul's hand. "It's wonderful." There is no question she means his carving. There is no question she means him. Her smile, all bright, and wide-toothed melts his heart.

"Really? For you, it's okay?" he asks.

"It's the best. The very best."

Paul pushes the pleasure down deep inside to savor later.

His mom says in a lilting, sweet voice, "The one thing I did love about your dad was his carving. I wish he were here. He'd have been so proud."

49

THE JUDGES MAKE THE CALL

The street of carvings is a fairyland of creatures: a mermaid and an eagle, a rhino and a giraffe, a pirate and a sea captain, a bear with cubs and a duck with ducklings, a contortionist and a juggler. The images appear to dance in a full circle. For some, the ice defied their skill and as they wait for the announcement an arm falls or a leg buckles.

The Florida carvers did best. They have spent many hours in hotels carving ice sculptures for gatherings of insurance men and Barbie Doll collectors. One has even repeated the Barbie Doll carving and there she stands, all torso and long legs in a ballerina dress.

The carving mishaps don't help Paul feel any more secure about what the judges will decide. Paul vaguely knows Judge Townsend and Judge Baker, but he has never heard of Judge Tulio. The judges make a final walk by each carving. They study their clipboards speaking to no one. The crowd waits in silence.

Paul worries that they are so used to wood that they won't realize how much more difficult is the detail. In the past, too much detail meant a carver was 'citified' or 'too professional' and would be marked down for his or her particular abilities.

The judges take their time. Everyone waits. Bystanders leave and come back with corndogs and cobbed corn, anything to keep them warm. Some even rush back to The Big Drinkers' Bar and return with Irish coffees. Finally, the three judges finish. Everyone gathers.

"Henry Hightop is the third place winner! Let's hear it for Henry and his ducks!"

"Jesse Anderson is our second place winner! Applause, please, for not only a great carving but that a woman did it!" People cheer extra loud to cover a few moans here and there from the crowd.

"It's an honor to give the first prize to Paul Whitinowsky! Pastor Paul! Whatever you want to call him. Paul has outdone himself with his carving of a bear!"

Probably the only person surprised by the announcement of the winner is Paul. He'd given up hope, especially after seeing the dexterity and originality of the Florida carvers. The announcement takes his breath away. He didn't just win. He won first prize and a ten-minute round of applause. By the time he walks up to the stand to accept the prize, everyone is warm from all the shouting and pounding of gloved hands.

Judge Tulio interrupts the cheering to declare that Paul's bear is even a 'welcome bear'. It meets all the qualifications. It has a sign. It has marble eyes. All in all it is a perfect 'welcome bear' with details never attempted in a carving before.

And once again, after this last announcement, the crowd cheers and cheers, for love of Paul, for the remembrance of Bear, for their hometown boy.

Back at the The Big Drinkers' Bar, Paul is made to sit at the front round table so that everyone can greet him. Elsie serves dozens of warm cups of cocoa and every few minutes someone makes a new toast and glasses are lifted. Most toasts involve Paul or Maria. Toasting, then eating, then drinking, continue well into the night. The church women order Elsie's hamburgers. Spitzky and Ace show Grandma Bella how to shoot pool. Big Bill Dumpster and Rex compete, telling stories of their youth to Spindler. Suzie sits between Saundra and Cruisewell, holding one hand of each, Sam snuggles next to Grandma Bella. Burps dreams rabbit-races at their feet. Brummer, eyes closed, hums along with Patti Page singing *Detour*, as if remembering the whole life of his Big Drinkers' Bar family.

Saundra gives Suzie a hug and goes to the stage in the corner of the bar. She adjusts speakers and plugs in amplifiers. She limbers her fingers in a series of runs over the accordion keys and the energy in the room quadruples. Cruisewell takes the microphone and leads everyone in singing. As eleven o'clock comes and goes, the last song is a raucous version of "Going to the Chapel and We're Gonna' Get Married." Cruisewell sings to Saundra, Paul sings, off key but with great enthusiasm, to Annabelle Lee. Grandma Bella and Big Bill's voices harmonize—a sweet and sour mix of molasses and lemon. Maria and Brummer sing but it's not time to look at each other.

Near midnight the floor fills with a last dance.

As the crowd leaves, Ace, Spitzky, Brummer, and Paul sing a rousing chorus of "Waltzing with Bears."

Much later when only a few people remain, Travesty and Elsie clean up the kitchen. Saundra puts away the speakers. Cruisewell admires Saundra. And Paul and Annabelle Lee hold hands in the back booth.

"So, how was carving? On ice?" Annabelle Lee asks.

"Interesting question," Paul answers, tucking a curl of hair behind her ear. "I think it's time you told me just how that 'ice thing' happened."

"It's a great story! You ready for this?"

"Probably."

"The judges weren't much for ice to begin with. I smiled a lot and told them what a great thing this event would be for Twist…and then…"

"Then?" Paul fears that their major disagreement will soon appear.

"First I had to deal with environmental regulations." Annabelle Lee speaks precisely. "I told the state chairman that the forty acres I was willing to purchase, I would put in a trust. That trust solves all of our problems. The primary requirement is that there be a non-profit campus for the benefit of the community. And, it just happens that Chainsaw Jack's illegally cut timber had been hidden on that very land. So, the trees are not trees, they're logs, and they will now become the basis for the buildings. Everyone wins! The very trees that would go to waste will now be the structure of a publicly used building. Any trees adjacent to my land, which will require a new fire lane, will also be used. It meets all the environmental specifications. I not only have the appropriate paper work for the land and the logs, but I promised them a major gift."

Paul can feel she is tiptoeing around the information she has just shared. "Isn't that a bribe?"

"Well, not according to Reverend Cruisewell. It's a gift. For which they are thankful.

"Then your land, the school, is a finished deal?"

"Yes, but let me tell you the ice story!" She looks at Paul with hopeful eagerness.

"I'm all ears," Paul says and tries to listen to her words, but it takes effort as he keeps drifting into the peppermint smell of her mouth.

"I took out the registration form the judges had provided for the competition and showed them that *nowhere* does it say the competitors have to cut logs. It just says the cutting has to be done with chainsaws. Then I smiled again and proceeded to sell them on what a grand and glorious idea an ice carving contest would be. Everyone would love the novelty of it. Then I told them I'd convinced *The Seattle Times* and *King Television* to do a feature about it and they gave in."

"That was all you had to do? Buy land? Get ice? Convince the media to come? Win over the judges?"

"Well, I lied a little bit. The judges were ready to hear, however, so they didn't question the fact that the land deal hadn't quite been signed and we weren't sure if the train with the ice would get here on time. And I did tell them that the reporter, was already here, busy at her typewriter. So impressed with Twist! Just waiting to interview every one of them. She would be submitting the story for the travel section. That last part was true."

"You are something!"

"Oh, I milked it even more. I told them the article would feature Twist, on the verge of becoming a national destination for investment. Like I said, they gave in. Happily."

Paul sighs contentedly. He wonders if maybe all their disagreements could be avoided. Maybe they'd never discuss tree cutting again. He'd just love her for the rest of his life.

"I also added I'd be needing some employees for the Twist Art Center and they thought that was a pretty good idea...and..."

"Honest?" Paul snaps back from his dreamy state. "This is *the* center? The one you've been talking about?"

"You knew I was here to look at land," she reminds him.

"Yes. But I thought for some day, some time."

"It's now."

"How?" Paul asks worried that her big ideas won't include him.

"Well, besides my grant, I've got a major donor."

Paul groans, "Don't tell me..."

"Cruisewell thinks it's for a very good cause," Annabelle Lee says, her voice calm, low, and sure.

Paul wants to ask if he is part of the plan. With his extra money, he will be free from his ministry thing and still have ten thousand dollars. For a minute he thinks about the ten thousand dollars he just won. With a double-sinking he realizes no one has even mentioned the money. Maybe it doesn't even exist.

He sits in silence. He doesn't say another word, fearful that once details of her project are known, her being his fiancée will become an afterthought.

"I'm curious," Annabelle Lee says, "How do things stand between you and Cruisewell?"

"With all my good fortune, I'll be able to pay him off. But, it doesn't look as if there's prize money, with Jack out of the picture..."

"Which brings us to..."

"...right, I'm one out-of-work, near-broke logger in love with a woman who hates men who kill trees and..."

"Mea culpa. My turn to apologize. I haven't had time, or I've avoided saying so, but your remark about using energy is right. We all do our thing and most of what we do takes energy. Takes away from the earth. That's why I grabbed on to that idea of using the trees already cut for the buildings we'll need."

Paul holds his breath, wondering what part of *we'll* is he.

"I guess what I'd like to see is both of us just doing our best to do the most good and the least harm by what we do."

"Not much worry about what I'll be doing. If you haven't noticed, there's not much call for loggers."

"Unless…"

"Unless what?" Paul asks, equal parts hopeful, equal parts fearful.

"Unless you come to work as a co-director of the Twist Art Center and teach chainsaw carving."

"Annabelle, Annabelle Lee, it's not going to work if I trade Cruisewell for you…just someone else to be taking care of me, making up some half-assed job."

"You don't understand. There won't be an art center unless you are the co-director."

"I'm lost."

"Well, just in time! Cruisewell. Reverend Cruisewell!" Annabelle Lee calls, "Please join us."

A second later she says, "Tell Paul how you think he is the best people-person you've ever seen. He also knows there's growing interest in chainsaw art across the country, right? You, Paul, can help make chainsaw carving a true art form. Here's the deal: we…not just me…we get an art center with Cruisewell's major donation, only if you are the co-director. His terms. Great terms if you ask me! Oh, one other thing. This is embarrassing, but the other part of the deal…well…is…" she stammers, "I was just mentioning to Paul there's a catch to the art center," she says to Cruisewell.

"Oh! I think it's a grand catch! Paul, guaranteed, you'll never regret it."

"Cruisewell, the last time you made me a deal I couldn't refuse, I ended up in a trailer court with eight widows in Seattle, doing absolutely nothing."

"And nothing but good has happened since," Cruisewell exclaims.

Annabelle Lee's hand reaches for Paul's.

"All I'm asking is that I can officiate," Cruisewell says with a mischievous grin covering his face.

"Officiate?" Paul turns to Annabelle Lee to see her blush and ask with the tilt of her head and the raise of her eyebrows.

"You mean? It's the real thing? Not just my fiancée, but my wife?" Paul asks, so pleased he feels he might burst.

"And Sam and Suzie already have agreed to carry the ring and throw rose petals, if you don't mind." Cruisewell adds.

Paul turns Annabelle Lee so that she faces him. He looks over her shoulder at Cruisewell. "I think we need a few minutes alone. This is one time I'd like to be in charge, totally in charge. So if you don't mind."

Cruisewell backs up, all the time talking, "I hate to miss such a moment but I guess I can't be everywhere at once. So, I'll leave, but only on the condition that I can announce your event first thing tomorrow morning, along with another announcement I'd like to make." Cruisewell's parting words are barely noticed.

Cruisewell leaves and heads back toward Saundra. He walks with purpose.

Paul returns to the moment. To the woman in front of him.

Cruisewell turns and comes back to Annabelle Lee and Paul. "Sorry, not to disturb you, truly, but I really want you to be the first to know. I'm going to propose to Saundra. I know she's going to say yes, and so when you're talking details, consider celebrating with us!"

Before they can speak, Cruisewell turns and marches toward Saundra, his arms outstretched.

Paul's hands hold Annabelle Lee's hands. He begins with the words, "Dear, lovely Annabelle Lee." He stands and then he kneels. "There's something I'd like to ask you, formally and correctly."

50

ALL IS REVEALED

One night, long after Paul and Annabelle Lee are Mr. and Mrs. and adding to the tribe of Whitinowsky; long after the Twist Art Center is open (where Spindler is the first to enroll to become the greatest chainsaw artist the Western world has ever seen); long after an adjunct building has been dedicated and has a gallery where on occasion Annabelle Lee shows magnificent collections of whimsical chainsaw art creatures she has carved and Paul shows his exquisite creatures in blown glass; and long after Randi Cruisewell has become the chairperson of the advisory board that does little but give money and find patrons for the Twist Art Center; and long after Paul's mother has returned from San Diego to become the bride of Brummer; and long after Grandma Bella and Big Bill Dumpster have settled into her new Airstream and visit Twist every summer for art camp; and long after Saundra and Cruisewell have built a giant house at the opposite end of Main Street where Suzie and Sam have front row seats to every year's ice sculpture contest; long after, Paul and Cruisewell have a talk.

Paul asks his old boss, "Cruise, old friend, tell me, no hedging, tell me what you are about. What was the ministry thing all about? And why me?"

And Cruisewell tells Paul, "Well, now that I've got what I wanted, what I tried to get all the time with all that money, now that I've got a family, I can tell you."

Paul sips a glass of milk and listens.

"We'll start with the easy questions. The ministry? Well, I checked the Washington State Employment numbers and at that time chefs and aerobic instructors were having the hardest time finding employment. I placed ads. The chef wasn't so good. The aerobics instructor was worse. And? Well, on the list, ministers were next. I placed another ad. Presto! There you were.

Or, more truthfully, there I was. And? I wanted to see Twist. Twist and Mt. Grizzly had made my granddaddy rich. I thought I'd get you settled and head back up here. But Annabelle Lee showed up with her great ideas...and I followed her lead."

"How did your granddaddy get rich?"

"In a minute...we haven't covered my ministry."

"Oh, yeah, all that white stuff."

"I'm of an age I can say anything I want...so here goes. You're the first to hear this. Confidential, between you and me?"

"Of course. Confidential."

"I love dressing up!"

"That's it? Dressing up?"

"Don't you laugh, Paul. Look at it this way. If you have money. If you like to dress-up. What are your options? Mafioso or a minister. I chose the logical choice. It's the one job in which one is expected to flaunt wealth. I don't think of it as flaunting so much as spreading. And so I did. I also had a little guilt problem and it seemed being a minister was the most direct route to saving my soul."

"So you dress up, and you still dress up."

Cruisewell touches his suspended-in-air hair. "I do look good. Saundra also thinks I look good!"

"And, no one doubts Saundra."

"Indeed."

"So where did the guilt come from."

"An interesting story. You see, my granddaddy was a little bit like your daddy. He loved the woods. He loved cutting trees. There was only one difference. He owned the land where all the trees were cut. Early on. He was what folks called a lumber baron. I grew up with a large quantity of money and a large quantity of guilt about the cut-down trees that supplied me with all that money. I swore when I came into my inheritance, I'd do good. But I also had this idea about creating a family. So, I decided to do both. It didn't happen quite like I planned. As you know, I floundered for a while. But now that I've got Suzie and Sam and Saundra, and you and Annabelle Lee are on your feet, doing good things for the arts and for lots of people, I think I've done what I set out to do.

"There's a question that's always puzzled me," Paul asks. "At the first ice carving competition, the wedding one, were you and Jack taking bets?"

Cruisewell throws back his head and laughs. "Funny you should ask. Jack was trying to rig the whole thing. You were his man. You were going to win. He'd hit you up for half of the ten-thousand-dollar prize. He just made the mistake of trying to get Ace and Spitzky and Brummer to place bets. By then, we were all involved in the land deal and your crew and I were pretty good friends. So, I'm afraid I rigged things a bit."

Paul's heart sinks. "You paid the judges? For my win?"

Cruisewell's eyebrows bounce up. His hair seems to grow another inch over the dome of his head. "Oh, Paul, no! I'd never do that! Oh, my goodness, never, never. No. Don't you remember? Don't you remember how Chainsaw Jack just kind of disappeared? Well, I did my usual thing."

"Your usual thing?" Paul says, fearful the conversation might strangely return to the Mafioso.

"Yeah. I used money for good. I know it's hard for you to understand, but sometimes giving money and bribing people aren't that far apart. I gave Jack ten thousand dollars. I told him he should use the money to leave town. He should use the money not to come back. He could still sell chainsaws, since that seemed the only thing that he was very good at, but if I ever heard his saws were used to cut trees not specifically designated for cutting, the money would jinx him. You know, I'm just a little bit superstitious. I'm also a hard man to turn down."

"You *are* a hard man to turn down, Cruise."

"And aren't we all the better for it?"

Paul chuckles, so easy to agree with Cruisewell.

"One very last question. For today. Where does faith fit in all of this?"

"Faith?" Cruisewell thinks and thinks. "You know that song, 'Now I'm a Believer?' I think it's something like that."

"That's it? Like a song? Do you know the rest of the words to that song?"

"Not so you could tell."

"It's a love song!"

"Great. That's it. Faith is a love song. You couldn't ask for more."

Paul smiles and sighs. He loves these discussions. He loves this crazy man. You definitely couldn't ask for anything more.

ABOUT THE AUTHOR

Karen Lorene spends one half of her life writing (*Buying Antique Jewelry: Skipping the Mistakes; Building a Business, Building a Life; ABeCedarian;* and now, *Dancing With Bear*). She also publishes *Signs of Life*, a literary journal, once a year. The other half of her life she maintains Facèrè Jewelry Art Gallery in Seattle, Washington. The in-between hours are focused on her husband, Don and a rescue puppy, Sam. They live happily together in a houseboat community on Lake Union. Oh, and her cat just jumped on her lap to remind her not to forget to mention her. Helga. All together.

(Photo credit: Aaron Briggs)